# THE GOAT-FOOT GOD

# The GOAT FOOT GOD

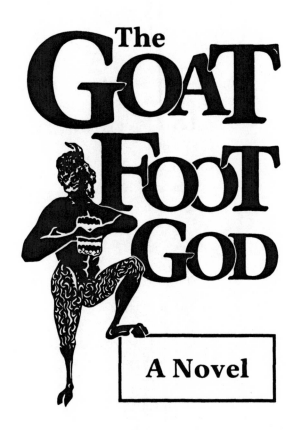

## A Novel

## DION FORTUNE

SAMUEL WEISER, INC.

York Beach, Maine

Originally published in 1936

First American paperback edition
published in 1980 by
Samuel Weiser, Inc.
P. O. Box 612
York Beach, ME 03910-0612
www.weiserbooks.com

This printing, 1999

Library of Congress Catalog Card Number:
73-27597

ISBN 978-0-87728-500-7

Printed in the United States of America
CCP

# THE GOAT-FOOT GOD

CAME the voice of Destiny,
Calling o'er the Ionian Sea,
' The Great God Pan is dead, is dead.
Humbled is the hornèd head ;
Shut the door that hath no key—
Waste the vales of Arcady.'

Shackled by the Iron Age,
Lost the woodland heritage,
Heavy goes the heart of man,
Parted from the light-foot Pan ;
Wearily he wears the chain
Till the Goat-god comes again.

Half a man and half a beast,
Pan is greatest, Pan is least.
Pan is all, and all is Pan ;
Look for him in every-man ;
Goat-hoof swift and shaggy thigh—
Follow him to Arcady.

He shall wake the living dead—
Cloven hoof and hornèd head,
Human heart and human brain,
Pan the goat-god comes again !
Half a beast and half a man—
Pan is all, and all is Pan.
　　　Come, O Goat-god, come again !

(From " The Rite of Pan.")

# CHAPTER I

THE double doors of 98 Pelham Street opened to the latch-key of their owner, who, to judge from his habiliments, had just returned from a funeral. The butler who advanced to meet him in the outer hall and take from him his neatly-rolled umbrella, his top-hat with the deep mourning band, and his close-fitting black overcoat, damp with rain—for one cannot hold up an umbrella during the actual committing of the body to the ground—endeavoured to put into his expression the exactly right proportions of sympathy and deprecation.

The problem was not an easy one, and he had given a lot of thought to it while awaiting his master's return. Too much sympathy was very definitely not called for ; but, on the other hand, too much deprecation would be in bad taste, and probably resented as indicating an over-intimate acquaintance with painful private affairs. He finally decided to have both expressions ready and take his cue from his master's countenance. But that impassive, cadaverous visage told him nothing ; in fact his employer might as well have been hanging his hat on the hat-stand as placing it in a human hand for all the indication he gave of recognising the presence of a fellow-being who presumably had an immortal soul.

Hugh Paston passed through the wide inner hall and into his study, shut the door behind him, and helped himself to a drink from the cocktail cabinet. He needed it.

He flung himself into an enormous arm-chair beside

the hearth, and extended his feet to the electric fire. The
soles of his shoes, wet with churchyard clay, began to
steam, but he never heeded them. He sat motionless,
staring into the glow ; endeavouring, if the truth were
known, to solve exactly the same problem that had so
severely taxed his butler.

He had just returned from the funeral of his wife, who
had been killed in a motoring accident. That is no
uncommon occurrence. Most men have wives, and
motoring accidents are frequent. But this was not quite
an ordinary motoring accident. The car had gone up in
flames ; and though the proprietor of the Red Lion
Hotel, at whose gates the accident had occurred, had
identified the bodies as those of a Mr and Mrs Thompson,
well known to him as frequent visitors for several years
past, an inscription inside the watch found on the man
had identified him as Trevor Wilmott, one of Hugh
Paston's most intimate friends, and an inscription inside
the wedding-ring of the woman had identified her as
Hugh Paston's wife.

What should be the attitude of a husband at once out-
raged and bereaved ? Should it be grief and forgiveness
or a disgusted repudiation ? Hugh Paston did not know.
He only knew he had had a severe shock, and was just
beginning to rouse from the dazed numbness that had
been a merciful anæsthetic against the full stress of the
blow. He had been hit on every tender spot on which a
man could be hit. If Frida had left a note on her dress-
ing-table to say that she was eloping with Trevor Wilmott, he would have pitied and forgiven. But they were
actually on their way home when the accident occurred ;
she had phoned to say she would be back in time for tea.
Trevor himself was dining with them that evening. The
thing had indisputably been going on for a considerable
period ; it must, in fact, have been going on from the
earliest days of the marriage, if the inn-keeper's chrono-
logy were to be relied on.

Sitting there, sipping his drink and gazing at the impersonal glow of the electric fire, Hugh Paston began to go over things in his mind, asking himself what he felt, and what he had better think.

The soles of Hugh's shoes had long ceased to steam and were beginning to crack by the time he had finished reviewing his life with Frida in the light of what he now knew. He had believed that there had once been mutual love between himself and Frida, even if it had not stood the test of marriage. And he asked himself again and again what it was that had killed that love? Had marriage with him been a disillusioning experience for Frida? He sighed, and supposed that that was it. So far as he knew, he had left nothing undone that he could have done. But evidently he had not filled the bill. He compared Trevor and Frida to Tristram and Iseult, and left it at that.

He rose suddenly to his feet. One thing he knew for certain, he couldn't stop in the house. He would go out for a walk, and when he was tired, turn in at some hotel and phone his man to bring along his things. He looked round at the room with its shadowless, concealing lighting and rectilinear furniture, which contrived at one and the same time to be so austere and so bulky, and the jagged points in the pattern of the carpet and hangings stabbed at him like so many dentist's drills.

He went hastily out into the hall. The butler was not about, and he got his hat and coat unaided. He closed the big doors silently behind him and set out at a brisk pace northward. But by the time he had crossed Oxford Street, and was making his way through the modified version of Mayfair that lies beyond it, he had slackened his pace. He had had precious little food or sleep since the inquest had revealed certain facts, and that is a thing which takes it out of a man.

Tired of going north, and finding that the district was beginning to get sordid, he turned sharp right, and in another moment found himself in a narrow and winding street of shabby aspect, given up chiefly to second-hand furniture-dealing and cheap eating-houses.

Hugh Paston made his way down this dingy thoroughfare slowly. His energy did not amount to a brisk walk, but he had no wish to return to the deadly emptiness of his home. He found the curious old thoroughfare interesting, enabling him to turn his mind away from the things on which it had been grinding for days. The rag-bag stock-in-trade amused him, and he stood contemplating it. No one bothered him ; no one importuned him to buy. Every one was completely indifferent to his existence. Which was as he wished it to be. Had he taken his walk abroad in Mayfair, he would have been hailed at every turn by his friends, inquisitive and eager for information, or embarrassed and anxious to be kind. Whereas the one thing he wanted was to be allowed to crawl away quietly and lick his wounds.

He sauntered on, dislodged from his contemplation of early Victorian mantel-piece ornaments and Oriental Brummagem by the reek of the eating-house next door, and paused in front of a second-hand bookshop across the front of which the words : ' T. Jelkes, Antiquarian Book-seller' showed faintly on the faded paint. The usual outside tables had been withdrawn owing to the heavy rain, but a kind of bin stood just inside the narrow entry that gave access to a half-glass door painted a faded green. The hard glare of an incandescent lamp immediately opposite supplemented the fading light of the stormy sunset and enabled the books in the bin to be examined in spite of the gathering dusk. It was an advantageous situation for a second-hand bookshop, thought Hugh, for the stock required no great amount of light for its display, and the owner could very well let the borough council do his illuminating for him.

He began to pick over the contents of the bin idly, previous experience having taught him that no lively

Latin or eager Hebrew would shoot out to try and sell
him something, but that everything was sunk in decent
Anglo-Saxon indifference to business. Picking over the
books in a twopenny bin is an amusing business, providing one does not mind getting dirty. The assortment
consisted chiefly of antiquated piousness and fly-blown
fiction. A local lending-library had apparently been dis-
posing of discarded volumes, and by the time a local
lending-library thinks a volume is ripe for disposal, it is
decidedly fruity. Hugh picked over the decomposing
literature doubtfully, but failing to decipher the titles,
decided not to imperil his eyesight with the contents.

A reasonably clean blue binding heaved up from the
welter like a log in rapids, and he fished for it hopefully.
It proved to be a battered library edition of a popular
novel, long since out in a pocket reprint. He dipped into
it by the light of the glaring incandescence behind him.
He knew by the name on the binding that it would be
readable, and the title intrigued him. ' The Prisoner in
the Opal '——. It raised visions.

He soon found the paragraph that gave the book its
title. ' The affair gave me quite a new vision of the
world,' he read. ' I saw it as a vast opal inside which I
stood. An opal luminously opaque, so that I was dimly
aware of another world outside mine.' There was a
curious fascination in the rhythm of the prose, and he
read on, hoping for more. But he did not find it. The
story then became, apparently, a detective novel, with
the amiable Hanaud prancing gaily through it. Hugh
began to wonder whether the wrong inside had got
bound up into those grubby blue covers. Such things
do happen at printing-works upon rare occasions. He
skimmed on, unable to catch the drift of the story from his
dippings, for it was as full of mystery as an egg is of meat.

He therefore turned to the end, knowing that there
has got to be a solution somewhere to even the most
mysterious of detective novels. A good detective novel

was what he wanted at that moment. Something sufficiently exciting to catch the attention, and sufficiently
intelligent to hold it. He dipped and skipped persever-
ingly, cursing the well-maintained mystery that baffled
him. He would soon have read the entire book if he
went on like this. And again and again he was puzzled
by the fact that the book appeared to bear no conceivable
relationship to its title, and had almost fallen back upon
his original hypothesis of a binder's error when he lit
upon the clue, and read, startled and absorbed, the
account of the Black Mass celebrated by the renegade
priest and the dissolute woman. Here was something
that would certainly both hold the attention and intrigue
the intellect.

He opened the dingy green door, hearing as he did so
the clang of a bell that gave warning of his presence, and
entered the shop, his discovery in his hand.

The shop was in darkness, save for such light from the
street-lamp as made its way between the volumes ranged
in ranks in the window. The characteristic smell of
ancient books was heavy on the air; but through that
smell came faint wafts of another smell; aromatic,
pungent, sweet. It was not incense; at least, it was not
church incense; and it was not joss-sticks or pastilles.
It contained something of all three, and something else
beside, which he could not place. It was very faint, as if
the draft of the opening door had disturbed vague wafts
of it where they lay hidden in crevices among the books.
Coming as it did immediately upon his reading of the
Black Mass and its stinking incense, and coming in darkness, it affected him to a degree that startled him, and he
felt with A. E. W. Mason's hero, as if ' the shell of the
world might crack and some streak of light come
through '. For a moment the obsession of the recent
happenings was broken; the memory of them was gone
from him as if a wet sponge had been passed across a
slate, and his mind was suddenly made new, receptive,

quivering, in anticipation of what was about to be given it.

He heard someone stirring in an inner room, and the sound of a match being struck. Evidently the bookshop did not run to electric light. Then a dim warm radiance shone across the floor in a broad streak, coming from under a curtain slung across a doorless gap between the books, and in another moment he saw the figure of a tall stooping man in a dressing-gown, or some such voluminous garment, thrusting aside the curtain and coming through into the front shop. The curtain fell back into place again, and everything was once more in darkness.

" Pardon me," said a voice, " I will strike a light. I was not expecting that anyone would call this wet evening."

A match scraped, and then flared, and he had a momentary glimpse of a vulturine head, bald, with a fringe of grizzled red hair ; a great eagle's beak seemed on its way to make junction with the prominent Adam's apple in the stringy neck, left bare by a low and crumpled soft collar, and a big Jaeger camel's-hair dressing-gown enveloped all the rest.

" Damn ! " said a voice as the match went out.

That single word told Paston that he had to do with a man of education, a gentleman, a man not too remotely removed from his own world. Not thus do the proletariat swear when they burn their fingers.

Another match flared up, and carefully shielding it with his large bony hands, the individual in the dressing-gown reached up to his full height and lit an incandescent gasolier hanging from the ceiling in the centre of the room. Only a very tall man could have done it, and the proprietor of the bookshop, if that were what he was, revealed himself as a great gaunt framework of a man, his loose clothes hanging slackly upon him ; his ungirt dressing-gown with its trailing cords making him look like a huge bat hung up by its hooked wings in sleep.

But Paston saw much in that single glimpse, even as he had heard much in that single word; the ancient and nondescript garments were not cheap reach-me downs, but honest Harris tweed. As the light flared up and his eyes took in the books ranged all round him, he saw at once that the twopenny bin was no criterion of the contents of the shop, but was filled with unregarded throwouts, and that the bookseller was a specialist and a scholar.

Hugh held out towards him the grubby blue volume in his hand.

" I got this out of your twopenny bin," he said.

The bookseller peered at it.

" Now how did that get into the twopenny bin ? " he demanded, as if enquiring of the book itself.

" Is it more than twopence ? " asked Hugh Paston, inwardly amused, and wondering whether he would be called upon to wrangle over odd coppers before the book was his.

" No, no, certainly not," said the bookseller. " If it was in the twopenny bin, I'll charge you twopence for it. But I wouldn't have exposed it to that indignity willingly. I have a regard for books." He looked up suddenly and transfixed his interlocutor with a piercing glance. " I have a feeling for them that some people have for horses."

" Are they ' wittles and drink ' to you ? " said Paston, smiling.

" They are that," said the bookseller. " Shall I wrap it up for you ? "

" No thanks, I'll take it as it is. By the way, have you got anything else in the same line ? "

It was as if an iron shutter, such as he might pull down outside his shop, came down over the bookseller's face.

" You mean something else by A. E. W. Mason ? "

" No, I mean something else about the—er—Black Mass."

The bookseller eyed him suspiciously, not to be drawn.

" I have got Huysmans' ' Là-Bas ' in French."

" I can't be bothered to read French at the moment. I want something light. Have you got a translation of it ? "

" There is no translation, nor ever will be."

" Why ever not ? "

" The British public wouldn't stand for it."

" Is it as French as all that ? "

" No."

" I'm afraid you're beyond me. Have you got anything else in English along the same lines ? "

" There is nothing written."

" Nothing written that you know of, I suppose you mean ? "

" There is nothing written."

" Oh well, I suppose you know. Here is your two-pence."

" Thanks. Good-night."

" Good-night."

Paston found himself outside in the dark, a light rain falling. He had no intention of going back to his own house that night, and as the light rain promised to be the forerunner of a series of squalls he cast about in his mind for the nearest hotel that would suit his mood of the moment. For on leaving the bookshop behind his previous mood had returned ; memories had risen again like ghosts in the gathering dusk, and he wished urgently to get back among bright lights and other people. But not his friends. The last thing he wanted was his friends. He did not want people to talk to him. ·He just wanted to see them moving about him in bright light.

There did not seem much hope of a taxi in that down at heel district, but it was apparently a short cut to a good many places, and at that moment a taxi turned into it. Paston signalled, and it drew in to the kerb.

He gave the driver the address of one of the big railway hotels, and got in. The cab swung round and bore him away into the width and straightness and brightness of a main road, and he heaved a sigh of relief.

Presently they arrived at the huge facade of the designated hotel, and he went into the lounge and ordered a whisky and soda, and lighting a cigarette, settled down to his book; the whisky and soda had soothed him temporarily, and his nerves were less on edge for the moment. He read rapidly, following the twists and turns of detectives and corpses with impatience. He was not reading for the story. He was reading for information. Information about the opal and its prisoner. Information about the Black Mass that had so caught his fancy and intrigued him.

He gathered from this hasty perusal that the Black Mass was a somewhat messy affair; that a renegade priest was necessary for its performance; also a lady of at least easy manners. He did not discover exactly what was done; nor for what purpose people went to all this trouble. The ceremony in itself did not particularly interest him; not being a believer, he was not especially scandalised; it was no more to him than a Parisian music-hall. The psychology of it escaped him.

The thing in which he was really interested, the thing for which he had bought the book—was its title, ' The Prisoner in the Opal '; the hint of escape— a glimpse of fire from the heart of the stone—the gates of life ajar—.

For he had come to his journey's end before the number of his days was fulfilled. Life had proved a blind alley, and unless a door opened before him there was nothing to do but fall over the precipice that is at the world's end. The symbolism of the fire flashing from the heart of the stone with its luminous opacity had fascinated him, but it was not elucidated in the course of the book, so far as he could see. The writer had had a glimpse, but had lost sight of it again. The idea of the Black Mass had intrigued him, but he had not followed up the trail. Now he, Hugh Paston, given that trail, would have pursued it ; and the idea occurred to him, Why shouldn't he pursue it? He had nothing to lose, no one to consider. If he threw his life away, that was his look-out. As for his soul, he knew nothing about it and cared less. Fortune had returned him his hostages and he was a free man.

He was intrigued by the idea of following up the clue that the author of ' The Prisoner in the Opal ' had dangled for an instant before the eyes of his readers and then snatched away again. He remembered the words of the second-hand bookseller, that there were no other books on the Black Mass in English, but one in French—very French French, Hugh Paston had gathered. He glanced at his watch. It was shortly after nine. Why not go round, and if there were a light showing in the shop, knock the fellow up, stand him a drink, and try and get him to talk? He had more than a suspicion the man knew something about the subject of Black Masses, else why had he first spoken upon them with authority, and then shut up like a clam? Hugh Paston got his coat, sinned against the tailor by pushing the bulky novel into a pocket, and left the hotel.

# CHAPTER II

THE night was clear at the moment, but scudding clouds across the face of the full moon promised more squalls. Hugh Paston turned up his coat collar and made his way through the sordid streets on foot. It seemed to him inappropriate to arrive in the narrow street in a taxi, creating a commotion and drawing attention to himself, and giving the visit an importance he did not wish it to possess. Moreover his head ached from the steam-heat of the hotel and his inner restlessness demanded an outlet.

The wet freshness of the gusty wind that he met at street corners was welcome ; it cooled his face and gave him something to struggle with. The dark, too, was welcome after the glare and publicity of the hotel. Just as, earlier in the evening, he had longed for light and crowds, so now he welcomed darkness and solitude, his moods following one another in rapid succession. He felt himself to be capricious, unstable, mentally and physically feverish. At the moment he walked vigorously, full of pressing life that could find no aim or outlet. He didn't know what he wanted, and if he got it, wouldn't like it. He felt irritable. If anyone jostled him, he would get shoved and sworn at. He suspected that his feverish energy would be short-lived, and that in a few minutes it would turn to a dragging weight, as it had done so often before, when the one thing he would want would be to drop into a taxi and be taken home. And once home, he knew the restlessness would renew itself and he would be too weary to sleep.

This was the cycle he had been repeating for the

last few days, and he had no reason to believe it had changed its track, save that as he got wearier the phases were shorter and more extreme and the changes more violent.

It came to him, in a moment of insight in the windy darkness, that the thing that had cracked him up was not the break-up of his marriage. That had been the occasion and not the cause. The trouble had been brewing for a considerable time. It amused him to realise that he who at one time had read psycho-analytical literature at the bidding of his wife in order that they might have something to talk about at dinner parties when such subjects were the vogue, was now getting a close-up of the disintegration of a personality.

Without knowing how he got there, he suddenly found himself outside the second-hand bookshop. Late as it was, it was all lit up just as he had left it. He laid his hand on the latch of the half-glass door. It yielded, and he entered, hearing its warning bell clang as he did so. He heard someone stirring in the inner room, the shabby serge curtain was thrust aside, and the bookseller appeared, blinking in the hard glare of the unshaded incandescence, and looking at him enquiringly.

For a moment Hugh Paston did not know what he had come for. His mind was slipping its cogs and it scared him. With a Herculean effort he pulled himself together and managed to say stumblingly : " You said you had another book—on the same subject— in French, I think it was——" and the situation was saved. At least he hoped it was. At any rate, the bookseller accepted him in a matter of fact manner as an ordinary customer. His face showed no surprise at the oddness of the demand or the lateness of the hour at which it was made. Had Hugh Paston had his wits about him, he would have known that the very absence of surprise indicated that he might just as well withdraw his head from the sand, as his tail-feathers were clearly visible. Though of course he had no means of knowing that shortly after his previous visit the vulturine bookseller had been out for his usual evening stroll after shutting-up time, and buying his usual evening paper, had found an illustration on the picture page in which the Press photographer had been lucky enough to catch one face clearly—the face of the chief mourner at a certain sensational funeral, and, staring at it, had murmured to himself: " Poor devil ! So that was why he wanted something exciting, but couldn't be bothered to read a foreign language ? "

The bookseller studied his visitor for a moment before replying.

" Ah, yes," he said at length, " Huysmans' ' Là-Bas ' is the book you are referring to. I have it here. Your mention of it roused my interest in it, and I have been dipping into it again myself. I have also remembered that I was a little rash in saying there are no books in English on the subject of the Black Mass, no books worth having, that is. I do not call sheer sensationalism a book. There is nothing, so far as I know, strictly on the subject of the Black Mass, but one or two interesting books on cognate subjects. ' The Devil's Mistress ', for instance ; and ' The Corn King and the Spring Queen.' Perhaps you would like to look at them. I have got them here, if you would be so good as to step this way." He drew back the tattered curtain that hung in the doorless gap between the bookcases, and Paston followed him through into the inner room.

He had never been in the room behind a shop, and the experienced intrigued him. Half the world does not know how the other half lives, and he was about to have a glimpse of a side of life that had never been opened to him before. He hoped it would distract his mind.

He found himself in a smallish room, too lofty for its size. There was a gas-bracket, but it was not lit, such light as there was came from a green-shaded oil-lamp that stood on a small table beside an ancient leather-covered arm-chair drawn up to the hearth. The lamp threw a small circle of gentle light onto the chair ; the rest of the room was in a dim, warm gloom, for the fire in the old-fashioned grate was low.

Serge curtains trimmed with a gap-toothed ball fringe were drawn carelessly across a long French window on the wall opposite the doorway by which they had entered, and beside them was a half-open door through which the corner of a sink was visible. The walls were lined to the ceiling with the bookseller's stock-in-trade. Piles of dusty books filled the corners of the floor. A small kitchen table covered with a coarse blue and white checked table-cloth occupied the centre of the room, and was the only bit of furniture in the place that was not cumbered with books. A wooden chair drawn up beside it indicated that it was the dining-table. The absence of a second chair indicated single blessedness.

The fire-place under its white marble mantel-piece was a beautiful bit of wrought-ironwork with high hobs at either side, on one of which a black earthenware tea-pot stood warming, and on the other a heavy, willow-pattern plate. An exceedingly ancient and mangy grey goat-skin hearthrug and an exceptionally heavy set of fire-irons completed the equipment.

Upon the opposite side of the hearth to the armchair with the lamp at its elbow was a big, broken-springed, leather-covered sofa of the same breed as the chair, its seat full of books. The bookseller disposed of the books by sending them to the floor with one sweep of his hand.

" If you will be so good as to take a seat——" he said, indicating the broken springs. Hugh Paston sat down and found them much better than he had antici- pated, discovering, to his surprise, that a sofa of this breed, even if broken-springed, was a very much better thing to sit on than the chairs in his own house. He sank back into its roomy depths and relaxed.

"I am afraid I am keeping you from your supper," he said.

"Not at all," said the bookseller, "I haven't begun to cook it yet. I have only made the tea. Might I— er—offer you a cup, if you would honour me? It seems a pity to let it stew and be wasted."

Hugh Paston accepted, not wishing to hurt his feelings. Tea was not one of his beverages at the best of times, and this was not the best of times with him. His mind turned in the direction of old brandy, and he wondered whether it would be after hours when he got back to the hotel, and felt pretty certain that it would.

The bookseller produced two large white cups with narrow gold lines round them and an odd little gold flower at the bottom of each. Hugh remembered having seen similar ones in the potting-shed of his boyhood's home. He believed they were used for measuring out weed-killer and insecticides. At any rate, no human being drank out of them. Into these roomy receptacles went some milk from a bottle. Soft sugar was shovelled in with what looked like a lead spoon, and then a stream of rich mahogany fluid was applied from the broken spout of the black tea-pot.

"This——" said the bookseller, handing him a cup, " is a man's drink."

Hugh Paston was rather startled to hear such an epithet applied to a cup of tea, but as soon as he sampled it he knew it to be justified. It was hot. It was strong. It was rich in tannin. And altogether it had as much kick as a cocktail and bore not the remotest likeness to tea as it was understood in his wife's drawing-room.

"By Jove," he said, "that's good stuff. I think you've saved my life."

"Have another cup?"

"I will."

Another cup was dispensed and drunk in a companionable silence : Hugh Paston in his tail-coat on one side of the hearth, and the old vulture in his dusty dressing-gown on the other. Hugh had a sudden flash of realisation that with this man one would not touch surfaces, as in Mayfair. If one touched him at all, one would touch the real man. And he felt that in some curious way he had touched him ; and to that human touch something in him suddenly clung desperately, like a child.

The old man had eyes of a very light bright blue, deep-set under superciliary ridges like a gorilla, and over-hung by eyebrows that would have served most folk for a moustache. He was clean-shaven, and his tanned leathery skin hung about his chops in folds, after the manner of a bloodhound. His mouth was large, thin-lipped and humorous, very like a camel's.

Hugh Paston, at first sight, had taken him to be somewhere in the eighties ; but in actual fact he was a battered and dilapidated sixty-five, looking much older than he need on account of his dressing-gown, a garment usually associated with the infirm.

He, for his part, looking at the man opposite him, judged him to be in the early thirties, but that whatever might be his actual age, he would never look a young man again. He wondered whether he had been deeply in love with the woman who had died with her lover, and surmised that he had not. There was a hungry and restless look about his face that is not seen on the face of men who have loved, even if they have been crossed in love. This was a man, he thought, who was unfulfilled. Life had given him everything he wanted and nothing he needed. Lack of spiritual vitamins and a rachitic soul, was his diagnosis. He judged that there was too much idealism in this man to start him drinking, but that he would prove rash and erratic in all his doings unless a steadying hand were laid on him at the present juncture, and probably rush into the wrong kind of marriage, or a ruinous

co-respondentship with some woman for whom he cared
not a single hoot.

He, for his part, had a hearty contempt for Mayfair
and all its ways and works, and the contempt was genuine
and not of the sour grapes vintage. For he held that
the average inhabitant of that district would never be
able to keep his head above water in a competitive world
unless he had a swimming bladder tied to it in the shape
of inherited money. Had he been kicked out into
life through the gates of a Council school, he would
have landed in the gutter and stopped there. So honest
and complete was his sense of superiority that he had
to overcome a kind of inverted snobbishness in holding
out a friendly hand to the man who had not been the
architect of his own fortune.

He was watching his visitor carefully, and observed
that he was settling down and relaxing, and being not
without experience in the ups and downs of life himself,
knew that a reaction was on its way, and the fellow
would soon feel more dead than alive. He wondered
what could be done to tide him over his bad patch.

" I wonder if I might offer you some supper, sir ?
It is getting late, and—I don't know what you are—
but I am getting hungry."

" Yes, by Jove, now you mention it, I am."

The old man moved off through the door beside the
French window, lit an incandescent burner, and Paston
saw a little built-on kitchenette, small as a ship's galley.
The pop of gas indicated a gas-stove behind the door,
and in a few moments there was a noble sputtering.

The old man came in with a second plate and put it
to warm beside the fire. The heavy black kettle was
restored to the hob.

" Eggs and bacon suit you ? " he enquired.

" First rate. Couldn't be better."

" Two eggs ? "

" Rather."

In a surprisingly short space of time the bookseller reappeared with a loaded tin tea-tray and began to shuffle a miscellaneous collection onto the table in the middle of the room. Everything was rough but clean, with the exception of the knives, which were not stainless, and had not seen a knifeboard for years.

The old man looked at them doubtfully. Then he went over to the mantelpiece, and clearing it of books by the same simple method that he had cleared the sofa, began to use one end of it as a knifeboard, slapping the knives backwards and forwards on its white marble surface, felt their edges with his thumb, and returned them to the table.

" There's one thing about marble mantelpieces for cleaning knives," he said, " it saves the Monkey-soap. Now we're ready. Will you come along ? " He plunged his hand into a huge pile of books that rose in a far corner, groped among them for a moment, gave them a shake that spilled them onto the floor in an avalanche, and drew out a second kitchen chair, which he carried to the table.

They seated themselves. Hugh Paston thought he had never smelt anything so good in his life as that bacon, or seen anything that looked as attractive as the crisp edges of the fried eggs as the bookseller served them out of the frying-pan in which they had cooked.

They fell to. The old man did not seem disposed to talk, and Hugh Paston, who felt as if he had not had a meal for a week, did not feel disposed to either. They ate in silence. At the conclusion of the meal his host put the black tea-pot back in its place on the hob and filled it up from the kettle. Then he shuffled everything onto the tray with a terrific clatter and deposited his load in the kitchen.

" I hate garbage," he said, having rendered this service to sanitation. Then he returned to the now blazing fire and began to fill his pipe.

# CHAPTER III

HUGH PASTON was half asleep over his cigarette, his feet stretched out on the fireside stool and a cup of the well-stewed tea beside him. The events of the last painful days, even his married life with Frida, seemed to have slid into the remote backward and abyss of time. The old bookseller, looking at him, saw that he was more disposed to go to sleep than to do anything else. He rose, went to the window, drew back the curtain by its snaggle-toothed fringe, and peered out into the darkness. Nothing was to be seen. Rain ran in long streaks down the glass. A furious draught drove through the cracks and swayed the tassel on the cord of an undrawn blind.

"A beast of a night," he said, dropping the curtain back into place and returning to the fire.

Hugh Paston roused himself wearily.

"What time is it? I suppose I can get a taxi?"

"Getting on for late. No, I don't know how you'll get a taxi in this district. I'm not on the phone, and the pub at the corner's shut. Have you far to go?"

Hugh named his hotel.

"Good Lord, what are you doing there?"

"God only knows. I don't. I couldn't stand the house so I cleared out." It never occurred to him that he had told the bookseller neither his name nor history, yet he took it for granted that the old man knew all about him, as in fact he did.

The bookseller looked at him thoughtfully.

"You can't go back there. No, you certainly mustn't go back there. Look here, sir, can I offer you a bed for the night? You're very welcome to one if you care to have it."

" That's dashed kind of you. Yes, I'd be very glad."
The old man took the lamp in his hand and led the
way into the shop. In one corner was a narrow wooden
stair with no hand-rail, no better than a glorified step-
ladder. Up this they mounted, coming out through an
unrailed hole in the floor like the entrance to a hayloft.
Apparently the shop was of the lock-up species, but its
owner was also the tenant of the maisonette over it, and
had solved the problem of having to go out to go to bed
in this simple but adequate fashion. Hugh Paston
wondered whether the landlord knew, and whether he
minded having his timbers cut in this happy-go-lucky
manner.

Looking round, he saw that everything was covered
with a thick layer of grey dust through which wound
paths made by the feet of the occupier ; where he had no
occasion to go, the dust lay undisturbed. Hugh wondered whether he had been wise to accept the offer of a
bed.

They went up another flight. A bit of faded old felt
carpeted the upper landing, but it looked as if it were
shaken out of the window from time to time. A fish-
tailed gas-burner, turned low, cast a faint illumination.
Through an open door he caught a glimpse of a high,
old-fashioned bath, badly in need of a coat of paint.

His host opened a door next to the bath-room,
entered, and set the lamp down on a bureau.

" Here you are," he said. " No bugs. I guarantee
that. That's all I can guarantee, though."

Hugh thought to himself that considering the state of
the stairs, he was glad to have this guarantee. His host
disappeared, to return in a moment with a faded old pair
of flannelette pyjamas, minus all the buttons and most of
the seat.

" Here you are," he said. " Sorry there's no buttons,
but the cord's intact, and that's the main thing."

Left alone, Hugh Paston took stock of his quarters.

The bed was not exactly a four-poster, but had two high poles behind, from which a canopy stuck out in a cock-eyed fashion, threatening to come down and hit the sleeper on the head at any moment. Curtains of faded red damask hung from it after the unhygienic fashion of an earlier age. Hugh got out of his clothes, and got into the seatless pyjamas, and slid into the bed, which consisted of a huge, fat old feather mattress, half a dozen washed-out blankets, and a faded patchwork quilt. Hugh had never slept in a feather bed before, and was immensely taken with it. He pulled the curtains forward cautiously, the canopy creaking ominously as he did so, and tucked them in under the mattress to keep off the draught from the dilapidated sash-window, against which the storm beat in howling gusts. From somewhere near at hand, presumably on the tiles, came the wail of a despairing cat. That was the last Hugh Paston remembered.

When he awoke it was broad daylight, and his host, still in the same old dressing-gown, but with pyjamas under it, stood looking down at him with an immense mug in his hand.

" Here's some tea for you. There's a can of hot water over there, tucked under the corner of the carpet. If you want a bath, you'll have to go out to the local wash-house for it. Bath's busted. I sat through it last summer. Anyway, there was no way of heating the water. Get up when you feel like it. There's no hurry. I've put my razor on the mantelpiece.

He waved his hand and departed.

Breakfast was one of the most agreeable meals, thought Hugh, that he had ever eaten. The tea-pot stood on the hob and kept really hot, and they made toast on their forks in front of the glowing coals. It only needed a dressing-gown like the old bookseller's, and a pair of carpet-slippers, to be perfection.

They were smoking peacefully, sharing the paper between them, when an old char-lady came in.

" Wot about food ? " she demanded.

" Sausage and mash, I think, for lunch. The usual for supper, and a beef-steak pudding for Sunday's dinner. That suit you, Mr Paston ? "

Hugh woke up with a start.

" Good Lord, are you going to keep me here over the week-end ? "

" You're welcome if you want to. You're not in my way. I reckon you won't care for the week-end at home very much."

" My God, no, I shouldn't think I would ! Nor in that blasted hotel. I'm everlastingly grateful to you."

The bookseller grunted.

The old dame grunted also, took up an enormous bag made of black American cloth, and sallied forth to do the week-end shopping.

As the shop-door clanged shut behind her, Hugh Paston turned to his host.

" I say, why are you doing all this for me ? "

The old man wagged his tufted brows at him.

" G.O.K.," he said.

Paston laughed. " Yes, He knows, but I'm not in His confidence. You've heard my story, I take it ? "

" I know what's in the papers, and guess the rest."

" There's no rest. The papers got the lot."

The old man did not answer.

" Well, I'm damned grateful to you, anyway. God knows what I'd have done to myself if I'd had to spend the night alone in that hotel."

" You probably wouldn't have spent it alone," said the bookseller with a slow smile.

" No, I probably shouldn't. Being after hours, that was the only resort left open to me. So much for Dora, God rest her soul."

The bookseller rose.

" I've got work to do," he said. " Make yourself at home. There's plenty to read. Don't let the fire out."

He disappeared through the curtain into the shop.

Left to his own devices, Hugh Paston put his feet up on the sofa and settled down to his cigarette. Uncommonly comfortable quarters, he thought. The general shabbiness and dilapidation counted for nothing. The old bookseller had got the essentials of real comfort. Among the grubby cushions lay the book that had been the alleged reason for his return to the bookshop the previous evening. He fished it out and commenced to flick over its pages.

Skipping skilfully, Hugh made his way through the novel. Bluebeard did not interest him particularly, nor the pointless French love affair ; it was Canon Docre he was after, ' *le formidable chanoine*,' and he found him as elusive as Durtal had done. Finally, however, he ran him to earth, and settled down to chuckle over the pages in which he celebrates the Black Mass, tastefully got up in a chasuble embroidered with billy-goats, socks and suspenders, and nothing else. He couldn't see anything horrific about it. It appeared to him simply funny.

Presently the old bookseller finished his chores and returned to the room behind the shop. Once the mail orders had been dealt with, there was apparently nothing to do for the rest of the day but sit around and wait for casual customers to drop in, and as the weather was worse than bad, it was improbable that they would drop.

" I say, Jelkes," said Hugh Paston, " can we do anything to this sofa ? I'm gradually going through."

" Certainly, my dear lad, why didn't you mention it before ? Always ask for anything you want here. It's yours for the asking," and he flung himself flat on his face on the hearthrug at the feet of the startled Paston, who thought the Black Mass had begun in good earnest.

But he was wrong. The old bookseller merely wanted to peer under the sofa.

" Ah," he said, " I see what's amiss. Springs have given way."

He reached out a long arm as he lay there, and drew towards himself a pile of loose books lying about on the floor and began to stow them scientifically under the sofa.

" There," he said, getting up and dusting his knees. " That's the best use I know for the modern novel."

# CHAPTER IV

THERE came a great pounding at the door as Paston
was about to seat himself on the now rejuvenated sofa.

"That's Mrs Hull," said the bookseller, and went to
admit the char, who came barging in like a ship in full
sail, hung about with purchases, mostly wrapped in
newspaper. The old bookseller gave her some loose
silver from his trouser pocket, without troubling to count
it, and she barged out again.

He flung the now bulging black oilcloth bag on the
table, where it disgorged everything imaginable, including a mouse-trap and a pair of braces.

"Absolutely trustworthy," he said, "and a great
comfort to me. That's the right sort of woman to have
about the place. No 'It.' Gets on with her job and
clears off when finished."

The bookseller began to get on with the preparations
for a meal. There was a pound of pale pink pork
sausages, showing through their damp bit of greaseproof
paper like a beach belle through her bathing-dress. There
was a large dollop of mashed potatoes in a basin, evidently
fetched from the neighbouring eating-house and only
needing warming. What a simple way of living, thought
Hugh Paston, with an envious sigh. And how efficacious !

He thought of all the elaborations that were considered necessary when he fed, and of the not always
admirable result. One thing was quite certain, nothing
that had to come up from the kitchen could ever taste as
it did straight out of old Jelkes' frying-pan.

He went and leant against the jamb of the door leading to the kitchenette and watched the old boy at his

cooking. The frying-pan presented quite a beach scene as the pale pink sausages gradually browned.

" Do you like 'em whole or bust ? " demanded Jelkes suddenly, waving a toasting-fork over the pan.

Paston, taken by surprise, answered without thinking :

" Well, I know it isn't fashionable to have much bust, but personally I prefer a reasonable amount. I think it's more feminine."

The old bookseller looked at him in bewilderment ; but before he could demand the meaning of this cryptic remark, the unpricked sausages settled the problem for themselves by splitting wide open, one after the other.

" Ah, well," he said philosophically, " you'll have to take them as they are. They've all bust now."

He turned them out of the frying-pan, and picking up the white china basin containing the mashed potato, held it out at arm's length and smacked its bottom, dodging skilfully back as the hot fat splashed out of the pan as the potatoes sploshed into it. Hugh Paston, cigarette between his teeth, was shaken with internal mirth. He thought of his butler. ·He thought of his chef. He thought of the head-waiters of fashionable restaurants. He wondered what his friends would make of him. He wondered what he made of himself. Changing for dinner in this establishment apparently meant putting on a dressing-gown and taking off your collar.

He suddenly realised that he was more intimate with the old bookseller than he had ever been with anybody in his life. With maturity, Hugh Paston had become a man of easy surfaces, but at heart he was still deeply reserved. Under his camaraderie there was a sensitive shyness, a disinclination to wear his heart in any spot where it might be pecked at. He had only saved the situation by refusing to look inside himself ; by forcing himself to live on his own surface ; by trying to make himself the man he appeared to be. He wondered how many were like him. It had often struck him how melan-

choly Mayfair faces were when in repose. The old bookseller, dilapidated and hard-bitten as he was, was cheerful
in repose.

It suddenly occurred to him that he positively loved
the old boy. What a priceless old bird he was ! He had
a feeling that the light-blue eyes under their thatch of
whiskers saw far more deeply into his soul than he was
capable of doing himself. He felt like a sick man feels
when he gets into the hands of a good doctor. He
wondered what the old boy, who was not of his generation, had made of the remark about the sausages. Had
he been brought up on Freud ? It certainly was a brick
and a half to drop on the toes of an elderly member of
the middle classes.

His meditations were interrupted by having the large
black tin tea-tray thrust into his hands. The old man
loaded the dinner onto it, and Hugh Paston lugged the
heavy load into the living-room. Without waiting to be
told, he filled up the big black kettle and set it on the
hob, ready for the everlasting tea. His highly polished
veneer had split and peeled off him like the husk off a
roast chestnut, and with it had gone his tensions and
bewilderments. He reckoned that the old bookseller,
with his tea-pot and his frying-pan, his broken-springed
sofa and his cock-eyed feather-bed, had saved his mental
balance and seen him safely through his time of crisis.
How it had been done he had no means of knowing. He
only knew that a human hand had been laid on him amid
all the hard, bright, impersonal surfaces of Mayfair, and
the human touch had in some curious way reassured him
about life, as if he were a child in the dark.

The old bookseller ate fast and never talked at meals.
The meal concluded with a slab of moist sultana cake
instead of pudding ; they brewed their tea, and Paston
was hoping to get down to a good chin-wag, when the
old bookseller suddenly put two grubby books into his
hands and said :

" Amuse yourself with these. I always have a snooze now," and suiting the action to the words, he settled himself back in his chair, opened his mouth, and went to sleep forthwith. Hugh Paston, who could not drop off to sleep like that, settled down to look at the books that had been given him.

They were the ones that the bookseller had previously recommended : ' The Devil's Mistress,' by Brodie Innes, who was a ' writer to the Signet,' whatever that might be, and ' The Corn King and the Spring Queen,' by Naomi Mitchison, a tale of ancient Sparta. He had a vague idea of having heard that Naomi Mitchison was the daughter of a professor of Greek, or some such classical subject, so probably her facts were correct, and provided she was not too heavy-handed with them, the book might be worth reading. He wondered why old Jelkes had recommended it as a useful adjunct to Huysmans' ' Là-Bas.'

He dipped into her first, and read the opening chapter upon the magic of the Scythian witch.

" That," said he to himself, " is just common or garden hypnotism."

He had learnt something of native magic during his big game-shooting expeditions, and knew the tremendous power of auto-suggestion upon the primitive mind. The only thing in which fiction differed from fact was in that the power was here represented as being used at a distance, without the immediate use of suggestion, on which he understood it depended. Induced auto-suggestion, he had heard hypnotism called by a well-known doctor, who always talked shop at dinner-tables as a means of advertising.

He thought of incidents which he had seen with his own eyes, and seeing is believing in such cases ; and he also thought of the long series of similar cases recorded in the ' Wide World Magazine ' month by month, a magazine that claims to print nothing but true stories, and takes care to verify them for the sake of its reputation.

It was odd, very odd, to find the same kind of witch-craft in modern Africa and ancient Scythia. He felt pretty certain that the archæology of this book was reliable ; and he himself had seen certain African inci-dents with his own eyes ; and even if his eyes misled him, there were the incidents recorded in the ' Wide World,' collected from all quarters of the globe. Every-body could not have been deluded.

Like all Mayfairians who go in for up to date dinner table conversation, he was an adept at skipping, and he was picking the gist out of the book as well as any reviewer. Presently, however, he came to something that arrested his attention, and settled down to read steadily the account of the rites of the spring ploughing. Naomi Mitchison was discreet ; she left something to the imagination, which was more than Huysmans did ; it was possible that a maiden lady might have read her book without noticing anything. Hugh Paston, how-ever, found here an interesting addition to his knowledge of human nature. He knew his Havelock Ellis, his Kraft-Ebbing, and his Forel, but he had never come across anything quite like this before. The ' Wide World,' in publishing its stories of native magic, did not publish stories of this kind of magic. It knew its public, its British public.

The dingy, cosy room disappeared from before his eyes as he saw in his imagination the woman lying nude in the centre of the great field, gazing up at the little white clouds of spring in the sky above her, and feeling the cold wind and the spring sun on her bare skin while the slow-moving, snow-white oxen dragged the primi-tive plough nearer and nearer as they circled the field.

He read on ; but the fate of the royal house of Sparta interested him less, and he put the book down and took up the other.

Here was a tale of an entirely different calibre, based on the account of the witch-burnings in the state papers of Scotland, and as the author was a 'Writer to the Signet,' which sounded imposing, he judged that it too might be considered as properly documented.

The old spell : ' Horse, hattock, to horse and away ! ' delighted him. It had the authentic ring. He chuckled at the picture of the handsome, vigorous Isabel Goudie putting the broomstick to bed with her stupid and boring husband and slipping off to the witch-coven in the old churchyard to enjoy herself with the Devil, who, it subsequently turned out, was a man, though ' very much of a man ', if the witches were to be believed ; and as they told their stories under torture, the truth was probably extracted from them.

He wondered what it was that made decent, sober Scottish matrons and maids kick up their heels and get their legs over the traces like this. He could understand their resorting to the rural Scottish equivalent of a night on the tiles, but why this adoration of the Devil ? Why the religious element in it all ?

He chuckled to himself at the idea of some respectable burgher playing the part of the Devil, complete with cow's horns, two on his head and one in his hand.

What a vogue, he thought, a well-run coven would have in Mayfair ! He chortled so loudly at the thought that he woke old Jelkes, who popped up his head, brisk as a bird, to enquire the cause of his mirth.

Paston told him.

" Humph," said Jelkes, " You stick to sausages," and Hugh Paston collapsed completely.

But while nominally snoozing, the old man had been doing a lot of thinking. He had brought Hugh Paston to shore in the thick of the storm, it was not in him to stand idly by and watch him slip back into deep water again. Yet what could he do with the fellow ? To invite him to prolong his visit, would, he felt, be an error of tactics. Paston belonged to a different world. He might be well enough content to picnic for a night or two on an old feather-bed in a bathless establishment, but he would not care to keep it up for long. No, Hugh Paston must be returned whence he came on Monday.

But what would happen to him then? There was something fundamentally wrong with the fellow. It was much more, and it dated back far earlier, than the wife's defection. That had been the occasion, not the cause, of his collapse. He wondered what inner emotional history lay behind Hugh Paston. Probably the real significance of his life was as much hidden from him as it was from the old bookseller at the moment. There were powerful undercurrents that were making the surface so choppy, and their owner was the last man to know what they were.

They made tea. Hugh Paston tried to count up the number of cups they had already drunk between them that day, but failed hopelessly. The storm had returned and was sheeting down the window, which was tight shut against it; and his cigarettes and Jelkes' pipe and the blazing fire all united to produce a most comfortable frowst in which the soul was set free to range the heights of fancy while the body sprawled, too enervated for movement.

They had allowed the fire to go too low for toast, and so they ate the soggy plum-cake that served Jelkes as ' afters ' for all the meals at which sweets are usually served. Conversation was impossible while this cake was being consumed, as it clogged the teeth.

Presently, however, they concluded their meal, and Jelkes cleared away. Untidy as he was, he never permitted the remains of a meal to lie about, but thrust it higgledy-piggledy into the kitchenette to await the ministrations of Mrs Hull next morning, who did one mighty wash-up every twenty-four hours, a practice that no doubt was responsible for the purchase of the mousetrap.

"Well?" said the old bookseller, returning to the fireside, this tribute to Cloacina concluded. "So you've read the books, have you? And what do you make of them?"

"There's nothing specifically Black Massy in them, so far as I can see."

"No, I told you there wasn't. But there are some very curious things if you read between the lines. Writers will put things into a novel that they daren't put in sober prose, where you have to dot the I's and cross the T's."

"You don't tell me that they worked the Black Mass in ancient Greece, or in Calvinistic Scotland? They wouldn't know how."

"No, precisely, they wouldn't know how. Huysmans brings that out clearly. You have to have a pucka priest for the job."

"Why so?"

"Because no one else knows how."

"But you can get the book of the words anywhere. It's all in the prayer-book."

"There's a lot more in it than the words. Do you know that it takes a priest a year after he's ordained to learn to say Mass?"

"How do you know?"

"Because I very nearly became one."

"Cripes!"

"Yes, I was educated by the Jesuits."

"What did you boggle at? Couldn't you manage the faith?"

"I could manage the faith all right. What I couldn't manage was the humility."

Paston looked at the craggy old vulture, and believed him.

"Could you work the Black Mass if you wanted to?"

"If I wanted to, yes, I know enough for that. But I don't want to."

" Then you have been actually ordained ? "

" No, I never got as far as that. But one couldn't be on the inside of things, as I was in the seminary, without picking up a good deal if you had your eyes open. I saw a lot then which I learned to understand later."

" What do you think of the Jesuits, if it isn't a tactless question ? "

" I think they are the most marvellously trained body of men in the world—and the most dangerous if you get on the wrong side of them. I think they make certain fundamental mistakes, but I admire them. They taught me a lot."

" What did they teach you ? "

" They taught me the power of the trained mind."

" Is that what makes the difference when a priest says Mass ? "

" Yes, that, and the tremendous momentum of the Church itself backing him up. That is why the Roman Catholic Mass has a kick in it that the Anglo-Catholic hasn't. The C. of E. doesn't know how to train her men."

" Then it isn't just a matter of theology ? "

" No, it's a matter of psychology—in my opinion, at any rate, though that's rank heresy, according to all the authorities."

" Is that why they've got to have a renegade priest for the Black Mass——? Because he's a trained man ? "

" That's it. He knows how to put the power behind it."

" Look here, Jelkes, will you work the Black Mass for me, for a lark ? "

" No, you bloody fool, I won't, it's much too dangerous."

" But you've just said it's only psychology."

" Maybe, but have you thought what you'd stir up with it ? "

" Stir up in what ? "

" In yourself."

" What do you stir up in yourself ? "

" Well, think ; think it out."

" I don't know that I can think it out.   I haven't got enough data."

" You've got plenty if you take the trouble to use it."

" Well, I can understand A. E. W. Mason's kind of Black Mass, where the villain had got this rather sporty female ' mid nodings on ' to act as altar, and did the job on her tummy.   One can see where the kick came in that, and its commonplace enough, and I know dozens of better kicks of the same kind.   What I can't understand is why Canon Docre's pals, after he had merely done everything backwards and upside down, all rolled about in heaps and bit each other.   He just struck me as being funny, him and his billy-goats."

" It wouldn't strike you as funny if you were a believing Catholic."

" No, maybe it wouldn't.   I suppose it would be a desecration of everything I held sacred.   And as there's nothing I know of that I hold sacred, Huysmans' kind of Black Mass wouldn't have any kick in it for me. And as there's nothing I'm shocked at, I don't suppose Mason's kind would have either.   So I must give it up as a bad job, then, and resign myself to a kickless life ? "

" I didn't say that."

" Now look here, T. Jelkes, you come clean.   You keep on dangling the carrot in front of the donkey's nose, and I keep on hee-hawing at it, but as fast as I try to close with it, you move it away."

" Well, what is it you want ? "

" Oh, damn it all, I don't know what I want.   But I want something, that's quite certain.   You know what I want a dashed sight better than I do."

" Do you ' yearn beyond the sky-line where the strange roads go down ' ? "

" No," said Paston, suddenly thoughtful, " and that's

my trouble, I believe. There aren't any roads in my life, not even strange ones. It would be better for me to have devil-worship than nothing ; only you won't let me, you disobliging old cuss."

Jelkes grinned his camel-grin.

" We may be able to manage something a bit better for you than devil-worship," he said.

" Who's we ? " asked Paston quickly, catching onto the plural.

The bookseller brushed him aside with a wave of his hand.

" I used the plural in a generic sense," he said airily.

" I'm afraid I don't know what you mean by that," said Paston.

" Neither do I," said Jelkes, " but it sounds well."

" Oh, come clean ! "

" Why should I ? I prefer being comfortably dirty, as you may have observed."

" You're a sore trial to me, T. Jelkes. Here, give me some more tea to sooth my troubled soul."

" But you still haven't told me what you make of these books ? "

" I told you what I made of ' The Devil's Mistress ' and you laughed at me. I shan't tell you any more."

" You've told me quite enough."

" I've told you too much, you damned old psycho-analyst, I'm going home."

Jelkes gurgled. " So you have discovered that these fantastic stories come home to men's business and bosoms ? "

" Yes, T. Jelkes, I have."

" And do they speak to your condition ? "

" Yes, damn you, they do."

" Why ? "

" I've no idea why, but they do, and in a very odd way. Jelkes, they're alive. These things are alive. There's a kick in them."

" You say these books come home to your business and bosom and speak to your condition. Now tell me, what is it about them that attracts you ? "

" The smell of sulphur, I think, if you want the sober truth."

" Well, my son, there are times when civilised men —and women too, for that matter, need sulphur, just the same as horses need salt."

" Was that what sent Isabel Goudie and Co. out to dance with the Devil in churchyards ? "

" It was. And it was the same thing that sent the Bacchantes out to dance with Dionysos on the mountains and tear fawns to bits."

" Ever read ' The Bacchae,' T. J. ? "

" Yes."

" You know, I've always wondered why a man of Euripides' calibre was so down on poor old Pentheus. After all, he only objected to all the respectable women in his kingdom going on the tiles, as any decent fellow would. I suppose the explanation is that they all went off for a sulphur-lick. Is that it ? "

" Yes, that's it. And Euripides, who had knowledge, knew it ; and that was what he was trying to tell his fellow-citizens. He knew that man cannot live by bread alone. He wants a pinch of sulphur occasionally."

" Yes, granted, from the psychological point of view. And it might have been all right for the Greeks, who took most things in their stride ; but if I go up to happy Hampstead, and take off my togs and tear a leg of mutton to bits, there'll be trouble with the police."

" Yes," said the old bookseller sadly, staring thoughtfully into the fire, " I'm afraid there will."

" Is the Black Mass the same sort of thing, T. J. ? A sort of break-away from convention ? "

" Yes, that's it. That's what it really is at bottom ; it's a reaction, my son, a reaction to an overdose of the true Mass."

" Can one have an overdose of that ? "

" One can have an overdose of anything that is strong enough to be medicinal. You take too much health salts and see how you feel."

" T. J., you're an awful old pagan."

" I'm a comfortable old pagan, my lad, and I thank God for it."

" Well, I'm a pagan, T. J., but I'm not comfortable."

" When were you happy last, Hugh ? "

" It's odd you should ask me that question, because it's one I've been asking myself. Do you know, I can hardly remember. I've had precious little happiness in my life, and yet I suppose I've had everything a fellow could want. I've always seemed to be sort of making the best of things and enduring them as philosophically as I could. Probably the trouble is that I've never had to exert myself. I honestly don't believe I've ever been happy, except when half-tight, since I left school."

" But you've played games and kept fit ? "

" I used to. But then I got so fed up with it I dropped it. The only thing I have got any kick out of, of recent years, is big game shooting. I should probably have got a kick out of flying if I hadn't been so dashed air-sick."

" You love danger then ? "

" Yes, I love danger. It wakes me up and makes me feel as if I were alive."

" Don't you feel alive at other times ? "

" No, not really, Or else I feel too much alive and don't know what to do with myself."

" Was your marriage happy till it cracked up ? "

" Yes, T. J., it was. Frida was the perfect wife. I had no fault to find with her until the inquest."

" And yet you don't impress me as having been particularly fond of her."

" Well, I was and I wasn't. I was loyal to her, and we got on all right. We never had a wrong word.

She'd always seemed perfectly contented. And yet the marriage could not have satisfied her or she wouldn't have stepped outside, would she ? "

" Did you ever step outside yourself ? "

" Well now, T. J., believe it or not, but I never did much in that line. Of course nobody'd have minded if I had, in the set in which I move ; but I'd had a good old Calvinistic Scotch nurse, and she brought me up in the way I should go, and it had always cost me a tremendous effort to run off the rails, and I don't enjoy it much when I do."

" Ignatius Loyola said : ' Give me a child till he is seven, and anyone who pleases can have him afterwards '."

" In the early days of my marriage I had a kind of upheaval ; I suppose everyone goes through it, like distemper in dogs. And I went over to Paris and got a pal to take me to call on a really high-class Parisian cocotte. I suppose it was my Black Mass, as you might say. But she didn't come up to expectation. I got the same feeling with her that I got with Frida, as if she wasn't there. The same feeling you get when you listen at the telephone and the line's dead. After that, I gave it up as a bad job and settled down with Frida. I reckoned I'd got as good as I could expect, and ought to be thankful she was even-tempered."

" Well, my son, you couldn't expect a professional to give you herself. You paid for her body, and you got her body, but naturally the *woman* wasn't there, and the line was dead."

" Well then, why wasn't it different with Frida ? "

" Ah, why wasn't it ? Was she forced into the marriage against her inclinations, or did you get her on the rebound from some one else ? "

Hugh Paston sat staring into the fire, his cigarette extinct between his lips. At last he removed it and said :

" T. J., you've put your finger on a point I've been

puzzling over ever since the inquest. Do you know who
it was introduced me to Frida, and practically made the
marriage ? "

" No, who was it ? "

" Her cousin, Trevor Wilmott, the fellow she subsequently carried on with."

Jelkes raised his massive eyebrows.

" Was it now ?   What was the game ? "

" I don't know.   It never struck me there was a
game.   Trevor was my great pal at college, and when
we came down, we were both rather at a loose end ;
he couldn't get a job, and I had nothing to do but
chew a silver spoon, and we went on an expedition
together."

" And you stood treat ? "

" Oh, yes, I stood treat.   Trevor hadn't a bean.
But that meant nothing to me.   He wasn't under any
obligation.   It didn't cost me any sacrifice."

" And then what happened ? "

" Well, Trevor's cousin joined the boat at Marseilles.
I was fresh back from womanless wilds, and I was
rather struck with her, and I suppose I showed it.
Anyway, old Trevor smelt a rat and he played match-
maker, and the next thing I knew, he was taking me
down with him for the fishing at her father's place.
Frida and I were thrown together a good deal.   Her
family smiled on me—or my silver spoon, I don't
know which.   That's the drawback of having a silver
spoon in your mouth, you never quite know what's
being smiled at.   However, I was young and unsuspicious, and when Frida made it clear that she liked my
society, I fell for it in one.   Her people were pleased
because they were as poor as church mice.   My people
were pleased because she was related to all and sundry.
Everyone was pleased, including me.   It couldn't have
been more ideal.   I concluded my best pal was pleased,
as he'd pulled off the match ; and I presumed she was

pleased, as she'd made the running. What more could anybody want ? "

" And yet it wasn't a success from the first ? "

" Well, T. J., I don't know. I've no means of judging. I've never been married before, or since. I thought it wasn't, and went on the binge to Paris to console myself. But I found Paris wasn't any better than London, so I came home with my tail between my legs and settled down. And then I found it wasn't so bad. Frida was a damn good sort. She was a good wife to me, T. J., I've no fault to find with her. We never had a wrong word."

" That's your trouble. If you'd been in love with each other you'd have had some fine old dust-ups whenever either of you fell short of perfection."

" You think I was married for my money, then."

" Looks like it to me."

" Yes, I suppose I was."

Silence fell in the dingy room, darkening to twilight. The fire was low, but the old bookseller did not stir to put coal on.

Finally Paston broke the silence. A considerable time had elapsed, but he spoke as if he were continuing a sentence.

" You know, that's a bitter thing, T. J. One gives of one's best——. There have been a lot of novels written about girls being forced into marriages with rich men, and what they suffer ; but I don't know anything that's been written about what a fellow feels like when he's fond of the girl and finds he's been married for his money."

" Does that explain a good deal to you ? "

" Yes, it explains everything. Except—— Why did Trevor go out of his way to make that marriage ? "

" Did you ever read a book by Henry James called ' The Wings of a Dove ' ? "

" No, what's it about ? "

" A man and a woman love each other, but they can't

afford to marry. They arrange between them that the man shall marry a rich woman who's dying of consumption."

Hugh Paston sat silent for a while. " Yes, I suppose that's it," he said at length. " That explains a lot. I suppose I was the milch-cow that financed the liaison. God, what a world! T. J., you've performed a surgical operation on me, I'm not sure whether I'll thank you or not."

" If I left it at that, Hugh Paston, like the Freudians do, you'd have little call to thank me. But I won't leave it at that. Having performed the analysis, we'll proceed with the synthesis."

" You'll have to leave it alone for a bit, T. J. I feel at the moment like one feels when one's been knocked out in boxing. I think I'll got out for a walk."

" It's raining cats and dogs."

" Doesn't matter. I want some air."

# CHAPTER V

At first Hugh Paston walked aimlessly about the dark streets, thankful for the cool, damp, rain-washed air after the stuffy heat of the room behind the shop. The revelation to which the old bookseller had led him had certainly been a tremendous shock. He knew that the old man had effectually lanced the abscess on his soul and it now ought to have a chance to heal. All the same, he harboured no delusion that he was out of the wood. He did not like the feel of himself. He still felt unnatural. He had heard of abscesses on the appendix bursting and causing peritonitis when they were operated on too late. He wondered whether the old bookseller had come on the scene too late to give him any real help and he was now going to have a peritonitis of the soul in addition to his original appendicitis. If he had known it, the old man whom he had left in the stuffy room behind the shop was wondering exactly the same thing, and was more than a little worried at the result of his playing with souls. It is one thing to have grasped the theory of psycho-analysis, but quite another to apply it in practice.

In a little while Hugh Paston ceased his aimless wandering and set out resolutely towards his house. It was no great distance, and his long legs carried him over the ground rapidly in the empty streets.

Arrived there, he admitted himself with his latch-key into the darkened hall. At the end of the hall was a swing-door, and passing through this, he found himself on the back-stairs. Going down a short flight, he came to a door on the half landing under which showed a line of light. He knocked, and a woman's voice with a slight Scotch accent bade him come in.

He entered a small room, much too full of knick-knacks, and a short square-set woman with greying hair rose to greet him. A lady, but not the kind of lady one found on the other side of the swing-door. She offered no greeting save : ' Good evening, Mr Paston ', but stood awaiting his pleasure.

He said, " Sit down, Mrs Macintosh ", and she did so, still silently, looking at him questioningly.

He sat down, too, not asking permission. For it was his house, and she was his housekeeper, even if she were a lady.

" Mrs Macintosh," he said, " I am going to give up this house."

She nodded, expressing no surprise.

(' I'll kill the woman if she makes any comments '), he thought. But she didn't. She had seen trouble herself in her time.

" I want you to pay off the servants. Give 'em all three months' wages. It's no fault of theirs the place is closing down. Take everything out of my bedroom and stick it into trunks—all my personal things, I mean, I don't want any of the furniture ; and take all my papers out of my desk and put them into deed-boxes, and put the lot into store. Then put the house in the hands of the agents and get them to hold an auction of everything, lock, stock, and barrel."

" What about—Mrs Paston's things ? "

Hugh Paston's face twitched.

" Sell them too."

" But what about her papers, Mr Paston ? "

Hugh sat silent for a long time, the woman watching him with pitying eyes.

Finally he spoke. " Yes, those have got to be dealt with, but I can't do it now. Can't be done. Look here, you put them all into deed-boxes and store them along with the rest of the goods, but keep them separate from my papers, you understand ? "

" Very good, Mr Paston," said the housekeeper quietly, " you can rely on me."

" Thanks, yes, I know I can," he said, and rising abruptly to his feet, he wrung her hand and was out of the front door before she had finished rubbing her tingling fingers.

He heaved a sigh of relief and cast no backward glance over his shoulder. He hoped never to look on that house again ; or on that district either, for the matter of that. All he prayed was that he might meet no one he knew before he could find a taxi. But taxis are as common in Mayfair as they are rare in Marylebone, and his prayer was granted.

Although it was after closing-time when he got back to Billings Street, he found the shop lit up, and the half-glass door yielded to his pressure. At the first ting of the bell the old bookseller was through the serge curtain, for the more he thought about the way his guest had taken things, the more anxious he had become.

Hugh Paston followed him into the room behind the shop, flung his hat on the table, and dropped into his old seat on the sofa. His action reassured the old man, for he could see he felt at home.

" Well," he said, " I've done the deed."

" What deed ? " cried Jelkes aghast, wondering if it were a murder.

" Given orders for the servants to be paid off and the house sold up. Got rid of everything except my duds. Oh yes, and my wife's papers. Those have got to be tackled sometime, but not now. No, not even to please you, T. Jelkes, however good you may think that abreactions are for me."

The old man heaved a sigh of relief.

" Well," he said, " I guessed you've earned your supper."

" Yes," said Hugh Paston, " I guess I have."

The frying-pan and tea-pot came into action, and the

amicable, silent meal was partaken of and cleared away.
But although relieved concerning his immediate anxiety,
for his guest had neither blown his own nor anyone else's
brains out, the old bookseller did not like the look of him
at all.  The hopelessness and apathy had given place to a
kind of repressed excitement that struck the old man as
being far from wholesome, and as likely to lead to rash
acts, the consequences of which might have to be paid
for heavily.

He cast about in his mind for something that should
not merely distract his guest's attention, but hold it.  He
had got over the immediate shock of the tragedy and
disillusionment, so Jelkes judged, but all that had
seethed within him so long was rising like a tide.  What
to do with this tide was the problem ; it had to go somewhere, and if no rational channel could be opened to it,
irrational ones would be found.

It was not easy for Jelkes to understand the viewpoint
of this man sitting silently smoking on his broken-down
sofa.  He was of a different class and traditions ; of a
different generation, and a totally different temperament.
Jelkes cast his mind back to the time when he was this
man's age, and tried to remember how he had felt.

But here he got no guidance.  The first fires of his
youth had gone up in a tremendous mystical fervour that
had burnt with a smokeless flame.

His mother had been left a widow in reduced circumstances, and though not a Catholic, had solved the problem of his education by sending him to the cheap but
excellent school in the neighbourhood run by some
Jesuit fathers.  She was assured that no attempt would
be made to convert the boy, and was satisfied with the
assurance.  No attempt had been made, but among the
teachers was, as always, a man of marked charm of
character, and to him the lad became deeply attached.
No attempt needed to be made to convert that boy, he
came knocking at the door of the fold of his own accord.

And not only did he enter the fold, he aspired to the priesthood. He felt he had a vocation ; and the very experienced men who judge of such things also thought he had a vocation. But he had been caught too late. A robust and rugged character had begun to be formed before he reached the seminary. The sports field of his preparatory school had done its work. He could not fit in with the whispering and influencing and routine humiliations. He bowed his neck to the yoke in the first flush of his faith ; but presently he began to ask himself whether he, when he was admitted, would be prepared to hand on this same treatment to others ? And something in the lad that had been formed on the football field rose up and said that nothing would induce him to do so. He asked to be released. His friend came and pleaded with him. And not only pleaded with him, but wept over him, wringing his hands in despair ; it was nothing more or less than a spiritual jilting. The whole experience made a terrible and searing impression on the adolescent lad. He had not taken the actual vows, being still in his novitiate, but the strongest admonitions of chastity had been impressed upon him, and these, together with his friend's heartbroken revelations of feeling, had prevented him from ever looking upon a woman to love her. A priest at heart, he had passed through life in complete spiritual isolation ; a mystic by temperament, he was denied all spiritual consolation by his critical brain.

Penniless, without any qualifications, he by great good fortune got a job as assistant to a second-hand bookseller, found the trade congenial, and developed an aptitude for it, for he was a lad of well above the average capacity, as his teachers at the seminary had seen. Spending nothing on girl friends, or making himself attractive to the feminine eye, he saved steadily, and by the time he was forty, had launched out into a shop of his own ; he soon prospered sufficiently to satisfy his simple needs, and these being satisfied, declined to exert himself any further, but enjoyed life after his own fashion, which consisted in a pot of tea on the hob, his toes on the fender, a book in his hand, and the collecting of the queer literature that interested him.

Although he had had no share in the kind of experience that had taken his new friend to Paris, he was well acquainted with the geography of the land where a man wanders after a severe emotional shock. His own trouble had taken the form of an acute crisis ; Hugh Paston's, he judged, had been of a chronic nature ; its cumulative effects gradually destroying his poise. Jelkes knew the thing that had saved him in his own time of trial had been the sudden opening-up of a new channel of interest. Made free of the shelves of his employer's second-hand bookshop, he had come across a translation of Iamblichos' curious work on the Egyptian Mysteries ; this, coming on top of what he already knew of the Method of St. Ignatius, gave him a revelation that was little less than a second conversion, for he saw here in a sudden flash that he had glimpsed the key to the technique of the higher consciousness. This served to start him off again on the ancient Quest—the quest of the light that never shone on land or sea. He had suddenly won to the knowledge that there was another kind of mysticism in the world beside the Christian mysticism, at which his manhood had rebelled ; his soul picked up its stride once more, and the man was saved. Ever since then he had pursued strange byways of thought, following up every bold speculation in science, every new viewpoint in philosophy.

His trade enabled him, though a poor man, to gather together a very remarkable collection of odd literature. Not very bulky, for there is not a great deal worth having in that line. Much that came into his hands after patient search passed out of them again to the first customer, having been weighed in the balance and found wanting.

He gradually learnt that he had to look for a viewpoint rather than a doctrine, and that it was in the *obiter dicta* and not the reasoned judgment that he would find what was of most use to him.

Novalis, Hegel, Hinton, he returned to most often among the philosophers ; Herbert Spencer he dismissed with a furious snort. Why should a thing be non-existent because it is inconceivable ? *Non est demonstrandum.* Is the average, the very average, human mind to set the standard ? To hell with you, Herbert ! and he pitched him into the fire, where he smelt so horribly that he had to be rescued, which is the end of many noble acts of vengeance.

The old bookseller had learnt at the seminary that when it comes to conceiving transcendent things, minds vary enormously in their capacity, and the trained mind is a very different matter to the untrained ; and the mind that is conditioned by music and incense and dim lights has very different capacities to the mind that goes at the job in cold blood. Herbert Spencer saw no further than his own pink-tipped, liverish nose.

The Search for the Absolute took hold of the untidy scholar among his dusty books, and kept him serene and happy as the years slipped by and brought him neither fame nor fortune but only the merest pittance, for he did not choose to exert himself.

He had had a good grounding in scholarship among the Jesuits and was familiar with the classical languages and had a working knowledge of Hebrew. Consequently he was able to go to the fountain-head of most things except Sanskrit. Though intensely irritated by her, he found Mme Blavatsky a useful pointer. She told one where to look, and pointed out the significance in a good many odd things. Maeterlinck compared her books to a builder's yard, and Jelkes reckoned he was about right, and wondered why it is that a mystic seldom has a tidy mind. It never occurred to him that his own establishment looked to most people as if it had been bombed.

Freud made him foam at the mouth at first, and he very nearly followed Herbert Spencer into the fire as a lop-sided outrager of the decencies ; then Jelkes' classical education came to the rescue, and he discerned in Freud the Dionysiac philosophy. Having a great respect for the Greeks, he gave Freud a grudging hearing after that, and it appeared to him that it was a great pity that the learned doctor had not also had a classical education, and learnt that Priapus and Silenus are gods, and not dirty little boys playing with filth. And learnt also that they are not the whole of Olympus, but that there are also golden Aphrodite and Apollo. He eyed the works of the great Austrian gloomily.

" These," he said, " are not paganism, they are decomposing Christianity," and he returned to Petronius, whom he considered wrote much better on the same subject.

But however much he might find his own satisfaction in playing chess with the Absolute, he realised it would be little use to offer this kind of bread of life to Hugh Paston in his present state ; or for the matter of that, in any state. Paston was a man who had been starved of life ; who had starved in the midst of plenty without realising what was the matter with him. A good old Calvinistic nurse had started him off in blinkers, and what passes for uplift at a public school had done the rest. Old Jelkes recalled Lytton Strachey's cynical comment upon the number of the great Dr Arnold's best boys who had gone off their heads.

He was relieved to find that his guest, having disposed of his more pressing affairs, seemed quite content to enjoy the homely concoctions of the frying-pan and amuse himself by browsing on the shelves. He watched him browse, knowing that here he would find the surest key to the man's character, and noted with interest the old armful he brought over to the sofa and settled down with.

He had got the treasured Iamblichos, he noticed; and an odd volume of Mme Blavatsky; and, of all incongruities, another book of Huysmans' ' A Rebours '. Jelkes watched him go from one to the other, and back again. ' A Rebours ' he reckoned Paston had picked up because of his interest in Huysmans' other book, and was surprised to see him settle down to read it. Time went by; the old bookseller started a fresh brew of tea that was to form a night-cap, and put a cup by his guest's elbow unnoticed.

Hugh Paston looked up suddenly.

" I've found my Bible, Jelkes," he said.

" Good God," said the old bookseller, " I like your taste in Bibles ! "

" It's nothing like as plain-spoken as the original."

" Maybe not. But even as literature, I prefer the original."

" You have it, Jelkes, you have it if you like it. This is my choice."

" If you were my son, you'd go face downwards across my knee."

" If I were your son, T. Jelkes, you would be pushing up the daisies by now, if you weren't pushing up a good-sized oak-tree. I'm no chicken."

" Then you're old enough to have a more mature taste in literature."

" Come, come, now, you wouldn't call ' A Rebours ' a kids' book, would you ? "

" I'd call it a pimply adolescent's book. Anybody who'd cut his wisdom-teeth ought to be sick over it."

"Now you mention it, T. J., this copy looks as if someone had. You do keep your stock badly. But joking apart, I really have seen a glimpse of daylight in my miserable condition. Don't take me too seriously, there's a good chap, but let me ramble if I want to. It amuses me, and takes my mind off worse things. Now see here, I've gone and shoved all my earthly goods into an auction sale, and I've got to re-stock, now haven't I ? I can't park myself here indefinitely, now can I ? "

" No, I'm afraid you can't. I've sat through the bath, and you've sat through the sofa ; and between us we'll go through into the cellar shortly. I'd like to have you, but it wouldn't work. We've both got enough sense to see that."

"I didn't mean that, T. J.; I love your ménage. I meant I couldn't take advantage of you indefinitely."

" Well, be that as it may. What are you proposing to do on the strength of that damned book ? I suppose you know how Des Esseintes ended up ? "

" Flat on his back and sick as a cat. Yes, I know. But then he took no exercise. Besides, he wasn't going any-where. He wasn't aiming at anything. Now I propose to aim at something."

" And what do you propose to aim at ? " the old book-seller's sandy eyebrows went up till they almost made junc-tion with the frill of grizzled hair just above his coat-collar.

" That's not so easily put into words. I'm not sure if I quite know what it is myself. Can you imagine a mixture of ' Là-Bas ', and ' A Rebours ', with a dash of Iamblichos and Ignatius ? "

" I can, but I'd sooner not."

" It's not as bad as it sounds. Let me put it this way. I've got to re-furnish, haven't I ? "

" No need, I'll lend you a frying-pan."

" No use to me. You've just admitted that my psychology demands a bath with a bottom to it. And you're right. I express myself in my surroundings. I'm not content to live inside myself and ignore them, as you are."

" You'd have to be if you had my income," said T. Jelkes drily.

" Well, I dare say there's something in that."

" There's a very great deal in it, as you'll know, my lad, if you ever accidentally swallow your silver spoon."

" A silver spoon isn't all pure profit, T. J.  It's a dashed difficult thing to own your money and not let your money own you if there's a lot of it.  It makes you feel as if you'd got a damn sight too big a spread of sail for your hull, if you know what I mean."

" I reckon you must pick up some pretty sticky friends."

" That's the least of my troubles.  They're welcome to what they can peck.  There's enough for everybody.  I'm not under any illusions nowadays, so my feelings don't get hurt any more.  You expect to pay your footing in any walk in life.  Now listen, T. J., if you've finished interrupting.  I've got to equip some sort of a place to live in, and your damned frying-pan won't go far with me.  And I'm going to do it à la Huysmans, not because I'm really a degenerate, like his blessed Des Esseintes, but because it amuses me and gives me something to do and to think about.  An empty mind's as uncomfortable as an empty stomach.  Believe one who knows, T. J."

" That's all right.  I've no objection to tortoises inlaid with precious stones to brighten up the drawing-room carpet, provided the tortoise is willing."

" I don't suppose the poor old tortoise was willing.  Being inlaid must be like having teeth stopped, if you come to think of it.  It went and died on him, anyway, and quite right too, I say."

" So there won't be a tortoise ?  You disappoint me."

"No, T. J.  Nor coal-black mammies with nothing on, waiting at an ebony dinner-table with all-black food."

" I'm glad to hear that.  I can't say I care for caviare.  It tasted to me like winkles stewed in sewage.  But I may be doing it an injustice.  I admit I ate it off the blade of a penknife without condiments."

"I expect it was the penknife spoilt it, T. J.  Perhaps you'd been using it for something else before you ate the caviare off it."

" Perhaps I had. It's quite likely. But anyway, what about this ménage you're planning, for which you do *not* require the loan of my frying-pan? And how the hell have you got Ignatius Loyola and Iamblichos mixed up with it? "

" That's quite simple when you understand it. Now look at it this way. You remember what Brodie Innes had to say in ' The Devil's Mistress ' about all these sober Scotch housewives breaking out and going for a dance with the Devil? Well, that's me, do you see."

" Yes, I see," said the old bookseller drily. " God help the Devil! "

" I don't mean it quite as literally as you seem to have taken it. What I really meant was the need of a moral salt-lick."

" You can do that without setting up housekeeping, my lad. In fact it's usually reckoned advisable to put the Channel between yourself and your moral salt-licks."

" You've got me wrong again. What I really mean is this. You remember what Naomi Mitchison said about the way they brought through elemental power in the rite of the Corn King and the Spring Queen? "

" Now look here, Hugh Paston, please remember you're talking to the beginnings of a priest."

" No, I don't mean what you mean. You keep on interrupting me before I've got time to make myself clear."

" Time to make yourself clear? What you want's eternity, from what I can see of you."

" All right, we'll drop Naomi and her pals since you're so particular. Well, you remember what Iamblichos said about the way they built up the god-forms in their imagination so as to get the invisible powers to manifest through them? "

" Yes."

" Well now, supposing I feel I want a salt-lick——
No, it's all right, I won't refer to Naomi. Supposing I
feel I want a salt-lick à la Brodie, don't you think I
could manage to have it à la Iamblichos without going
to the trouble of erecting a platform in the middle of
a ploughing-field ? "

" Hugh Paston, if you talk like that any more I'll
chuck ye out."

"Go on! T. J., I'm as pure as the crystal spring.
It's your filthy mind that's your trouble. What I'm
trying to say is this, What did they get out of the Eleusinian Mysteries ? They got a kick, didn't they ? Well,
what sort of a kick ? That's what I'm after."

" You won't find the Dionysian kick mixed up with
Des Esseintes and his turtles. He was more than half
dead."

" I should have said he was actively decomposing.
I'm not taking him as my model. I'd sooner have
Canon Docre, billy-goats and all. What I mean is
this—what Loyola called a composition of place in
your imagination and see yourself there, and by gum,
you jolly soon begin to feel as you would feel if you
were there ! Now supposing I furnish my place à la
Iamblichos ; that is to say, I build up a ' composition
of place ' with a view to getting in touch with the old
pagan gods, and then express it in furnishings ?
Supposing I live in the middle of those furnishings,
day in and day out——"

" You'll get so used to 'em you won't notice 'em
after a bit."

" I'm not so sure. Seems to me they must have
some effect on you. But supposing I put my imagination
behind it all, as it were, like a priest saying Mass—
won't I get some sort of a Real Presence—of a pagan
kind ? "

" My God, Hugh, do you realise what you're talking
about ? "

" Yes, I do, but you don't. You think I'm talking about the Black Mass. But I'm not. I'm simply saying that there's more than one sort of contact with the Unseen."

" I'd be glad if you wouldn't say it in my hearing."

" T. J., I believe you're scared! Really, genuinely scared. What are you scared of? Do you expect me to raise the Devil on the spot?"

" Laddie, I know a lot more about these things than you do. I *am* scared, and I don't mind admitting it. Now tell me seriously, do you really believe that these antics you propose performing will yield any genuine results, or are you just playing at them?"

" T. J., I don't know, and I want to find out. I can tell you one thing, however, if there is no invisible reality, and everything is just the surfaces I've always thought it was, I shall blow my brains out and go peacefully into oblivion, for I just can't stand it, and that's the sober truth, and I'm not joking."

" I thought you had something like that in your mind," said T. Jelkes.

# CHAPTER VI

" I THINK I'd better make some fresh tea," said Jelkes.
" We've neglected this, and it's stewed."

Not that stewed tea would have troubled him in the
ordinary way, provided it was hot, and the tea-pot on
the side-hob was practically boiling, but he wished to
have a chance to do a little thinking before he committed
himself in words to the psychological box of tricks sitting
on his broken-down sofa. He pottered about in the
kitchenette, boiling up a kettle from cold on the gas-ring
instead of using old black Sukie sitting on the hob, as
was his usual economical habit.

It certainly needed some thinking out. He could see
exactly what Paston was driving at. He proposed to
imitate Huysmans' decadent hero by making every object
that surrounded him minister to his moods and have a
definite psychological value. His aim, however, was not
to produce æsthetic sensibility, but to get into touch with
those old, forgotten forces hinted at in the various books.
Hugh Paston, he saw, believed them to be objective, and
Jelkes did not think it wise at the present juncture to disillusion him ; he himself, however, knew from his thirty
years' strange reading and experimenting, that they were
subjective, and God only knew what hells and heavens a
man might open up in his own nature by such means as
Paston proposed to use.

But he certainly could not open any hell that was not
already there ; and if there were a hell there, according
to Freud it was best to let the devils out for an airing
occasionally. But even so, the old man was aghast at
the possibilities that opened up. But it was too late to
stop it now. Hugh Paston had got the bit between his

teeth, was impatient of all control, and would go on from sheer bravado.

It seemed to him that the best thing he could do would be to throw himself into Paston's plans, and lay at his disposal the vast stores of odd knowledge that he had acquired, but never used, in the course of a lifetime's reading. Hugh would be exceedingly busy for months to come collecting his impedimenta from the ends of the earth ; that would give him something to occupy his mind, and by the time the house was equipped, he might have returned to normal. Jelkes bore the tea-pot triumphantly into the sitting-room, having arrived at this solution.

Hugh Paston, with a very flushed face as if he had been drinking, though the old bookseller knew that he had not, was busy turning over the pile of books that lay beside him on the sofa.

" T. J.," he exclaimed as the old man entered, " I'm on the trail of something. I don't know what it is, but I can feel it in my bones."

Jelkes grunted and slammed down the tea-pot.

" You're on the trail of a hell of a lot of trouble if you don't watch out. I reckon you'll be glad of the loan of my frying-pan before you've finished. You'll want to get out of the fire and sit in it to cool off. Now look here, Hugh, there is a way of doing what you want to do, a way of doing it properly, not in this hit or miss fashion you've got in your mind, and I'll show you what it is, provided you'll handle it the way I say, and not let us both in for a pickle."

" I thought there was, you old devil, and that if I burnt enough sulphur under your nose, you'd come clean. Right you are, I accept your conditions. Flying with dual control to start with. But afterwards I want to fly solo, mind you. Now where do we start ? "

" You start with that cup of tea. I don't want to see another pot wasted."

" Right. Now I'll tell you what's in my mind, and we'll see if we both have the same idea. I think we ought to start by invoking the Great God Pan."

The old bookseller groaned inwardly, shades of the seminary gathering about him. He did not repudiate the idea however.

" How do you propose to make a start ? " he enquired mildly.

" I propose to get hold of a suitable house, one of those big, left-over country mansions with lots of huge rooms, that are white elephants to everybody, and fit up the different rooms as temples to the different gods of the old pantheons. Make a really artistic job of it, you know. Have some first-class frescoes done, and all the rest of it ; and I'm inclined to think that if we make the temple ready, the god will indwell it, and we shall begin to learn something about him—or her."

The old bookseller groaned again.

" Now, T. J., I'll provide the wherewithal—it's about the only thing I can provide, God help me—if you'll provide the ideas, and then we want someone to do the designing and chase about after the oddments. I know various firms who go in for designing houses from the attic to the cellar in any period or a mixture of 'em all, but I don't know of anyone who could do this job, do you ? I expect we'll have to wrestle with it ourselves, and get hold of a tame artist who'll do as he's told."

" That sort isn't usually much of an artist," said T. Jelkes.

" Well, can we get hold of an artist who's along this line of thought ? "

That was the exact crux of the matter, and that was what T. Jelkes had touched upon and discarded while he was brewing the tea. Paston had put his finger upon the spot ; they must have their master-craftsman for the making of any temple of the Mysteries. The things they wanted are not to be bought in the Tottenham Court

Road.  There was another thing Hugh Paston must have,
only he didn't know it, he must have his priestess ; they
two men couldn't work the thing between them.  And
God only knew where the thing would end if they introduced a woman into it.  He knew where it usually ended
in pagan times.

And he had the priestess ready to hand if he chose to
lay his hand on her.  But did he choose ?  No, he did
not.  Paston could go to hell before he'd do that.  But
on the other hand, the work would be a godsend to the
girl, who needed it badly.  He was very anxious about
her.  Things had not been going well with her lately.
Two of the papers she worked for had closed down,
owing her money.  He suspected she was not getting
anything like enough to eat.  Would it be possible to get
her the job of doing all the craftwork and designing,
which was her trade, and yet keep Hugh Paston from
playing the fool with her ?

He considered his guest critically.  He did not think
he would be a man especially attractive to women.  That
had probably been his trouble.  Women would want a
lick at his silver spoon, but they wouldn't want the man,
which was not surprising.  He was singularly lacking in
' It '.  He was tallish, loosely built, and carried himself
badly, with awkward, jerky, nervous movements.  He
had the long-fingered, bony hands of a psychic and sensitive, and Jelkes guessed that the rest of his physique was
to match.  His strength, he guessed, would not be muscular, but would depend upon nervous energy ; and he
judged by the jerky, awkward movements that at the
present moment everything was dis-co-ordinated, and
the fellow had no stamina or staying-power.  He would
go up in brief flares of nervous excitement, and burn out
as quickly, like a fire of straw.  He judged that it would
be fairly safe to give him his head and let him pelt away
at his new scheme because the first burst would exhaust
him, and the new toy would be broken and thrown aside,

after the manner of Mayfair. It might therefore be all right to give Mona a chance at the job.

He thought of Mona. He did not anticipate much danger there. Hugh Paston was probably accustomed to highly decorative females; he did not think his little brown mouse would be classed as a female at all in Paston's eyes.

His visitor suddenly broke in on his thoughts, and in the odd way he had done two or three times before, he voiced the very thing that the old bookseller had been turning over in his mind.

" Jelkes, can we run this show with men only, just you and I, or shall we want some women ? "

Jelkes grunted non-committally.

" Got your eye on any women for the job ? "

" I know of plenty who'd like to join the—er—witch-coven when we get it going, but I don't know of any who'd be any use as priestesses. But I know various folk connected with the stage, and I thought we'd probably be able to find a young actress of the right type, one of these classical dancers, you know, and teach her the job, and she could teach the others."

Jelkes heaved a sigh of relief. That solved one of his problems anyway.

" If you can find the right sort of priestess, I think I can lay my hands on the right sort of artist."

" That's fine. I really feel we're getting under way. T. J., I'll be a different man if I have something to do, and feel that I'm really getting somewhere instead of chasing my tail in circles down the arches of the years. Now then, let's get down to practical politics. What's the first move ? Find a house ? "

" No, not quite, the first move is to decide exactly what you want to do, and then see how we can best set about doing it."

" We, T. Jelkes ? Did I hear you say ' we ' ? You impenitent old heathen, I believe you're getting quite keen on the scheme."

" I'll try anything once," said T. Jelkes grimly.

" Well, what do we want to do ? You note I say we, T. Jelkes."

" You can leave me out of it. I'll hold your coat, and I'll flap a towel at you between rounds, but as soon as the gong goes, I'm through the ropes before you can turn round. This isn't going to be *my* funeral. What is it *you* want, Hugh Paston ? By what particular route do *you* want to attend the Harrying of Hell ? "

" What in the world's that ? "

" Don't you know that King Arthur, in the days before he was taken on as a Christian king and an ideal of chivalry, set off with his warriors to harry Hell because the Devil had overstepped the limit ? And they chased all through Hell, and upset everything, and Arthur came away with the Devil's big cooking-pot tied on behind as his share of the spoils. And he gave it to Keridwen, the Keltic earth-goddess, and she minded it over a fire that never went out, high up on the flanks of Snowdon ; and it was an inexhaustible source of supply for all and sundry. However much they ate out of it, and whatever sort of parties Arthur gave, the cauldron always filled up again, and everyone found it contained his favourite recipe. Then when Arthur was duly whitewashed when civilisation began to be the vogue, he became the very perfect Christian knight and model of chivalry, and the Devil's cook-pot, that Keridwen used to mind, became the Graal."

" You do take the gilt off the gingerbread, T. J."

" Well, my lad, you can trace that story every step of the way through Keltic folklore and literature."

" Are you suggesting that future generations will canonise me ? "

" No, I wouldn't go as far as to suggest that. You're more likely to end up on the same grid as Simon Magus, to my way of thinking. What I mean is this, if we're lucky in our harrying of Hell, we *may* get away with the cook-pot."

"That is all Greek to me, T. J."

"It's meant to be, my lad, at your present stage of development."

"You're an irritating old cuss, I must say. You try me sorely."

"If you never get anything worse than me to try you, you won't do too badly, laddie. Now tell me straight, what are you trying to get at with your invocation of Pan and all the rest of it?"

"Well, it seems to me, T. J., that if I get Pan, I'll get all the rest of it. Now don't think that I'm suffering from delusions. I know perfectly well that no cosmic billy-goat is going to materialise on your hearth-rug : but it's my belief that if I can break out of the luminous opacity of the opal, something in me that is septic, or ingrowing, or got corns on it at the present moment, is going to touch something in the spiritual world that corresponds to it, and yet that isn't exactly spiritual. I don't want anything spiritual, it isn't my line, I had an overdose of it at Oxford. What I want is that something vital which I feel to be somewhere in the universe, which I know I need, and which I can't lay my hand on. It was that I went over to Paris after when I didn't find it in my marriage, where I expected to find it. Now I call that 'something' the Great God Pan ; and you know, T. J., if I don't find it, I believe I shall go off in a decline and peg out."

The old bookseller looked at him intently with his light, bright eyes under their sandy brows.

"People don't die of psychological troubles," he said.

"Don't they, T. J.? Well I don't intend to live with them, I can tell you that."

# CHAPTER VII

HUGH PASTON, chased off to bed by the sleepy book-seller, found sleep far from him. His mind was roused to alertness by the talk of the evening in a way that it had never been roused before, and images chased each other through his brain. The house he proposed to buy and equip as a marvellous temple of the Old Gods—in fact more than a temple, a monastery, for there must be others who would delight to join him on his quest—took various forms in his imagination as the dark hours went slowly past. First it was to be of classical architecture, with a front entrance resembling the Parthenon, over the door of which Jelkes' artist friend should carve the motto : 'Know thyself'. Entering, one should find oneself in a vast pillared hall to impress the imagination. Everything was to be of white marble. Then he discarded the marble as too like a bathroom, and the house took on a designedly commonplace exterior ; but as soon as the front door opened, one found oneself in the mysterious gloom of an Egyptian temple, with vast shadowy images of the gods looming over one. He decided to take a leaf out of ' A Rebours ' and have a coal-black negro to open the door. But then he decided that that would not work ; the negro would bolt like a rabbit at the first sign of anything supernatural. Perhaps a Chinaman would be more suitable. But a Chinaman wouldn't go with the Egyptian temple. Hugh Paston gave it up. He must wait for Jelkes' artist.

He lay on his back on the feather-bed and stared up at the shadowy outline of the cock-eyed canopy, dimly revealed by the faint light that always shines through a London window, and wondered where his quest would

end, if there were any end to it. He had spoken with
great assurance to old Jelkes concerning his quest of Pan,
but did he really believe in it himself? One thing, and
one thing only he knew, he had a desperate need that
was eating him up and destroying him, as if something
were feeding on his tissues, and that something could
only be appeased by the thing he chose to call Pan, whatever that might ultimately prove to be. It was the x in
his calculation. He wasn't obliged to define it at the
present moment. He could erect an altar to the Unknown
God if he chose.

The fancy temples passed from his thoughts and he lay
along the soft hummocks of the feather-bed wondering
exactly what was going to happen now that he had deliberately and with malice aforethought unleashed the Pan
Within and sent it forth in search of the Cosmic Pan in
the same way as Noah sent out the dove from the Ark.
Surely it would return to him with at least an ivy-leaf in
its beak? He wondered what manner of thing in reality
sympathetic magic might be ; as described by the anthropologists it was just plain idiocy ; but he had a shrewd
suspicion the anthropologists never really got at the
heart of anything. In sympathetic magic one imitated
a thing and so got into touch with it. How superstitious,
said the anthropologists. What childishness the mind of
primitive man is capable of ! But Ignatius Loyola said :
Put yourself in the posture of prayer, and you will soon
feel like praying ; and the founder of the Jesuits was
reckoned a very profound psychologist. If some of the
methods taught in his ' Exercises ' were not sympathetic
magic, well, Hugh Paston would like to know what was !
And if sympathetic magic was the basis of the Jesuits'
training, perhaps there might be something to be said for
the viewpoint of the ancients, who at least knew enough
to build the pyramids.

Hugh Paston had browsed to some purpose on the
tangled shelves of the dusty library. All the books that

Jelkes most highly esteemed, his private library, one might say, were in the inner room, safe from sacrilegious hands, and in these Hugh had dipped and skipped extensively. It was not in his nature to work systematically ; studying, annotating, collating, experimenting, as the old bookseller had done ; but he was an expert at picking up the drift of a book with the minimum of reading, which is the only way to keep up to date in Mayfair. One thing, and not much else, he had picked out from four tattered, dog-eared, paper-backed volumes on magic spelt with a K— the magician surrounds himself with the symbols of a particular potency when he performs a magical operation in order to help himself to concentrate. That was a useful practical point, thought Hugh Paston ; it bore out his theory that the sympathetic magic of Loyola's ' Exercises ' could be usefully reinforced by all the deckings of a temple. And if, in addition to the decked-out temple, one lived the life—one had every object within one's sight, every garment one wore, every word one spoke, or that was spoken to one, tuned to the same key over a period of time—surely the effect would be reinforced a hundredfold ? Was not that the idea underlying the retreats that High Church people disappear into round about Easter time ?

He was determined to seek Pan by the same methods that other people use to seek Christ. Was it a horrible blasphemy ? That would certainly be the opinion of most people, but he didn't mind that. Was it the Black Mass ? In a way he supposed it was, and yet it did not seem to him black. He certainly had no intention of desecrating anything that anybody held sacred. It would not give him the slightest kick to throw the sacred Wafer on the ground and jump on it, as ' *le formidable chanoine* ' appeared to amuse himself by doing. He might try working his Mass on the tummy of an undraped lady, provided he would find one that wasn't ticklish, but he doubted if this would amuse him after the novelty had

worn off. There was not much kick left in that for anyone who was used to cabaret. No, he thought all that
sort of thing was only one remove from writing dirt on
walls. Those who were given that way might abreact
their complexes by so doing, but it didn't appeal to him
because his complexes did not lie along those lines. He
felt that the Black Mass, whether of Huysmans' or of
A. E. W. Mason's variety, was a destructive and negative
thing, not a constructive one ; it was a symbolic freeing
of oneself from one's inhibitions ; it called through no
power. Maybe Isabel Goudie managed something a
little more constructive when she went out to dance with
the Devil in churchyards, but there was a big measure of
abreaction there also. He could picture the mediæval
women, repressed by religion and custom, stealing out of
the narrow streets of the walled towns by twos and threes
at the dark of the moon to go to the terrible Sabbat and
taste of its dear-bought freedom, so often paid for with
the faggot and rack. He also thought of the hint picked
up from another book, how the witches that could not
attend the Sabbat rubbed themselves with the drugged,
aphrodisiac ointment, lay down and concentrated on
what was going on out on the moor or in the forest,
and presently found themselves there in dream or vision.
This again was Ignatius done backwards. The more he
thought of it, the more he saw that all the methods were
really one and the same method. The broom-stick flying
of the mediæval witches was first cousin to the temple
sleep, or incubation, of the Greeks, in which the wor-
shipper, sleeping in the temple, was blessed with a vision
of the god. Was it along this track that he would find
Pan ?

He composed himself for sleep on his back, for he had
always understood that this position induced dreams, and
sent his mind ranging out over the vales of Arcady in
search of Pan. In his imagination he performed the
' composition of place ', reconstructing the scene from

what he could remember of the classics, so laboriously
and unprofitably rammed into his head at Harrow. The
sparse woods of oak and fir; the wine-dark sea beneath;
the sound of the bees in the cistuses, the basking lizards,
and above all, the flocks of leaping goats springing from
rock to rock. He imagined the thin fluting pipe of the
goatherd that at any moment might change to the pipes
of Pan; he smelt the smell of the pines in the rare dry
air; he felt the sun warm upon his skin; he heard the
surf of the loud-sounding sea on the rocks far beneath.
He heard the crying of gulls. Were there gulls in the
isles of Greece? He did not know, he only knew he
heard them; they had come of their own accord.

But the act of attention and question had broken the
magic, he was back in bed again, with Greece far away,
as if seen through the wrong end of an opera-glass. All
the same he had seen enough to satisfy him. Those gulls
had been extraordinarily real, and he hadn't phantasied
them as he had the goats, he had actually heard them.

He turned over and lay passively waiting for sleep, his
mind drifting idly over what he had just experienced;
over his talks with old Jelkes in the dusty brown bookshop; he remembered a particular race he had run in at
school, when he had been in particularly good condition;
the sun had been warm on his back through the thin
running singlet as he had crouched waiting for the start,
just like the sun in ancient Greece. His wife's face came
to him, as she sat before her mirror, making-up; her
frock off, her backless scanties revealing the satiny skin
with its softly-moulded muscles, so different to a man's.
She turned her head to speak to him, and he suddenly
realised with a start that it was not his wife, but a stranger.
But in that brief glimpse he could discern no more than a
flash of eyes, nose and mouth. He could not identify the
face, save that it was not his wife's.

Then he found himself out on the hillside among the
thin woods of oak and fir, and ahead of him moved

through the light shadow the satiny back. He followed it, springing after it; it kept ahead. He quickened his pace; he was sure that when it came out into the sunshine, as come it must in those sparse woods, he would see the face; but it did not come, and he lost sight of it, and found himself in deeper woods, a dense growth, dark with laurels. And through that darkness there came a curious cold exhilarating fear, a touch of panic.

He found himself sitting up in bed, tense and startled. Something must have wakened him suddenly. What was it? He listened, eyes staring into the darkness. His ears took in nothing, but his nose did. There was a distinct smell of burning.

He leapt out of bed, flung open his door, went out onto the landing and shouted for Jelkes. The old house would burn like tinder if it once got a start. A bump upstairs told him that the old man had roused, and the light of a candle over the banisters immediately followed.

" I say, Jelkes? " he called out. " I woke up smelling smoke. I think we'd better have a look round your establishment."

Jelkes joined him, and they stood on the stairs sniffing, trying to see whether the smoke came up from below. But it didn't. They went into Paston's room, and there they met it, faint blue wreaths of it, and a very distinct smell. The old man stood still and stared at those blue wreaths revealed by the candle-light, making no attempt to do anything about it. Hugh was round the room like a questing hound; head under the bed, head in the fireplace, flinging up the window to see whether the smoke had come in from outside. But he found nothing. Still old Jelkes did not move.

" There's smoke all right," said Hugh, shutting the window. " But I can't trace where it's coming from."

" No," said Jelkes, " and you won't either, because it isn't here."

" Where is it then? In the next house? "

The old man shook his head. " No, it isn't on this plane at all. Do you notice that it is the smell of smouldering cedar-wood ? "

He suddenly found himself seized by the shoulders and swung around his dusty landing in a wild dance. Hugh Paston, regardless of the seatless state of his pyjamas, was performing a saraband.

" T. J.," he cried. " Do you realise we've made a start ? We've really made a start ! "

" Damn ! " said T. Jelkes, as the candle fell over and spilled hot wax on his thumb.

## CHAPTER VIII

Upon the two men in the old bookshop the cold light of morning had its usual sobering effect. Hugh Paston wondered how much of last night's experience was pure imagination, and T. Jelkes wondered how in the world he was going to steer between the Scylla and Charybdis that confronted him. Every dictum of common sense told him to leave well alone ; he would embroil himself in a pretty kettle of fish if he went any further. Occultism was all right between the covers of books, especially novels ; but in real life, if it were not such stuff as dreams were made of, it would probably prove to be pretty explosive. He himself was by nature the dreamer, the contemplative ; the mystical philosophy appealed to him for the understanding it gave, and as a way of escape from the limitations of life as it is lived on a meagre income. But Hugh Paston was no mystic ; whatever he learnt he would immediately put into practice. Old Jelkes saw himself being dragged in out of his depth when the duckling he had hatched took to the water, as it showed every sign of doing.

He believed that the final cord had been cut when he made Hugh Paston face the fact that he had never been loved but had been tricked from the beginning, and in so doing had torn the last rag of self-respect from him. Such treatment was kill or cure. He had smashed the man down to his foundations. For all the brave face Hugh Paston might put on things, he was lying with his head in the dust. The old bookseller had dealt with him by the homœopathic method of rubbing his nose in it in the hope of making him lift his head out of sheer resentment, if nothing else. If there were any capacity for

71

reaction left in Hugh Paston, now was the time to apply stimulants, and they must be drastic stimulants. He daren't stop now or he would have a pretty bad wreck on his hands. The old bookseller sighed, and wished to God he had never started playing with souls.

He looked at his *vis à vis* across the breakfast table, and saw that he was staring glumly into the fire. Serious conversation was impossible, for the char was still bumping about like a colossal bluebottle, and in any case it was inadvisable to go any further until he knew exactly what he could do. It would be fatal to raise hopes and then dash them. He determined that there should be no further conversation until he had every-thing ready for what must inevitably transpire.

Hugh solved his problem for him by saying abruptly :

" I shall have to tackle my mother today. Can't leave things hanging about any longer."

Jelkes nodded. " Back to lunch ? " he enquired.

" No, back to supper—if I may."

Having seen his guest safely off the premises, Jelkes discarded his dressing-gown for an ancient Inverness cape and sallied forth. He had not far to go. A couple of turns, and he was at his destination. He pressed one of a number of bells at the side of a shabby door under a pretentious portico. A visiting-card stuck up beside it with a drawing-pin announced that Miss Mona Wilton, Designer and Craft-worker, was the owner of the bell. Jelkes lodged his shoulders against the pilasters flanking the portico and set himself to wait, for he knew that even if Miss Mona Wilton were in, it would take her a little time to get from top to bottom of that tall narrow house to admit him. Presently his patience was rewarded ; he heard a step on the bare tiles of the hall, the door opened, and a girl in a faded blue linen smock presented herself.

He looked at her sharply, almost suspiciously, and saw what he expected to see—a pinched look about the nostrils, a hollowness about the eyes ; early in the day as it was, the girl looked fine-drawn and exhausted, and there was about her a curious air of apprehension. It is the appearance that is produced by fasting. Jelkes blamed himself bitterly that he had not been round before to see what was happening.

At the sight of the old bookseller the girl's eyes filled with tears and she was unable to speak.

" Why didn't you come round and see me ? " demanded Jelkes, glaring at her.

" I'm all right," the girl answered brokenly, ushering him into the dusty, empty hall, whose only furniture was a smelly pram.

He followed her up the wide, uncarpeted stone staircase. Up and up they went ; and presently the bare stone gave place to echoing wood and the stairs grew steeper. Each landing was decorated with milk bottles, full and empty ; also ash-cans—full.

Finally they came to the narrow winding stairs that led to the attics. At the top was a flimsy, glass-panelled partition. They passed through it, and the girl closed the door behind them.

" Heavens, what a climb ! " said the panting bookseller. " No wonder you keep your figure, my dear."

" It's worth it," said the girl. " You see, I can shut my door behind me and have privacy up here, and no one else in the house can. Besides, there's the view and the sunsets."

Jelkes thought to himself that the sunsets must be poor consolation for grilling under the tiles during a London summer.

The girl led him into a little sitting-room lit by small dormer windows in the sloping walls, and placed him in the one arm-chair as the guest of honour. There was no fire in the grate, but an eiderdown that had slipped to the floor behind the chair showed how she had been keeping herself warm.

Miss Wilton sat down on a small pouf, folded her arms

round her knees—to keep herself from shivering, he suspected, and smiled up at him with a gallant attempt at cheerfulness.

" What brings you here at this time of the morning ? " she enquired.

" A job of work," said Jelkes.

Her face brightened eagerly.

" For me ? "

" Yes, if you'll take it on."

" What is it ? "

" It's a very odd job, but I think there's money in it."

" It will have to be very odd indeed if I don't take it on. My last paper has let me down."

" Why didn't you tell me ? "

" Oh, well, one can't tell that sort of thing, can one ? You haven't got much more than I have, you know."

" I've got enough to give you a meal," said Jelkes savagely.

" Well, as a matter of fact, I did look round last night, but you had got someone with you, so I did not come in."

Jelkes snorted, and rose to his feet resolutely.

" You are coming round with me now to have a meal," he said, " and you'll get no information till you do."

" Well, Uncle Jelkes, I won't say no. I've done about as much slimming as I care for."

She hung the smock up on a peg behind the door, appearing in a shabby brown jumper and skirt that emphasised the sallowness of her skin and the dullness of her dark hair ; put a little knitted cap on her head ; pulled on a brown tweed coat with a worn coney collar, and slipped her latch-key into her pocket.

Jelkes, looking at her, felt relieved. It was improbable that Paston would get into mischief in that quarter.

They went round to the bookshop, and Jelkes warmed her by his fire, and filled her with sausages and tea, till the fine-drawn look gradually faded from her face and she settled down in the corner of the sofa that Hugh Paston had made his own, and helped herself to one of his cigarettes.

" My word, Uncle Jelkes," she said as she inhaled the fragrant smoke, " you are doing yourself well. These must have cost you a pretty penny."

" It's all right, my dear," said the old bookseller, grinning, " I did not come by them honestly."

" Well now, what about this job ? "

" Yes, what about it ? " said Jelkes, scratching what was left of his hair. " I hardly know where to begin. It's a fellow that wants a house furnishing."

" You mean he wants me to design the decorations, and choose the furniture, and generally see the job through ? "

" Yes, that's it," said the bookseller hesitatingly. This description, though true so far as it went, was so far from being the whole truth that it was a lot more misleading than most lies.

" And the rest ? " said Miss Wilton. " You're looking very guilty, Uncle Jelkes. I'm sure there is a nigger in the wood-pile somewhere. Isn't this individual respectable ? "

" Yes, yes, he's all right. At least I hope so."

" Then where's the snag ? "

" I don't suppose there really is one. I'm afraid I'm old-fashioned. I suppose you can take care of yourself as well as any other girl of your age."

" If I couldn't," said Mona, " I'd have become extinct long ago. I'll keep my end up with this individual as long as he's solvent. But I don't want to let any firms in for bad debts, because that will queer my pitch for next time."

" He's solvent right enough. He's the grandson of the man that founded Paston's, the big tea merchants. I suppose it practically belongs to him, and a lot more beside."

" Is he anything to do with that man whose wife was killed in a motor smash just recently when she was eloping ? "

" Yes, it's the same man.  But she wasn't eloping.  No such luck.  She was keeping two homes going."

" I call that a dirty trick."

" An uncommonly dirty trick.  And it's made a nasty mess of the man.  I'm exceedingly sorry for him."

" What is he starting furnishing for ?  Has he consoled himself already ? "

" No.  It's not that.  I think it's partly because he can't stand the sight of the furniture, if you ask me.  He's put the whole place in the auctioneer's hands, lock, stock, and barrel."

" And he wants me to fit him up with a new one ?  Hasn't he got any womenfolk to look after him ? "

" I don't know anything about that.  I haven't seen any signs of them.  But anyway, he wants the place specially designing."

" That ought to be interesting."

" Very interesting," said Jelkes drily.  " I only hope it won't be too interesting by the time you're through with it."

" What is all the mystery ?  Do come to the point, Uncle."

" Well now, I'll tell you, Mona.  He's been dipping into Huysmans' books, ' A Rebours ' and ' Là-Bas ', and he wants to amuse himself by going and doing likewise."

" Does he want to work the Black Mass ?  How entertaining ! "

" Now, Mona, I won't have you talking like that, even in fun.  He certainly isn't going to work the Black Mass or I wouldn't have put you on to him.  What he wants to do is to furnish a house on—er—esoteric lines."

" What exactly does he understand by that ? "

" Hanged if I know.  And I don't believe he does, either.  So there ought to be some pickings in it."

" There certainly ought, if he's as vague as all that,"
said Mona. " But even so, I can't rook the poor man.
It is really my job to see that nobody rooks him."

" Yes, that's exactly it. You see, my dear, he's had a
very bad shake-up over this business with his wife ; and
I think that if he doesn't have something to occupy his
mind, he'll go completely balmy. And it struck me that
you might as well have the pickings as anyone else."

" Thanks very much, Uncle Jelkes. I'll be very glad
of the job, and I won't rook him more than is just and
right, and I'll be a mother to him generally. I suppose
that's the idea ? Have you taken him under your Jaeger
wing ? "

" Well, as a matter of fact, I have. I'm sorry for the
fellow."

" What is he like ? Is he nice ? "

" He's not bad. One of these society fellows, you
know."

" Does he wear an old school tie ? "

" No, he doesn't need to. His clothes are all right."

" You *are* cynical, Uncle Jelkes."

" Well, my dear, if a man looks like a gentleman, he
doesn't need a label. It's only when he looks like a sand-
wichman that he has to hang out a sign to say : ' I'm a
gentleman, though you mightn't think it.' "

" Is he handsome ? "

" No. Plain as a pikestaff."

" Are you nervous for my morals, Uncle Jelkes ? "

" No more than usual, my dear. But you know what
these society men are."

" I suppose he reckons parlourmaids are his perks.
Oh, well, I'll soon disillusion him. By the way, where is
his house ? "

" He hasn't decided yet. I believe you will be wanted
to help with the house-hunting."

" Uncle, this is going to be fun. I've never had a
chance to choose the house before. I've always had to

make the best of what someone else has chosen."

" It will be more than fun, Mona. It will be a really useful piece of work if you handle him the right way. The fellow wants taking out of himself or I really think he will go on the rocks."

"It appears to me that I shall have to redecorate him as well as his house. When am I to meet the poor young man ? I take it he's young, or you wouldn't be so apprehensive about my morals."

" You ought to be ashamed of yourself."

" I can't help it, Uncle. You shouldn't dangle your leg within reach of my hand. How can I help pulling it ? But you needn't worry. I'll be most professional with him. I know better than to go about asking for trouble."

" Very well then. You come round this evening about seven and have a spot of supper with us. And put on that green frock of yours. I can't stick you in that ghastly brown. You look mud-coloured all over. Why ever do you wear those dark colours ? They make you look like the dead."

" I wear them because they don't show the dirt, Uncle Jelkes. And I can't put on my green frock because my other uncle's got it. The three brass balls one, you know. So I am afraid this will have to do. And anyway, it's no use my dressing up for a man like Mr Paston, because the best I could do would only look to him like the housemaid's afternoon off."

Miss Wilton had hardly got out of the door when in came Hugh Paston.

" Well, T. J.," he said, " I've done my duty by my family. I've lunched with my mother. Poor old mater. She's terribly fed up about this business. She can't exactly blame me, and yet she's furious with me. She said I ought to have looked after Frida better. I told her that it's only because I did not look after Frida that things have lasted as long as they have. They'd have gone up

in flames long ago if I'd tightened the reins. But anyway, the mater blames me. It is rather feeding for her.
You see, all her social aspirations have gone west. We
don't come out of the top drawer, you know. Only
one remove from retail trade. Frida's friends can't very
well keep up with me after what's happened ; so there
we are, back where we were when we started."

The old bookseller grunted his disapproval.

" Do you know, they've got their eye on my second
already ? My eldest sister came in, and began to talk
about some duke's daughter, very down at heel, that she's
picked up with. I could see the mater knew all about it,
but we had to hear it all over again for my benefit.
What a life ! Given away with a pound of tea. Paston's
Tea. That describes me exactly. Damn it all, Jelkes,
surely they don't expect me to repeat the dose ? "

" What do you propose to do, then ? Shake a loose
leg and enjoy yourself ? "

" Yes, that's it exactly. Once bit, twice shy. I don't
want social advancement, so what have I got to marry
for ? "

" What indeed ? " said Jelkes.

" Well, have you thought any more about my
scheme ? "

" I've done more than think, I've got a move on."

" Good man. What's the move ? "

" I've seen that artist I told you of." He handed Hugh
Mona's professional card.

" Oh, a woman ? " said Paston.

" Yes. Plain. Thirtyish. Competent. You'll find
her all right. She knows her job."

" Good God, T. J., you don't suppose I'll be starting
off again already ? Give us time to breathe. You're as
bad as my sister."

T. Jelkes blushed scarlet all over the top of his bald
head.

" I don't care whether it's a man or a woman or a

' giddy harumphrodite ' so long as it knows its job,"
said Hugh.

" She's coming in this evening to supper."

" Good.   We don't change, I take it ? "

" No, we don't change."

# CHAPTER IX

JELKES was busy dishing up the ready-made beefsteak pudding, which was half in and half out of its basin when there came a sound of knocking on the half-glass door of the shop.

" Go to the door, will you, Hugh ? " he called from the kitchen, wondering whether Paston had ever answered the door before in his life, and what he would make of this sort of treatment. It was his fixed conviction that anyone of Hugh's walk in life was incapable of wiping his own nose.

He heard footsteps crossing the oilcloth floor of the shop, the clang of the bell as the door opened, and voices —the man's pleasantly cordial, the woman's impersonal and business-like.

Mona Wilton, coming in hatless through the door of the shop, was surprised to find herself confronted by a stranger. The hard glare of the incandescent light was not kind to the looks of either of them. She saw before her a loosely-built man whose well-cut suit did what it could towards disguising his stooping shoulders. His sharp-featured face looked haggard, and his black tie reminded her why. Except for his good clothes he was a nondescript individual, she thought, lacking personality. She was not surprised that this man's wife had been unfaithful to him. What was there in him to hold a woman faithful ?

He, on his side, saw under the hard white glare a youngish woman, tired-looking, with a sallow complexion and rather unkempt dark hair. She had a square face, with a strong jaw and wide mouth, innocent of lipstick. The only thing that struck him about her was the strong, muscular neck, the muscles showing moulded like a man's under the olive skin.   She had hazel eyes, set wide apart under heavy black brows that almost met over the bridge of the short, straight nose.   Her brows were much blacker than her hair, which was a rusty brown, like the coat of an ill-kept cat.   She wore it *coupé en page*, with a straight-cut fringe in front, and a straight-cut bob behind.   Hugh Paston, who had never known a woman that wasn't permed, thought she looked rather like Mrs Noah out of Noah's Ark.

She went through into the room behind the shop, and as he lingered behind to secure the door, he heard her being grunted at by the bookseller.   He was not particularly struck with Jelkes's choice.   In fact, to be candid, he was disappointed.   He had hoped for something much more exotic than this—a bit of old Chelsea on the loose. If he could have had his way, he would have had her inlaid with precious stones to brighten her up, like Des Esseintes' turtle.   She looked competent, however ; and there would obviously be no nonsense about her.   It would be difficult to imagine a woman about whom there would be less nonsense.   She was rather Mrs Macintosh's type.   Frida had always been a good judge of housekeepers.

He joined the party in the room behind the shop. Jelkes wasted no time in introductions.   He took it for granted they had become acquainted.   They drew their chairs up to the table, and he ceremoniously laid before them an old willow-pattern dish, burnt almost black in the oven, instead of serving the food out of the usual frying-pan.

Conversation was stilted.   Old Jelkes did not bother with it, but shovelled down his food in silence, as was his usual custom.   The girl seemed equally ready to sit in silence or to answer any remark that might be addressed to her, just as did Mrs Macintosh in the presence of her employer ; but Hugh, who had been well-trained by his womenfolk, worked hard at the conversation.

He tried to get the girl to talk about her work, and this she did impersonally and without enthusiasm, telling him what her qualifications were, and what experience she had had. He saw that she was not prepared to make friends, but was keeping him on a purely business footing. He was inclined to resent this. Surely if she accepted an invitation to a meal she should accept also the implied social relationship, instead of keeping a shop-counter between them, as it were ? But he supposed she had probably had some trying experiences in her time, though she did not appear to be a person who called for them, and if she preferred to keep her male clients at arm's length, well, it was to her credit. He felt a little sore, however, and vaguely defrauded, as if he were not getting proper value for the money he was prepared to spend.

The meal was despatched expeditiously under such circumstances ; Jelkes moved them over to the fire to drink their tea, and with an airy wave of his hand, said :

" Now, you two, get on with your business while I clear away," and disappeared into the kitchen and left them to it.

Hugh, taking his cue from the girl's attitude, came straight to business.

" Has Mr Jelkes told you anything about what I want doing ? " he enquired.

" A little," said the girl. And then suddenly the wide colourless lips broadened into a smile, " I hear you have been reading ' A Rebours '."

The sudden humanising of the girl startled Hugh Paston, she changed so completely. But before he had time to respond, her face settled back again into its impassivity. He followed up his temporary advantage, however. He must humanise this girl. It was impossible to explain what he wanted to an impersonal business woman ; impossible to get her to co-operate with him.

" I suppose Mr Jelkes had told you I'm half mad ? "
he said.

The smile hovered at the corners of her mouth.

" No, he didn't exactly say that," she said.

" Well, take it from me, I am. At any rate, I'm very
eccentric."

The smile hovered again for a moment, and then suddenly the whole face changed and softened and became
almost beautiful, and Hugh Paston knew that the story
of his tragedy had been told to this woman. A wave of
uncontrollable emotion surged up in him ; his mouth
quivered and his eyes stared into space, seeing his muti-
lated dead. It was a moment or two before he could
recover control, but when he did, and met the woman's
eyes again, he knew that the barriers were down between
them.

He moved uneasily in his seat, seeking desperately for
some remark that would serve to break the silence and
bring the atmosphere back to normal.

It was the woman, however, who picked the situation
out of the fire.

" I gather that the first thing to do is to set to work
and find a house ? " she said.

" Yes, rather," said Hugh, grasping thankfully at the
life-line. " I'd be awfully glad if you would."

" What sort of a house do you want, and where ? "

" Do you know, I haven't the remotest idea," said
Hugh, and the girl burst out laughing. The intolerable
tension was relieved, and Hugh leant back in his corner
of the sofa and laughed too.

" I told you I was loopy," he said, and the girl laughed
again. But behind the laughter was the knowledge why
it was that this man had torn everything he possessed
from himself and flung it aside, and what torments of
the soul lay behind the eccentricity. To laugh at him,
and make him laugh at himself, was the only safe thing
to do at the moment. There is nothing to equal laughter,

either as camouflage or safety-valve.

Mona Wilton leant forward, resting her elbow on her
knee and her chin on her hand, and considered him.

" It is to be a mixture of ' Là-Bas ' and ' A Rebours ',
is it ? " she said.

" Yes, that's exactly it," replied Hugh eagerly, his
facile attention distracted and caught, as she had meant
it to be.

" Does access to town, or anything like that matter ? "

" Not a ha'porth."

" Very well, then, the best thing we can do is to get
out a map and pick a district that will give the right conditions.   Uncle Jelkes ! " she called, and the old bookseller popped his head out of the kitchen.  " Have
you got a big atlas ?  One that has a geological map
in it ? "

Jelkes ambled over to the far corner of the room,
pushed some books aside with his foot, and extracted an
enormous and very dilapidated tome.

" Here you are," he said, lugging it across to the sofa
and depositing it between them.  " It's pretty ancient,
but I guess the geological strata haven't changed much
since it was published."

" And I want a pencil and ruler, please."

" Huh," said the bookseller.  " So you're at that game,
are you ? "

He gave her what she required and disappeared into
the kitchen again, apparently getting on with the washing-up, an unheard-of performance.

" Now look," said Mona, opening the atlas at the map
of England.  " There are certain places that are more
suitable than others for what you want to do, just as
there are some places where you can grow rhododen-
drons, and some where you can grow roses ;  and the
places that will grow the one, won't grow the other."

" Oh, you're a gardener, are you, in addition to all
your other accomplishments ? "

" I used to be. Now look at this map. You see Avebury ? "

" Yes."

" That was the centre of the old sun-worship. Now draw a line from Avebury to any other place where there are the remains of ancient worship, and anywhere along that line will be good for what you want."

" Good Lord, what's that got to do with it ? "

" You want to wake the Old Gods, don't you ? "

" Yes."

" Well then, go where the Old Gods are accustomed to be worshipped."

" But then surely one would go to Avebury itself, or Stonehenge ? "

" Too much of a tourist show. You would get no seclusion. No, the lines of force between the power centres are much better for your purpose. You will get quite enough power without being overwhelmed by it."

" If there is so much power knocking about, why aren't the local yokels bowled over by it ? "

" Because they don't think about it. You only contact these things if you think about them. But you will find that people living at these power-centres simply hate any mention of the Unseen. It rubs their fur the wrong way and makes them writhe. That is their reaction to the invisible forces. Ask Glastonbury what it thinks of Bligh Bond if you want to see people really savage."

" I'd as soon ask them what they thought of John Cowper Powys. It's been my experience that a prophet is not only without honour, but without reputation in his own place."

" You aren't expecting to preserve any reputation, are you, if you go in for this sort of thing ? Because if you plant yourself down in a country place and do anything out of the ordinary, people will think the very worst."

" The worse, the better. The one thing I want to be spared is local society."

A slow smile spread over Mona Wilton's face as she bent over the map.

" You will be spared that all right," she said.

" Well now, look here, I've got my finger on Avebury, what next ? "

" Put the edge of the ruler on it and revolve it slowly. Where is it now ? "

" One end's on Cornwall and the other to the north of London."

" Can you see Tintagel ? "

" Yes, it's just north of my ruler."

" Then bring the ruler onto Tintagel. That's the western power-centre. Now draw a line right across the map to Avebury."

Hugh ran the pencil down the ruler.

" Now project your line to St Albans. Is that straight ? "

" Dead straight. It's one line."

" St Albans is the eastern power-centre. Now take St Albans Head in Dorset, and lay your ruler from there to Lindisfarne, off the Northumberland coast. Does that pass through Avebury ? "

" Yes."

" Lindisfarne is the northern power-centre. So you see, if you take a line through Avebury from either Lindisfarne or Tintagel, you end up with a St Albans. Odd, isn't it ? "

" Yes, it's odd. But I don't quite see why it's odd."

" St Alban was the first British saint."

" Look here, we don't want any saints in this business."

" Don't you realise that these prehistoric saints are really the Old Gods with a coat of whitewash ? Do you know that somewhere in the neighbourhood—sometimes actually in the crypts of the oldest cathedrals—the ones with some Saxon work in them, you invariably find traces of the old sun-worship ? "

" What's the reason for that ? "

" It's quite simple and natural if you think it out. The old pagan Britons were in the habit of having fairs when they assembled at their holy centres for the big sun festivals. The fairs went on just the same, whether they were pagan or Christian, and the missionary centres grew up where the crowds came together. When the king was converted, they just changed the Sun for the Son. The common people never knew the difference. They went for the fun of the fair and took part in the ceremonies to bring good luck and make the fields fertile. How were they to know the difference between Good Friday and the spring ploughing festival ? There was a human sacrifice on both occasions."

" ' *Plus ça change, plus c'est la même chose* '," said Hugh.

" Precisely."

" So when you want to get on the track of the Old Gods, you sniff round the heels of the dean and chapter because you know they won't be very far off ? "

" Yes, that's it. You see, where people have been in the habit of reaching out towards the Unseen, they wear a kind of track, and it's much easier to go out that way."

" But surely to goodness the dean and chapter would exorcise the whole affair with bell, book and candle if they knew ? "

" Of course they would, and that's why we who worship the Old Gods use the lines of force between the power-centres, and not the power-centres themselves because those power-centres have all been exorcised long ago. But they didn't know enough to know of the lines of force, so they never exorcised those."

" How did they exorcise them ? "

" They put up chapels dedicated to St Michael, whose function is to keep down the forces of the underworld, and had perpetual adoration there. There is one right on top of Glastonbury Tor ; and another on St Michael's Mount in Cornwall ; and a third on Mont St Michel in

Brittany, and those three make a perfect triangle. And I'll tell you a funny thing about the one on top of Glastonbury Tor. The body of the church fell down in an earthquake and left the tower standing. And a standing tower is one of the symbols of the Old Gods, so the Devil had the best of it down there."

"Are the Old Gods synonymous with the Devil?"

"Christians think they are."

"What do you think they are?"

"I think they're the same thing as the Freudian subconscious."

"Oh, you do, do you? Now I wonder what you mean by that?"

"Shall we get on with our house-hunting? Now the best place to get the kind of experiences you want is on the chalk. If you think of it, you know, all the earliest civilisation in these islands was on the chalk. Turn over the page and look at the geological map, and see where that line of yours runs through the chalk."

"It runs through quite a lot of chalk, doesn't it? Avebury's on the chalk; and St Albans is on the chalk."

"Well, anywhere on that line, where it runs through the chalk will serve your purpose."

"That's narrowed the field of search down very satisfactorily. Now what's the next move?"

"Get a large-scale ordnance map and look for standing-stones and hammer-pools."

"What in the world are standing-stones?"

"They are supposed to be the altars of ancient sacrifices, but as a matter of fact, they are the sighting-marks on these lines of force between the power-centres. The stones on the high places, and the hammer-pools in the bottoms."

"I thought hammer-pools were to do with ancient forges."

"You get hammer-pools in parts where there is no iron, so they can't be."

" Then what did ancient man dam the streams for ? "

" Because water shows up in a valley bottom among trees, where stones wouldn't. Then, you see, he sights from one to another, and gets a dead straight line across country. You know the Long Man, cut out of the turf on the chalk downs ? You remember he has a staff in each hand ? Well, those are the pair of sighting-staffs that are used for marking out these lines. These lines criss-cross all over England just like a crystalline structure. You can work them out on any large-scale ordnance map by means of the place-names and standing-stones and earthworks."

" But look here, you know, my idea is to do an invocation of Pan. What has all this got to do with Pan ? "

" Well, what is Pan ? "

" God knows. I don't."

" You don't suppose he's half a goat, any more than Jehovah is an old man with a gold crown and a long white beard, who made man out of mud, do you ? "

" To tell you the honest truth, I've never thought about it. The one's just as much a name to me as the other."

" But they both represent something, you know. They're—they're factors."

" They can please 'emselves about that. I only know I get a kick out of the idea of Pan, and I get none out of the idea of Jehovah since I outgrew Hell. But never mind the metaphysics. Let's get on with the house."

" But it's applied metaphysics you're aiming at."

" I don't know anything about that either. I'm afraid it's beyond me. I must leave that to you and Mr Jelkes. Now look here, what's the next item on the programme ? Go house-hunting along this line of villages on the chalk ? Who's going to do it ? "

" I will, if you wish."

" How will you manage about transport ? "

" Green Line buses, and then walk."

" That's a slow and weary business. Supposing I run you round in my car, and then we can look at them together ? "

" That is very kind of you."

A movement in the background caught Mona's eye, and glancing up, she saw the old bookseller's vulture head come round the jamb of the kitchen door and eye her reproachfully.

Jelkes evidently considered he had done enough washing-up for one night, and that it was his duty to return and keep a hand on things, so he sat himself down in his usual chair and registered all the psychological symptoms of a hen whose ducklings take to water. After that, conversation languished.

# CHAPTER X

AT ten o'clock precisely Mona Wilton presented herself at the second-hand bookshop, clad in her brown tweed coat with the coney collar and her little knitted cap. Outside the door stood an open two-seater of the kind that is used for racing. It had the minutest windscreen and no hood. Mona gazed at it apprehensively; her tweed coat was of the cheapest, with little warmth in it, and the day was bleak.

She entered the shop and found Hugh and the old bookseller still at their breakfast. She was offered a cup of tea, and accepted it. Old Jelkes quietly cut her a thick slice of bread and marmalade, and she accepted that too.

Hugh rose from the table and girded himself into a heavy leather motoring coat; fitted a leather racing helmet onto his head, and pulled a big pair of wool-lined gauntlets onto his hands.

" Now we're ready," he said. Mona acquiesced.

They went out into the street.

" I must apologise for the car," said Hugh. " I had forgotten I'd only got this one when I offered you transport."

Mona remembered what had happened to the other car, and she guessed from his face that he was thinking of the same thing.

They entered the two-seater. She had a beautiful llama-wool rug round her knees, but the cold wind cut like a knife through the upper half of her as the car whipped into the main road. To her surprise, they turned east instead of west. The car twisted through the traffic like a hound, and then came to an abrupt standstill outside the magnificent premises of a firm of motor

accessory dealers. Hugh Paston got out. Mona, supposing he was going to get something for the car,
stopped where she was.

"Come along," said Hugh, opening the low door for
her. She got out meekly and followed him. One does
not argue with clients.

He led the way through the region of lamps and horns
and came out where rows of leather coats hung on stands.

"I want a coat for this lady," he said to the shop-
walker.

Mona gasped. Opened her mouth to slay him. Shut
it again in bewilderment and stared at him in speechless
protest. He turned to her with a melancholy smile on
his face.

"Don't worry," he said. "This means nothing to
me. I've got a lot more than I know what to do with.
You can leave the coat in the car if you don't want to
take it, but I can't stand watching you shiver."

Mona could not find a word to reply. Every instinct
of the independent professional woman was against
accepting the gift, and yet she was profoundly touched
by the way it was done. The man's manner conveyed
the impression that he had not the slightest expectation
of being liked for himself; that he had not the slightest
expectation of receiving any gratitude for anything he
might do. Before she could find her tongue, the assistant
returned with an armful of coats.

Mona's eye fell on a sober nigger brown, but Hugh
Paston put out his hand and picked up a fold of vivid
jade green.

"I rather like the look of this, don't you?"

"Oh no," said Mona. "It's much too bright for
me."

"You are a funny person. You're supposed to be an
artist and know all about colours, and yet you go and
wear the things that kill you dead."

"I know. Uncle Jelkes is always grumbling at me.

But it isn't because I like them.  It's from motives of economy."

"Let's cut a dash for once.  Try this green.  I think you'll like it."

She allowed herself to be strapped into the jade green coat.  In the pocket was a soft leather helmet with a chin-strap which gave a curiously elf-like effect, framing the girl's straight-cut black hair and olive-skinned face.

Hugh Paston looked down at her thoughtfully.

"Do you know, I think that's a very appropriate kit in which to go and look for Pan," he said.

It was a very different matter, driving in the camel-lined leather coat to what it was driving in her thin little worn-out wrap.  The car, roaring in second, whipped in and out of the traffic.  Mona was interested in watching how Hugh Paston handled it.  One can learn a great deal about a man by watching the way he handles a car. She saw that he knew exactly what he was about with a car, what he could do with it, and what he could ask of it, and that he relied quite as much on his accelerator as on his brakes to get him out of a tight corner, which is a thing that reveals the calibre of a driver.  He was in sympathy with the car, and seemed to rely on the car's sympathetic response.  He was, in fact, in far closer touch with the inanimate machine than with human beings.  The one thing he did not appear to expect from human beings was sympathy.  His whole attitude seemed to say : 'I know I bore you.  I don't expect you to like me ; but I am quite used to not being liked, and I don't mind it.'  There was no resentment, no reaction ; just a tacit acceptance of solitude.  She wondered what experiences had made him what he was, and what rebellion against life had led to this breaking-out in the quest of Pan.

She realised very clearly that the man beside her was by no means in a normal state at the moment, and wondered what he might be like when he was himself.

Between his sudden flare-ups of animation he was curiously negative. She got the impression that this negativeness was his habitual attitude ; and yet it did not seem to her that it could be considered normal. He gave her the impression of a man who had given life up as a bad job ; and yet in his position he had only to formulate a wish in order to gratify it. Now she had been on the point of giving life up as a bad job because the struggle to keep her head above water was too severe. If she had had this man's resources, she thought, she would have lived with a most amazing fullness of life. She had no realisation of the enervating effect of great wealth, or the victimisation to which its owner is subjected. She knew that the usual attitude of a rich man, especially one who has not been the architect of his own fortune, is to suspect everyone who is more than decently civil of trying to get a hand in his pocket. But Hugh Paston's attitude seemed to be : ' It is only natural for you to have your hand in my pocket, and I don't expect it to be anywhere else. My money is very little use to me. If it is any use to you, you are welcome to it.' She felt that he gave freely to all who asked, expecting no return—and got what he expected. There suddenly arose in her an ardent desire to protect him from exploitation.

With a car like Hugh Paston's, and handled in the way he handled it, they were not long before they got clear of the London streets into an arterial road. Hugh changed into top gear, the car settled down to a steady snore, and conversation became possible.

" How far out shall we run before we start house-hunting ? " said the man to his companion as the scanty weekday traffic thinned out behind them.

" We must run clear of London's aura," came the answer in an unexpectedly rich speaking-voice that rang above the rush of the wind and the roar of the car without effort.

" How far is that ? "

"It varies on the different roads. Barren soil and rising ground both break it. I will tell you when we clear it."

They travelled on for some time in silence.

"Are we clear of it yet?" said Hugh presently.

"No, not yet. It strings out along this valley bottom with the ribbon-building. I expect all the folk in these little red houses go up to London every day. Look, turn down one of these lanes. We'll soon get away from it now if we leave the main road."

Hugh swung the car into a narrow by-lane that dipped to the valley bottom where a marshy stream ran amid osiers, crossed a hump-backed bridge, and began to climb steeply up the far flank of the valley. Presently they found themselves coming out onto a wide common. Everything was brown and sear up here, though first green had been showing in the hedges of the main road. The sparse growth of Scotch firs broke the sky-line; a scanty sprinkling of birches marked the wide expanse here and there, and the blackened stems of a burnt-out patch of gorse writhed as if in perpetual agony, the tins and bottles of many picnics revealed among them. It was not a prepossessing spot.

"We are still too near the main-road," said Mona. "This is where London slops over on a Sunday."

They left the common behind them and dipped into another but shallower valley, little more than a depression between two ridges, and found themselves suddenly in rural England. The average picnicking motorist had gone no further than the first bit of open ground. Here was unspoiled country. They followed a winding lane between high hedges that opened every now and then to give a glimpse of plough-land. Then the ground rose again, and plough gave place to pasture. The gradient grew steeper, and pasture gave place to open common with a few geese walking about. A hamlet strung out along one side of the common, and as they drove towards it an old dame in a sun-bonnet waddled slowly down the road with a bucket in her hand and began to agitate the handle of a pump.

" By gum," said Hugh, " this is primitive if you like."

" Not as primitive as it might be," said Mona. " They are lucky to have a pump. They might only have a bucket and windlass. Now keep a look-out for the village shop, for that is where we shall be able to pick up some information."

" Why not the pub ? Are you an ardent teetotaller ? "

" Not a bit. But the kind of information we shall get at the pub will be different to what we get at the shop. You see, when the shop-keeper sees you coming, he will want to help you to a house in the neighbourhood in the hope of getting some, at any rate, of your custom. But if the publican sees you coming, he will try to do his cronies a good turn by running up the price on you, then they will have more to spend with him."

" Right you are. We will avoid strong drink."

They drew up opposite the inevitable tiny general store. Mona marched in, and was greeted by an elderly gentleman who ledged his corporation on the counter and his backside on the shelves that held his stock. His ruddy countenance, smoothly shaven, was encircled by that curious form of whiskerature known as a Newgate fringe. Chilly as the day was, he wore no coat. The sleeves of a spotless pale pink shirt were carefully folded above his elbows. A grey waistcoat encircled his enormous front, the lower buttons apparently acting as a kind of sling, and round his middle was a white fringed towel such as grocers affect. This towel, spotless as his shirt, was slung over an endless piece of tape, which disappeared into the shadows behind him and ended in a bow. But his front elevation was so extensive that the towel, which would have gone round an ordinary man's hips, was no more than a panel to him. Hen-food, veterinary medicines, hardware, haberdashery, stationery, tinned goods, braces, overalls, children's pinafores, a large cheese in cut, a side of bacon ditto, a canary in a cage and a cat with family occupied such portions of the shop as were not overhung by its owner's waistcoat.

He seemed pleased to see them, and a smile of immense geniality creased his vast pink countenance with its perfect schoolgirl complexion.

" And what can I do for you, sir ?—madam ? "

" There is not much you can do for us at the moment," said Hugh, " except for some milk chocolate ; but we are looking for a house, and were wondering if you could put us on the track of one."

" A 'ouse, now, a 'ouse ?  Now what sort of a 'ouse ? "

At this very reasonable question Hugh turned and looked helplessly at Mona.

" An old house, roomy, that can be modernised and adapted."

The old man shook his head sadly.

" We only 'ad two big 'ouses about 'ere," he said, " and they're both schools now."

" And I suppose they get all their goods from London ? "

" Yes, that they do," said the grocer with sudden fierceness.  " Unless they 'appen to run out of something, and then it's :  ' Mr 'Uggins, will you oblige ? ' and on early closin' day, as often as not."

" Too bad," said Hugh.  " People shouldn't do that sort of thing if they live in a place."

" That's what I sez," said Mr Huggins.  " And if we 'ad another railway strike, they'd know it.  *I* shouldn't put in for more'n I needed for me regular customers. Now an 'ouse, sir ?  A large 'ouse ?  MOTHER ! "

His yell was so loud and sudden that both Hugh and Mona recoiled into the hen-food.

" Yes, Pa ? " came a mild voice from behind a pile of biscuit-tins, and a little old lady, her spectacles pushed up onto her forehead, her hair pulled back as if she were about to have a good wash, and a clean white apron round her waist, appeared.

" Mother, do ye know of any large 'ouses about 'ere that's empty ? "

" No, indeed I don't," said the little old lady thoughtfully. " They all go for schools, nowadays, there's no gentry left, like we used to serve."

" Yes, that's it. No gentry left. Everything gone. The farmers, they can't keep body 'n soul together."

" That's an idea. Any farms going begging ? " said Hugh. " How would a farm do, Miss Wilton ? "

The Hugginses opened their eyes at this mode of address, having taken it for granted that if a man and a woman went about together they must be married, or at least engaged.

" A farm would do very well indeed, as long as you don't mind spending a good deal on it."

" No, I don't mind that," said Hugh. The Hugginses registered approval.

" Now I'll tell you where you'll find a farm that's empty," said Mr Huggins animatedly. " Monks Farm. The people what 'ad it went out last Michaelmas. It belongs to old Miss Pumfrey. That's 'er 'ouse you see through the trees. She wouldn't do no repairs to it, and they wouldn't stop no longer ; and she can't get no one else 'cos of the state it's in. I reckon she'd be reel glad to sell it, sir."

" That sounds promising. We might have a look at it. How do we get there ? "

" What about water supply ? " interrupted Mona before Mr Huggins could reply.

" Ah," said the old gentleman, rubbing his nose. " You're all right for that. Them old monks, they knew what they was about. You got a fine spring just above the 'ouse, and the water comes down of it's own weight, as you might say. That was the only reason the folks that was there stopped as long as they did. No pumpin'."

" I don't know that I should like a monastery," said Hugh, flinching.

" It ain't haunted, sir, it ain't reely," said Mrs Huggins anxiously.  A prospective customer like Hugh, who didn't care what he spent on his house, was to be hung onto desperately.  Ghosts might have run about like blackbeetles, but she would have sworn all was normal.

" I don't know of anything wrong with a monastery," said Mona.  " In fact it might be quite good."

" All right.  Lead on.  You're the one that knows.  Whereabouts is it, Mr Huggins ? "

" You go straight on down this road, and keep to the left on the top of the ridge when the road forks.  Then you come a little further on to a wood, and in the wood you'll see a lane with the gate off its 'inges.  You go down that, see, and you'll come to the 'ouse.  It's a tidy way from the road, but it's a good lane all the way, and you've got the water, and that's the main thing."

" Thanks very much, Mr Huggins, it sounds first-rate.  We'll have a look at it."

" And when you go to see Miss Pumfrey, you tell 'er Mr 'Uggins sent you."

" Yes, you tell her that," added Mrs Huggins emphatically.  " She did ought to sell that place, even if it has been in the family for years and years."

" Now why have we got to tell Miss Pumfrey that Mr Huggins sent us?  Can you tell me that, Miss Wilton ? " said Hugh as they went out to the car.

" I expect she's owing them money, don't you ? " said Mona, smiling.

" Good Lord, is this what the landed gentry have come to ? " exclaimed Hugh.

They followed the road as directed, and presently, in a thick belt of firs, came to a gateless gap.  They turned in, and bumped their way over a sandy surface till the firs gave place to open, moorlike pasture, dotted with clumps of gorse. It all looked pretty barren. They crossed the pasture and came to another belt of firs, and saw through them the loom of whitewashed buildings. They drove through a gap in the trees, and found themselves in the farm-yard.

Hugh was not familiar with the anatomy of farms, but even to his urban eyes that farm-yard looked odd. Round all four sides of it, with gaps here and there for ingress, ran a low, penthouse roof; rough tarred weather-boarding rose to meet it, evidently forming a long narrow cow-house or stable. Across one end of the yard was a very large barn with a very steep roof of ancient, lichen-blotched tiles. Across the side was a long range of old stone buildings, evidently used as living-quarters, dairy, store-rooms, and anything else that the work of a farm requires. It was much too large for a dwelling house, anyway. At the other end was a smaller and more roughly-built barn, evidently of later date than the rest of the buildings. A raffle of pigsties, calf-pens and cart-shelters occupied the extensive yard round which these buildings stood; the yard itself was unpaved, and must have been a quagmire in wet weather.

Everything was boarded up and fastened with enormous padlocks, which probably came from Mr Huggins, so they could readily be opened by anyone else who had purchased a padlock from the same source. All the lower windows were shuttered, so they could not get a look-in anywhere.

"Miss Pumfrey appears to be a lady of suspicious nature," said Hugh. "I say, shall I get a tire-lever out of the car and bust some of these boards off?"

"Shall we all go to jail?" said Mona.

"I may. You won't."

Hugh inserted the lever under the edge of one of the boards shoring up the penthouse, and prised. The board was rotten, and almost fell off. He put his head through the gap.

"I say, do you know these stables are cloisters?
They're all fan-arched."

"No, are they really? How perfectly marvellous. Do
let me look."

Hugh drew back, and Mona popped her head through
the gap.

"Do you know that behind those mangers are stone-
mullioned windows?"

"Are there really? This sounds gorgeous. Let's rush
off and find Miss Pumfrey, shall we?"

"You can't live on stone mullions. Let's trace the
water-supply."

They passed through a gap in the cloisters and came
out in front of the house. It was a beautifully propor-
tioned building of two stories, rising to a high attic gable
in the middle and stretching away on either side in long
wings. High up under the gable was an empty niche that
had evidently once held a statue. A few gloriously golden
daffodils tried to make a garden against the grey stone
walls, and then unfenced, barren pasture stretched away
to a far belt of trees. No other human habitation, nor
any sign of the work of man, was in sight. It seemed a
most unpromising spot to try and do any farming.

A heavy door, just like a church door, filled a pointed
arch in the centre of the long low front. High, stone-
mullioned, gothic-arched windows flanked it at regular
intervals. The whole effect was very ecclesiastical.

They strolled slowly round the building. Nothing
could be seen through the windows as the lower parts
were boarded up. It looked, however, as if a high room
had had a rough floor thrown across it, making it into
two low rooms, for they could see the edge of the boards
through the upper parts of the high narrow windows.

They turned the corner and found themselves beside
the bigger of the two barns.

"Obviously a chapel," said Mona, pointing to the
remains of a mouldering cross on the gable-end.

They went on in their circular tour, following a path that led through the small fir-wood at the back of the house through which they had passed on their arrival. The path ended abruptly in a miniature bog.

" Well, we've found the water-supply, anyway," said Hugh, " only it doesn't look very wholesome to me. I don't know what you think."

" I expect there's a culvert somewhere that's blocked up or broken down," said Mona. " The water's all right, look how clear it is ; and this bog hasn't been here very long ; it hasn't killed the grass."

" Well, I think we've seen as much as we can expect to see unless we commit a burglary. Shall we go back and call on Miss Pumfrey and ask her what about it ? "

" No," said Mona, chuckling. " We'll go back and call on Mr Huggins, and ask him to ask Miss Pumfrey what about it."

" You cruel woman. I believe that old chap is quite capable of giving her an awful bullying."

" Well, somebody ought to, and you obviously aren't that person."

" No, I'm no good as a bully. I just leave people alone."

As they returned down the road to the village they saw from afar Mr Huggins standing outside the door of his shop waving what looked in the distance like an agricultural implement, but which, as they drew nearer, proved to be a huge key.

" I've seen Miss Pumfrey," he cried as they came within hailing-distance. " She'll sell. But don't you give 'er a penny more'n four 'undred. It's all falling to bits, and as bare as the back of your 'and."

They gathered that Miss Pumfrey had called to buy candles, and had been stood in a corner and lectured till she agreed to sell. From the heated appearance of Mr Huggins it looked as if considerable pressure had had to be brought to bear before she could be got to agree.

Behind him stood Mrs Huggins, as if in support, with a grim look still lingering about her mouth.

They took the key, and returned.

" I say," said Hugh, " we can't go far wrong at four hundred. Let's close with the deal right away."

" Let's have a good look round first," said the practical Mona. " If there's dry rot in the main timbers you can go wrong at fourpence-halfpenny. I know. I've had experience."

The great ecclesiastical door creaked open unwillingly, and they entered. The place smelt musty. Unswept stone flooring stretched away on either hand, and what had once been large barn-like rooms had been roughly partitioned with heavy boards plastered with wall-paper. A fine stone staircase wound up in a wide spiral opposite the door. They mounted it, and found themselves in a broad passage that ran the whole length of the upper storey of the building. Out of it opened a number of small low doorways.

" By Jove, the monks' cells ! " said Hugh.

They entered one that had evidently been used to store apples, to judge by the smell of it.

" Why, there's no window," said Mona, " only a little grating up near the ceiling. They must have been a very austere order indeed."

Up again there led a small, narrow stone stair, winding in the thickness of the wall. Up this they went. At the top was a miniature church door, they pushed it open and entered, and found themselves in what had obviously been a small chapel.

" Gosh, there's a queer feeling in here ! " said Hugh. " I don't believe Mrs Huggins spoke the truth when she swore the place wasn't haunted. It is, and she knows it."

" It struck me she was a bit slick in her denials," said Mona. " Still, it's none the worse for that, for the purposes for which you want it."

" I don't want any second-hand spooks," said Hugh

hastily. " If anything is going to be raised, I want to have the raising of it myself."

" That's all right," said Mona. " You needn't worry about that. But it will help to keep the price down."

They descended to the ground-floor again, and saw cellar steps leading down into the depths.

" We'd better have a look down here," said Mona. " This will tell us whether the place is dry or not."

They found themselves in a large groin-roofed cellar around three sides of which were low arched doorways, similar to the cell-doorways on the upper floor.

" Good Lord," cried Hugh, " those are prison cells ! "

" No wonder the place has a funny feel," said Mona. " It must be a penal house belonging to one of the old monasteries."

" What in the world's that ? "

" Some of the monasteries were as big as small towns. Naturally not all the monks were saints. They generally used to keep one priory where they sent the monks who wouldn't behave themselves so that they shouldn't corrupt the others. Sometimes the monks were just mad and harmless. Sometimes they were—not harmless."

" Why didn't they just turf the bad lots out and be rid of them ? "

" I suppose they didn't want monasticism to get a bad name. There are more ways than one of being bad, you know. I say, do you think you will be able to stand the feel of this place ? "

" Why ? What's wrong with it ? It only feels melancholy to me, as if the last folk here had gone smash before they left."

" It feels queer—uncommonly queer—to me, but not inimical. Let's go and see Miss Pumfrey and find out its history."

# CHAPTER XI

THE house whose chimneys Mr Huggins had indicated proved to be a Georgian structure, imposing, but much in need of paint. An elderly parlour-maid opened the door. Her manners were perfect. The hall contained some fine old furniture. The drawing-room into which they were shown contained some very fine old furniture, but the coverings were threadbare. There was no fire, and the maid made no gesture of lighting one.

A lady entered. She wore a sagging tweed skirt; a flannel shirt-blouse; a baggy, home-knitted jersey coat, and a pair of gold pince-nez. Her greying hair was twisted into a jug-handle at the back of her head and she wore a curled fringe.

She greeted them coldly, did not ask them to sit down, and enquired their business.

" I am looking for a small property about here," said Hugh. " I have just seen Monks Farm, and I think it might be suitable. May I ask the price ? "

" I really could not say," said Miss Pumfrey. " That is a matter for my solicitor."

" Are you willing to sell ? "

Miss Pumfrey hesitated.

" I should prefer to let," she said.

" I do not wish to rent a place. I prefer to buy," said Hugh.

" I am prepared to sell," said Miss Pumfrey sullenly, " provided the price is adequate."

" What would you consider an adequate price ? "

" That is a matter for my solicitor."

" Would you consider six hundred pounds an adequate price ? "

Miss Pumfrey's eyes glistened.

" You had better see my solicitor."

A gong sounded somewhere in the house. Miss Pumfrey looked towards the door. The interview was at an end.

" Gosh ! " said Hugh when they found themselves safely back in the car. " Didn't you feel as if you had been caught stealing apples ? "

Mona began to laugh.

" I was too overcome to ask any questions about history," she said. " Wouldn't she have made a magnificent abbot to keep the unruly monks in order ? "

" I don't think I'm going to be troubled with local society," said Hugh.

" You weren't wearing your old school tie," said Mona.

" Thank God for that," said Hugh. " I'll wear a bootlace when I go to sign the deeds. What about a meal ? Aren't you peckish ? That old dame's gong made me feel hungry. I think I'd have offered anybody a bite of something if they'd been in my house when the gong went."

They went back down the road by which they had reached the village, crossed the hump-backed bridge, and made their way to a near-by country town. There they found some tea-rooms of Ye Olde Oake variety and had a meal of sorts. Very much of sorts.

" This isn't a patch on Uncle Jelkes and his frying-pan, is it ? " said Hugh.

Mona laughed. " He's wonderful with his frying-pan ; but a frying-pan has its limits, you know. I think you'd get rather tired of it after a bit. I know I should."

" He seems to thrive on it."

" He survives on it. I shouldn't say he throve. He's a darling, isn't he ? "

" He's a dashed good sort. I owe a lot to him."

" I owe everything to him.  He's been like a father to me.  I think I would have gone under if it hadn't been for him."

" I believe I should, too," said Hugh, and silence fell between them.

" I wonder what he'll say to our monastery," said Hugh at length.

" He'll be frightfully interested.  Did you know he once studied for the priesthood ? "

" Yes, he told me.  And he's still a priest at heart. You can see that.  Tell me, is he a Christian or a pagan ? I can't make him out."

" He's a Christian at heart, but he won't stand for the narrowness of Christian theology."

" What is there in Christianity beyond the theology ? "

" Why, there's just as much power as there is in Pan, only of a different kind."

" Would you call yourself a Christian ? "

" No, I shouldn't.  But I'm not anti-Christian.  I see it as one of the Paths."

" Paths to what ? "

" Paths to the Light."

" You wouldn't get a Christian to admit there was more than one Path."

" I know.  And that's the pity of it.  That's what spoils Christianity.  It's too limited."

" What does Uncle Jelkes say to your pagan proclivities ? "

" It was he who put me on to them.  I had a terribly strict upbringing and it disagreed with me most actively. I used to get dreadful headaches that simply laid me out. The doctors said they couldn't do anything for it and I just had to put up with it.  Of course I couldn't keep a job.  It was too dreadful trying to struggle round with those headaches on me.  And I would sooner have died than go home again.  In fact, I don't think they'd have taken me in.  Father thought an art school was an abode of sin. Then I met Uncle Jelkes, and he made me understand a lot of things I'd never understood before. He made me see that my acquired self and my real natural self were fighting with each other, and that was what was knocking me to pieces. My natural self said : ' I'm jolly well going to be an artist ' ; and my acquired self said : ' It's a deadly sin. You ought to be a missionary.' Uncle Jelkes said : ' You'll have to give up Christianity. It's disagreed with you. It isn't for everybody.' And he put me on to the old Greek gods, and I simply loved them. My headaches got better, and my drawing improved out of all sight. He says, and I'm certain he's right, that there is a tremendous lot in the old Greek gods. There are great truths there that we have forgotten."

" Does he propose to scrap Christianity ? "

" Oh no. But he thinks the Greek viewpoint is a very valuable corrective to it."

" It certainly needs something done to it," said Hugh.

" It does indeed," said Mona. " It is not meeting the need of the world as it is at present. And it isn't just the worldly people who are leaving it. Nor the sceptical. It is people like Uncle Jelkes and you and me, who want more of God than they can find in it."

" What of God do you want that you can't find in it ? "

" I want God made manifest in Nature—that's Pan, you know."

" What does that mean ? "

" It means a lot, but we can't discuss it now. We must go on and see this solicitor person before he shuts. They shut awfully early in country towns."

They found Mr Watney as directed, and he proved to be a sprightly old gentleman who had a twinkle in his eye as he talked to them. He did not say very much, however, until Hugh had handed over to him a cheque for a hundred as deposit. Then he opened out.

" It is a custom with country lawyers to seal a land-deal with a glass of port.  I have often wondered whether it is a relic of a Christian sacrament or a pagan libation, but I have never been able to discover.  Some odd old customs linger on in the law.  Did you know that when a case is settled out of court, the brief is always marked with the Sign of the Cross ? "

" I know there's an odd scribble on it," said Hugh.

" Well, that is actually the Sign of the Cross.  And did you know that no priest can be a barrister ?  If a parson wants to change his cloth, he has to give up his orders.  We got rid of the domination of the Church, but we kept the blessing on a settled case.  Odd, isn't it ? "

" You are interested in archæology ? "

" Yes, very.  In fact I am the president of our local archæological society.  The country round about here is most fruitful ground.  We have Saxon, Roman and ancient British remains in layers one below the other."

" Can you tell me anything about Monks Farm ? "

" Dear me, yes, I can tell you a lot.  It is one of our most interesting relics.  There are some very curious stories attached to it.  Do you know we had an inquest there once, on the bones of a monk who was found walled up in the cellar ?  Most interesting.  I was able to identify him.  He was a very famous sub-prior of the parent foundation.  A friend of Erasmus, at any rate he corresponded with him.  He was one of the first Englishmen to study Greek."

" What was his offence ? "

" I've no idea.  It must have been something pretty scandalous because there is not a word about it in the records of the monastery.  Merely a remark that he was replaced in his office by someone else.  No reason given. It must have been something they did not care to put on record.  Monks Farm, you know, was a kind of penitentiary.  Bread and water and peas in their shoes,

I believe. They had a lot of trouble at that monastery.
We have never been able to find out what it was all
about. The records have some very odd silences. Men
removed from their offices and no reason given. A
new abbot appointed by the Pope instead of being
elected by the monks. Then a lot of monks distributed
among the other houses of the Order and all the new
officials brought in from outside. A clean sweep, as it
were. But there were a number of monks who weren't
accounted for. They weren't sent to other houses,
their names just disappeared off the rolls. We've
accounted for one of them, however, at our inquest, so
perhaps the others went by the same route. You may
find some interesting things if you excavate."

"I may find some pretty grim things if I excavate,"
said Hugh. "I think I'd better leave it alone."

"Nonsense, nonsense, you'll enjoy it," said Mr
Watney, who suddenly seemed to realise that he had
been telling too much.

They drove back to town in the gathering dusk, and
landed in upon Mr Jelkes just as he was getting his tea.
It would have been difficult to have landed in on old
Jelkes at a time when he wasn't brewing tea, but this
tea was distinguished from all other brews by the fact
that he ate a bit of cake with it.

"Well, T. J., we've done the deed. We've bought
a house."

"You haven't been long about it," said the old man.
"I hope you've not been rash. What have you let him
in for, Mona?"

"I've let him in for a monastery, Uncle Jelkes."

"My God!" said the old man. "Why didn't you
let him in for a nunnery while you were about it?"

"Do you think it will be a suitable place for the
invocation of Pan, T. J.?"

Jelkes scratched his nose.

"It's suitable enough," he said. "The psychic

atmosphere has been worked up.  You will have to do a kind of banishing, you know, before the Old Gods will settle down ; but they'll get going all right once they make a start."

" Will you do the banishing for us, T. J. ? "

" No.   Damned if I will."

" Uncle Jelkes, do you remember once telling me about the penal houses attached to the big monastic foundations ?  Well, it's one of those.  And do you know, the prior was found walled up in the cellar, and they had an inquest on him."

" What's all this you're telling me, Mona ?  It must be the penal house attached to the big Abbey.  They had a lot of trouble at that Abbey.  One of the big Catholic historians made a valiant attempt to whitewash it of recent years.  Shows there was something wanted touching up.  So they walled up the prior, did they ?  Now that must have been for something pretty serious.  They usually reduced 'em to the ranks and shoved 'em into other houses of the same Order when they ran off the rails."

" The solicitor was telling us that they did that with a lot of the monks, but there were some who just disappeared, and this man they held the inquest on was one of them.  He was one of the earliest Englishmen to study Greek, Mr Watney said."

" Then that probably explains his trouble.  You think what it must have meant to these monks, shut up in their monasteries, when they got to work on the Greek manuscripts that the Renaissance brought to Europe.  They were careful what Latin ones they let come into the libraries, because the old abbots could read those.  But they couldn't read the Greek ones, and the smart young fellows in the scriptorium got to work on them—the younger chaps, like your walled-up prior— and they must have had an eye-opener.  Supposing they got hold of the ' Bacchae,' for instance, with the invocations to Dionysos? That must have livened up the cloister a bit. Do you know what I think must have happened? This prior, Ambrosius, I believe his name was, is known to have corresponded with Erasmus. His letters are extant. There is a letter from him about the purchase of a batch of Greek manuscripts for the Abbey library. The abbot was a very old man, in his dotage, I gather, and this Ambrosius practically ran the place. A prior is the second in command, you know. Then the Pope sent a visitor to have a look at them. That made them wild, for they had a special charter that made them exempt from inspection, and they chucked the visitor out. But the next thing was that the Pope sent them a new abbot, and the civil power enforced it. The old abbot was dead and Ambrosius was expecting to get elected. But he never was. He just disappeared and they got an Italian in charge of them. Then there was that clean sweep you've been hearing about. Something pretty bad went wrong with that monastery, I'll bet. And I'll bet another thing, that the Greek manuscripts were at the bottom of it. They bought a job lot, and some of 'em probably weren't exactly canonical."

" I say, T. J., do you suppose that poor old Ambrosius was playing about with an invocation of Pan, and got dropped on ? "

" How do I know ? I can only piece two and two together. All I've read is the whitewashing and the reprint of the records. But you can guess a good deal when you put the two side by side. Why the gaps, and why the whitewashing ? In come the manuscripts, and up goes the monastery. We know what Greek literature is like, and we know what monasteries are like. Then we find the smart young prior who worked on the manuscripts bricked up in a lonely grange, and we smell sulphur."

" Was he a young chap ? "

" He was about your age, Hugh, when he disappeared

off the map."

" Poor devil, he has my sympathy. I wouldn't have fancied being bricked up with the best part of my life before me."

" I wouldn't have fancied being bricked up at any stage of my career," said old Jelkes drily. " It's an unpleasant end."

Sleepy from the fresh air, Hugh got off to bed early. But sleepy as he was, he determined to try and recapture the trail of the previous experience. He felt somehow that he must do this thing regularly if he were to succeed with it. He turned onto his back, crossed his arms on his chest, and called up before his mind's eye the picture of a sunny hillside above the sea in ancient Greece. But before he knew where he was, he was sliding off into dreamland. He dragged his mind back once, but it slipped again immediately, and this time he failed to recapture it.

It seemed to him that he was lying on his back on a narrow plank bed. It was pitch dark, and the roof seemed to be pressing down on him and the walls closing in on him. And all the time he could hear the tolling of a bell. He felt a hood of some coarse woollen material like serge around his head, and folds of coarse serge material under his hands that were folded on his breast. In his dream he sat up on the narrow plank bed and pushed the hood off his head to wipe the sweat from his face. He passed his hand over his sweat-soaked hair, and found a round bald patch on the top of his head, as if the thick hair had been shaved away. Then in his dream he lay down again and drew the hood over his face, and concentrated his mind on one idea—to die with dignity and without struggling. Then it seemed to him that the sound of the tolling bell became merged in the beating of his own heart. The heavy beats grew louder and louder, and slower and slower, and then, all of a sudden, he found himself in the fresh air and full sunlight on the Grecian hillside, and ahead of him was the figure of the woman with the satiny back and softly moulded muscles.

He leapt after her. Round his loins was a goatskin, he could feel the rough hairiness of it, but the upper part of his body was bare. The woman ahead had a fawnskin slung over her shoulder. She had an olive skin and her body was strong and muscular. In particular was he struck by the strong firm column of the neck. He pursued, but she did not so much flee as go on ahead of him.

Suddenly sleep left him, and he woke up to find himself in a bath of sweat.

" By Jove," he said to himself, getting up and groping for a towel to have a rub-down with, " this won't do. I'm giving myself nightmares."

His mind played over the dream-symbols, trying to pick up the threads of them after the manner of psycho-analysis.

The first part was obvious. The story of the walled-up prior had impressed itself on his imagination and reproduced itself in the dream. The origin of the second part was equally obvious. It was a reproduction of the vision that had made such an impression on his imagination the night before last. Hugh Paston got back to bed and slept peacefully till morning.

# CHAPTER XII

REAL estate is not a thing that ever gets itself transferred from one owner to another expeditiously. Miss Pumfrey was not a person of whom one could ask favours in the way of obtaining possession, and Hugh reckoned he would find himself at a loose end for at least a fortnight.

At breakfast next morning he said to old Jelkes :

" I say, what do I do about paying Miss Wilton? I'm taking up a devil of a lot of her time, and I suppose time is money with her."

" Does she suit you ? "

" Yes, first-rate. She's a dashed good sort. I like her."

" Then I should put her on the pay-roll, if I were you. Give her a weekly salary, and have the call on her time."

" That's a good idea. There are various jobs I'd like her to do for me. What shall I offer her ? "

" Three pound a week ? " said old Jelkes tentatively.

" Right you are. I suppose she'll pick up a bit on commission from the various firms we deal with ? "

" Yes, she'll expect to do that. What are the jobs you want her for at the moment ? It's too soon to start furnishing isn't it ? "

Hugh was nonplussed. He hadn't thought of any particular jobs for Mona to do. What he really wanted was to get some money into her hand without hurting her pride ; the jobs had been faked up on the spur of the moment to give him an excuse for paying her. At least, so he told himself. He had often faked up jobs for people before, so why not now ? God knows, the girl needed it if appearances were anything to go by. But at the back of his heart was the feeling that it would be a very empty fortnight before he could get to work with her.

" I —— er —— I had an idea that she might do a bit of research for me," he said, improvising hastily.

" Yes, she'd do that all right. She's done a good deal of work at the British Museum for me. I can't leave the shop during business hours. What is it you want her to look up ? "

" I'd like to trace out the history of Monks Farm. I believe it will prove to be rather exciting."

" It's certainly made a promising start. Yes, I can put her on the track of that. She needn't go much further than my shelves for the moment. I've made rather a speciality of the queer side of monastic history. After she's got through with that, she could go down and see this archæological solicitor, and follow up the trail locally. Besides, there is sure to be a good collection of stuff in the library of the local museum. I bet there's plenty of material available for piecing together by anyone who knows as much as we do of the queer side of things."

" By Jove, that's a bright idea. I'll run her down to see old Watney and we'll have a rootle round in the local museum."

It was on the tip of Jelkes' tongue to say : " Why don't you let her get through with my books first ? " but he restrained himself.

Consequently Jelkes went round to collect Miss Wilton, leaving Hugh in charge of the shop. Returning in ten minutes' time, he found Hugh immensely elated at having sold three books out of the twopenny bin in his absence.

Once again the racing-car took the road north with Mona Wilton, hooded and clad in green, seated beside its driver.

She was amused to see that he had forgotten all about his quest of Pan, and was absorbed in the pursuit of the walled-up prior.

They called on Mr Watney first, who threw up his hands in horror at the sight of them and cried :

" Good God, do you want possession already ?  What do you take me for ?  A steam-engine ? "

However, he was not merely pacified but enraptured when he learnt that Hugh was bent on unearthing the antecedents of his new property.  The one thing Mr Watney's soul yearned for was to dig over the ground and find more corpses.  Hugh, however, was interested only in the circumstances that had led up to the mysterious crisis at the monastery.

Mr Watney gave him a list of books to refer to, and a note of introduction to the curator at the museum, and off they went.  The curator, a Mr Diss, proved to be just such another as Mr Watney, and the two were apparently cronies, being respectively president and secretary of the local archæological society.  Mr Diss murmured something about the printing of transactions, and Hugh took up the idea enthusiastically.  After that the museum and all it contained was his to do as he liked with.  There are more ways than one of corrupting public servants.

The museum was the proud possessor of the Abbey rolls, and they had the interesting experience of looking at the actual entry of the purchase of the Greek manuscripts from Erasmus' agent.  The monks had paid thirty pounds for them—a substantial sum in modern money.

" I expect Ambrosius thought those thirty pounds were thirty pieces of silver before he had finished with them," said Hugh in Mona's ear.

" Eh, what's that ? " said the curator.

" It was a lot of money for those days," said Mona, tactfully heading him off.  Then he was called away, and left them in the hands of a youth with instructions to get them whatever they wanted.  Hugh gave him the list Mr

Watney had furnished, and the youth deposited a pile of books before them and disappeared.

"Now then, we'll share these out," said Hugh. "I'm an adept at skipping."

They got to work, and silence fell between them.

Mona was the first to break the silence.

"This is interesting," she said. "It's the ghost at the farm. The one Mrs Huggins swore wasn't there."

Hugh left his chair and came round to her side of the table and sat down beside her, reading over her shoulder.

The book that was open before them was an old bound volume of the proceedings of the local archæological society, and the paper in question concerned local superstitions.

According to the writer, Monks Farm bore a sinister local reputation, and was about as thoroughly haunted as any place could be, and in order to justify his thesis, he gave an account of its history.

It appears that it was not originally a penal house, such being unknown in England, though common enough on the Continent, English abbots contenting themselves with penancing the lives out of recalcitrant monks. It had been built by the famous—or infamous— prior, Ambrosius, as a special place of retreat and meditation to which certain picked monks retired at certain seasons. It was not until the trouble broke out that it was turned into a penal house by the simple expedient of blocking up the cell windows and making the monks who were there, stop there, whether they liked it or not. Ambrosius was taken to his own special priory and bricked-up below-stairs as a warning and an example. The other monks were kept in their cells on a low diet till they died more or less naturally. They never saw the light of day again. In darkness and solitary confinement they waited their end. One man lived to be over eighty —fifty-five years' imprisonment. Their jailers never spoke to them, and jailer replaced jailer till the last monk

died, and then the place was abandoned.  The ghost of
the prior was supposed to walk round the cells, talking
to his monks and consoling them.  At any rate, it was a
well-established fact that the monks in solitary confinement talked to someone, but then men in solitary confinement often do that.  There are always naturalistic explana-
tions of supernatural phenomena to be found if one will
only look for them and doesn't mind their being far-
fetched.

The discussion that followed the reading of the paper,
and which was recorded in all its wordy fullness, somewhat took the gilt off the gingerbread, however, for it
was pointed out by persons familiar with local customs
as well as local superstitions, that the empty buildings of
Monks Farm had long been a favourite haunt of lovers
without benefit of clergy.  This apparently disposed of
the ghost of Ambrosius once and for all, and though the
speaker was thanked for his paper, no one said they
believed him.

"That's a useful clue," said Hugh.  "What do you
suppose they were up to at that priory?  Raising the
Devil?"

"I shouldn't be a bit surprised if they were trying to
do exactly the same thing that you are trying to do——"

"What is that?"

"Break away from their limitations and find fullness of
life."

"I don't blame them.  A monk's life must be a pretty
empty life for an active chap."

"That is where you are mistaken.  A contemplative
life can be an extraordinarily vivid and interesting life,
provided one is getting results."

"What did the old boys do, besides saying their
prayers?"

"There is more in prayer than just asking for what
you want.  We Protestants don't know anything about
it, but with the Catholics it's a fine art.  You can get

wonderful experiences from prayer and meditation if you know what you are about. If you once get on the track of those, a contemplative life is lively enough for anybody."

"I don't think it would suit my style of beauty. I am out after Pan."

"Well, aren't you approaching Pan through prayer and meditation?"

"Now you mention it, I believe I am. In fact, I tried to apply to him the Method of St Ignatius. And I got results, too. I've had them twice now."

"Do tell me, what are they?"

"Well, I made a mental picture of ancient Greece, and it came alive, and for a moment I found myself there. And then, last night, when I tried to do it again, I was too sleepy to keep control, and first I slipped off into nightmare from going to sleep on my back, and then I escaped from the nightmare into the very scene I had been imagining, and do you know what the nightmare was? I dreamt of poor old Ambrosius. Or rather, I dreamt I was walled-up, like him, and very unpleasant it was, too. Then I bust out of that dream onto the Greek hillside in the sunshine, and someone was going up the hill ahead of me, and I believe it was you. At any rate, it was someone with your build and walk."

"That's interesting," said Mona noncommittally, apparently absorbed in an account of the way in which the ancient Romans laid their drains.

At that moment the curator returned.

"I am sorry to have had to leave you," he said. "Would you care to see the illuminated manuscripts?"

They acquiesced, and he led them to a glass case, unlocked it, raised the lid, and began tenderly to turn over the heavy vellum pages of an exceedingly fine psalter.

"This is particularly interesting," he said, "because all the initial letters are set in little scenes of the Abbey."

He pointed out to them the high altar, the cloisters, the bell-tower, the great gate, the monks at work in the scriptorium. Then he turned another page, and pointed to a little picture of a black-robed monk sitting at his desk writing.

" This is the man," he said, " who laid the foundations of the famous library. A great scholar in his day, but died young. Life was short in those days."

They saw a minute but diamond-clear portrait of a youngish man, round-shouldered at his desk. Sharp-featured, clean-shaven, tonsured. Mona glanced up involuntarily at the face of the man beside her, bending over her shoulder. Feature for feature, the faces were identical ; even the scholarly stoop of the shoulders was reproduced.

" That was one of the priors, Ambrosius," said the curator.

There was dead silence for a moment, Mona holding her breath and wondering what was going to come next.

Hugh broke it, and Mona thought his voice sounded rather odd.

" That's interesting," he said. " Can you tell me anything about him ? "

" Yes, there's a good deal about him in the library, scattered here and there. It is all gathered together in one of these Transactions, however, and by our mutual friend, Mr Watney, too. I expect he is greatly excited by your purchase of Monks Farm. He has always wanted to excavate there, but Miss Pumfrey would never allow it."

" He said something about it," said Hugh, " but I am afraid I did not encourage it. I did not fancy the idea of having my future garden all dug up."

" But my dear sir, a garden has to be dug up. If I were in your place I should tell Watney he can dig up the garden provided he'll manure it while he's about it. Let him have any bones he finds in return for the manure."

" Sounds good value," said Hugh. " By the way, where did they plant Ambrosius after they held the inquest on him ? "

" Ah, now, that's a curious story. There is a small monastery in the town of the same Order as once owned the Abbey. The coroner offered the bones to them to inter in their graveyard, but they declined them, so they were buried in the churchyard in the village. Evidently Ambrosius died in bad odour, but you would not have thought they would have carried on the feud all these centuries, would you ? "

" I couldn't say. I know nothing about their habits. But whatever he had done, they might have let his bones rest among friends after all this lapse of time."

" Ah well, you know, they have very strict views. I have no doubt they were right according to their lights. If you will excuse me, I must get back to my work. Perhaps you will return these books to the desk when you have finished with them."

Hugh took the chair Mr Diss had vacated and sat staring into space, making no attempt to start on the volume lying open in front of him. Mona, watching him, saw that he had gone very white and his eyes had a startled look in them.

He looked up.

" Do you know, it gave me quite a turn seeing that picture of Ambrosius."

" It did me, too," said Mona.

" It made me realise what that bricking-up meant. There was the fellow sitting quietly at his desk studying the things that interested him, and all the time there was this bricking-up business hanging over his head. What with seeing the actual place and dreaming about him last night, well—it gave me quite a turn."

" You have been extraordinarily lucky in the way you have struck his trail."

" Yes, haven't we ? Now let's have a look at this

paper and see what else there is to be seen."

He began to skim rapidly, reading out excerpts to Mona, who listened, watching him, and wondering what Mr Jelkes would have to say to the transaction. Mona felt a strong sense of responsibility to old Jelkes for Hugh Paston. It was as if she had been allowed to take some-one else's baby out for an airing.

" ' Born in 1477 '," read Hugh. " ' The illegitimate son of a huckster's daughter.' (Possibly got a bit of good blood in him somewhere.) ' Showed such marked pro-mise in scholarship that he was admitted to the Abbey school without fee. Received the tonsure while still a youth. Was in great favour with the abbot. His rapid promotion caused much jealousy. A special mission was sent to Rome to protest against the appointment of so young a man as prior. The old abbot lived to be eighty-six, and for the last few years of his life was bedridden. Ambrosius as prior had complete control. Much jealousy and opposition. Ambrosius, a man of strong character, overbore the opposition and carried out his own policy. He was not a great building ecclesiastic, but he was a great scholar and collector. Much criticised for using funds to buy Greek manuscripts instead of a piece of the True Cross that was on offer to the monastery. Influence of his enemies finally prevailed with Rome after the death of the old abbot, a mission of enquiry was sent to the Abbey, and he was removed from his place as abbot-elect. Nothing further is heard of him. There is no record of his fate, death, or place of burial.' (I suppose this was written before they found the bones up at the farm.)

" ' Although he added nothing to the structure of the Abbey, he built a daughter-house three miles away at Thorley, and there he appeared to have founded a sub-sidiary community of his own ; nothing is known of its nature, however, the records of this period of the Abbey's history having been destroyed in a fire which burnt out a part of the famous library, and in which perished all the Greek manuscripts purchased from Erasmus.'

"Well, that doesn't say much, but it tells us a good deal. I wonder who lit that fire? Their new Dago abbot, probably. I should say there is not much doubt about it that Ambrosius was up to some queer games, and as Uncle Jelkes says, the Greek manuscripts were at the bottom of the trouble. Corrupted his mind, I expect. But can't you see the fellow getting shoved into the Church as the only possible outlet for a poor scholar in those days, and not belonging there a bit, and breaking out good and proper when he struck those Greek manuscripts? Come on, let's go home and ask Uncle Jelkes what he makes of it."

Hugh deposited Mona at the bookshop and went to put the car away.

"Uncle Jelkes," said Mona, as soon as he had disappeared, "Mr. Paston has gone completely mad on Prior Ambrosius and forgotten all about Pan."

"Splendid," said Jelkes. "I'm exceedingly glad to hear it. I had hoped something of that sort would happen if you took him in hand tactfully."

"But that isn't all. We've traced out the story of Ambrosius pretty completely, and Ambrosius was also after Pan, or something uncommonly like it. And I'll tell you another thing, we saw a little picture of Ambrosius at the museum, and it might have been a portrait of Mr Paston."

"Gorblimey!" said the old bookseller, and sat down in his chair with a flop. "I knew it was going to be bad, but I never dreamt it was going to be as bad as all this!"

"Uncle Jelkes, I think it wouldn't take much to send Mr Paston off his head, if you ask me."

"Well, my dear, we can't stop now we've started. That would make the devil of a mess. All we can do is to hang onto his coat-tails and hope for the best. But where is the thing going to end? It struck me when he was talking last night that he felt very strongly about Ambrosius, but I put it down to his having just heard that ghastly story and seen the place where it happened. After all you know, some people have such vivid imaginations that they will react to a novel. Ambrosius' death was a pretty dreadful one. Are you sure you aren't imagining things, Mona ? "

" The facts about Ambrosius are history, Uncle, and you can verify the portrait for yourself if you don't believe me. And I'll tell you yet another thing, Mr Paston had nightmare last night, and it must have been a pretty vivid one, because I could see that it upset him to talk about it, and he dreamt that he was Ambrosius, walled-up and dying, and then he escaped from there into Greece, and was wandering over the hills in the sunshine."

For some reason best known to herself Mona did not mention that in his dream Hugh had a companion.

The old bookseller scratched his bald and vulturine head.

" Any single one of those things one would pay no attention to," he said. " But when you get them all to-gether like that you have to take notice. The interest in Ambrosius would mean nothing by itself ; nor even the interest and the dream together, because the interest might have caused the dream. But when you get the interest, and the dream, and the same sort of history in the two men, and on top of that, the likeness—well, you can't get away from it that something is afoot. I've known things like that happen before. When a man who has been on the Path comes back to it again, circum-stances often take him to the place of his last death. Now we will watch and see what happens. Hugh may start recovering the memories of his last life."

" Won't that be rather trying ? " said Mona. " They must be pretty awful memories. And what is going to happen when we get Pan and the monastery all mixed up together ? Is a monastery a good place for the invocation of Pan ? "

" Goodness only knows," said the bookseller. " This one ought to be ! "

At that moment Hugh returned, and they all sat down to one of the queer, scratched-up meals that the bookseller produced out of his hat, as it were, at any moment.

# CHAPTER XIII

ONE subject, and one subject only, interested Hugh at that moment, but he found that neither Mona nor the old man were willing to talk about it. Whenever he introduced the name of Ambrosius they simultaneously and with one accord talked of something else. Hugh, who was an unsuspicious person, found this irritating. He was not sorry, therefore, to get off to bed early, and once warm under the eiderdown, he lit a cigarette, and set himself to have a good think.

He was not particularly anxious to attempt the experiment of the previous night and risk another such nightmare—that was an experience not to be repeated. Hence the cigarette and the candle.

It was extraordinary the way that the recreant prior haunted his imagination ; he could not get rid of him. Again and again the memory of his terrible death came back, and of the circumstances that led up to his death. From the scanty materials they had obtained, and his still more scanty appreciation of their significance, he tried to form a picture of the man's personality and of the true inwardness of his history.

He could imagine the brilliant son of the huckster's pretty but none too virtuous daughter, and wondered whether the abbot's interest in him had been genuinely paternal. It was quite likely. Rome has always taken a humane view of human nature. He could see the lad accepting the monastic life with its intellectual opportunities readily enough ; throwing himself heart and soul into it in fact, and winning rapid advancement at the hands of the all-too-complacent abbot. Then he could see the sudden wakening of another side of the man's nature at the touch of Greek thought. God only knew what vivid play or daring poem had been among that job lot of Greek manuscripts purchased untranslated from Erasmus. He could imagine the tentative experimenting with some chant of invocation, and the sudden and unexpected obtaining of results, just as he himself had obtained them that night when he applied the Method of St Ignatius to the invocation of Pan. A man trained in the cloister would get results quickly and very definitely because mind-work, though otherwise applied, would be familiar to him.

He could imagine the fascination of the pursuit growing on Ambrosius; the guarded sounding of others as to their fittedness for the enterprise; and then the cautious organisation of the special daughter-house where the new and absorbing interest could be pursued, safe from prying eyes.

Then he could imagine suspicion gradually being aroused; the spying and watching; the gradual piecing together of the damning evidence; finally, when the death of the old abbot removed his influential protector, the sudden swoop of Rome; the clean sweep of all sympathisers; the quarantining in their own priory of those who had actually participated in the pagan rites; and the walling-up of their leader in the cellars under their feet as a terrible warning, the slow tolling of the bell informing them of the slow approach of his death. Then the long dragging years of silence and solitude and darkness till to one by one came the still slower but inevitable end. And finally the old, old man of over eighty, on whom the cell-door had shut as a lad in his twenties, found at last his release, and the priory was abandoned to the wind and the rain and the work of the rats.

There was one gleam of light that comforted Hugh in the utter gloom of the tragedy—the return of the prior's spirit to stand by the men who had trusted him. He could imagine the shadowy figure, tall and gaunt in its heavy black habit, moving on sandalled feet along that upper corridor and pausing to talk to each monk in turn through the small barred wicket that alone remained open in the nailed-up doors of the cells. It never occurred to Hugh to ask himself how he knew that the cell-doors were nailed up. He just imagined it that way, and that was good enough for him.

He could imagine the amazement of the monks when first this spectral visitant greeted them through the narrow aperture ; then their terror when they realised that their prior was indeed dead and that this was his ghost that had come to them. Then their gradual reassurement as they realised that the spirit was kindly —that death had in no way changed the man they had trusted. And finally, the establishment of regular communications between death-in-life and life-in-death so that the spirits of the imprisoned men rose out of the narrow confines of their cells and breathed a wider air, even such air as Hugh himself had breathed in the sunshine of the Greek hillside.

Suddenly Hugh roused from his reveries to find the old bookseller standing over him, looking at him reproachfully and saying :

" Laddie, you'll set the house on fire if you go on like this."

" By Jove, T. J., do you know, I was actually at that priory, walking up and down the passage with Ambrosius and talking to the monks ? I say, do you realise that the fellow came back from the dead every night and had a chat with them ? And do you know what has just occurred to me ? That if he could come back to them, would it be possible to persuade him to come back for me ? You know, I've been at séances when something came back which I would swear was not the medium's subconscious. You can't prove it, of course, but all the same, you know it. Now if I got hold of a good medium, do you think I could get in touch with Ambrosius ? "

The old man stood looking down at him with a very queer expression on his face.

" I should leave mediums alone, if I were you, Hugh. You'll get no good from them."

" T. J., do you know, I believe for two two's Ambrosius would come back to me, I feel so much in sympathy with him. His history is so much like mine. Doing your best to carry on on wrong lines till you feel you will burst, and then suddenly getting the clue that opens everything out to you. Now he was shut in. He didn't get through with it. Circumstances were too much for him. But the world has moved on since then. Now I believe I could get through with it. I could do what he failed to do——"

A curious change came over the figure lying propped on its elbow in the bed. The rather boyish, eager, hesitating manner of a man uncertain of himself, who had never found himself, gave place to something entirely different. The air was that of a man accustomed to be obeyed. A man aloof, purposeful, resolute. The keen eyes gazed at Jelkes, but without any look of recognition in them.

" *Pax vobiscum*," said Jelkes.

" *Et tibi, pax*," said the man on the bed.

He looked into Jelkes' eyes for a minute, then a shudder passed through him. He blinked dazedly at the lighted candle in the old man's hand.

" Hullo ? " he said vaguely. " What's up ? "

" What do you imagine is up, my son ? " said Jelkes.

" I've no idea, but I'm in a muck-sweat. Chuck us a towel, there's a good chap."

Jelkes did as requested, and sat down on the foot of the bed while Hugh swabbed his dripping chest. He wondered how much Hugh remembered of what had happened ; how far the two modes of consciousness had made any sort of contact with each other. But there was no glimmering of awareness in Hugh's rather nondescript grey-green eyes, so he waited till the towel was cast aside, a sodden rag, and then extinguished the candle and bid his guest good-night.

The next morning found Hugh perfectly normal, with no recollection whatever of the incidents of the previous night. He was all agog, however, to go down to the museum again and arrange to have the picture of Ambrosius in the illuminated psalter photographed.

" There ought to be a photographer capable of the job in a town that size," said he.    " If you could get hold of Miss Wilton for me, we'll run down and tackle it."

Jelkes looked at him.   Why was Miss Wilton wanted for the job ?   Why couldn't he go down himself ?

" Is she on the telephone ? "

" Yes, I think she is, unless it's been cut off."

" Why should it have been cut off ? "

" Well, she's been rather hard up lately, so she may have had to dispense with it."

" I say, do you think she'd let me stick it in again for her ?   It would be a great convenience to have it. And I say, Jelkes, will you let me put one in here, too ? "

" Good Lord, you'll be through with the job long before you get the telephone in.   Remember you're dealing with a government department."

" That's all right, I can ginger them up.   I've got friends in high places."

Jelkes went round to fetch Mona while Hugh went to fetch the car.   Arrived at her house, he stepped inside the front door when she opened it to him, and drew it shut behind him.

" My dear," he said, " we're in for the devil of a time. Ambrosius turned up last night in person."

" What do you mean ? " said Mona, startled, as much by his manner as his words.

" I guessed that Hugh had gone to sleep with his

light still on, and I went in to him.  And he woke up and began talking about Ambrosius—I think he had been dreaming of him—and for about five seconds Hugh *became* Ambrosius, and, my God, he startled me! He didn't know me from Adam, and he looked as fierce as a hawk.  I addressed him in clerical Latin, and he answered me.  And then he swung back to Hugh again, and, thank God, he doesn't remember a thing about it this morning."

" If he has done it once, he will do it again, Uncle Jelkes, especially when he gets to the farm, and what will happen then ? "

" The Lord only knows.  I don't.  We shall have to hang onto his coat-tails and do the best we can.  If he looks at you like he looked at me, you'll run a mile.  He must have been a terror of a prior."

Mona went up and got her leather coat and hood, and they walked round to the shop together, where they found Hugh outside on the pavement, tinkering at the car.  He straightened up at their approach, and greeted them with his usual diffident air, like a school-boy greeting his family in public—much more pleased to see them than he dared to admit.  It was an odd scene. There was old Jelkes in his ancient ulster, his tumble-down, paintless shop-front as a background, both he and the shop looking so much the same colour that from a little distance he appeared to melt into it and disappear under the protective coat of London grime that covered them both.  Then there was Mona Wilton, the handsome vivid leather coat enveloping her from chin to ankle and revealing only the ancient pair of brown brogues on her feet, mercifully concealing the shabby, dingy jumper and skirt.  Finally there was Hugh Paston and his car.  Hugh in a chrome leather racing coat ; the car a vivid but battered blue, still bearing the great black numerals that had distinguished it in a famous race. The dingy street and the dingier bookseller all faded into a neutral drab, but Hugh and Mona and the car stood out like the brightly coloured vignettes in the illuminated manuscripts of the ancient monks. To the old book-seller, standing back and looking at them, it seemed that everything Hugh Paston touched at the present moment turned bright-coloured. His own life ; Mona's life ; the grey farm on the bare hill—everything suddenly became vivid, exciting, perilous. It was the touch of Pan all right, thought the old man with a sigh, and where the devil was it going to end ? Hugh had about as much control over it as he had over a sunset. Pan had taken charge.

Hugh and Mona drove off in the car, the powerful engine making a fearful shindy in the narrow street. Jelkes watched them go. What was going to be the end of that also ? Hugh Paston was a wealthy and well-connected man, still young, and, at the moment, very unbalanced. Mona, the daughter of a Nonconformist minister in a small manufacturing town in the Midlands, was a young woman with a stormy emotional past behind her. She had lived as girl artists breaking out from such homes into England's Bohemia are apt to live—going from one extreme to the other. It was his hand that had steadied and saved her when the inevitable reaction had set in, and he had hoped that she had settled down. Left to her own devices, he thought that she had ; but was she going to be left to her own devices ? Jelkes did not at all like the way Hugh was looking at her. After all, she was a young woman of an entirely different class who was in his employment, and he had no business to be looking at her like that. Hugh had been educated at Harrow and Balliol, Mona at the local high-school and one of the private ateliers in which London's Bohemia abounds—the prestige and security of the Slade were beyond her reach. Hugh was accus-tomed to a very sophisticated type of feminity ; if Mona managed to be clean and tidy, that was about as high as she aspired, her early upbringing effectually preventing her from adventuring into the slipshod garishness that girl artists often affect, and which is not without its effectiveness. Jelkes judged that Hugh's present mood was a reaction to the shock and disillusionment he had been through, and that when it wore off he would revert to normal and return to his own kind. He would no longer be willing to put up with the discomforts of the bookshop or the limitations of Mona's society.

At the moment Mona appeared to be taking things impassively and impersonally. She had had experience of men of Hugh's type before when she had been doing designs for the interior decorations of Mayfair, and had a pretty good idea what their attentions were worth. Her attitude was that of a woman humouring her employer, falling in with his mood, and at the same time keeping him at arm's length. Jelkes entirely approved. But he knew from experience that underneath her impassive exterior, Mona Wilton was a young woman of stormy emotions, and apt to get the bit between her teeth in pursuit of them. He could not imagine her falling for Hugh, however; Hugh seemed to him an exceedingly unlikely person for any woman to fall for, with his diffident bearing and general unsureness of himself and lack of personality. All the same, he did not like the way that Hugh kept Mona continually at his heels, taking advantage of the position of employer and employee. Mona, it is true, stalked after him impassively enough in her heavy brogues, her downright manners giving no encouragement to romance. Jelkes could not quite see how romance was going to come into it, in view of all the circumstances, but all the same, he wished Hugh would give Mona a list of what he wanted and send her out to attend to it, instead of running round with her like this.

In the meantime Hugh was putting the car along in the way to which it was accustomed, and they were not

long before they arrived in the little town and had sought
out the inevitable photographer whose fate it was to
perpetuate features much better forgotten.  They took
the scrubby, disillusioned little man and his gear into the
car.  He had to have the seat as he was elderly, so Mona
in her vivid green perched on the tapering back, holding
on by Hugh's collar while he took the car carefully round
the bends of the narrow, winding, mediæval streets so
as not to shoot her off.

Arrived at the museum, the photographer did his
job and departed; but Hugh, as Mona expected,
remained bent over the illuminated pages of the ancient
book.  She watched his face as he studied them, and it
seemed to her that his features changed as she watched
him, taking on the same air of a watching hawk that was
worn by the sharp features of the tonsured head rising
from the black folds of its thrown-back cowl in the four-
hundred year old picture.  The two men were certainly
extraordinarily alike, and as the living man stared at the
dead one, he grew more and more like him.

It seemed to Mona as if her employer were hypnotising
himself with the picture of the dead monk, and she felt
that she had better break the spell before it took altogether
too much hold on him.

She leant forward, intending to touch him on the
sleeve, but the leg of her chair slipped on the uneven
floor, and instead she touched him on the bare skin of
his wrist.  He looked up suddenly, and met her eyes,
and the man who looked up was not Hugh, but Ambrosius, and he had reacted to her touch as a cloistered monk
might be expected to react.  Mona found herself looking
into the eyes of a bird of prey.

She knew well enough that she had Ambrosius and
not Hugh Paston to deal with, but she had no means of
knowing whether the monkish celibate was infuriated
by her touch, or stirred out of all reason by it.  She was
alone with him in a large empty upper room of the

mediæval house that served the town as a museum.
From the ordinary point of view she was dealing with a
madman—a man who imagined himself to be a dead and
gone monk of sinister history. She was not even sure if
a man of his epoch would understand modern English if
she spoke to him—he must be a coeval of Chaucer. Not
knowing what to do, she very wisely did nothing. The
eminent churchman, whether real or imaginary, was
unlikely to resort to any sudden violence or unseemliness.

Fra Ambrosius—it was impossible to think of him as
Mr Paston—stared at her with the fixity of a snake at
a bird. It was probable that he was just as much
surprised as she was by the encounter. The room would
appear familiar enough to him—it was a room of his
own period, carefully preserved and restored ; the book
under his hand was one of his own books. The table
on which it rested was a refectory table out of the
monastery itself. The only thing, beside Mona herself,
that was out of the picture was a notice on the wall
requesting people not to smoke—a request which could
have conveyed nothing to him even if he were able to
decipher the modern script.

But he was not paying any attention to notices. He
was entirely occupied in attending to what was before
him. Mona in the vivid green of the dyed leather was
sufficiently incongruous to eyes accustomed to the crude
dyes of the Middle Ages. She had an elfin face at the
best of times, and in her quaint green hood she looked
even to modern eyes, accustomed to freakish fashions,
like something strayed from the greenwood—how must
she have appeared to the cloistered eyes of the ecclesiastic,
accustomed to the soberly coifed heads of the mediæval
women, and only to those at a distance ?

As she watched him, Mona saw the expression of
stupefaction with which he had first greeted her gradually
give place to a look of exaltation, as if he had been
vouchsafed some miraculous, other-world vision. Mona

wondered whether he was under the impression that he was having a vision of a saint. But the expression in his eyes disillusioned her. Ambrosius was under no delusion that he was seeing a saint. She thought of the Temptation of St Anthony, and wondered how Ambrosius was in the habit of dealing with devils. Was she going to be exorcised or strangled? Was Ambrosius going to do his duty as a monk and say: ' Get thee behind me, Satan ? ' or was he not ?

She felt, from the amazed, exalted expression with which he was regarding her, that he did not believe her to be of any earthly nature, and had jumped to the conclusion that she was something come to him from another world in answer to his ungodly experiments with the Greek manuscripts. To say that Ambrosius was agitated would have been but half the truth. The mediæval mind of the man returned from the dead knew no half-lights or compromise in the doctrines of sin and hell. According to all the standards of his world, he had sold his soul to the Devil and an eternity of hell-fire awaited him. However much one may think for oneself, the standards of one's world are not easily thrown aside, and they are apt to come back whenever one is taken by surprise.

The minutes went by, and neither of them moved. Mona, watching the expressions following each other on the face of the man bending towards her—the face of a stranger though the features were familiar—had a profound realisation of the tragedy of the cloister for those who have no vocation for it. The tragedy of Abelard and Eloise. Was this an English Abelard who was bending down to look into her face across the narrow table ?

She gazed back at him. The minutes were slipping away one after the other. A town clock chimed the hour. How much longer were they going to stay like this ? She dared not move lest God knew what should be let loose upon her. She could conceive of Hugh Paston falling dead if the occupant of his body withdrew suddenly. Come what might, the first move must not come from her.

Then the man, without taking his eyes off hers, slowly stretched his hand and touched the back of hers with the tips of his fingers, as if feeling her pulse. The finger-tips were icy cold. It was indeed like the touch of the hand of the dead. Mona did not stir, but continued to hold his eyes with hers. He was evidently trying to ascertain whether she was flesh and blood or phantasy. He had probably known many such phantasies.

Then the other hand began to move and came towards her. Mona could see it coming, though she never took her eyes from those that gazed into hers unwavering with their bird of prey regard. What was that hand going to do ? Was it coming for her throat ? But no, it came to rest on her shoulder. Then the finger-tips that had rested so lightly on the back of her hand closed round her wrist. Mona could not move now if she wanted to.

So firmly had the phantasy of Ambrosius taken hold on her imagination that the modern dress disappeared from her view, and this man bending over her actually was to her the renegade Churchman, desperately risking hell-fire. To a Catholic the situation would have appeared one of horrible blasphemy and indecency, but Mona's nonconformist upbringing gave her no sympathy with, or understanding of, the Catholic point of view, and all she saw was the natural man hideously cut off from natural things. She knew life as it was lived in Bohemian circles, and she understood male human nature, and she was sorry for that man. Instinctively, unthinkingly, her free hand went out and rested on his arm in a touch of sympathy. She watched the eyes of the renegade, imaginary monk slowly fill with tears. It made no difference whether the man before her were a dead man come back from the past, or whether it was a madman phantasying the tragic history, the results were the same, and sprang from the same roots in frustrated human needs. Whether it were Ambrosius vowed to the celibacy of the cloister, or Hugh Paston wasting his manhood in a loveless marriage—the same causes were producing the same effects. There are loveless marriages sometimes when the nun weds the Church, and not every monk is able to get an effectual transference onto the Virgin Mary. The literature of mysticism leaves us in no doubt whatever as to the nature of that transference.

What would have been the end of the encounter, heaven only knew, but a step was heard on the stairs and the man hastily let go of Mona and rose upright, the keen, commanding air telling Mona that it was still Ambrosius who was present. The footsteps crossed the bare boards of the landing and came in at the doorless arch, and Mona turned to greet the curator, wondering how in the world the situation was to be carried off.

But as she turned, the spell broke, and a startled exclamation from Mr Diss caused her to turn again, to see Hugh Paston swaying with closed eyes, and then go over backwards with a crash.

They rushed round the table, but before they could get to him, Hugh was sitting up, rubbing the back of his head where it had made contact with the floor-boards.

" Good Lord, what's the matter ? " he demanded, looking at them dazedly. The only thing he could think of was that he had been in a motor smash. He seemed little the worse, however, except for a sore head. The sudden collapse of all the muscles that takes place when the controlling entity withdraws from a medium is a very different matter to the heart-failure that causes a faint.

Mr Diss, however, was thoroughly alarmed.

" My dear sir, allow me to assist you. Sit down a moment, and I will get you some brandy from across the way."

Hugh, nothing loath, sat down and blinked at Mona.

"What happened?" he asked, as soon as Mr Diss's back was turned. "Did I faint?"

"I think you must have done," said Mona.

"That's odd. What did I faint for? I was feeling perfectly all right."

"How are you feeling now?"

"A bit swimmy. As if nothing were real and I didn't know quite where I was. I shan't be sorry for the old boy's brandy."

But Hugh did not get his brandy as quickly as he might have done, for Mr Diss despatched the youth for it, and then got busy on the phone to Mr Watney.

"I wish you would come round," he said. "Your new client has just gone off in a dead faint, and I think the young lady is badly frightened."

Consequently when the brandy arrived, it was brought upstairs by the pair of them, and they jointly stood over Hugh, now thoroughly ashamed of himself, while he drank it. They likewise gave a dram to Mona, for which she was truly thankful. Every time she looked at Hugh's shy, nondescript face, she felt that at any moment the burning eyes of Ambrosius might stare out at her from it.

It was immediately decided that all four of them should go round to Mr Watney's house and have some lunch before Hugh undertook the drive back to town. Mr Watney was a bachelor, and things can be done with a housekeeper that cannot be done with a wife.

During the short walk Mr Watney contrived that Mr Diss should walk with Hugh while he himself companioned Mona.

"Does Mr Paston suffer with his heart?" he enquired of her.

"I have no idea," said Mona. "I only know him very slightly."

"You are not a relation, then?"

" Oh dear no, I am a professional designer. It is my job to design all the decorations for the house and see the contracts through. I know nothing whatever of Mr Paston personally. I only met him a couple of days ago."

" Dear, dear. Rather a trying experience for you, my dear young lady."

" It was, very," said Mona. " However, he does not seem much the worse for it."

" It is very dangerous for him to drive a car if he is subject to these attacks."

" Yes, it certainly is," said Mona, wondering what Ambrosius would make of modern traffic if he suddenly appeared when Hugh was at the wheel.

" Can you not persuade him to employ a chauffeur ? "

" It is none of my business, Mr Watney. I can't interfere in a thing like that. I only know Mr Paston very slightly. If he chooses to take risks, that is his look-out."

She felt that Mr Watney was probing to discover the nature of the relationship between them, and so she diligently emphasised its casualness and her total indifference to Hugh's fate.

" It may be a very unpleasant matter for you, not to say a dangerous one, my dear young lady, if you go driving about in that car of his with him."

" Business is business, Mr Watney. I cannot dictate to my clients."

He appeared satisfied as to Mona's entirely utilitarian interest in Hugh Paston. They came out of a narrow passage and found themselves in the Abbey close. Mona's heart was in her mouth as they crossed it lest Ambrosius should put in another appearance, or, in other words, lest Hugh should have another seizure ; but though he stared up hard at the ancient towers, nothing happened, and they reached the low ivy-covered house looking onto the monks' graveyard in safety.

It was a house of great interest and charm and contained a wonderful collection of antique furniture ; but although Mona was a connoisseur of fine furniture, she had no eyes for it, for she was all the time obsessed by the idea that Hugh Paston was Ambrosius, and she could not get out of her mind the way that Ambrosius had looked at her. She could see those burning eyes still, whenever she looked at Hugh. She also saw that he had noticed that she was upset and nervous with him, and that in its turn made him nervous with her. It did not take much to shake Hugh Paston's self-confidence, his mother had been a dominating woman and his wife a self-centred one.

It was obvious that Hugh was still dazed and hardly knew what he was doing. Not only had he been through a startling psychic experience, but he had also had a good hard crack on the head. Mona felt that if Ambrosius looked at her out of Hugh's eyes again, she would rush from the room, so terrific an impression had the renegade prior made upon her. She could not keep herself from watching Hugh all the time in case he should suddenly turn into Ambrosius again. She felt that he was conscious of her scrutiny, although his social training saved him from showing his embarrassment. Mr Diss and Mr Watney did not increase Mona's peace of mind by endeavouring to entertain them with tales of the Abbey. They never got actually onto the subject of Ambrosius, however, for which she thanked heaven, but as every time they came anywhere near it she held her breath and waited, she did not make a very good lunch. However, they were both plied with Mr Watney's best port. Mona took all she was given. If she were going to be murdered by Ambrosius, or killed in a car-crash by Hugh, the less she knew of it the better.

Finally the meal came to an end, and Mona, perspiring from the port and the heat of the low-ceilinged, stuffy dining-room, for she had not dared to remove her leather coat owing to the shabbiness of her frock, took her place beside Hugh in the car, and they turned homeward.

He took the car out of the difficult streets of the town without speaking. Then he pulled in to the roadside and stopped the engine.

" I say, I'm frightfully sorry," he said. " I am afraid I gave you a rotten scare. I've never behaved like that in my life before. I suppose I must be run down after all I've been through."

Mona, what with the port and the shock, had all she could do to refrain from bursting into tears. The one thing of all others she desired to avoid was being alone with Hugh in a lonely place where he might suddenly turn into Ambrosius.

" It is quite all right," she managed to say at length, " as long as you are not hurt."

" I'm all right," said Hugh, " except for a bump on the back of my head. It is you I am worried about. I am afraid I have upset you."

" It isn't that. I—I think I have got one of my headaches coming on."

" Which is due to the scare, I suppose," said Hugh. " Well, I can only say how frightfully sorry I am, and take you home."

He started up the engine and they travelled home in silence, the headache gradually taking hold on Mona till she felt as if her skull were held in a vice while knives went through her brain. By the time they arrived back at the bookshop she looked ghastly. Hugh looked at her as he helped her out of the car, and was horrified at her appearance.

" I wonder what in the world Jelkes will say to me for bringing you home like this," he said, " I can only say how frightfully sorry I am, Mona."

Mona was too far gone to notice what he called her, nor did she notice that he put his arm round her as she walked unsteadily into the shop.

Old Jelkes, wrapping up books, raised his eyebrows at the sight of the pair of them.

"I am afraid I've brought you back a wreck," said Hugh to him.

"Got one of her headaches ? Well, that's no fault of yours," said the old man.

"I am afraid it is my fault," said Hugh. "I distinguished myself by fainting, and scared her to death."

"Good Lord, are you given to that sort of thing ? "

"Never done it in my life before, and don't know why I did it now."

"Well," said the bookseller, looking at Mona, "I suppose it's tea and aspirin, and so to bed ? "

She walked into the room behind the shop without answering, and dropping down into his own armchair, huddled herself over the fire.

"Let me take your coat off, my dear," said the old man.

"No, I don't want to take it off just yet, I'm cold."

Jelkes went off to put the kettle on for the inevitable tea and Hugh stood staring miserably at Mona, feeling himself to be responsible for her state. He had had no experience whatsoever of illness in women ; his wife had been as strong as the proverbial horse ; any illness there was in his house had been provided by himself.

Mona had not been huddled over the fire many minutes before she suddenly flung off the heavy leather coat that she had been hugging around her.

"I'm boiling hot," she said peevishly.

But in a few moments she wanted it on again. Hugh put it over her shoulders as she groped for it, and as he did so, discovered that she was shaking in a violent fit of the shivers.

He went quietly into the kitchen to Jelkes.

"I say," he said, "this is something more than a headache. It looks unpleasantly like pneumonia to me."

He had had charge of porters at high altitudes, and was familiar with the sudden onset of ' the captain of the hosts of Death.'

Jelkes whistled. " That's a nasty job if it is," he said. " But it may only be one of her headaches. She has uncommon bad ones. I'll have a look at her. I'll soon know. I've seen plenty of her headaches."

He returned with the tea.

" Well, lassie ? " he said. " How are you feeling ? "

" Rotten," said Mona. " I think I've got a chill as well as a headache."

" I think we had better put you to bed and get your doctor to you," said Jelkes.

" I haven't got a doctor," said Mona. " I'm not on the panel."

" You little goose, why aren't you ? " exclaimed the bookseller, aghast.

" I work on my own now, I don't have to be."

" But why for God's sake, child, didn't you keep up the contributions ? "

" Couldn't spare them."

Hugh listened in amazement to this revelation. It had never entered his imagination that any woman whom he could treat as a friend would even be ' on a panel,' let alone unable to afford to be on a panel.

" Look here," he said. " Don't you worry about that. I'm responsible for your chill, so the least I can do is to stand treat with the medico."

" That's damned good of you," said the relieved bookseller, who had seen himself saddled with the expenses of Mona's illness.

" Look here," said Hugh, " what about a nursing-home ? "

" No ! " said Mona, suddenly waking up. Of course she couldn't go to a nursing-home, she had hardly a rag to her back in the way of night-gowns and such like. " I'm not really bad. I'm just chilled on top of my headache, I shall be all right in the morning. I'll go home as soon as I've drunk my tea."

"Oh no, you won't," said the old bookseller. "You'll stop here."

"No, I shan't."

Jelkes went over to her and put his hand on her forehead.

"Shut up," said Mona angrily, brushing aside his hand. "I hate being pawed."

Jelkes took no notice, but caught her two hands and held them so that she could not push him aside, and then felt her forehead at his leisure. Hugh, who had never in his life seen a woman dealt with like this, gasped.

"You've got a temperature all right," said Jelkes. "Now the problem is, what are we going to do with you? To bed you must go, that's quite certain. I think you had better have my bed, and I'll doss down on the sofa. You certainly can't go round to your place by yourself. It's not to be thought of."

"No," said Hugh, "and you on the sofa is not to be thought of either. Look here, I have a suggestion. Let me ring up my housekeeper, Mrs Macintosh, she's a dashed good sort, and let's get a bed and whatever's needful, and shove them in your front room, and keep Mona here till we know what's wrong with her, and let Mrs Macintosh tackle the situation."

"I call that dashed sensible," said the old bookseller. "Yes, that's what we'll do."

"You won't, you won't!" cried Mona hysterically. "I am going round to my own place. I don't want to stop here."

"She's always like this when she has a headache," said Jelkes aside to the agitated Hugh. "Go on and phone your housekeeper while I keep her quiet."

Mona rose to her feet unsteadily.

"I'm going home," she said. How could she explain to these two men that she would not dare to close her eyes in the same house with Hugh Paston lest suddenly she should find herself in the presence of Ambrosius? Involuntarily she raised her eyes to Hugh's, and he saw the fear in them.

"Look here," he said quietly. "I believe Miss Wilton is scared that I'll treat her to another faint if she stops here. If I clear out, will you stop? I can easily go to a hotel."

"Oh no, it's not that. It's too ridiculous."

"Well then, what is it, Mona?" said Jelkes.

"It's nothing. I'm just being silly. I wish you'd let me go home quietly. I shall be quite all right."

"We're not going to let you go home in the state you're in. Will you stop if Hugh clears out?"

"Yes, yes, I'll stop. There's no need for him to clear out. I'm just being silly. Don't take any notice of me. I get like this when I have a headache. I'll be all right presently."

Bad as she was, Mona had enough wits left not to offend a client. She huddled up into a heap in the big chair and hid her face miserably in the dirty cushion.

"Go on and get your phoning done," said Jelkes to Hugh, and Hugh vanished.

"Well, lassie, what really is the matter?" said Jelkes to Mona as soon as Hugh had departed.

"He turned into Ambrosius," said Mona huskily.

"I thought as much," said Jelkes. "What happened when he turned into Ambrosius?"

"He—he just looked at me for ever such a long time without moving, and then someone came into the room, and he fell over backwards in a faint and woke up normal."

"That wasn't a faint, it was the change-over from Ambrosius back to Hugh. What are you scared of, lassie? Did you find Ambrosius alarming?"

"Yes, terrifying."

"Well, well, I don't suppose he'll do it here. Any-

way, you'll have that Scotch housekeeper of his with
you, and I'll keep an eye on Hugh.   You ought to know
enough not to be scared of the dead, Mona.   A dead
man's no different to a living one, except that he hasn't
got a body."

"It's not that, I'm not scared of the dead, any more
than you are.   It's—it's Ambrosius I'm scared of."

"Why ? "

"I—I don't know."   How could she tell him of the
strange passage between them ?   How, above all, tell
him that Ambrosius had 'received encouragement'?
And without that fact any explanation would be more
than misleading.

Hugh Paston returned.

"O.K. chief, she's coming round forthwith, and
bringing a bed and bedding with her.   I told her to hire
a Daimler and toddle round in that.   The chauffeur's face
ought to be worth seeing when they arrive."

"I'll get a fire going upstairs," said Jelkes, and
signalling to Hugh to follow him, he led the way out
of the room.   He knew Mona would not want to be
alone with him.

"Look here," he said, as soon as the fire was under
way, "don't talk to her about Ambrosius, he's got on
her nerves."

"Does she think he'll come back from the dead and
chase her ? "

"Yes, that's it."

"Do you know, T. J., I've had an awfully strong
feeling myself that he's about somewhere, but I don't
think he's inimical.   I think the poor devil had a rotten
time and would be glad of a kind word from anybody,
if you know what I mean.   Personally, I'd like to give
him one, just to cheer him up, you know.   I think he
must have had a pretty poisonous life of it."

"That's all right," said the old bookseller, "but
don't do it while Mona's seedy, or she'll go all to pieces.

You keep your mind off Ambrosius while you're in this house.  We don't want him manifesting here."

"Right you are, T. J.  It's your house.  It's for you to say who comes here, whether from this world or the next.  But as soon as I get settled in at the farm, I'm going to have a jolly good try to get into touch with Ambrosius, and I've a sort of feeling that he knows it."

# CHAPTER XIV

MRS MACINTOSH arrived, and without fuss or comment, took charge of the whole situation.

"What about getting Dr Johnson?" said Hugh.

"Certainly not," was the reply. "If that man comes into the house, I go out of it."

"Good Lord, what's the matter with him? Mrs Paston always thought no end of him."

"I know she did. But he's not coming near Miss Wilton, all the same. What we want is a good, sensible, reliable general practitioner. I know exactly the man, if you will allow me to send for him."

"A Scotchman?"

"Yes."

"I thought as much," said Hugh, laughing. "All right, have your Scotchman. He's not a relation, by any chance, is he?"

"He is my late husband's second cousin."

Mrs Macintosh's Scotchman arrived, looking rather like a pocket edition of old Jelkes. While he was examining the patient, Mrs. Macintosh joined Hugh downstairs.

"Mr Paston," she said quietly. "It would be much easier for me to deal with things if you would tell me frankly what the position is."

"There's not much to tell, Mrs Macintosh. I came across Mr Jelkes quite by chance when I was feeling rotten after the funeral, and palled on with him, and I've been stopping with him ever since. He pulled me round a pretty nasty corner. I think I'd have gone smash if it hadn't been for him. Miss Wilton is a protégée of his—he's a kind of father confessor to the district, I fancy.

She's an artist. I have been setting to work to get another house, and I wanted the furnishing and decorating done, and Jelkes put me on to her for the job. It's her line of work. Then she went sick on our hands. She's got no one to look after her, and we've been doing the best we can for her."

" I see," said Mrs Macintosh. What she thought could not be discerned. She was a woman who believed in keeping herself to herself.

A call from upstairs summoned her, and she departed, leaving Hugh to his own thoughts.

He was very distressed indeed about Miss Wilton's illness, blaming himself for it. But even if he took the whole responsibility upon himself, and he could hardly blame himself for fainting, he was distressed far beyond what he reasonably ought to be. He had believed that he had long since reached a point when all emotion passed him by and he simply felt nothing. This recrudescence of the power to feel was a decidedly painful affair, like the blood returning to a numbed limb. On the other hand, however, it reassured him that he was still alive ; a point he had sometimes come to doubt of recent years. It seemed to him that life was definitely coming back to him, and even if the process were painful, it was a distinctly healthy sign.

He heard the doctor being ushered out, and then Mrs Macintosh returned to him.

" Well ? " said Hugh. " What's the verdict ? "

" A touch of bronchitis. Nothing serious in the chest. The real trouble with her is malnutrition."

" What is malnutrition ? "

" Insufficient nourishment."

" What is the cause of that ? "

" Lack of money."

" What do you mean ? "

" Miss Wilton has had no food for the last five days except the chance meals of most unsuitable things that you and Mr Jelkes have given her."

" But, good Lord alive, what do you mean ? Why hasn't she had proper meals ? "

" Because, Mr Paston, the girl is out of work and starving, and you and Mr Jelkes have not had the sense to advance her any money to go on with till her wages became due, and she was too proud to ask for it. She has been trying to manage on the one meal a day she has been having with you and Mr Jelkes, and you know the kind of things he gives her—sausages, kippers, cheap cheese. In her condition she can't digest them. They simply upset her."

Hugh said nothing. There was a dead silence between them, Mrs Macintosh watching him out of inscrutable eyes.

At length he said : " Get whatever is necessary, Mrs Macintosh."

" Very good, Mr Paston. By the way," she added, " Miss Wilton has begged that Mr Jelkes should not be told, as she thinks it would upset him so much. She did not want you to be told either, but I thought it was as well that you should know."

" My God, yes, I am truly thankful you told me. I hadn't a suspicion."

Mrs Macintosh smiled. " No," she said, "I don't suppose you would have. You have never seen anything like that before at close quarters, have you ? "

Hugh looked at her in surprise. It was the first time he had seen her anything approaching human.

" Do you know," he said, " I feel as if I had never in my life seen anything really at close quarters. Everything seems to me as if it were on the other side of a pane of thick glass, if you know what I mean."

" It is a very artificial life you have always led, Mr Paston."

" Yes, I suppose it is. I didn't realise that, because I have never known any other. Didn't know there was any other. It always seemed natural to me, but I suppose it wasn't."

" I think it would have killed you if you had gone on much longer. I have watched you going steadily down-hill ever since I have been at the house."

" I say, Mrs Macintosh, did you ever suspect about—about my wife and Mr Wilmott ? "

" I knew there was someone, Mr Paston, but I did not know it was Mr Wilmott. They were always most careful. Of course it could not have lasted so long if they had not been."

" Do you think it was generally known ? "

" I could not say. It was a lady who always did the telephoning. Wilkins, who went to the inquest, tells me he thinks it was Miss Wilmott's voice, he recognised it when he heard her giving evidence."

" Good Lord, fancy that girl being a party to it ! And I set her up in her hat-shop ! "

" I think if you knew the truth you would find that the hat-shop was a favourite meeting-place."

" But, my God, have people no decency ? "

" It is quite exceptional among the people I have worked for since my husband died, if you will forgive me for saying so."

" But what is wrong with them ? "

" Too many stimulants, in my opinion. The highly-spiced food ; the constant alcohol ; the women's clothes —no one can stand it and keep their decency. The decent ones withdraw from it ; those who remain are—not decent. That is my candid opinion, and I have had good opportunities for forming it."

" Well, I suppose I can't be particularly decent, for I didn't withdraw from it."

" Oh yes, you did, Mr Paston. You withdrew com-pletely. You were like a waxwork. This is the first time I have ever seen you look alive."

" Do you know, Mrs Macintosh, I believe I have been

suffering from malnutrition quite as much as Miss Wilton."

Mrs Macintosh smiled. " I only hope Mr Jelkes won't feed you on as unsuitable things as he gave to Miss Wilton. He is a very funny old man. He has got some very queer books."

Hugh gasped. Mrs Macintosh, who evidently thought she had better resume her professional mask, asked his leave to withdraw upstairs to attend to her patient.

The next few days were very boring ones for Hugh. He saw nothing of Mona, whose bronchitis was running its course, and he was of too active a nature to be content to sit indefinitely on old Jelkes' broken-down sofa and talk philosophy. He was not interested in occultism from the philosophical side, as the old man was. He wanted phenomena. Jelkes, discoursing of relative realism and the psychological value of symbolism, left him cold. He got all outstanding legal business through his hands, and then, finding himself at a loose end once more, got out the car and ran down to call on Mr Watney, who was delighted to see him—who would not be delighted to see a client of Hugh's calibre?—and invited him to lunch.

The conveyancing, it seemed, was going on as well as could be expected.

" Look here," said Mr Watney in a hushed voice, as if compounding a felony. " You go on and take possession. You've paid your deposit. We can neither of us back out now. Miss Pumfrey isn't to know we haven't finished with the deeds. Unless you get to work at once, you won't be able to make a start on your garden this summer, and—er—while you are having the ground dug, I should very much like to have a look at it."

Hugh readily acquiesced. Mr Watney was welcome to dig up Australia, if he could get at it, so long as something was going on to fill the endless days.

They parted with what were almost endearments on

the part of Mr Watney, Hugh having in his possession an enormous key. It was only three miles to Monks Farm, a mere step in a car. In Hugh's car, one arrived almost before one started. He went round the place at his leisure, and found to his delight that what he had first taken for a second and smaller barn, proved to be a dwelling-house of much more modern structure than the rest of the buildings. Fallen plaster littered the floors ; rotted window-frames let in the weather, but the main structure appeared to be sound, and he saw that it could fairly speedily be rendered habitable.

He returned to the car and sped down the road to the village at his usual gait. There Mr Huggins received him with open, pink-sleeved arms. Yes, he could recommend a builder, a really reliable man, who worked himself alongside his men. Hugh was led round behind the houses to the most amazing hugger-mugger tumble-down raffle of sheds in a cluttered yard, from which, at Mr Huggins's hail, a bearded elder appeared, who was introduced as Mr Pinker.

Yes, Mr Pinker could undertake the work—" And glad to do so, sir. It's a shame to see a lovely bit of building like that going to rack and ruin. You seen the fan-archin' in the cattle-sheds, sir ? "

Yes, Hugh had, and had appreciated it at its proper worth. Mr Pinker was delighted.

" It's a good job you came to me, sir. Now there's many would have spiled that archin' for ye. But I understand 'clesiastical work. I go all about here, sir, I go right up to close to Lonnon sometimes, wherever there's a bit of old work wants handlin'. It's not every mason that understands old work. They spiles it. They pulls it about as if it didn't matter. You shouldn't do that, you should respec' it."

Hugh saw that he had to do with a genuine craftsman, and was delighted. He had read of such men but had never met one before, and believed them to be creatures of romance, along with the Mark Tapleys and the like. He saw before him a delightful prospect of long days while the old fellow pursued his leisurely but honest way and the farm gradually returned to its original likeness under his reverent hands. He was immensely cheered by the prospect, and his depression left him.

He loaded the old boy into the car and returned to the farm.

" That's a bit of plain sailin'," said the old man, viewing the dwelling-house. " My son, he'll do the plumbing. But why you want two baths, I don't see. There's only one Saturday in a week. Howsomever, have it as you've a mind to."

" I dunno what you'll do with this," said he when shown the rest of the buildings. " Girt big rooms they'll be when all this here boardin' is pulled away. And then them little rooms upstairs. There ain't one will make a decent bedroom. Like horse-stalls, I call 'em. I should knock two or three into one, if I was you."

" No," said Hugh, " I don't think we'll do that for the moment. I'll have the big room upstairs made into a bedroom for my own use, and leave the rest of the place alone."

They climbed up the winding stairs to inspect it.

" That's bin a chapel," said Mr Pinker. " Sure you don't mind sleepin' in a chapel, sir ? "

" Not so long as it's no longer used as a chapel," said Hugh

" There's some as wouldn't like it," said Mr Pinker.

" I'm not one of them," said Hugh.

" Well," said Mr Pinker reflectively, " they do say as bein' born in a stable don't make ye a hoss, so maybe sleeping in a chapel won't affect ye. Anyway, sir, I'll have all the timberin' pulled away forthwith, and when next ye come, ye'll be able to have a reel look at the place."

" Do you know what I think I shall do ? " said Hugh,

" I think I shall run back to London and get my gear, and put up in the village till the house is ready.  It will be tremendously interesting to see it taking shape.  Is there anywhere in the village where I could put up ? "

" They'll put ye up at The Green Man, sir, if you ain't too pertickler.  It's rough-like, but it's clean.  Of course it's only meant for the likes of us.  They don't get no gentry, not bein' in the road to nowhere."

Hugh ran the old man back to the village, the long mile trudge disappearing in a flash under his wheels.

" This be a grand machine you've got," said Mr Pinker as the super-charged car ate up the ground.  " I did be thinkin' of gettin' one meself for use in the business.  I 'ad one offered me once for five pun, and I wish I'd taken it now I seen what they can do."

Arrived at the village, Hugh pulled up in front of the ancient bowed frontage of The Green Man.  It was a genuine old hostelry, not one of ' Ye Olde ' variety.  The landlady, a stout and determined-looking widow, had her doubts about her power to accommodate gentlemen, but a little persuasion on the part of Mr Pinker, who was enjoying refreshment at Hugh's expense, helped to reassure her, and by the time Hugh had asked her to have one with him, and she had been treated to a ladylike port, she was not only sure, but certain.  It seemed that in her far-away youth she had been scullery-maid to Miss Pumfrey's mother, so she knew exactly how gentry should be treated.  Hugh wondered how she had managed to graduate into the refreshment trade.  The Pumfrey ménage did not look a likely jumping-off place.

Everything being arranged to everybody's satisfaction, Hugh went racketing off down the London road.  He reached the bookshop to find Mr Jelkes and Mrs Macintosh in conclave.  The abrupt break-off of the conversation at his entry told him that he must have been providing the subject-matter.

They discoursed platitudes for a few minutes, Hugh

telling of his doings and his plans, and enquiring concerning Miss Wilton's progress during the few short hours he had been away.

" That's what we have been discussing," said Jelkes. " She's not getting on as well as she should. Got a certain way, and then sticks."

" Do you think she ought to get away to the sea for a change ? " asked Hugh.

" She's not fit for that yet. Her temperature still keeps up."

" What's the cause of that ? "

Jelkes looked at Mrs Macintosh. She grasped the nettle firmly.

" I think, Mr Paston, that when she saw you faint she had a far more severe shock than we realised. She has been a little light-headed, once or twice, and talked about it. She thinks you are going to do spiritualistic experiments, and she is afraid of that also. It is my belief that she is dreading meeting you again, and yet does not want to break with you because she needs the work."

" I say, I'm frightfully sorry. What can I do about it ? "

" The best thing you can do is to go up and see her, and talk to her as if nothing had happened."

" Right-oh, I'll go as soon as she'll see me."

" Very good, Mr Paston, supposing you come up after you've had your tea ? "

" Hugh," said old Jelkes, cocking a sandy eyebrow at his guest over a tea-cup, " do you know what it is that has bitten Mona ? "

" No good Lord, what is it ? "

" Ambrosius."

" What in the name of glory do you mean ? "

" She's scared to death of him. Thinks she'll see his ghost. Keep off the subject, see ? "

" Right you are, T. J. But what's made her so scared ? "

" Goodness only knows.  There's no sense in women."

" I'm not so sure of that.  You know, I've had a very strong impression of Ambrosius several times ; but whereas I welcome it, it scares her.  It's pretty strong when it comes, and if you didn't like it, as I do, I can quite believe you'd be badly scared."

" Well, anyway, leave it alone for the present, Hugh, for the love of heaven."

Having finished his tea, Hugh presented himself upstairs as bidden, and was duly ushered in by Mrs Macintosh, who then withdrew, leaving him to his own devices.

Mona, sitting propped up in bed, a washed-out pink shawl about her shoulders, had that fine-drawn, transparent look that any chest trouble always gives.  There was no question whatever about it, she was scared of him all right.  He could see it by her eyes and the way she was holding herself together.  Hugh, who had never seen any human being scared of him before, and could not imagine how they could be, felt, to his immense surprise, deep down inside him a curious glow of satisfaction, even while his one desire was to reassure her and restore her to peace and happiness.

It was an extraordinary thing that Mona, who at first sight looked a very self-willed creature, was really and genuinely scared of him, and had to take her courage in both hands in order to talk to him.  There was something in this that delighted Hugh profoundly, and made him esteem Mona's companionship very highly.  Something that gave him the first inkling of the self-confidence he had always lacked.

He sat down in the chair placed in the correct position by the foot of the bed—Mrs Macintosh always did everything correctly——.

" Well, how goes it ? " he said.

" Not too badly," said Mona.  " I'm much better than I was."

" But not as well as you might be ? "

" No, I'm afraid I'm not. Tiresome, isn't it ? Especially after everyone's been so good to me. I feel it's ungrateful."

" Don't you worry about that. We'll hang on to you till you're quite all right."

Silence fell between them. Hugh cast about in every direction for some remark that would prove of interest and not lead round to Ambrosius, and he could not find it. If he spoke of the farm, it led straight to Ambrosius. If he spoke of her work, it led on to the farm, and so to Ambrosius. Suddenly the problem was taken out of his hands. Mona Wilton fixed her eyes on him and said :

" Have you found out anything more about Ambrosius ? "

Hugh gasped. " I—I thought you did not like Ambrosius," he said.

" I never said that," said Mona. " He made me feel perfectly awful because of his dreadful end, but I never said I didn't like him. As a matter of fact, I—I feel most awfully sorry for him. I think he must have had a rotten time."

" That's exactly how I feel about him," said Hugh eagerly, and then stopped hastily, for he knew the subject was a forbidden one, and he had a vision of Mona's already high temperature rising towards boiling-point if it were pursued.

" Tell me about him. Have you found out anything more ? "

" Er—no, I haven't been looking for it. But you know I don't think it is very good for you to talk about Ambrosius while you're still seedy. He's rather a harrowing subject, don't you think ? You mightn't sleep after it."

" He's the best possible subject for me to talk about, and I probably shall sleep after it. I certainly shan't sleep properly till I do. Ambrosius has got on my nerves, you know, and I've got to talk about him to get him off them."

" All right, go ahead.  What do you want to know about him ? "

" Where do you think he is now ? "

" Good Lord, I don't know.  Safe in the churchyard where they planted him after the inquest, I suppose."

" That's where his body is, but where is *he* ? "

" How should I know ?  Do you think his ghost walks ? "

" Not exactly walks, that implies an earthbound spirit, and I don't think he's that.  But I think he would manifest, given half a chance."

" So do I," said Hugh, and then could have bitten his tongue off.

" Do you know what we've got to do ? "

" No ? "

" We've got to help him to manifest."

" What do you mean ? "

" We've got to make him welcome and bring him back. There will be no peace for anyone until we do.  I've made up my mind to that.  That's the thing I've been turning over in my mind while I've been ill.  It was that that sent my temperature up.  But now I've made up my mind to it, and told you, I think it will go down.  If you see Ambrosius, give him my love."  Mona smiled at him very curiously as she said the last words.  He had never seen a woman smile like that before, and could not imagine what it meant.

There came to him a most extraordinary sense of peace and relaxation, as if something he had been straining against had given way and released him.

" That's most awfully good of you," he said, and then looked at himself in surprise.  Why should he return thanks on behalf of Ambrosius ?

" Now tell me all the news," said Mona.  " How are things going at the farm ? "

" First-rate.  Do you know that what we thought was

a smaller barn is really the farm-house, and quite habitable ? It only wants a lick of paint and a few tintacks
knocking into it. We could move in next week if we
wanted to."

"But how gorgeous! Oh dear, I must get well
quickly and get to work on it. It will be the greatest fun
getting things into shape. You have no idea what possibilities that place has got from the decoration point of
view. It is the most perfect background one could
possibly have."

"So you have fallen in love with it too, have you ?
So have I. There is a queer fascination about it, isn't
there ? One would expect it to be gloomy and sinister
from its history, but I don't get that, somehow. It seems
as if all that were superficial, and the real thing there,
that's coming to the surface now, is what Ambrosius set
out to do. Have you tumbled to what that is ? "

"No, what is it ? "

"The same thing we're going to do—invoke Pan.
And the house knows it. That's why we feel welcome
there. It was awfully pleased to see us. That house was
no more cut out for a monastery than Ambrosius was cut
out for a monk. I bet you anything that all these centuries Pan has been waiting to keep that appointment the
Pope's visitor interrupted."

"That explains a good deal," said Mona thoughtfully.
"I have been addling my brains to discover why
an invocation of Pan landed you in a monastery. It
seemed the most unlikely spot one could possibly imagine.
But it is coming clear now. The same path leads to both
Pan and Ambrosius."

"That has been my guess all along. That old chapel's
not Christian ; it is got up on conventional lines to cover
its tracks ; but if it was ever meant for anything orthodox, I'll eat my hat. But all the same, I don't think
Ambrosius was a bad lot, even by the local reckoning. I
believe he was suffering actually from a deficient spiritual

diet, and he was trying to get some vitamin P. into it."

" What a lovely name ! "

" Original and copyright.  When he got hold of the Greek manuscripts he realised what was wrong with him, and how to remedy it, and he set to work to develop the thing on the quiet, knowing he'd be burnt as a witch ——"

" Wizard——" said Mona.

" —If he were caught out.  I think Ambrosius really meant to be a reformer, given half a chance.  He wasn't just abreacting his complexes by playing with dirt.  He knew, whatever they liked to say, that Pan was clean and natural."

There flashed before Mona's memory the expression on the sharp-featured face of the stranger who had bent over her in the empty upper room of the museum, and she wondered what chains upon the soul Ambrosius would have to break before he reached the relative freedom indicated by Hugh Paston's viewpoint.  A sudden pang of fear shook her ; for although she did not fear Pan, she feared, and not without reason, the overwhelming rush when barriers go down.

" If our hypothesis is right," Hugh went on, " Ambrosius was trying to raise Pan.  At least, his contemporaries said he was trying to raise the devil, and Pan and the devil were the same thing to their mediæval minds."

" But you don't think Pan and the devil are the same thing, do you, Mr Paston ?  You haven't said to evil, be thou my good ? "

" Good Lord no, I don't feel that Pan is evil ; though, mind you, I think he might be a bit of a devil if he got out of hand.  I think he is something that is missing from modern life—a kind of spiritual vitamin.  But you can have too much of a vitamin.  I've seen it done with kids who were supposed to be leading the healthy life. Loaded too much of half the alphabet into them and brought them out in spots.  Odd, isn't it, that you can have too much of a good thing, but you can."

" It's the same with everything," said Mona. " You'll find it's just the same with Pan. If you get too much Pan, you see red, and if you get too much church, you feel blue. Funny, isn't it, that temperance has come to mean total abstinence instead of not taking too much. But tell me, when are you going down to Thorley ? "

" I'm going down tomorrow, to put up at The Green Man."

" Is that the name of the pub there ? I suppose you know who the Green Man is ? He's Pan."

" Good Lord, you don't say so ? "

" Yes, he is. He's Jack-in-the-green, the wood-spirit —the fairy man who runs after the maidens on mid-summer eve—— What's that but Pan ? The British Pan ? And do you know the meaning of the name of the village—Thorley ? It's Thor's ley, or field. You're in the thick of the Old Gods there ; the Scandinavian old gods, because it's towards the east side of England. In the west it's the old gods of the Kelts you get. But you will like the Norse gods best because you're fair. Now I'm dark. I belong with the Kelts. But it's all one, you know—the same thing with different names. Pan is the same everywhere. He's elemental force—that's all he is. He comes up from the earth under your feet, just as spiritual force, the sun-force, comes down from the sky over your head."

" Well, I'll be hanged ! But look here, you mustn't go on talking like this. You'll have a temperature as high as a house."

" Oh no, I shan't. I'm feeling better already now I've got it off my chest."

The door opened, and Mrs Macintosh entered.

" I think she has talked enough for one visit," said the housekeeper, and Hugh went like a lamb. Mrs Macintosh was a woman to be obeyed, as many Mayfair staffs had found.

# CHAPTER XV

LEFT alone, Mona dropped back on the pillows and clasped her hands behind her head and asked herself what in the world they were doing and where in the world they were heading. There were two relations to be considered—the relationship between herself and Hugh Paston as man and woman, and the relationship between the pair of them and Ambrosius, both jointly and separately.

She considered first the relationship between herself and Hugh Paston, that being the obvious and incontrovertible one—the relationship with Ambrosius being open to more than one interpretation. Hugh liked her, that was obvious ; he seemed to want her with him all the time ; he referred everything to her. But all the same, he did not give her the impression of being attracted to her as a woman. He liked her as a friend, she felt. But is that relationship possible between a man and a woman to any great degree without the sex factor entering into it ? Only, she knew, if both were adequately mated elsewhere. Old Jelkes had taught her a good deal of the secret knowledge on the subject of sex that is so important a part of the Mystery Tradition—one of its secret keys, in fact. He had steered her round a very difficult corner by means of his knowledge, and what she had learnt was standing her in good stead now. She knew that there must be some degree of reaction between a man and a woman whenever any appreciable degree of sympathetic relationship is established between them, but under Jelkes' tuition she did not make the mistake of thinking it need be crudely sexual. She knew the subtle interplay of magnetism that goes on all the time in every relationship between the more vital and positive of the pair and the more pliant and dependent, quite irrespective of sex. She knew that, so far as magnetism went, in her relationship with Hugh Paston she was far the more positive of the pair. Hugh was peculiarly negative; peculiarly lacking in any sort of magnetism, and that was probably at the bottom of the trouble with his wife. She could not imagine him attracting or holding any woman, or for the matter of that, wanting to attract any woman. He was the most sexless male she had ever met.

But then there was Ambrosius, who was a very different matter. But who, or what, was Ambrosius ? First of all, he could be the dissociated personality of Hugh himself, and there was no need to look any further than abnormal psychology for his explanation. Secondly, he might be the spirit of the dead and gone monk manifesting through Hugh, who was quite negative enough for any sort of mediumship. Or thirdly, the explanation might lie in the far-reaching doctrine of reincarnation. But in the latter case, how did it work ? There were two distinct personalities inside Hugh Paston's suit, neither of them apparently knowing anything about the other, and behaving in the exact manner that is described in the text-books of psychology that Jelkes' queer tastes and queerer collection had introduced her to. Mona had read widely in that field because it interested her and enabled her to understand some of her own problems.

It was easy enough to explain the whole affair as one of those multiple personality cases that were produced in bulk at the Salpêtrière at a time when suggestion and dissociation were less well understood than they are now. It was easy to see how Hugh's repressed subconscious mind might have split off bodily from his conscious personality and built up for itself an Ambrosius fantasy. There were all the makings of such a happening. Hugh, already shaken by his own tragedy, suddenly found himself face to face with the tragic history of

Ambrosius and was struck by the similarity between their aims. ' There, but for the grace of God, goes Hugh Paston'—he might quite well have said to himself. Were Hugh Paston and Ambrosius the conscious and sub-conscious minds of the same man ? And if so, where did she stand between them ? Where she stood with Ambro-sius was not merely obvious, but blatant.

Where did she stand with Hugh ? Mona had no delusions about Mayfair, or its morals. She knew that if Hugh were true to type, it was exceedingly unlikely that she stood for marriage with Hugh Paston. A few week-ends—a wrist-watch—a pendant—She doubted if it would run to a flat in these economical days when the girls of his own class gave themselves for the asking. Now Mona, though entirely unconventional in her manners and speech, of which latter Jelkes frequently complained bitterly, had very definite views as to what was clean and what was not in conduct. If a man who were free to offer her marriage offered her anything else, she would consider herself grossly insulted. If, on the other hand, a man who were not free to offer her marriage asked her to make a home with him, she would have considered herself entirely justified in doing so ; the divorce laws being so far removed from the national conscience, no great odium attends upon being a law unto oneself in such matters nowadays. Equally, how-ever, the offer of a clandestine flat by a man who desired to save his face with the world would have been turned down contemptuously. Mona had been through the bitter experience that awaits the woman who gives her all for what she thinks is the great love to a man who has not the slightest intention of risking his reputation. She learnt, as all the daughters of Eve must learn, that passionate love is a fire that burns itself out, and unless it is replaced by the love of comrades, there is nothing left. Never again would she make the mistake of giving herself for love unless the man were also willing to give himself

for love and face the music with her and make a home
for her.    To have passing affairs of the senses she would
have considered utter degradation.

It was on the reaction from this affair that Jelkes had
found her, and had helped her to pull herself together
again.    She too had been consoled with cups of tea and
put to bed in the old feather-bed in Jelkes' spare room.
It was, in fact, Mona herself who had knocked the canopy
cock-eye, slaying clothes-moths.    She had tremendous
confidence in Jelkes' wisdom in matters of human nature,
having found him a true prophet in her own affairs of
the heart—a reputation he had earned simply by knowing
that human nature is made after a certain pattern in such
matters and will run true to form.    At the very outset
of her acquaintance with Hugh, Jelkes had taken her
aside and given her a very straight talking-to, and warned
her that Hugh was in an abnormal condition, and not
to be taken too seriously.    Mona herself had seen enough
of the world to know the reactions of a man who had had
an emotional shock and disllusionment, and she had
nodded her acquiescence.    But now she was not quite
so sure.    The negative, purposeless, gentle-natured Hugh
might be putty in anybody's hands, easily managed, and
quite content with Platonics, but Ambrosius was another
matter.    He was anything but Platonic, and promised to
be a very awkward handful, whether he were a dissociated personality or a separate entity.

Mona did not know what to do with him because she
could not be sure exactly what he was.    How could one
tell a dissociated personality from a spirit-control, and a
spirit-control from a previous incarnation of the same
person ?    Anyway, the practical results were the same,
whatever theory might be chosen to explain them.

At that moment the door opened and in walked Jelkes,
looking uncommon grim.

" Where's Hugh ? " he exclaimed in surprise, finding
Mona alone.

" I've no idea. Mrs Macintosh turfed him out some time ago."

" Has he been gone long ? "

" Yes, ages. Good Lord, did you think he was spending the night with me ? "

" Mona, I wish you wouldn't talk like that. I don't like to hear it."

" Don't take any notice of me, Uncle Jelkes, my bark is a lot worse than my bite. You ought to know that by this time."

Jelkes grunted and flung a piece of coal on the fire with a crash.

" Mrs Macintosh had quite made up her mind he'd be spending the night here. And she wasn't at all anxious to disturb him, either. I was surprised to hear she had come in after all."

" She's been trained in good places. All the same, she met with a disappointment. Hugh went like a lamb. That ought to teach her not to judge others by herself."

" So you're calling him Hugh, are you ? "

" Not to his face. I only called him that because you did. I know my place—

" ' *God bless the squire and all his rich relations,*
*And teach us poor people to know our proper stations.*' "

" I hope you know it, for your own sake, Mona."

" Good Lord, yes, I know it all right. I've seen his sort before. You needn't worry about me. I've no use for Mayfair or any of its ways and works. All the same, Uncle, I think the poor chap's in a devil of a mess, just as a human being, quite apart from his old school tie."

" What sort of a mess ? "

" A mess inside. I say, Uncle, what is Ambrosius really, do you think ? "

" That's exactly what I have been addling my brains over, Mona. I'm dashed worried about the lad. If it's mediumship, there will be the devil to pay. He's in no state to stand it. The kind of mediumship that develops under strain is always pathological, in my opinion. I think it's a dual personality, myself. I've seen it before. There was a case at the seminary. A little lay-brother washing dishes in the kitchen. Mildest little creature in the ordinary way. Then, when he'd had enough of dish-washing, he turned into no end of a dog with the vocabulary of a bargee. I expect the invocation of Pan has stirred up all Hugh's repressions, and Ambrosius is the result."

" Yes, Uncle, but why Ambrosius ? Why not Henry VIII, or Solomon, or any other respectable polygamist he might fancy ? Why Ambrosius, who was just as repressed as Hugh ? He's no wish-fulfilment for anybody. Do you know what I believe, Uncle ? I believe that Hugh was Ambrosius in his last incarnation, and what we know as Hugh today, all nerves and inhibitions, is what was left of Ambrosius after the Pope's visitor had finished with him. Then, when he invoked Pan, he opened up his own subconscious, which is what Pan always does, and the first thing he struck was the layer of memories belonging to Ambrosius, all full of emotion because Ambrosius died a terrible death. It's a psycho-pathology all right ; it's a dual personality all right—two men under one hat, but it doesn't start in this incarnation, it goes back to the last."

Jelkes sat for a long time deep in thought. At length he spoke.

" I believe you're right, Mona. That explains a lot of things that fit in with each other. Anyone with any knowledge knows that psychology doesn't begin with this life. You can't account for any innate qualities if it does, except by a special act of creation, and I should have thought that was out of date since Darwin."

" Never mind the academics," said Mona. " What's to do about it ? "

" But it is upon the academics that the question of what to do is based," said Jelkes. " Until I am sure what is wrong with the fellow, I don't know what to do with him. All I can do is to pursue expectant treatment, as the doctors say when they're flummoxed. We have got a choice of two things ; we can lance him or let him burst naturally. The one thing we can't do is to turn Ambrosius back now he's come so far. If I had known the way things were going to work out, I'd have shoved Hugh down a drain as soon as I set eyes on him. But being as things are, we've got to do the best we can for him, damn him."

Mona smiled. She knew so well how much worse Jelkes' bark was than his bite.

And Jelkes knew it too. His snarling at Hugh was to cover his own emotion. He knew that in tackling the problem in psycho-pathology presented by Hugh Paston he was taking on a very nasty job—particularly nasty, because the girl was inevitably involved in it. In order to get invocations of the old gods to work, something in the nature of a self-starter had to be provided. As St Ignatius so truly said in another context : ' Put youself in the posture of prayer, and you will feel prayerful.' Country-folk, when a pump won't suck, pour a little water down it ; this seals the valve, and the pump gets going. So it is with invocations. Rouse the Pan Within, and he makes contact with the Great God, the First-begotten Love, who is by no means merely a cosmic billy-goat. Mona Wilton had caused sufficient reflex stir of the instincts in Hugh Paston, whether he knew it or not, to serve as water down the pump. Old Jelkes, whose ideals were not of the kind that leads to self-delusion, knew that if Mona chose to follow up her advantage, the invocation of Pan would be an unqualified success. But would she ? And even if she would, could

he let her ? It was a tricky business. There would be
a sudden rush of repressed emotion, like the bursting of
a mill-dam, and then Hugh would rapidly come back to
normal ; and once back to normal, it was exceedingly
unlikely that he would have any use for Mona Wilton,
but would shake her by the hand, and thank her warmly,
and return whence he came and never give her another
thought.

If he could be sure that Mona would keep her head,
and neither panic at the manifestation, nor get her
personal feelings involved, the way to handle Hugh was
deliberately to wake the Inner Pan till it burst its inhibitions and the two sides of Hugh's nature joined up.
And Jelkes knew how it could be done. Steadily, deliberately, under control all the time, as the ancient
priests did it—by means of ritual. But it was Mona
who would have to do it. He had no word of power
that would evoke Pan to visible appearance in the soul
of Hugh Paston. It is one thing to tackle a nasty job
oneself ; but it is quite another to put someone else on
to do it. Jelkes was doing some pretty hard thinking,
and was inclining towards the decision that Hugh Paston
was a structure that was not worth the repairs, when
Mona's voice interrupted him.

" Do you know what I believe is the only solution of
Mr Paston's problems ? Do a ceremony of invocation
and bring Pan through. You will have him under control
then, whereas if he goes on leaking through in the way
he's doing at present, he will be all over the place."

" That's just what I was thinking myself, Mona. But
if we do that, who's going to do the invocation ? I can't.
Pan won't come for me."

" Me, I suppose," said Mona. " Lord, what a life !
I never thought I'd come to this. But it is the only thing
that will straighten things out. Mr Paston will go on
the rocks if we can't do something for him. And his
family will have him certified if they get half a chance.

They've been on the verge of it several times. That was why Mrs Macintosh wouldn't let the family doctor be sent for. He'd had a finger in the pie. He's an awful swine, I believe. Did an abortion for Mrs Paston to cover her tracks. Mr Paston seems to have been thoroughly let in by everybody."

" Yes, poor lad, he's got bones that are worth picking. All the same, I don't see what they stand to gain by certifying him. He doesn't need it."

" If they certify him, he can't go and get married again and raise a family, and then all his money will go to his little nephews and nieces. Mrs Macintosh is certain that's the game. They came round to see her, and cross-examined her up hill and down dale, trying to get evidence about his eccentricities. I believe he is pretty eccentric, at least they think he is, judged by Mayfair standards. I don't suppose he'd be considered so in Chelsea. Anyway, if we don't do something for the poor chap, he'll be in the soup, for he's an awfully defenceless sort of creature, for all his cash. From what I've seen of them I should say that millionaire's children are like Michaelmas chicken—not worth rearing. If he'd had to knock about like I have, he wouldn't have lasted long."

" If he'd had to knock about like you have, he wouldn't be like he is, he'd probably have been all right. But everyone he comes near exploits him, and the lad hasn't a chance."

" I'd like to give him a chance, Uncle, if you're willing. There's something awfully decent about him, in spite of his money."

" I'd like to give him a chance too, Mona, but what you're proposing is no joke, and you're the person who is going to have to stand the brunt of it. You'll have to lead him up the garden path, and then nip from under at the critical moment. I don't see any likelihood of Hugh settling down with us for keeps ; we're not his sort, and he's not our sort. We'll have to put him on his feet and then say good-bye. Are you game for that ? "

" Oh yes, I'm game for that all right, Uncle. In fact, that's the only thing I am game for. I shouldn't care to have Hugh for keeps either. He wouldn't amuse me."

" Well, my dear, I take off my hat to you. You're saving a soul, and not cheaply, either."

" We must mark time till I get fit again. I can't tackle a job like this while I'm under the weather."

" Good God, no, child, of course you mustn't. And I don't want to move either until I'm absolutely certain as to what I'm handling. We must watch Hugh for a bit, and make sure of our diagnosis, and even then we must insert the thin end of the wedge very gently. It doesn't do to bring these things through to consciousness with a shock. Let him adjust himself gradually."

" But on the other hand, don't let him flounder," said Mona.

" He's all right. He's stood it so long, he can stand it a bit longer—until you're quite fit, anyway."

" I don't know about that. Once things begin to stir they soon get up pace, and if you haven't got them in hand, well, they're soon out of hand."

# CHAPTER XVI

HUGH would have liked to have said good-bye to Miss Wilton before he took his departure next morning, but this Mrs Macintosh would not permit, alleging that the doctor was expected. He was vouchsafed the information, however, that Miss Wilton had had a good night, and was much better this morning. Although her prescription had worked well, Mrs Macintosh had no intention of risking an overdose. Hugh, therefore, had to content himself with ordering a large bunch of flowers to be sent in from a very expensive florist who could be relied on to do the thing in style and not work off stale stock, knowing that the recipient of a present is unlikely to report the dudness of the gift.

A fearful smash-banging greeted Hugh as he approached the farm, and he discovered that Mr Pinker had been as good as his word, and the place looked as if it had been bombed. All the raffle of unsightly shacks in the courtyard was piled in a heap in the centre, giving promise of a noble bonfire. Even as he crossed the muddy expanse, a couple of youths came out of a doorway laden with dilapidated planks to which the garish remains of flowered wallpapers still clung. Things were moving.

It was now possible to see the fan-arching and the delicate pillars of the cloisters surrounding the four sides of the yard. To the east there were no buildings backing onto the cloisters, and the grove of Scotch firs overhung them with their branches and dropped cones and needles onto the lichened stone of their roof. To the north they were overshadowed by the steep-pitched roof of the chapel. To the south, the dwelling-house backed on to them ; to the west, the main building of the ancient priory.

He entered the main building by a big door that stood wide open, and found that the last of the partitioning lay on the floor and it was possible to get a view of the big rooms. They lay one either side of the large hall with its groined roof and fine curving stone stair. The whole place appeared to be built of stone, the only timber being the doors. Hugh thought of the cold during the long winters, and the imprisoned monks in their unheated cells ; there were big stone fireplaces in the two large rooms, but he doubted if the prisoners got much benefit from them.

And yet the place did not seem melancholy to him. It was as if the terrible happenings that marked the close of its ecclesiastical career had been swept away and it was back at the days of its building, when its master, full of new hope, got his risky enterprise going.

Hugh walked round his domain. The labourers were busy smashing out the rough woodwork that defaced the older portion of the building, but in the dwelling-house the skilled men were at work on the repairs. Old Pinker himself was busy with the window-frames.

" You do want to make a place weather-tight before you does aught else," said he as Hugh greeted him.

The ancient kitchener was up by the roots already, revealing the fine fire-back behind it.

" I got a pair o' dorgs will do ye fine here," said Mr Pinker. " Fire-dorgs," he added, as an afterthought, in case Hugh mistook him for a fancier. " It's a shame and a sin to hide a fire-back like that. Now what about dis-temper ? Myself, I'd fancy a nice cheerful pink ; or a good green. But you have it as you've a mind to."

Hugh took up his fascinating little book of patterns.

" I'll take this with me, if I may," he said.

" That's right," said Mr Pinker. " It's allus best to ask the missus. Then she gets what she wants and there's peace. If she don't, there isn't. And it don't matter to a man what's on the walls. I suppose ye want the white-wash gettin' off'n the beams? It will be the heck of a job, but we kin do it if you want it. And they're oak, they are, and it's a shame and sin to hide 'em."

Having arrived at Thorley, Hugh did not keep on running backwards and forwards to Billings Street, as he had planned to do. Things were happening inside him that made him think, and made him wish to be alone while he thought.

He was very puzzled as to exactly what had happened in the upper room at the museum, where he was supposed to have fainted. But had he fainted? The last thing he heard before he lost consciousness had been the great bell of the Abbey striking the hour, and he had recovered consciousness to hear the chiming of the quarter. He had been sitting down when he had lost consciousness, and he had been flat on his back on the floor, well clear of any chair, when he recovered it. It does not take a man a quarter of an hour to fall from horizontal to vertical when he faints. Moreover, there had been a marked change in Mona Wilton's attitude towards him from that moment; she had registered fear in no mistakable manner. Jelkes, too, had cooled off appreciably. Hugh was amazed to find that the defection of these two new friends cut far deeper than his wife's disloyalty or his mother's lack of sympathy had done.

The one thing he had to hold on to was Mona's curious remark: 'We must help Ambrosius to come through. Give him my love', and the extraordinary lifting of the cloud that had followed her words. He had done the usual promiscuous surface reading of his kind, and was familiar with spiritualistic thought, and there imme-diately came to his mind the idea that the disincarnate Ambrosius might have turned up and made use of him as a medium. Was it possible to go into trance without knowing it? He didn't know.

The idea left him cold, however. It would not in the least amuse him to be a trance medium. He had always considered that a job for women. For Ambrosius, however, he had an extraordinary sympathy. An overwhelming rush of sympathy, for Ambrosius was the last thing he remembered before losing consciousness. It seemed to him that, just as on the night when fantasy turned into nightmare, he had realised so clearly what Ambrosius was trying to do and how he must have felt, that for a moment he had actually identified himself with the dead monk, and was himself feeling, rather than thinking of the feelings of another.

And at that moment Mona Wilton had laid her hand on his. Now Hugh reckoned himself as a married man whose moonstruck days were far behind him, and he was quite accustomed to do his share at a necking party, though he was never considered to shine, and a woman's casual touch meant little or nothing to him. But when Mona laid her hand on his wrist, he had reacted as Ambrosius would have reacted. Now what was the meaning of that? He had experienced the tremendous upheaval that might have been expected to take place in the soul of the monk, totally unaccustomed to women, who had secretly broken with his religion and all its inhibitions, and was pursuing the cult of Pan.

It was a bewildering problem, and Hugh, sitting over the fire in the stuffy little parlour at the Green Man, gave himself up to the contemplation of it.

And as he did so, he felt the same change coming over him again. And for a brief moment he *was* Ambrosius. And he felt the tremendous concentration of will and energy, the daring, and at the same time the subtlety and wariness, that had characterised the renegade monk. Once again he was adrift in time and space and was afraid. But at the same time he felt a strange exhilaration and sense of flowing power. It was like being at the wheel of a racing-car when the greatest risks are being taken and

are coming off successfully. Or like the critical moment
on a rocky face as one comes up and over the cornice. It
was for this that he had loved danger and pursued dangerous sports—for these tremendous moments of exhilaration when he was another man.

Was it possible, simply by thinking hard of the dead
and gone monk, to produce this feeling at will ? It certainly looked as if it were. He must ask Jelkes. The
feeling had gone again, though leaving an aftermath of
excitement behind it. He concentrated once more on
the idea of Ambrosius, trying to summon him before his
mind's eye and picture him as he must have been in his
black habit, with his ascetic hawk's face, but failed to get
anything clear. It might be easier if he had the picture
of Ambrosius to remind him of his appearance. He
reached for the cardboard-packed parcel that he had
picked up from the photographer's on his way to Thorley, but which, in his obsession with his new idea, he had
forgotten to open, tore off the wrappings, and held in
his hands a full plate photograph. He examined it
critically.

The brushwork was extraordinarily fine ; held a little
way off, as one must hold a modern picture if one is to
see it properly, he found that the enlargement gave the
same striking effects of luminosity as an Impressionist
work. The light and shade of the photograph revealed
the formal, massive draping of the black robe and the
stiff folds of the cowl, as if the material had been harsh
and unyielding, as it probably was. The bold, impres-
sionistic effect which enlargement had lent to the minia-
ture-painter's brush-work, threw up in strong relief the
modelling of the face and head and the long-fingered
hands. A bare sandalled foot showed under the hem of
the robe. It gave him a strange sensation to gaze upon
the flesh of the man who had been horribly done to
death.

He studied the pictured face closely. It was seen in

profile, as the sitting man bent over his sloping desk, pen in hand. Hugh wished it had been full face so that he could have looked into the eyes. From the features thus revealed he strove to reconstruct the nature of the man. The forehead was high under the close-cropped hair, and he judged that it would be narrow, like his own. He judged that Ambrosius had a rather lantern-jawed face altogether. What little hair appeared round the skull-cap that protected the tonsure appeared to be dark, so far as he could tell, whereas his own was of the nondescript, light mousey brown that is effectually peroxided by alleged blondes. Hugh contrasted his own indefinite countenance with the hawk-like features of the pictured face ; his own vague purposelessness with the intensity of that figure, even when seated at a desk. He realised with abundant clearness that it was the intensity of the man's nature that give his driving-force to Ambrosius ; whereas he, Hugh, having no intensity, simply slipped into a negative condition that was death in life when things became difficult.

It seemed to him that Ambrosius was everything that he was not, and a far better man into the bargain. But then Hugh always felt that about people he liked. The moment he saw anything to admire, he realised how lacking it was in himself, and how hopeless it was to try and develop it in his negative, useless nature.

At that moment Mrs Pascoe came in with his tea, and he laid aside the picture to help her clear a place for the tray among the books and papers with which he had littered the table. As he did so, the picture caught her eye.

" My, is that you in fancy dress, Mr Paston ? " she said. " Ain't it a speakin' likeness ! "

The moment she had withdrawn, Hugh went upstairs, regardless of the stewing tea, and got his shaving mirror. Then, manœuvring till he got the right angle, he managed to see his own profile reflected in the fly-blown glass over the mantel-piece. There was no question whatever about the likeness. Even its owner could see it.

He dropped back into his chair, the tea completely forgotten. This was a most extraordinary thing. Here was he, the living image of the dead monk with whom he felt such a profound sympathy and whose house he had got! What did it all mean? He rose, pulled on his leather coat, went and fetched the car from the shed that housed it, and sped down the long mile to Monks Farm.

There was no one there when he arrived, Mr Pinker having called his men off to give first aid to a cowshed that threatened to fall down upon its occupants. The first faint dusk was gathering as Hugh made his way round the buildings, and going well out into the rough field, stood still and considered them.

He was gazing at the west front, with its high gable that roofed the small chapel, its statueless niche showing like an empty eye-socket in the pale reflection from the western sky. It was planned that the niche should come out to make way for a window, but this had not yet been done. He could see the small gratings up under the eaves that marked each monk's cell. Through the high windows of the rooms on either side of the door he could see the skeleton outline of ladders and planks such as decorators use. He did not desire to go in there, among all the impedimenta of the modern builder, so he turned left, and using his duplicate key, let himself into what had once been the large chapel of the priory.

Last time he had seen it, the west end had all been boarded up, and he took it for granted that the wall had at some time fallen out and been subjected to this rough repair. The unpaved floor, too, of poultry-droppings trodden as hard as cement, he had also taken for granted. But a great change met his eyes as he entered.

The rough boarding at the west end had been taken down, and revealed the skeleton of a stone-mullioned rose-window of lovely proportions, with fragments of stained glass still clinging here and there in the highest angles. The dirt floor had been dug out, and revealed patterned tiles. In a corner under the window, carefully laid on an old sack, was a pile of bits of broken, multi-coloured glass, that had evidently been picked out of the dirt of the floor as it was shovelled away. Mr Pinker had truly said that he knew how to deal with old buildings.

Hugh was delighted. He would have a fascinating time piecing the bits together like a jigsaw puzzle and having them restored to their place in the tracery.

Standing beneath the west window, through which the last of the light struck upwards from the sunset, he was able to see the roof, which he had not been able to do at his previous visits, with the west window still boarded up. He saw that the roof was steep-pitched, and very lofty for the size of the building, and that it was divided into five bays by buttress pillars. In each bay, as the last light struck upwards from the western horizon, he could just discern the dim lines of a vast winged figure, evidently an angel.

The east end, contrary to the custom of churches, presented a blank wall instead of a window, and upon its great height Hugh could see the shadowy outlines of a painting. He walked slowly up the aisle, and as he advanced, the picture became clearer, and he saw that it represented a vast green tree bearing multi-coloured fruit. Ten of them, he counted, in the faded remains of crude primary colours, arranged in stiff triangles, three by three, with the odd one low down on the trunk at the bottom.

Immediately in the centre, as if it were a pot for the tree to grow in, was a square stone pedestal like a short pillar, waist-high. Hugh wondered what in the world this had been, for it was exactly where the altar ought to have stood, and supposed it was to carry some statue. On the stonework of the wall he could see clearly the marks where the altar had been fastened, and it evidently completely enclosed the stone pedestal.

Three steps led up from the nave of the chapel into the sanctuary, and there the tiling ended and mosaic began. He saw that the design on the mosaic represented the twelve signs of the Zodiac, with the seven planets within their circle, and the symbols of the four elements of earth, air, fire and water in the centre. It was an exact reproduction of a picture in one of Jelkes' books.

" This doesn't look to me a very Christian church," said Hugh to himself.

Then the solution of the curious stone pedestal, enclosed in the altar, suddenly dawned on him. He had been reading about exactly the same thing in another of Jelkes' books. One of the charges against the Knights Templars was that they had made cubical stone altars to the goat-god, Baphomet, and concealed them underneath orthodox wooden table-altars, made to open up like cupboard doors, so that the uninitiated suspected nothing.

Hugh was thrilled to the marrow. This chapel, outwardly Christian, was inwardly pagan. No wonder they bricked up Ambrosius !

It was fast becoming too dark to see any details of the shadowy building, and Hugh sat down on a builder's barrow that stood conveniently to hand and asked himself what it was all about. And as he sat, he felt a curious sensation. It seemed to him as if the chapel were the focus of all the forces of the universe and they all converged upon it. He sat listening, as it were, to the sensation, and it went on steadily, like the sound of a waterfall. The chapel grew darker and darker, but he felt as if he could have sat all night, just listening. Then the thought crossed his mind that it must be getting late, and he ought to return to the supper Mrs Pascoe was preparing for him, and instantly the sensation vanished and he was back to normal in the empty barn. He rose, groped his way round the buildings, switched on the car headlights with a sense of relief, and returned to the Green Man, where Mrs Pascoe stood over him to make sure he ate his supper, as he had neglected his tea.

Settling down over the fire after his meal with a cup of tea and a cigarette, a trick he had learnt from Jelkes, Hugh set to work to puzzle out the situation. Unquestionably, Monks Farm was more than filling the bill ; it had, in fact, got the upper hand completely. He had wanted the Old Gods of Greece, not mediæval monasticism kicking over the traces. Then there was Ambrosius, whom he had found to be such an absorbing topic, and who finally, when he got his portrait enlarged, turned out to be his own double. And then there was Mona Wilton, whom at first sight he had not found to be particularly prepossessing, but who was gradually becoming—he did not quite know what. A friend, unquestionably, but that was an odd relationship to have with a youngish woman.

Hugh was accustomed to women who took love-making as a matter of course, but Mona obviously did not want him to flirt with her, in fact, would have strongly objected to any attempt at so doing. He also suspected that even as a friend, she intended to keep him at arm's length, for which he respected her, for he knew what friendship under such circumstances might be expected to imply, and how was Mona to know that that was not his game ? In one way he liked the unacknowledged friendship, with its steady sense of fidelity and goodwill, better than any more explicit and open relationship, which might have proved embarrassing ; but on the other hand, the manhood in him, waking up for the first time since it had been knocked on the head and left for dead on his honeymoon, wanted to press on with the friendship, though it was very careful not to call it anything save friendship.

Ambrosius, Pan, and Mr Pinker receded together into the limbo of things forgotten as Hugh studied the problem of Mona Wilton, for it slowly dawned on him that he was getting awfully fond of her. Not in love with her, as he had been with his wife, who had been a very beautiful and very sensual woman, but just fond of her, he couldn't describe it in any other way, even to himself. Mona Wilton was very far from being a sensual woman. She treated him like a brother man, and nothing more. Hugh was so used to that deep, inner, spiritual loneliness of the soul which lies so heavily upon those who live in an unsympathetic environment, that he had accepted it as the natural lot of man, never having known anything else. The lines he had read as a schoolboy stuck in his head when all the Imagists were forgotten—

> " *Yes, in the sea of life enisled,*
> *With echoing straits between us thrown,*
> *Dotting the shoreless, watery wild,*
> *We million mortals live alone.*"

These seemed to him, even when he read them first, to enshrine an ineluctable truth, and life had confirmed it. As much contact as he had ever had with anybody he had had with Trevor Wilmott—because Trevor knew just how to handle him. Naturally Trevor would keep in touch with the milch-cow! And then, when the revelation of the inquest had torn from him the last shreds of any human contact, had come the meeting with old Jelkes, and the instant, unreasoning upspringing of affection between them. And the odd thing was that Jelkes wanted nothing from him, but on the contrary considered himself as the bestower of benefits—and so he was. Even Hugh's offer of a telephone had met with a poor reception. Hugh was accustomed to hear the offer of anything, from a cocktail to a car, greeted with riotous applause. He had gradually acquired the state of mind when he could not conceive of any way of pleasing anybody save by giving them something far handsomer than they had any right to expect. He had speedily discovered, however, that if he applied this method to Jelkes and Mona, Mona would be embarrassed and Jelkes would be rude.

Wanting desperately to make friends with Mona, he did not know how to approach her. His one attempt at a gift, the green coat, was religiously treated as a loan— " Oh dear, I've marked your coat——! " said Mona when she found some engine-oil on the hem—and carefully folded and left in the car after each run. He knew that Mona was tacitly saying, ' Not for sale ' ; he knew that her code was entirely different to the one to which he was accustomed, whereunder, having given a coat, he was surely entitled to put his arm round it. Mona would simply throw the coat back at him if he did that. Hugh felt more acutely than ever that the only thing he had to offer anybody was his money, and if they did not want that—well, poor lad, what had he to give them ?

Hugh went to bed very depressed ; lay on his back and tried to dream of Greece, but only succeeded in dreaming of his mother, who seemed to be angry with him. It is a curious, and melancholy, fact that uninteresting people have the same capacity for suffering as attractive ones.

# CHAPTER XVII

MR PINKER, under the stimulus of Hugh's constant presence, bestirred himself in a way he might not have done if left to his own devices, and the smaller house was fast approaching habitability. Hugh dropped Mrs Macintosh a line requesting her presence, and that lady duly turned up in the local taxi, dressed in impeccable housekeeper's black, as was her invariable custom. She had entirely recovered her poise, and expressed neither approval nor disapproval when Hugh introduced her to the farm, but merely acquiesced. She measured and took notes as bidden, and finally, equally professionally, took her seat in Hugh's unhandy racing car and permitted him to run her down to the station. He lacked the courage to invite her to lunch at the Green Man in the face of her unyielding professionalism.

As they waited on the platform for the train, she said to him : " How much longer do you think you will want me, Mr Paston ? "

" I was wondering whether you would care to take charge at the farm, Mrs Macintosh ? "

" No," said Mrs Macintosh emphatically, "I would not."

" Why ever not ? " demanded Hugh, startled, and rather annoyed, by her emphasis.

" I don't like the feel of it. I could never settle there."

" What's wrong with it ? "

" It feels sinister to me. Sinister and wicked. I don't know how you can stand it. I wouldn't live there for anything you could offer me."

Hugh, who had not counted on Highland psychism

backed by Highland Calvinism, was nonplussed.  His plans were going astray.  How was he going to get Mona Wilton to come to the farm unless Mrs Macintosh were there to play propriety and look after her while she was still convalescent ?

" I think I ought to tell you, Mr Paston, that Lady Paston came to the bookshop to enquire after you, and Mr Jelkes was very short with her.  She is very anxious about you, and I do not think that Mr Jelkes' attitude allayed her anxiety."

Hugh groaned.

" Does she know about the farm ? "

" She knows nothing.  Mr Jelkes refused to tell her a thing, and was, if you will pardon my saying so, very rude to her."

" What did she say to your being there ? "

" She did not know of my presence, nor Miss Wilton's. I thought it wiser that she should not.  Miss Wilton and I sat in the kitchenette with the light out while she was there."

" Why ever did you do that ? "

" I thought the position of Miss Wilton might be misunderstood, and involve you in unpleasantness."

" I don't see why the dickens it should be."

" Well, it will be, to a certainty, Mr Paston."

" Oh, well, no good worrying about that.  Here is your train."

" Thank you very much, Mr Paston.  And if it is convenient to you, I would like to get off at the end of the week.  I have the offer of another post, and I want to pay a visit to some friends in Scotland before accepting it.  I do not think Miss Wilton needs me any longer."

" Yes, certainly, Mrs Macintosh.  Get off by all means."

Hugh put her into the train with a sigh of relief.  She was a good woman.  She was a kind woman.  She was trustworthy.  She was efficient.  He liked and respected her. He classed her with his old nurse as one of the best women he had ever known. And yet he heaved a sigh of relief as he put her into the train. He wondered what would have been the upshot if she had accepted his offer to housekeep at the farm. And then it suddenly occurred to him to wonder why he had made such an offer to such an utterly unsuitable person. One could not associate Mrs Macintosh with attendance at a rite of Pan. If she came at all, she would bring her knitting. She represented to him duty and the fear of God. She was awfully like his old nurse, who had really stood to him in the place of the mother who was always out. He supposed psychologists would call his offer the fruit of a mother-fixation. The presence of Mrs Macintosh at the farm would have been a sop to what was left of his conscience—and effectually prevented Pan from appearing even if invoked. His conscious mind might desire her as a housekeeper, but his subconscious wanted her as fire-insurance.

He was greatly cheered by the news that she would be leaving the bookshop at the end of the week. He had a feeling that the estrangements would clear up when she went. She was a prayerful woman, and he fancied that she did not do the atmosphere any good. He wondered how she had got on with Jelkes. There had been a veiled tone of disapproval in her voice, and she had never referred to Miss Wilton, save to answer his enquiry primly and briefly.

In response to his instructions, sufficient mass-production furniture arrived in the course of the week to make the small house habitable for three people. There were also cretonnes covered with rosebuds.

Knowing that Mrs Macintosh meant to go North, and that she had a long journey before her, for he believed she came from Ross-shire, or thereabouts, he thought he would be quite safe in putting in an appearance at the bookshop round about lunch-time on Saturday, and seeing if he could cadge a week-end out of the old bookseller. So with Mrs Pascoe's help he got a few things into a suit-case, for it was a terrible effort for Hugh to pack, and set off for London ; to be delayed, however, by a screaming figure rushing across the common waving its arms and crying : " You've forgotten your 'air-oil, sir ! " It was Hugh's one social asset to awaken maternal feelings in the souls of the motherly.

Arrived at the bookshop, he found that Jelkes, who interpreted the Shop Hours Act in a liberal spirit, had already bolted the door against customers, and knocked in vain, Jelkes concluding that someone wanted some Sunday reading, and not being of an obliging disposition, declined to let him have it. Hugh was seriously considering smashing a pane of glass in order to get in, when he heard a window overhead being raised, and looking up, saw Mrs Macintosh's head coming out. She smiled her non-committal smile, as if trying to make it appear orthodox for a person in Hugh's position to be applying his toe to the door while his housekeeper surveyed him from a point of vantage. She withdrew her head, and in a moment he heard her on the stair.

But it was not Jelkes' chicken-ladder she was descending, but the stair of the maisonette, which led down outside the shop, and Hugh turned in surprise to find the door behind him opening instead of the one at which he stood.

" Might I have a word with you, Mr Paston ? " said Mrs Macintosh.

Hugh acquiesced, wondering what in the world the word might be. Mrs Macintosh led the way up the maisonette stairs by which she had just descended, and then was nonplussed. She could not take him into her bedroom to talk to him, for that would not have been proper, though what harm either Mrs Macintosh's reputation or her person were likely to suffer at his hands was unimaginable. So they stood up solemnly on the dusty landing while she prepared to say her say, Mrs Macintosh bolt upright and Hugh draped over the nearest piece of furniture, as was his invariable custom.

" I wish to apologise to you, Mr Paston," she said.

" Good Lord, there's nothing I know of for you to apologise for."

" I wish to apologise for the way I spoke of your new house.  And I hope, I hope very much, that I have not put you to inconvenience if you were counting on me to look after it for you, but I couldn't—I really couldn't go there, Mr Paston.  You know, we have second sight in our family, and I am certain I should see things."

" Did you see anything there ? "

Mrs Macintosh flinched.  She would not tell a lie, and she did not want to tell the truth.  Such people are at a great disadvantage.

" I did not exactly see anything in the house," she said hesitating.

" Did you see anything outside ? "

" No, nor there either."

" Well then, what did you see ? "  Hugh was too eager in his quest to heed her discomfort.

She hesitated, then came to the point.

" It was your face I saw, Mr Paston."

" My face ?  What do you mean ? "

" Your face changed completely as you went into the old part of the house."  She looked at him sharply. " Did you know that ? "

The tables were turned on Hugh, and he too had either to lie or give information he had no mind to.  For as he had crossed the threshold he had thought of Ambrosius, and for a brief second the curious sensation had come to him that he sometimes got when he thought of the renegade monk.

" I think it must have been this that Miss Wilton spoke of when she was light-headed one night," continued Mrs Macintosh.  " I could not think at the time why it had frightened her so badly, but I understood as soon as I saw it. It is very alarming, Mr Paston, I don't think you quite realise how you look when you do that."

" But look here, Mrs Macintosh, you've been with us over two years, and I've never done anything desperate that I know of, why are you suddenly getting scared of me now ? "

" I am not scared of you, Mr Paston." Mrs Macintosh bridled indignantly at this aspersion. " But when you change before my very eyes into somebody else—I think you will admit that is enough to alarm anybody."

" Did I change into someone very alarming ? "

" Not exactly—. Well, Mr Paston, I'll tell you how it impressed me : I went to a circle once, very much against my better judgment, and the medium went just like that."

" Oh, so you think I'm mediumistic, do you ? "

" Well, really, I don't know what to say. It was gone in a minute. I hardly had time to look at it. But it was very marked while it lasted. You were certainly somebody else for a moment."

" You think that was what scared Miss Wilton ? "

" Yes, I'm certain it was. You seemed to get into her dreams when her temperature was up, and she called out in her sleep, not once but several times, ' Don't turn into Ambrosius again—— ! ' She was badly frightened, Mr Paston ; and I don't mind telling you, so was I when I saw you do it."

Hugh was thankful he was draped over the furniture, for he was certain he would have staggered if he had been standing without support. But before he could reply, even had he been able to, a battery of knocks sounded on the shop door.

" Excuse me," said Mrs Macintosh, " I expect that is the man for my luggage," and she went down the narrow, dusty stairs. Hugh heard her open the door at the bottom, and an exclamation of surprise followed.

" Mrs Macintosh, *you* here ? " he heard in the voice of his eldest sister.

" Yes, Lady Whitney," came the noncommittal tones of the Scotswoman.

" I want to see my brother.   His car is outside, so it is no use saying he isn't here."

Hugh thought that the best thing to do was to bow to the inevitable.   He did not want Alice to have a stand-up row with old Jelkes.   Knowing them both, he thought they would come to blows.

He came down the stairs.

" Hullo, Alice ? " he said.

" So there you are, Hugh ?   We have been looking for you everywhere.   Whatever is the meaning of all this nonsense ? "

" Well, I thought I would like to get away from everything and be quiet for a bit."

" You might have let us know where you were.   It has been most inconvenient.   Everybody asking, and no letters answered, and there have been such a lot.   Where were you, all this time ? "

" Never mind where.   I'd sooner not tell you.   Just a place of retreat that I want to keep quiet."

" By yourself ? "

" Yes, of course."

" There's no of course about it, that I know of. Hugh, who's this Miss Wilton ? "

" She's an artist I've been employing to do the decorations for my new house."

" So you've got a new house already, then ? "

" Yes."

" Where ? "

" That's not your business."

" What has come over you ?   I've never known you like this before.   What's all this secrecy about ? "

" The secrecy is because I don't want to be bothered.

That's all there is to it."

" Do you expect me to believe that ? "

" No, I don't expect you to believe it.   And I don't
care whether you believe it either."

A tide of anger utterly unlike anything he had ever
known before, had been rising in Hugh while they were
wrangling, and suddenly it brimmed over in a flood
of rage that held him speechless.   A curious heat and
burning went through him, and he found himself staring
down into the face of a strange woman whose flushed
angry cheeks gradually went dead white under her paint.
He pointed to the door and said one word :  " Go ! "
She went.

He walked up the stairs again, there did not seem to be
anything else to do, and at the top saw another strange
woman, and heard her calling to someone in a terrified
voice.   The place was unfamiliar, he did not know where
he was.   A  man came, and behind him yet another
woman, peering anxiously round his shoulder.   And he
knew that woman !

For the first time he saw in the flesh the face he had
so often seen in his dreams.   The succuba that had
haunted his sleep for years.   Now he saw her.   And he
could not take his eyes off her, nor could she take hers
off him.

He knew the risk ;  and yet he felt that nothing mattered
compared to that one thing, and that at all costs he must
grasp it lest it slipped out of his reach for ever.   He
stepped forward, put the man aside, and gripped the
woman by the arm, drawing her towards him.   He
looked down into her eyes.   Greenish eyes, as one would
expect in a succuba ;  but he realised instantly that this
was no evil demon sent to lead men's souls astray.   The
eyes were steady and sincere, and looked straight back
into his.   The eyes of a woman, not a fiend.

And he realised with a dreadful hopelessness his
isolation ;  the bondage of his vows ;  his powerlessness

to escape from the life to which he had been given before he knew life's meaning.  He was cut off from all this.  He must let go of this woman or he would ruin himself.  And then something fierce and terrible rose up in him and said that he might ruin himself, but he would not let go of her.

A sound behind him made him turn round, and there stood the woman he had already driven off, and with her another and older woman who looked like her mother.  They spoke to him, but their dialect was incomprehensible save for a word here and there.  His wits had returned to him, however, and with them, his dignity.  He put the succuba behind him, though he still kept tight hold of her, and saluted them gravely, as became a churchman of his standing.  He could see that they were non-plussed.  The old man then took a hand and talked with them animatedly in their dialect, of which Hugh understood enough to gather that some learned person was to be summoned forthwith.  They departed, plainly very angry and upset, and the old man took him by the shoulders and said :

" Hugh, you damn fool, you stop this nonsense or I'll punch your head ! "

A sudden giddiness passed over him.  He felt himself sway, and if someone had not caught him, would have fallen.  Then he recovered himself, and found Jelkes and Mrs Macintosh confronting him with consternation written all over their faces.

" Hullo ? " he said, feeling very foolish.  " Have I been having one of my seizures ?  I suppose this is what you have been complaining of ? " turning to Mrs Macintosh.

" Yes, Mr Paston, that is exactly it," was the reply.  " And if you would let go of Miss Wilton, I think she'd be relieved."

Hugh turned round startled, to find Mona behind him.

" What's it all about ? " he demanded.

" That's what we'd like to know," said Jelkes, grimly.
" And that's what someone else means to know, too,
in the near future, if I'm not very much mistaken."

He led the way down into the shop, and they all
followed. Hugh felt he had never been so glad to see
anything in his life as he was to see the warmth and
cosiness of the little back parlour. It seemed to him as
if he had just come out of a long and vivid nightmare of
cold, and stone walls, and loneliness, and frustration.

" How are you feeling, Hugh ? " said the old bookseller, turning to him abruptly.

" All right. A bit shaken. What happened ? "

" Goodness only knows what happened. A change
of consciousness of some sort. But they've gone to
fetch the doctor, and if you don't watch your step, they'll
get you certified. For the love of God, Hugh, keep
your hair on when the doctor comes."

" If it is Dr Johnson, I shouldn't let him in, if I were
you, Mr Jelkes. He's a thoroughly unscrupulous man,"
said Mrs Macintosh.

" Right," said Jelkes, " I'll give him a kick in the
pants."

" I don't know about that," said Hugh, " I could do
with a bit of doctoring. I feel as sick as a cat."

" He couldn't do anything for you, laddie. I can do
as much for you as anyone."

" Will you ? " said Mona abruptly.

" Yes, I'll have to. They'll certify him if I don't."

" So that's the game, is it ? " said Hugh. " That's a
new one. They've tried a good many things, but they've
never tried that before. I say Jelkes, tell me frankly,
as a pal, any likelihood of their being able to do it ? "

" Well, laddie, frankly, there is, if they give their
minds to it. Not that you need certifying, or anything
like it, but you've got bones that are worth picking,
Hugh, and that's what has always been your trouble."

" What did I do, T. J. ? "

" Went off in a day-dream, laddie."

" Thinking I was Ambrosius ? "

" That's about it."

" By Jove, T. J., I *was* Ambrosius too, for the moment. It was a weird experience."

" Don't you do it too often, for if the wind changes, you may stick, as my mother used to tell me when I pulled faces."

They all laughed, a trifle feebly, for they were all thoroughly shaken.

A resounding bang at the door startled them. Jelkes girt his dressing-gown about him with a determined air, and went striding off through the bookshop, murder in his eye. He returned in a moment, crestfallen.

" It's the man for your box," he said to Mrs Macintosh, and together they departed upstairs, leaving Hugh alone with Mona.

He sat down on the sofa, facing her.

" I say, Mona," he said. " Will you tell me the truth, as a friend, for I'm in the dickens of a hole if I can't get things in hand. I know that certification game. I've seen it played before. Tell me frankly, was what happened just now the same as what happened in the museum ? "

" Yes."

" That was what scared you into your illness, wasn't it ? "

" Yes, I'm afraid it was."

" I say, I'm frightfully sorry. I hope I haven't upset you again. I'm frightfully sorry, Mona."

" No, I'm all right this time because I know what it is, or at least I think I do. Things are all right when you understand them, aren't they ? "

" I hope so. I'd be truly thankful to understand this. Tell me, Mona, tell me all you can."

" I'd sooner Uncle Jelkes told you. Wait till he comes back from seeing Mrs Macintosh off."

" By Jove, is she going ? I must say good-bye to her, she's a dashed decent sort."

He rose from the sofa, but a sudden sound of altercation in the front shop made Mona catch his hand and pull him back. Uncle Jelkes was evidently denying admission to someone who was demanding it with authority. Jelkes settled the argument by telling him to go to hell and slamming the door with such force that all the books in the window fell down. After that there was silence, save for distant bumpings which announced that the man had made junction with Mrs Macintosh's box.

" I say," said Hugh, " I've been desperately busy at the farm, I've got it pretty nearly straight, one end of it, anyway. Let's all pack up and go down there, shall we ? and have a good holiday, you and I and Jelkes. It'll be no end of a lark. We can just camp out there and picnic. Mrs Pascoe, that's my landlady, has got some skivvy that she's been trying to foist on me which she swears is a paragon. Say you will, Mona, and we'll shunt the whole party and leave no trail. We'll be dashed hard to trace if we get off promptly. They haven't sold the big bus yet. She's sitting at the garage. I had her bill the other day. Her in'ards were out when they had the auction, that's why she's been spared. I'll run this little brute back, God knows why I ever try to drive her on the road, and I'll get the other. Say you will, Mona ? It will be no end of a lark."

Mona looked at him. It might be a lark for him, but it was a job of mental nursing for her.

" I will if Uncle will," she said.

At that moment Jelkes reappeared.

" She got off all right," he said. " Asked me to say good-bye to you for her. She'd cut it rather fine."

" Sorry to have missed her," said Hugh. " She was a dashed good sort, but a trifle oppressive. I don't believe she'd have fitted in with Pan, do you, Uncle

Jelkes ? "

"Who said I was your uncle ? " demanded Jelkes, cocking a be-whiskered eyebrow at him.

"I say you're my uncle. If you're Mona's uncle, you've got to be my uncle too. Why should girls always have the best of everything ? "

"All right, I don't mind," said Jelkes, "I can stand worse than that." He looked at Hugh with affection. "I think you could do with an uncle, laddie, even if you don't happen to want to pop anything at the moment."

"Hugh's got a suggestion to make, Uncle Jelkes," said Mona.

Up went Jelkes' eyebrows again at her use of the Christian name.

"I was suggesting," said Hugh, "that we all go down to the farm for, say a fortnight, and have a jolly good holiday, and throw all these blighters off our trail. I've got another car at the garage, a great brute of a bus, and I can load you and Mona and all you both possess into it, chuck it in loose, no need to pack—that's the advantage of a car—and run down to the farm here and now. They'll never trail us if we get off promptly."

Jelkes looked at Mona.

"That's what we're going to do, Uncle Jelkes," said she quietly. "It's the only thing to do. We shall have all sorts of trouble if Hugh stops here."

"Yes," said Jelkes, "I know we shall. But, Lord, I wish it wasn't the farm ! "

"It's got to be the farm, Uncle Jelkes. There's nothing to do but grip the nettle. You know that as well as I do."

"Magnificent," cried Hugh, leaping to his feet. "You two sling a few things together, and I'll go and get the car," and he vanished before they had time to change their minds.

Mona Wilton, looking out of the window as she packed, thought that someone had built a row of cottages in the street. She came down with her arms full of her belongings to find Hugh eyeing a superb Rolls-Royce with distaste.

"Here she is," he said. "Isn't she a brute? My Lord, I'm thankful I'm not a chauffeur. Fancy having to take this through traffic! She's a procession in herself. However, she's all right on the open road, especially on long runs. I must say I like her then. Not as fast as my little bus, but sweeter."

Jelkes appeared with a rush basket under his arm.

"As it's for a fortnight," he said, "I suppose I'd better bring a clean collar."

"And a toothbrush," said Mona firmly.

"Toothbrush be hanged. I just take 'em out and rinse 'em under the tap."

# CHAPTER XVIII

HUGH slammed the huge car through the traffic, cursing her at every bend. Mona and Jelkes, sitting at the back among their belongings, were immensely amused. They had never seen Hugh in this mood before. He had always seemed to be permanently apologetic. But when it came to cars he knew what he was about and felt sure of himself. It amused Mona in particular to hear Hugh grumbling at the luxury car as she grumbled at the second-hand cycle she had bought in the hope of reducing expenses, and that had let her down so badly. Most people think, when they get into a Rolls of their own, that they are free to drive straight to heaven. Mona herself would have lived for years in the lap of luxury on the price of that Rolls, and here was Hugh grousing at it and knocking it about ! Life looks very different when seen from different angles.

" I am afraid I'll have to put you in the dark," said Hugh, as they reached the open road and left street lamps behind. The lights inside the car went off, and the great headlights went on ; the car settled down to her beautiful gait, and peace appeared to be restored in the driving-seat.

The rhythm broke, however, when they turned off the main road, and the cursings began again as the big car had to be coaxed down narrow lanes, Hugh blackguarding her for an unhandy brute to an accompaniment of swishings and rendings as the untrimmed hedge-plants slashed at her panels. However, she got to the end of her troubles in due course, and slid silent as a ghost across the common and down the lane to the farm. Hugh pulled up beside the dark and silent buildings, switched on the inside light, and turned in the driving-seat to speak to his companions.

There, in his corner, sat Jelkes, looking like an old cock gone broody, with Mona asleep on his shoulder, worn out by all the alarums and excursions.

The sight affected Hugh in an indescribable manner. It seemed to him that the deepest springs in his nature would be fed if a woman did that to him. Mona woke up and raised her head and their eyes met. Hugh turned away hastily lest his face should say too much, and so lose him her friendship.

" Well, we get out here," he said, suiting the action to the word. He opened the car door and held out his hand to help Mona to alight. She took it, and put her foot on the running-board ; but the foot, numb from sleeping in a cramped position, gave way under her as she put her weight on it, she fell forward, and Hugh caught her. She laughed, but for a brief moment Hugh had his wish.

" Come on," said Hugh, taking a key out of the guttering over the door, which is the time-honoured place to keep a key in the country. " I know it's like burgling a tomb at the moment, but we'll soon have it more cheerful. You aren't scared of Ambrosius, are you, Mona ? He's a great pal of mine. I'll introduce you presently."

They entered, the air striking cold and dank and smelling of fresh plaster, which is not a pleasant smell. Hugh, who had no matches, struck a light on his pocket lighter, and held up the dim blue flame to illuminate their surroundings. They were not too bad. The mass-production furniture was inoffensive, and its limed oak went well enough with the old farm-house kitchen. Hugh lit a battered hurricane lamp hanging from a beam, a lamp which bore in clumsy lettering the words, ' J. Pinker and Sons ', in case the light-fingered should be tempted, and the place began to look more like a human habitation and less like the family vault.

" Now for a fire," said Hugh.

" Got any fuel ? " said the practical Jelkes.

" Haven't we just ?  I should say we just about had !
I'd thought of giving a Guy Fawkes party to the whole
district."

Jelkes followed him through a door that led into a
scullery, and thence into what had been the farm-yard,
and there, in the centre, they saw dimly in the moonlight
an enormous pile.  They each gathered up an armful,
returned to the living-room, and deposited their loads
in the great empty fire-place, for Mr Pinker's dawgs had
not yet come to occupy it.  Hugh went out to the car
and returned with a grease-gun and shot black oil all
over the pile.  He touched a match to it, and it went up
like a volcano.

" Now then, T. J., I'll leave you to stoke.  Get the
place really warm and blow the expense.  I'm going to
the village."

Arrived at the village, he was faced by the delicate task
of breaking it to Mrs Pascoe, who had made a thorough
pet of him, that he was about to desert her.  However,
he reckoned he could soften the blow by confiding in her
and asking her advice.  Things were not made any
easier, however, by the fact that she apparently had company in her sanctum behind the bar, for someone was
singing a languorous and long-drawn-out ditty to the
accompaniment of an accordion in there.  However,
there was nothing for it, and Hugh overcame his shyness
and knocked on the door.  The accordion died away
with a wail like a despairing tom-cat, the door opened,
and a man stood there, obviously a seaman of the roughest
type.

" Hullo ? " said Hugh, too taken aback to think of
anything else.

" Hullo yerself," said the stranger, " and what might
you be wantin' ? "

" I wanted a word with Mrs Pascoe," said Hugh.

" She's gone across to the shop.  Back in a minute.

Anything I can get yer ? "

" No, thanks very much," said Hugh. " I'll wait till she comes back, if I may."

" Come inside and sit down," said the man.

Now he, like old Jelkes, had been put off at first sight by Hugh's voice and bearing, which were those of his caste, but he in his turn had quickly sensed the simple humanity that underlay the veneer that his environment had plastered on to Hugh, and metaphorically speaking, clasped hands with the man underneath. He ushered him into the lamp-lit, smoke-clouded, low-ceilinged snuggery.

" 'Ave one with me ? " he said, taking up a stone jug that stood on the table amid the remains of a meal.

" I don't mind if I do," said Hugh, " I've had no lunch."

That was the way straight to the heart of the blue-jerseyed individualist confronting him. Had Hugh accepted fulsomely it would have been only one degree better than declining ; but to admit that he was glad of the beer—well, that was man to man.

" 'Ave a bite of supper ? " said the seaman.

" No, I won't do that," said Hugh. " I've got some people waiting for me, and I want to get some supper for them too ; that's what I want to see Mrs Pascoe about."

" She'll be back in two tweaks, or if she isn't, I'll fetch 'er. Where are your folk, Mister ? "

" Up at Monks Farm."

" Cor, so you're Mr Paston ? Ma wasn't expecting you back till Monday."

" I wasn't expecting myself back either, but here I am, and two people with me, one of them just been ill. And there's the place up there, all in darkness and nothing in it, and I want to get Mrs Pascoe to lend me a hand."

" We'll lend yer a 'and all right, Mister. What'll yer want ? "

" I haven't a notion.  That's what I want to ask your mother, she'll know."

" You bet she will," said Mr Pascoe junior, winking, " and I'll get it up from the cellar ! "

A bumping in the passage announced the return of Mrs Pascoe, her arms full of parcels, having evidently been to call on Mr Huggins.  Hugh explained his predicament.  He had an old gentleman and a young lady, his niece, Hugh added hastily, up at the farm, and the young lady was only just out of bed, having been ill.

Mrs Pascoe was horrified, and not without reason. The poor young lady !  She'd get her death.  What things men were !  She flew round like a hen in a corn-bin.  Hugh was immensely amused to see what was her notion of the primary necessities of life.  A case of bottled beer, two bottles of port and a bottle of whisky made their way into the car almost of their own volition. Then at his suggestion, she got in too.  Without waiting for any suggestion her nautical offspring added himself to the party, and they set off in the Rolls-Royce for Mr Huggins.

The amazement of that gentleman when he saw them beggars description.  A heavy swell developed itself in his waistcoat, and it surged about like a captive balloon. They formed a human chain, with Mr Huggins and Mrs Pascoe at the business end and himself and Bill as mindless links in outer darkness beside the car, and it seemed as if the entire contents of the shop were being passed out to them.  In fact, it was only Bill's scientific stowage that enabled the Rolls to hold the stuff.  Hugh expected momentarily to see the kittens coming out from hand to hand.  Finally Mrs Pascoe came out and climbed in among the dunnage with a ham in her arms.  Bill got in beside Hugh, and off they went.  Hugh thought of the kind of cargoes that the Rolls was accustomed to carry, and wondered, if cars have souls, how it felt.  Anyway, it was no stranger to alcohol.  It was a Mad Hatter's Tea-party, and he thought he might consider himself lucky if nobody stuffed him in the tea-pot.

Firelight shone out of the farm windows so brightly that Hugh wondered whether it had caught alight. But no, Jelkes had merely done as instructed, and stoked efficiently. A furnace roared up the chimney, throwing more light than the lamp.

Introductions were effected, and everybody seemed to know everybody else at once. Bill and Hugh winked at each other, and got out the bottled beer ; but Mrs Pascoe suddenly spotted them and turned on them both impartially. Hugh, however, skilfully saved the situation by suggesting that Miss Wilton needed a small port ; this roused Mrs Pascoe's professional instincts, they had one all round, and life took on a more normal hue. Jelkes and Bill went upstairs to get the beds put together, and Mrs Pascoe disappeared into the kitchen.

Mona, her toes on the hearth, looked much more like herself than she had done since things began to go wrong with her and her papers stopped payment. It was impossible to think shudderingly of Hugh after one had seen him caught out over the bottled beer. He drew a chair up to the hearth beside her, and dropped into it.

" I don't know that I can do anything more useful," he said, " than entertain you. How are you feeling these days ? "

She told him.

" It's going to be a great lark here," he said. " I'm having the time of my life." He had completely forgotten his hours of black depression, when his only friend was Ambrosius. " I say, Mona, you haven't got to hurry back, have you ? "

" I haven't got to, but I expect Uncle Jelkes will have to."

Hugh fell silent. Dare he risk it ? Supposing she resented the suggestion, would it finish the friendship ?

" You know Mrs Macintosh has let me down ? " he

said at length.

"Yes, so she told us. I think she was right, you know. It wouldn't have worked. You want to break right away from everything connected with your old life."

"Yes, that's my instinct. I don't know why I swerved from it. You see, I thought it would be so awfully handy if you could put up at the farm while you were working on it, and I didn't suppose I could get you to unless I could offer you Mrs Macintosh, or someone like her. Look here, supposing I get you this prize skivvy of Mrs Pascoe's, will you stop on after Uncle Jelkes goes home ? It would save no end of bother and fuss if you would."

Mona thought for a minute. "I don't see why I shouldn't," she said at length. Her Bohemian soul cared nothing for the unconventionality of the situation. There had been a momentary flutter of fear at the thought of coping with Ambrosius single-handed after Jelkes had left, but she steeled her heart. After all, what prospects had she beyond her job with Hugh ? She must try and separate the employer from the human being in her mind. But that, unfortunately, had been her difficulty all along, for nothing would induce Hugh to separate the human being from the employée. Mona put the problem aside. She was too tired to cope with it at the moment. This was her first outing since her illness, and it had been a pretty strenuous one.

Hugh, a thoroughly impractical person, achieved organisation when left to his own devices by a curious kind of unconscious cunning. He picked some person he liked, whom he felt would have the requisite know-ledge, and threw himself on their mercy ; and as Hugh had the same kind of flair for character as is reputed to be possessed by dogs and little children, his method suc-ceeded. His female relations, all of whom were managing, designing women, were exasperated to fury by this

manœuvre of Hugh's ; Cassandra-like, they prognosti-
cated woe the moment Hugh was off his lead ; but
instead he always turned up smiling, propped up by some
kind-hearted, competent person, who took a delight in
being a mother or brother to him as the case might be.
It was enough to annoy any female relation.

Mrs Pascoe had taken Hugh so thoroughly in tow that
he hardly realised he was in motion. A domestic organisation grew from the ground, as it were, almost without
his knowledge. She got him and his visitors fed, and
their beds aired, and metaphorically, (in fact, literally, in
the case of Mona) tucked them into them without his
quite realising what was happening. Then she and her
offspring thoughtfully took the tarpaulin off Mr Pinker's
circular saw and tucked the Rolls-Royce up in it, and
trudged back the long mile to the village, and so to bed.

Mona was the first to awake next morning, Hugh and
Mr Jelkes being constitutionally late risers. She looked
out of her window and saw the first young green on the
birches, and the first sunlight over the firs, and as soon
as might be she was out of doors. Living in London so
long, she had hardly realised what the spring and the
morning could mean to her. Some polyanthuses, velvet-
brown and wine-purple, had joined the daffodils in the
coarse grass at the foot of the old wall, and Mona, made
sensitive by her illness, stood and looked at them. Dew
sparkled on every grey blade of the dry winter grass, the
heavy dew left behind by late frosts, and the little velvety
faces of the polyanthuses looked up through it un-
harmed. The sky was the pale blue of early spring and
early morning ; a little mare's tail of clouds to the south
showed the way of the wind, which came in soft breaths,
blowing away the chill of the dawn. Dark gorse with
yellow bloom dotted the unthrifty pasture, silver birches
rising among it made a fine lace of twigs against the sky,
shot through as the light caught them with a faint haze
of new green. The dark firs stood against the skyline

as they had stood the year through, unchanging. Against the winter grey of the pasture broad stretches of bracken lay tawny ; unfenced, the field stretched away and dropped into a wood with the fall of the ground. The sylvan Pan held his own here, and gave no inch to Ceres. It was a sight to break the heart of a landlord, but Mona gave God thanks for it.

A hand through her arm made her jump nearly out of her skin, and she turned round to see Hugh looking down on her from his ungainly height. He smiled, and gave her arm a squeeze. " Lovely, isn't it ? " he said.

" Very lovely," said Mona, and they stood together silently.

" Everyone talks about a garden round here, Mona, but there isn't going to be any garden. This is good enough for me."

" There ought to be some old-fashioned, cottagy flowers in the garth," said Mona.

" What's a garth ? " asked Hugh.

" The ground inside the cloisters, the present farmyard."

" So you'd like to make a garden, would you, Mona ? All right, you shall."

A clop-clop on the drive attracted their attention, and they saw Mr Pinker arriving in an old-fashioned gig with a most extraordinary load on board, which included Mrs Pascoe, Bill Pascoe, the foreman, a boy, a quantity of planks, and in Mrs Pascoe's motherly arms a steaming glue-pot. Bill was nursing a milk-can as if it were his first-born. The Green Man could go to hell with all its clientèle ; once more was exemplified the truth to human nature of the parable of the ninety and nine sheep safe in fold that weighed as naught against the one forlorn stray. Technically, Hugh Paston was not a ewe-lamb, but he was the next best thing—a male who would allow himself to be managed.

Jelkes, who had left his dressing-gown behind out of

politeness, ambled down in his Inverness cape and lent a touch of picturesqueness to the assemblage. Mona, whose neutral-tinted clothes seemed so drab in London, looked here as if she had risen from the grey winter pasture like Aphrodite from the foam of the sea, so perfectly did she match her surroundings.

They set the door of the living-room wide open and carried the table into the patch of sunshine that came streaming in. Mona picked some of the polyanthus and set them in a rough little earthenware jar she found on a shelf in the scullery, and placed them on the table among the gay cottage crockery, and a bee came bumbling in and got the honey from them. Hugh suddenly realised that there was a kind of happiness that had almost the quality of inebriation.

It was a great joy to them both to show Jelkes all there was to see of the interesting old buildings. Jelkes, for his part, was amused to observe that Mona was quite as possessive as Hugh in her attitude towards them.

Mona had not seen them since the general clearance of partitions and other impedimenta had taken place, and she was now able for the first time to appreciate the possibilities of the two beautiful big rooms with their fan-arching and fine fire-places. Ambrosius had evidently been a gentleman of taste who had done himself well—within the limits of ecclesiastical architectural conventions.

Jelkes looked at the chapel, but said no word : but it was obvious that, like the parrot that was a poor talker, he thought a lot.

Returned to the dwelling-house, they were confronted by Mrs Pascoe, who had rallied all her forces with a view to planting upon them the prize skivvy, whom she was determined they should have. It appeared that there were wheels within wheels in this matter, and it gradually transpired that Miss Pumfrey was in the habit of running her establishment with the help of girls from ' Homes '. Now the chief thing about a Home is that it is not a home in the usually accepted sense of the word. And girls from Homes bear very little resemblance to home-reared stock when they first issue forth into the world from their cloistral retreat. They resemble, in fact, the old-fashioned ideal of what a servant should be, and this was the kind that Miss Pumfrey liked to get hold of. In varying periods of time, however, these unhappy fledglings became full-fledged, realised how they were being imposed upon, and gave in their notice. Consequently they had to be replaced. Miss Pumfrey, therefore, ran her establishment with a steady succession of ignorant orphans, which the village took a malicious delight in educating in the ways of the world, for Miss Pumfrey was not popular.

The latest orphan, however, had stuck. She had been with Miss Pumfrey over a year, and in all this time she had never been out alone, but always in the company of either the elderly parlour-maid or Miss Pumfrey herself. It then happened, and it is difficult, on the surface, to see the connection between the two matters, that Mrs Pascoe applied for an extension of hours on the occasion of the Xmas Eve share-out of the slate-club ; the matter had come to Miss Pumfrey's ears ; Miss Pumfrey had spoken to one of the magistrates, who had been a friend of her father's, and the application was refused. Mrs Pascoe wanted to get Miss Pumfrey's perfect orphan another job.

Of course Mrs Pascoe did not put it as bluntly as all that, according to her, the girl was a deserving girl, being imposed upon, who wanted to better herself, but information leaked and percolated in the course of her loquaciousness. After she had withdrawn, the three of them looked at each other.

" If you take that girl, you've made an enemy for life of Miss Pumfrey," said Jelkes.

" Do you know," said Mona, " I don't think I've ever

met anyone I've disliked quite as much as Miss Pumfrey.
I'd love to snitch her skivvy."

"That's all right for you," said Jelkes, "but what
about Hugh ?  He's got to live in the village after you're
gone."

There was a sudden, blank silence, as if everybody
were taken completely aback, and Jelkes' eyebrows
slowly rose higher and higher.  Then everybody talked
at once.

Mona went to tell Mrs Pascoe they would have the
girl, and see what arrangements could be made for her
transference, to learn that arrangements had already been
made, and the girl was practically sitting on her box
waiting to be fetched.  Hugh began to sniff a rat, but he
was so amused at the spite-fight between Mrs Pascoe and
Miss Pumfrey that he declined to take sides with Jelkes
in discouraging the scheme, and backed up Mrs Pascoe
for all he was worth.

Finally it was arranged that he should run Mrs Pascoe
back to the village, drive the Rolls into a thick wood by
a track used by the village sewageer when he emptied
Miss Pumfrey's cess-pool, and wait there the coming of
the fugitive orphan.  Huge, enormously amused with
the whole affair, readily agreed to the tryst by the midden,
and drove off with Mrs Pascoe in the Rolls forthwith.

Left alone, Jelkes cocked a sandy eyebrow at his ewe-
lamb, and said :

"Well, Mona, what are you brewing ? "

"I had been going to tell you, Uncle, only I haven't
had the chance.  Mr Paston was talking to me just before
you came down, and he suggested that if I had this girl
with me, I could stop on here after you had gone back.
It would be far handier like that while I am getting the
place ship-shape."

Jelkes sat in thought for a few minutes.

"Well, Mona," he said at length.  "It's your
funeral."

" Are you against it, Uncle ? "

" I don't know what to say. It's a bit of a puzzle. I don't see what other alternative you've got. I suppose, providing you keep your head and handle things shrewdly, you'll be all right, but I can't say I'm happy about Ambrosius. You could have the hell of a mix-up with Ambrosius, whether he's Hugh, or spooks, or whatever it is, and the girl would be no protection to you. Look here, why don't you work up a job for Bill here ? He's been sounding me about it. It seems there's a lot of shipping laid up at the moment, and berths hard to come by. He'd be very useful as handy-man, gardener, and general roustabout. I'd be happy, at least, much happier, about you, if you had Bill around."

" You do amuse me, Uncle, proposing a regular cutthroat like Bill as protection from Hugh, who's the mildest of souls."

" Not so damn mild, Mona, don't you believe it. No man who goes in for the kind of games Hugh has gone in for—mountaineering, motor-racing, and risky cabaret —is altogether mild. And anyway, the milder Hugh is, the bigger handful Ambrosius will be."

" It strikes me that one would obtain an awfully nice result if Hugh and Ambrosius were melted and mixed and divided into two equal halves."

" That is exactly what wants doing, but how it is to be done is more than I know. We'll just sit tight for a fortnight and see how things pan out."

" Then you'll stop here for a fortnight, Uncle ? How are you going to manage it ? "

" I'll hop up to the shop twice a week. It's mainly a postal trade. I'll manage all right. It's shoal water we're in, Mona, more than you realise. I don't blame Mrs Macintosh for bolting. I'd bolt myself if I could."

" What are you scared of, Uncle ? "

" I'm scared of two things, child. Ambrosius is either a previous incarnation of Hugh's or a split personality.

For all practical purposes it doesn't matter which. Everything that's shut down in Hugh is in Ambrosius—unchecked. Hugh is pecking his way out of his shell, and as he comes out, Ambrosius is coming out too—with a rush, if I'm not very much mistaken ; and the trouble is going to be while Ambrosius is in a transition state, and it's you who are going to get the brunt of the trouble. If you don't handle Ambrosius just right, there'll be the devil to pay."

" If I don't——? What do you mean, Uncle ? "

" I ceased to count in this transaction some time ago, Mona. I spotted that early on, and that's what's been worrying me. Mrs Macintosh spotted it too, in fact it was she who put me wise to it.

" I thought as much," exclaimed Mona bitterly. " I felt certain Mrs Macintosh had been messing things up."

" Well, Mona, she knows Hugh pretty thoroughly, and she knows his kind of world pretty thoroughly. I've told you from the beginning that it doesn't do to take Hugh seriously in his present condition. As soon as he steadies, he'll go back to the life he's used to, you can make up your mind to that. As long as you do make up your mind to it, it will be all right, but what I've been afraid of all along was that you'd take Hugh seriously, and get hurt."

" I don't take Hugh seriously," said Mona. " He wouldn't amuse me. He's much too neutral. If it were Ambrosius, now, it would be a different matter."

" Mona, you're absolutely shameless. If I didn't know you were talking nonsense I should say you were an abandoned hussy."

" Yes, Hugh and Ambrosius, mixed in equal parts, would really be rather nice ; but I wouldn't take Hugh neat if he were the last man on earth. I know my own nature better than that. I am not surprised his wife played him up, I'm not, really. I'm awfully sorry for Hugh, and all that, but—well, being sorry for a man won't hold a woman that's got any guts in her."

"Well, my dear, may be you're right, but I lament your language."

Hugh, meanwhile, was waiting beside an ominous-looking mound, like a prehistoric pit-dwelling, out of which stuck a length of stove-pipe. Luckily for him, he had not long to wait, for that stove-pipe was not a pleasant neighbour. Hugh had just begun to speculate upon its analogue at Monks Farm, and the amenities of country life in general, including the opportunities for feuds in a circumscribed society, when he heard a crackling in the undergrowth, and there appeared Mrs Pascoe and a girl, staggering along with a tin trunk between them. Hugh wondered what might be the reason for all this secrecy. Surely the girl could walk out at any moment provided she did not mind abandoning the wages due to her. In fact, he had always understood that the thing to do in such circumstances was to get your wages and then walk out, together with anything you could lay your hands on. At least, that was Frida's idea of the modern domestic. Why, therefore, the secretive get-away?

But the moment they came alongside, he knew. He had only to take one look at the pair of vague brown eyes gazing up from that moon-like face to know the kind of Home that Miss Pumfrey, in despair, had got her latest servant from. He wondered what were the penalties for kidnapping idiot orphans, and his heart sank into his boots. It was a judgment on them for being so spiteful as to snitch Miss Pumfrey's skivvy; there might be something after all in the Christian ethic of returning good for evil—at any rate, it prevented one from saddling oneself with weak-minded servant-girls.

But it was too late to back out now. Mrs Pascoe hurled the trunk into the car, hurled the girl in after it, and then scrambled in herself. Hugh sighed, and drove back to the farm by a devious route, as instructed.

Leaving Mrs Pascoe and her protégée to dispose of
the tin trunk, he stalked into the living-room and
announced :

" Mona, she's loopy ! "

Mona leapt to her feet in horror.   " What, my new
skivvy ? "

" Serve you jolly well right, the pair of you," said
Jelkes.   A knocking at the door caused Hugh to stand
aside and open it, and there was Mrs Pascoe.

" Now it's all right, Mr Paston, sir, you've nothing to
trouble about.   I see'd by your face what you felt.   I
know she comes from the Silly Home, but you've nothing
to worry about.   Them sort make the best kind of servants provided you get 'em with just the right amount of
silliness.   There isn't a better servant to be had than a
silly girl who ain't too silly.   They do as they're bid, and
none of the others does."

" I see," said Hugh, who was in internal fits at the
débâcle, and the faces of Mona and Mrs Pascoe, and Mrs
Pascoe's viewpoint.   " They're like medlars, are they,
not ripe till they're rotten ? "

" I couldn't say about that, sir, we don't grow medlars
round this way.   But she's a real good girl, and that
respectable, you wouldn't believe."

" Well, you'd better settle it between you," said Hugh,
and headed for the door, feeling he would disgrace himself if he stopped a moment longer.   He was followed
equally precipitately by Jelkes, who appeared to be in
the same predicament.

Safely out in the yard, they leant up against the wall
and exploded.   Bill sauntered up.

" 'Ullo ? " he said.   " Has Ma stuck you with Silly
Lizzie ? " and joined shamelessly in the guffaws.

Presently Mona joined them.

" You're not to laugh," she said.   " It's very naughty
of you.   I've had a word with her, and she's a nice, well-
spoken little thing.   I think she'll be just what we want."

" That's what I sez," said Bill.   " Only Ma don't think so when I'm about."

Jelkes went off in fresh fits.   Here was an additional complication.   Mrs Pascoe had evidently not contemplated a shore job for her son when she laid her plans. It was a judgment on the lot of them.   A special Providence evidently watched over Miss Pumfrey.

The three at the farm settled down into peaceful domesticity.   To everyone's surprise, for Mona had only been singing her praises to save her own face, Silly Lizzie turned out, within limits, to be the paragon for which she was vaunted.   She did everything she was told. The only drawback to her was that she did nothing she wasn't told, however obvious.   What she knew, she knew.   But what she didn't know, she left severely alone, regardless of the gaps occasioned in the domestic service.   Told to roast a leg of mutton for an hour and forty minutes, she roasted it for an hour and forty minutes, and very good it was.   But left alone with the chops for supper, she roasted them for an hour and forty minutes also, with results that can be guessed.   However, provided she got the supervision she needed, she was the perfect servant.

# CHAPTER XIX

JELKES and Hugh were both watching Mona from their different viewpoints. She was entirely absorbed in regulating the menage. Before she broke out and took to art, she had had a thoroughly sound North Country up-bringing, and now that she found herself responsible for the running of a household, all her old house-craft, so resented in the learning, returned to her. Hugh watched her with interest. The kind of housekeeping he was accustomed to see done in his household was a very different affair to this, and consisted mainly in snatching up the inter-house telephone and saying how many people would be coming to dinner. This absorbed interest, this joyous pride, was something quite new to him. Incidentally, it was new to Mona also. She would never have believed it of herself. But she found it to be a very different matter, running her own show, to helping her mother. Which is one of the reasons, perhaps, why the totally undomesticated maiden is not always a sloven when she marries.

Jelkes also watched proceedings with interest, for he knew that the household machine Mona was so laboriously getting into running order would fall to bits the moment her hand was removed. Lizzie and Bill would do anything for her, but without her they would slow up, come to a standstill, and then get into every sort of reverse. Monks Farm would not merely be chaos, but Hades when Mona left it, thought Jelkes. Now if Mona played her cards cleverly—thought he—But would she ? He was pretty certain she wouldn't. Mona valued all sorts of imponderables, and like most women with ideals, could be extraordinarily stupid where her own interests were concerned. He sighed. Mona was neither to hold nor to bind by any male. He could manage Hugh, however, Hugh was easy. So he made up his mind to slip into the background and bide his time.

Mr Pinker was getting towards the end of his activities for the moment. There were no internal decorations to do because everything was plain worked stone. Guided by that expert in ancient buildings, Hugh had not subjected the old priory to the indignity of central heating, but had contented himself with putting an enormous stove in the cellar where Ambrosius had met his end.

" There's some," said Mr Pinker, " as would have run ye into hundreds of pounds, sir, to warm the place, and then it wouldn't hev' bin warm. Ye can't shove central heatin' into a place that ain't built for it. It don't do no good. It's against nature. But you spend ten pun' on a big stove for the cellar, and leave the cellar door open, and you're all right. Heat's bound to rise. Can't help itself."

Hugh thanked the old craftsman, and admired his honesty. Perhaps, however, if Mr Pinker's plumber son had been a better hot-water engineer it would have been a different story.

When the muck was excavated from the cloister garth, they came, eighteen inches below the surface, upon the broken flag-stones of what had once been a paved courtyard. These, re-laid, made a fine crazy paving. Once the gutters were up—Miss Pumfrey scorned gutters —on her tenants' houses, anyway—Hugh had an inspiration, and led the rain-water from the roof to a lily-pool in the centre of the garth. Then they all packed into the car and went off to a near-by nursery, and if Mona had not been exceedingly firm, not to say a trifle caustic, Hugh would have had the entire stock sold to him, including all the old shrubs too big to move. Jelkes watched it all, and wondered where the pair of them were going to end. Hugh leant his weight on Mona, and Mona watched over his interests with the eye of a hawk. But even so, as Mona had truly remarked, that wasn't enough for a woman with—Jelkes would not avail himself of the word ' guts ' and was at a loss for another.

So far as Jelkes could see, Hugh and Mona were settling down to Platonic domesticity. All the same, he had his doubts. He knew his Mona. She had no delusions, even if Hugh had.

And the sands were running out. Jelkes couldn't stop on indefinitely. As he truly said, " I don't believe in spending too much energy on money-making, but a business is like a baby—you've got to attend to it sometimes, or you have trouble with it."

But into their Eden the Serpent irrupted, and his name was practically legion, for from a big Daimler descended Lady Paston; her eldest daughter, Lady Whitney; her younger daughter, the Hon. Mrs Fouldes, and an urbane, professional-looking gentleman who was not Dr Johnson. That fact alone filled Jelkes with profound uneasiness. For if it had merely been Hugh's health they were concerned about, the person in whom they would have trusted would have been the family physician who knew him. Two signatures, and only two, are necessary on the certificate that loses a man his freedom for life. Jelkes had heard what Mrs Macintosh had had to say about the kind of doctor that ministers to Mayfair, with its drugs and its abortions, its imaginary ailments and its by no means imaginary venereal disease. If he had had his way, he would not have permitted the new-comer to set eyes on Hugh, for a man may only certify on what he sees, but Silly Lizzie showed the whole party in on top of them without demur, Miss Pumfrey's parlourmaid never having succeeded in teaching her how to answer the door.

Hugh looked distinctly annoyed, but was polite after the first surprise. Mona was introduced, and received with freezing coldness; Jelkes was introduced, and repaid the coldness with interest. The three women sat round like small boys at a pig-killing, and the doctor began to chat to Hugh, getting him onto the subject of Ambrosius almost without preamble. Jelkes wondered how he knew what to look for. Had Mrs Macintosh been indiscreet or unfaithful? Hugh, on his absorbing topic, opened up and forgot his constraint, and Jelkes marvelled at his unsuspiciousness.

They all professed themselves as exceedingly interested, and asked to view the scene of Ambrosius' death, and Hugh led them down into the sweltering cellar where Mr Pinker's ten pun' stove was putting in overtime to dry out the building. Jelkes, determined that they should not linger here unduly, surreptitiously opened the coal-hopper and pushed in the damper.

Lady Paston, coughing, commented on the unhealthiness of stoves.

" It'll be all right when the chimney gets warm," said Jelkes, determined they should have nothing to use against Hugh; but as the stove-pipe already glowed a dull red, he appeared to be setting an exacting standard.

Hugh not having risen to the bait of Ambrosius, Lady Paston, on their return to the upper regions, suggested a family conclave on business matters. Hugh sighed, but agreed.

Jelkes rose. He couldn't very well do anything else. He looked at the only other person present who wasn't a member of the family, and said : " Perhaps Dr Hughes would care to join me in a stroll while family matters are being discussed ? "

Dr Hughes blinked at this mode of address, for he had been introduced as plain Mr Hughes. He bowed politely, however.

" I am afraid I shall be needed," he said, " if you will excuse me."

His manners were perfect Mayfair, and Jelkes did not

love him any better on that account. Sulkily he withdrew, and walked up and down outside the window so
that he could hear if voices were raised in altercation;
for he knew that if, having turned his mind on-to Ambrosius, they baited Hugh up with a family row, they would
probably get Ambrosius, which he guessed was what they
wanted. Profoundly uneasy, he walked up and down,
glancing in through the lighted window each time he
passed.

Hugh was uneasy too; quite apart from the fact that
his family always made him uneasy when they descended
on him in bulk for the purposes of a family counsel;
the peculiar sensitiveness that is the heritage of all negative natures told him that something out of the ordinary
was afoot today, and that the presence of Mr Hughes,
or Dr Hughes as Jelkes had chosen to call him, was as
much a danger signal to him as the arrival of a butcher at
the farm is to the calf. Dr Hughes was very kind in his
manner, not wishing to deteriorate the veal, but Hugh
could almost see him surreptitiously trying the edge of
his knife with his thumb. Altogether, Hugh was in
much the frame of mind of a frightened horse, and was
showing the whites of his eyes in much the same manner.
He saw Dr Hughes watching him, and began to get his
head back like a horse getting ready to rear. Dr Hughes
edged his chair round little by little, till the table was
between them.

The ladies of the party, however, seemed quite
indifferent to the tension in the atmosphere. They were
used to Hugh and his ways, and knew that these symptoms of impending trouble never ended in anything
worse than a profound attack of depression. Frida had
been warned that Hugh might commit suicide some day
in one of these bouts of the blues, but nothing ever came
of it. Hugh had been too well brought up by his old
Scotch nurse even to commit suicide.

" Won't you sit down, Hugh? " said Lady Paston

with that acid sweetness that had taken the place of
authority since he had got too large to be smacked.
Hugh sat down, not being able to think of any excuse
for refusing on the spur of the moment.   In some curious
way he felt he had lost a point in the game by so doing,
although he had yielded out of nothing save politeness.

"We have been very worried about you, Hugh," went
on his mother.

"You had no need to be," muttered Hugh sulkily,
shuffling his feet and not meeting her eyes.   "I was
quite all right."

"We are very uneasy about these people you have
got in with.   We have had enquiries made about them,
and they are not at all satisfactory."

Hugh muttered something that he couldn't even hear
himself.

"I suppose you know that the old man is an unfrocked
priest?"

"No, he isn't," said Hugh.   "He just didn't go on
with his training."

"We have heard otherwise.   And they don't do that
to them for nothing."

Hugh sat miserably silent, knowing the uselessness of
argument, and quite unable to argue, even if it had been
any use.

"I wonder whether you also know that the girl has
got a very dubious reputation?"

Hugh sat up and looked her in the eye.

"I know nothing whatever about her history," he
said.   "I have always found her straight to deal with,
and that is good enough for me."

"What terms are you on with these people, Hugh?
It seems to us a most extraordinary menage."

That was a facer.   What terms was he on with them?
He didn't know himself.   He loved old Jelkes.   He
worshipped Mona.   He was utterly dependent on the
pair of them, jointly and separately: but he had the

melancholy certainty that he meant nothing to them ; that they were doing him a kindness for the sake of common humanity, and that they would expect him to get onto his feet and stop there after a reasonable time, and would not allow him to hang on-to them indefinitely. How could he explain all this to his family ? How, for the matter of that, could he face it himself ? He fell back on the bare truth, which was quite inexplicable enough to baffle anybody.

" Jelkes is just a pal of mine," he said.   " Miss Wilton is a kind of adopted daughter of his whom he looks after as she's got nobody else.   She's a designer and house furnisher by trade and has been doing this job for me. Mrs Macintosh was to have come to take charge here, but she let me down at the last moment, and Miss Wilton stepped into the gap temporarily.   It's only temporary," he added desperately, feeling his heart sink within him at the words.

" I'm not so sure of that," said Lady Paston.   " You may find it a lot easier to get her in than to get her out."

Hugh mumbled a disclaimer, wishing to God that she were right.

" What does she get for whatever it is she is doing for you ? " pursued Lady Paston.

" Three pounds a week," said Hugh.

" And the old man ? "

" He gets nothing.   He's here on holiday."

" And what are you going to do with the girl when he goes home after his holiday ? "

Hugh didn't know.   He stared blankly into space, his mind distracted from all other problems by the contemplation of the problem thus presented.

" Is she going to stop on here with you ? "

Hugh knew no more than she did, and continued to stare miserably into space.

" That is a matter on which I have no comment to make," said Lady Paston.   " The day is long past when one even pretends to be shocked at such things. I have no doubt it is much better for you than sitting and brooding—isn't that so, Dr Hughes?"

"Oh, yes, yes, much better," said Dr Hughes hastily. "Never repress, always abreact your complexes."

"What we are troubled about, however, and very troubled about indeed," continued Lady Paston, "is what will happen to you, Hugh, in the hands of these harpies."

"They haven't shown much sign of being harpies," said Hugh.

"That is only to win your confidence. They will soon. You needn't worry about that."

Hugh shifted his position wearily in his chair. "When they do, I'll let you know. At the present they are uncommon useful to me."

"And then it will be too late," said Lady Paston irritably. "We have had so much of this sort of thing. You are so easily influenced, Hugh. Anybody can get anything they like out of you."

"There's plenty for everybody," said Hugh sullenly.

"That is exactly what there isn't, if you fritter it away. I have only a life interest, there is nothing I can leave your sisters. And there are Alice's two children, and Letitia's three, and Moira's baby."

"Well, what about them? Won't they ever be able to earn a living? Have I got to support them permanently? Isn't anybody ever going to get a job?"

"There is no need to be offensive about it, Hugh. You know perfectly well how difficult things have been for everybody. Surely you are prepared to make some provision for your sisters' children?"

"I should have thought their own fathers might have done something in that line."

"There is no need to be offensive, Hugh, as I have already told you once. Now this is my suggestion, my dear boy, and as it is unlikely that I shall be with you very

much longer, I hope you will do it to please me, and then
we can all be happy together for the few short years that
remain to me.   I suggest that you make your affairs into
a trust, Hugh, with Robert and Cosmo as the trustees ;
then capital cannot be frittered away, and there will be
something for everybody.   When I persuaded your father
to leave everything to you instead of dividing up the
estate, it was always understood that you would look
after your sisters."

" So I will," said Hugh.   " But I don't see the fun of
doing more for the third generation than educating it.
I'm damned if I'm going to pension it."

" But Hugh, who else have you got to leave your
money to, except your sisters' children ?   You aren't
thinking of leaving it to charity, are you ?   I never heard
of anything so absurd, with the three girls unprovided
for.   If I had known you were going to turn out as you
have, I would never have persuaded your father to leave
everything to you.   If you can't make a mark in the world
yourself, you might at least enable others to do so.
What do you propose to leave your money to, Hugh, if
not to the girls ? "

" Hang it all, mother, why do you take it for granted
I am going to peg out first ?   I am the baby of the family.
I ought to bury the lot of you if I have my rights.   Why
do they expect to get more out of it if there is a trust,
with their husbands as trustees, than if I disburse largesse
myself ?   Are the trustees proposing to misapply trust
funds ? "

" Hugh, you are not to speak like that, I won't have
it.   It is only to prevent the capital from being frittered
away that I want things put into the hands of trustees,
so that there will be something for the children even-
tually.   It makes a very great difference to the opportunities children get, especially girls, if there is something
in prospect for them.   You might just as well get things
settled, Hugh, and then we can all be easy in our minds.

What can you possibly leave your money to, if not to your sisters' children ? "

" Has it never occurred to you that I might marry again ? I'm no Methuselah, you know."

There was a dead silence.

" I thought as much," said Lady Paston, at length. " So she has got you to that point, has she ? "

" Will she have you, Hugh ? " came the voice of his youngest sister from his left.

" Judging on type, I should say she wouldn't," came the voice of his eldest sister from his right. " She looks to me a passionate, full-blooded type. Personally I shouldn't think she would have you if you were the last man left alive."

Hugh was too bitterly appreciative of the truths contained in these remarks to realise the *volte face* they indicated.

His mother's voice interrupted his thoughts as he sat staring out of the window into the fast-deepening twilight, oblivious of his companions, who were watching him like so many cats at a mouse-hole.

" We would be only too happy for you to marry, dear," she said, " provided the girl was suitable ; but you are very foolish to involve yourself with this Wilton woman, who believe me, is more than unsuitable. We have had enquiries made about her, and quite apart from being very middle-class indeed, she has led a thoroughly loose life, living with various men."

" Is that my business ? " said Hugh.

" It is if you are thinking of marrying her."

" You remember that Lady Doreen something you were talking about last time I saw you ? "

" Alice's friend ? Yes, dear, of course I do ; we have been seeing a good deal of her lately."

" I wonder what her record would prove to be like if you got that detective to look it up."

There was a deadly silence that was unbroken even by

Lady Paston's assertion of maternal authority.

"We know what Frida's record was, don't we?" said Hugh with a harsh laugh.

"Whether you care about records or not, Hugh," said his eldest sister, "you are a fool to let yourself get at all deeply involved with this Wilton girl, for she is only too obviously taking advantage of you."

Hugh looked up, startled. "What do you mean?" he asked sharply.

"Look at her type—and look at yours. You don't suppose you have got a chance with a girl of that type, do you, Hugh? Vital, intense, accustomed to men of the artist type? My dear boy, have some sense. Look at the thing from her point of view and read between the lines. Don't be a goose, Hugh, keep your freedom. You have been married for your money once, and you know what came of it. Don't make that mistake a second time."

"I don't suppose she'd marry me even for my money," said Hugh bitterly, and the company pricked up its ears as one man.

"Have you asked her?" asked Lady Paston tartly.

"No," said Hugh.

"Are you going to?"

"I don't know. I think not."

Then all of a sudden something seemed to snap like a harp-string inside Hugh's head; for a moment the room swam round him; then it steadied again and he gathered his wits together; but they were not the wits of Hugh, but of Ambrosius.

The two minds overlapped, like two exposures on the same film, and the resulting man was neither one thing nor the other. There came upon him a horrible nightmare feeling of confusion and bewilderment. He did not know where he was—and yet the place was familiar. He did not know who these people were, and yet their faces were not strange. He knew, however, with both sides of his mind, that he was in a very tight corner, but what his peril was he could not be sure.

He knew that a net was closing round him, that suspicion was hardening into certainty ; that the power of Rome had been invoked by certain of the senior monks, and that at any moment one who could not be denied might arrive. But these people did not look like the delegation from Rome ; then who were they ? He was utterly perplexed, dreading a mis-step that might precipitate the very danger he was striving desperately to ward off. The very uncertainty, the very bewilderment of mind, made things a thousand times worse, and he feared that at any moment he might lose his head and start flailing around wildly. There came to him the feeling that it was not real at all, but just a nightmare ; and then the feeling that he was dead, and this was one of the dreams that come in the sleep of death. It was as if time were flowing the wrong way round and space were stretching and twisting like a wet hide. But whatever else was unreal, he knew that the danger was real, and he felt the cold hand of fear on throat and heart.

But whereas in this crisis Hugh would have been as helpless as a bird before a snake, as they very well knew as they sat waiting for him to betray himself, something that was not Hugh was also present, and as they watched him they saw his face change, and there was looking at them a man who, whoever he might be, was certainly not Hugh. They gasped. The eyes of the stranger were steady and cold as a swordsman's. The three women were dumb ; whatever they might do to Hugh, they dare not tamper with this individual ; by sheer weight of personality he dominated them. Dr Hughes, too experienced to precipitate a crisis, kept quiet and took mental notes ; he was familiar with the classical cases of dual personality, and had seen some minor ones in his own experience, but he had never come across anything like this before. The personality that was now present was putting the fear of God into him in a way that no pathology ought to do.

Then, even at the very moment when the situation lay in his hand, there came to the man standing there in the midst of them the knowledge that he was broken—that this was the end. Those who sat round him, whoever they might be, were the representatives of a power he could not resist ; the inner protection that had been his ever since he had first contacted the great God Pan was withdrawn, and he waited for death unarmed.

And yet the god had not deserted him. He had only retreated, and stood a little way off beckoning him to follow. The time was not yet ripe, they could not make head against a world embattled against them. The Goat-god had come at his call, but the end was forbidden ; he must beat a retreat.

Then he knew with an inner certainty that there was that in the soul which could rise above the bondage of the age and go free. Outwardly he had failed, but on the inner planes he had made the conditions that would assure success at the next attempt. He would go now, and he would come again. He would offer no resistance of casuistry or counter-charge against his accusers ; he would not take refuge in flight. The inner resistance withdrawn, they could take his life and be done with it. But in his heart were the promises that had been made to him in the strange visions and writings that had been his, and by those he held the god pledged. When he came again, conditions would be right ; the god would manifest as promised : the dreams would come true. It seemed to him, as these thoughts went through his mind, that the god, standing a little way off on a mound, lifted his hand in affirmation.

Then there arose in him an overmastering desire to go once again to his own place, his priory. Would they let him go there, or was he already under arrest ? He put it to the test, walked boldly out of the door, and none stayed him.

To his surprise he found that he was already at his own priory, whereas he had thought that he had been in the justice room at the Abbey. Confusion descended on him again. A moment before he had been with Pan in a wood. Where was he? What was happening? Was it all a dream? Yet the peril was real enough, he felt certain of that. But it did not matter, now that he had given up hope. Let the end come quickly, the quicker the better; but he was glad that it was coming at the priory—his own place that was friendly to him, not alien and hostile as were the very walls of the Abbey.

He turned and went towards the chapel. He would stand in the centre of the great Sign that showed forth the created universe, he would stand at the point of the concourse of forces, and there he would surrender his soul to the powers that created it, and withdrawing, leave his body to those who had authority over it; they could do their worst, it could not be for long.

Some one spoke to him as he crossed the dew-soaked grass to the chapel door; he did not know who it was, but the feel of the man was friendly, so it must be one of his own monks, not the strangers from Rome with their Italian subtlety and cruelty. He gave the curt blessing of peace expected of an ecclesiastic of his grade, and passed on and entered the darkness of the chapel.

As he took the great doors in his hands to close them, he stood still and looked back. The sun had set, but the afterglow lingered in the sky over the dark trees, at its verge one silver star. He stood long and looked at it. He would not see it again, he knew that. This was the end. He had a strange feeling as if it had all happened before—as if he knew exactly what was coming. They would seek him here; they would take him down underground; and before dawn death would find him. He went up through the darkness to the high altar and took his stand as he had planned. Around him were the

symbols of the heavenly houses ; behind him the great
Regents of the Elements, winged like archangels, stood
in their buttressing bays. He stood for a while, and
then knelt down and laid his hands on the cubical altar
of stone. Those who would come for him should find
him here.

# CHAPTER XX

BACK in the room he had left, a rather heated conference was in progress.

"Do you think," said Lady Paston, "that you can certify on what you have seen?"

Dr Hughes rubbed his chin. "It's a little difficult. I should have liked to have had something more definite. One has to be so very careful."

"But there is what Miss Pumfrey told us," said Lady Whitney.

"We cannot make use of that, I am afraid, it is only hearsay evidence. She pumped it out of the girl, and the girl is admittedly subnormal. It may guide us in coming to an opinion, but I cannot put it into my certificate. I can only certify on what I actually see."

"Well, haven't you seen enough? I should have thought we had seen enough today for anybody to certify on. I never saw anything that looked madder in my life."

"Yes, but he hasn't *done* anything, dear lady."

"It isn't what he does. He has never done anything in his life—and never will——" said Lady Paston bitterly. "It is what other people do when they get him into their hands. Dr Johnson is prepared to certify him, if you are, and he knows him very well."

"Mm. Ah. One has to be very careful."

"Well, if you don't certify him, there won't be a penny left for anybody. Most unfortunately his father left everything to him so as to give him the best possible chance in life, and you see how he has turned out. Quite subnormal mentally, Dr Johnson tells me."

"Mm. Ah. Yes. He'll certainly never set the

Thames on fire.  Very eccentric too, I take it.  Likes to associate with the lower classes.  Defectives often do."

"Well, what do you suggest?"  Lady Paston was beginning to get a little tart.  Dr Hughes had been brought for a special purpose, and knew it, but he did not seem disposed to get on with the job.

"Of course if I had Mr Paston under my care for a time——"

"That's no use," snapped Lady Paston.  "That won't enable us to take his affairs in hand and look after them."

"I was about to say, Lady Paston," said Dr Hughes with dignity, "that if I had Mr Paston under my care for a time, I could form a better opinion of his condition, and if I see anything that made certification appear advisable I could advise you in the matter."

"What would your fee be for having him under your care?"

"Twenty guineas a week."

"Twenty guineas a week?  Why, that is a thousand a year."

"It is a little more than that, dear lady.  I said guineas, not pounds, and there are fifty-two weeks in a year."

("If he calls mother 'dear lady' again, she'll kill him!") whispered the younger to the elder of the two sisters.  But it looked as if Lady Paston would not wait for that eventuality, but would slay him forthwith.

"Do you mean to say I have got to pay you twenty guineas a week indefinitely?"

"He has got to live somewhere, dear lady, and he will spend a great deal more than that on himself if he—er—remain in the hands of these—er—persons."

"I am not prepared to do that," snapped Lady Paston.  "I am prepared to pay a fee for the consultation, certainly, but not to go on paying indefinitely."

"I think we had better have another opinion," said Lady Whitney icily.

"Then in that case," said Dr Hughes, equally icily,

" my opinion will be available for the other side. You cannot go from doctor to doctor till you get a man certified. If one doctor has declined to certify when asked, any other doctor is exceedingly chary of certifying, in the existing state of the law."

" You can't change horses while crossing a stream, mother," said Mrs Fouldes, with a laugh.

" This is sheer blackmail ! " exlaimed Lady Paston.

" That statement is actionable," said Dr Hughes.

This was an eventuality they had never bargained for. Hugh could be certified all right, and his affairs got into their hands, no difficulty about that ; but apparently he would only remain certified as long as Dr Hughes drew his twenty guineas a week ; if that came to an end, Hugh would promptly be de-certified, and his trustees would then be called upon to render an account of their stewardship. And would Dr Hughes demands be limited to twenty guineas a week ? Blackmail is a thing that grows with what it feeds on.

But if they went to any other doctor for the putting away of the unhappy Hugh, Dr Hughes would promptly turn round and say that Hugh did not need certifying, and then where would they be ? In for a penny, in for a pound. Desperate situations required desperate remedies. They set to work to drive the best bargain they could with Dr Hughes.

" Twenty guineas a week is a very high fee," said Lady Paston, but her voice was much milder than it had hitherto been.

" You are asking me to take a very heavy responsibility," said Dr Hughes.

" I should have thought twelve guineas a week would have been ample."

" I could not possibly undertake it for that money. Mr Paston is the kind of patient who will always be trying to escape, and might be very violent when prevented. He will have to have special attendants. I shall also require an indemnity against any legal expenses I might be involved in by him; these kind of patients often have a mania for litigation."

"There is not the slightest likelihood of that with him. He has never been known to do anything on his own initiative."

"But supposing a friend stirs up trouble?"

"He has no friends worth mentioning. They were all his wife's friends, and of course that is all over now."

"His solicitors, then?"

"I have already been to see them. They are quite agreeable; they only stipulated that they should continue to handle his affairs, to which I agreed."

"Mm. Ah. Yes, I see. It might, on the whole, be in his best interests to certify him. There do not seem to be any difficulties in the way. I will have a word with Dr Johnson, and see what he thinks. He has known him longer than I have. We will give him the casting vote. If he thinks it advisable, I will not say no."

So all arrangements were made once more for walling Hugh up alive, and history was about to repeat itself, when in walked Jelkes and stood in the centre of the circle with his hands on his hips, glaring at them.

"What the hell do you think you're playing at?" he demanded of Dr Hughes, who jumped as if he had had a pin stuck in him. "What is it you propose to do that is worth twenty guineas a week till the cows come home?"

"My dear sir, my dear sir, I don't know what you are talking about, but your tone is most offensive. I must really take exception to it."

"Have you had your ear to the keyhole?" snapped Hugh's youngest sister, her temper getting the upper hand of her mother's attempts to signal discretion and denials.

"No, not the keyhole; but the window is open and you've all got voices like peacocks."

" Then why didn't you move out of earshot when you realised that private matters were being discussed ? "

" Because Hugh Paston's got one friend, anyway."

Dr Hughes recovered his wits first.

" I do not think any *disinterested* person would deny that Mr Paston is not quite normal."

" May be not. I don't dispute that," said Jelkes, scowling at him under his bushy brows and contriving to look pretty formidable. " All the same, no *disinterested* person would try to get him certified, because he doesn't need it. Psycho-pathology is a thing I happen to know something about. And I'll tell you another thing too, in case you don't know it—there was a feller a little while ago who got let in for twenty thousand pounds damages for certifying a chap that didn't need certifying—but perhaps you do know that, as you put in for an indemnity. If you'll pardon my saying so, I think you're sailing damn near the wind."

Dr Hughes looked down his nose. His twenty guineas a week was going to take some earning. It requires considerable nerve to sail near the wind in front of witnesses of the ram-you-damn-you type of Jelkes.

He turned to his female companions.

" I think, dear ladies, we might as well be going. There is nothing more we can do for the moment."

They all filed out, giving Jelkes awful looks as they went.

Jelkes went hastily to the chapel as the dying sounds of the car assured him that they had really gone. He looked in, but it was pitch dark and dead still. All the same, he fetched a lamp from the living room and looked in again. Then, as he expected, he saw, kneeling in front of the altar that was not a Christian altar, the figure of a man, and that man, whoever he might be, was calling upon strange gods.

Jelkes groaned, withdrew quietly, and returned to the house.

He called to Mona, who had retreated to her bedroom under the irruption of Hugh's womenfolk, and told her what had happened. Ambrosius had arrived in front of witnesses—hostile witnesses, as they had expected would happen sooner or later, and had probably come to stay. Jelkes made no secret of his expectation that the morning would see the arrival of a large car, first cousin to a hearse, containing three or four of that curious variety of gentleman's gentlemen who minister to a mind diseased, and that would be the last they would see of Hugh; and if Mona succeeded in collecting from the persons who would take charge of his affairs the salary actually due to her, she would be uncommon lucky. As Hugh was at present, certification could hardly be disputed.

It was at this moment, as they were debating the gloomy prospect, that the sounds of a car on the drive were heard once more.

" My God ! " said Jelkes. " What is it now ? "

He went to the door, and there confronted a short, dapper, elderly man, who got out of a coupé as neat and small as himself.

" Good evening," he said. " Is Mr Paston at home ? "

" No, he isn't," said Jelkes curtly, eyeing him with unconcealed hostility, at which the new-comer looked rather taken aback.

" That's a pity," he said. " I thought I could have saved him a trip into town. I have just been with Miss Pumfrey, getting her signature, and I thought perhaps I could get his, and hand over the deeds and be done with it. Perhaps you would be good enough to ask him to call at my office at his convenience. My name is Watney."

Jelkes looked at him for a moment. " Is it ? " he said. " Come inside," and held the door open.

Mr Watney entered, and passed into the living-room, where he saw Mona, obviously agitated, standing before the fire. He greeted her, and Jelkes was formally introduced to him, though without explanation, so he was none the wiser. He sensed the tenseness of the atmosphere, however, and noted the absence of Hugh. He wondered why the impersonal Miss Wilton, whose interest in Hugh Paston was purely commercial, should look so very agitated.

She offered no explanation, however, but gazed at the old man, her alleged uncle, as if wondering what his policy might be.

" Sit down," said Jelkes curtly.

Mr Watney sat as bid.

" We're in the devil of a mess," said Jelkes.

Mr Watney looked at him enquiringly, but with true legal caution uttered no comment.

Jelkes suddenly turned to the girl.

" You tell him, Mona, you'll put it better than I will."

The girl hesitated. " What is it you mean to do, Uncle ? " she asked.

" We've got to have someone to help us, Mona, they'll shove Hugh in an asylum if we don't."

Mr Watney raised his eyebrows.

" This is the position, sir," said Jelkes, turning to him again. " My friend Hugh Paston, has recently been through a good deal of trouble—lost his wife in rather tragic circumstances."

Watney nodded. He evidently knew. (" Now how did you know ? " thought Jelkes.)

" The result has been to upset him a good deal, and to bring on—er—split personality. I dare say you have heard of such things ? "

" Yes, I have heard of them," said the man of law, dry and non-committal.

" There are times——" Jelkes struggled on, " when he shifts from his normal self into a—er—secondary personality."

" And the time at the museum was one of them," said Watney, looking at Mona.

" Yes," said Mona.

" I knew that wasn't an ordinary faint," said Mr Watney.

" The point is this," said Jelkes. " In my opinion, and I know something of abnormal psychology, Hugh will soon right himself, and anyway, he's harmless. But the trouble is, his family seem to want to get him certified."

" Why should they wish to do that, if it is not necessary ? "

" Because if he were certified, they would have the control of a very large estate, and their children, that is, his sisters' children, would come in for it. Whereas, if he remains at large and—er—should marry again, he might have children, and then his children would come in for it."

" Is he likely to marry again ? "

Jelkes hesitated.

" Not that I know of," said Mona.

Something, he could not say what, made Mr Watney look behind him, the others followed his glance, and there, in the doorway, stood Hugh, and, Jelkes thanked his stars, it was Hugh, and not Ambrosius.

" I am afraid I have been an involuntary eavesdropper for the bulk of your conversation," said Hugh, coming slowly into the room. He never looked at Mona.

" Then," said Jelkes, " you know the lie of the land ? "

" I am beginning to grasp it. So this is the explanation of the—seizures—that alarmed Miss Wilton ? " He looked at Mona for the first time.

" Yes," said Mona miserably.

" I am not surprised," said Hugh. " It must have been a very alarming experience."

He turned to the solicitor. " Well, Mr Watney, it looks as if I were in for a life sentence if I don't watch my step. What about it ? You are a man of law, can you suggest anything ? "

" I can only suggest that you consult your lawyer and your family physician, Mr Paston."

" That would be just walking into the lion's den. It is our family physician who is in on this thing. As for my lawyers, well, I don't know. I shouldn't be surprised if I were worth more to them locked up than loose."

" Is there no person, no friend of the family, of your late father for instance, upon whose disinterestedness you can rely ? "

Hugh waved his hand towards the old book-seller.

" Jelkes, here," he said. " I don't know of another soul. Unless, maybe——? " he looked at Mona and hesitated.

" I would do what I could," said Mona quietly.

" I am glad to have that assurance," said Hugh, " and I shan't——" he hesitated, seeking the word that would express what he meant, " I shan't overstep my welcome."

There was high tension in the atmosphere, and everybody felt acutely embarrassed.

Jelkes broke it. " Do you know what I should do, if I were you, Hugh ? I should take your affairs out of the hands of your solicitors, if you don't feel you can trust 'em, and get Mr Watney to look after them for you."

" That's just what was in my mind," said Hugh. " That is, if Mr Watney is willing ? "

" Er—well, of course I—er—I—er—should be very pleased." Who wouldn't be ? But, to his credit, the little man had not fished for it. " But—er—family lawyers, Mr Paston ? Things may be complicated. Did your father tie things up with them in any way ? "

" Not with these lawyers. I shifted to them to please my wife. She couldn't abide the others. Had no end of a row with them. We disentangled all the legal knots then. I haven't been with these folk much over three years."

" Then in that case, I shall be very pleased to take charge of your affairs, though I should have felt some diffidence in taking them out of the hands of family lawyers."

" And I'd like you to have them," said Hugh, suddenly smiling at him. The little old bachelor beamed back. Hugh had pulled off his stunt once more. Mr Watney had followed Mrs Pascoe into the cohort of those who looked after Hugh far better than he could look after himself.

" Now, Mr Paston," said the little lawyer, suddenly losing his diffidence and becoming authoritative. " I should advise you to give me the necessary authority to take over all your papers from your present firm, and I will send a clerk up first thing tomorrow morning, before they know what is afoot, and collect 'em. Possession is nine points of the law. Secondly, if you feel sufficient confidence in us, I suggest that you give me your Power of Attorney, to come into effect in the event of your incapacity. They'll contest that, of course, if we ever have to use it, which I hope we won't. But again, possession is nine points of the law, and they will have to dislodge us from an entrenched position. A High Court job, Mr Paston. Plenty of publicity. The right counsel could make 'em wish they were dead. Bargaining power, my dear sir, bargaining power is never to be despised. Say to a man, ' If I can't, you shan't ', and he often becomes reasonable. Applied psychology—a very useful thing. More useful than law sometimes. Lawyers concentrate on law and forget the psychology of litigants. That, in my opinion, is foolish. I have won quite as many cases with psychology as I have with law.'

He beamed at them all through his horn-rimmed glasses, in his element. He loved litigation for its own sake. It was never his choice to see the Sign of the Cross go onto a brief. It sealed a hard bargain on any brief of his that bore it.

" What is the point in giving you Power of Attorney ? " said Mona curtly.

" It is this, Miss Wilton. Supposing they did certify Mr Paston, they would not obtain control of his affairs without a tremendous struggle. I'd fight them tooth and nail through every court in the country. They'll know that, without being told. I think you will find that as soon as they know there is a Power of Attorney in existence, they will drop the idea of certification, especially if Mr Paston places himself in the hands of a doctor. As we all know, there is no point in certifying our friend here for his own sake, and no disinterested person would try to ; and with you and Mr Jelkes to look after him, I am sure it won't be long before even an interested person wouldn't be able to."

He looked round with a beaming smile, but had a sub-conscious feeling that he had said the wrong thing.

" I think that's O.K.," said Hugh wearily, as if bored to death with the whole transaction. " Who'll we get for the disinterested doctor ? Mrs Macintosh's husband's cousin ? "

" No," said Mona decisively. " He's all right for a cold on the chest, no one better, but he'd be no good for this job. He'd be like Mrs Macintosh, incredulous and scared at the same time."

Mr Watney pricked up his ears. He had sensed all along that there was much more in the whole transaction than met the eye.

" Now that I am definitely acting for you, Mr Paston," he said, " I may as well tell you that your previous soli-citors asked a great many questions in connection with the conveyancing of this place. Questions which I thought rather odd. Naturally I did not answer them. I told them that their client was their business, and my client was my business. In the usual legal terminology, of course."

" What did they want to know ? " said Jelkes, looking at Hugh, who seemed to be sunk in thought and to have lost all interest in the discussion.

" They wanted to know through whose introduction Mr Paston had got in touch with Miss Pumfrey. I told 'em I didn't know. I don't, either. Then they asked me, over the phone, as a favour, to try and find out. I said : ' He's your client not mine. I can't act for both sides. Ask him, if you want to know, and if he wants you to know, he'll tell you '. They don't know a blessed thing about conveyancing. It's they who've hung us up all this time. They're divorce and criminal lawyers. What you're doing in that galley, I don't know, Mr Paston."

" What's their standing ? " said Jelkes.

" I'd sooner not express an opinion," said Watney.

" I told that lad he wanted an uncle," said Jelkes with one of his sudden camel-grins. " He will call me uncle, you know, though I run a book-shop, not a pop-shop."

The two old men exchanged smiles and looked at Hugh affectionately, who took no manner of notice of them, being sunk in thought. They looked back at each other anxiously.

" I presume you are an old friend ? " said Mr Watney.

" Not a bit of it," said Jelkes. " No older than you are. He drifted into my shop after his wife's funeral, on his beam-ends, and I took him in and looked after him, as no one else seemed disposed to."

" Well, well, well," said Mr Watney. " What a state of affairs." He looked at Mona, but no further information was forthcoming.

He turned to Jelkes, and spoke in a low voice :

" With regard to the doctor, I should get him to run up to town first thing tomorrow morning if I were you, and see someone really first-class, whose opinion cannot be gainsaid."

" No," said Jelkes. " We'll have the local saw-bones in tonight. I'm taking no chances."

" I know the man we want," continued Mr Watney in a low voice. " A young chap who's just set up in the district. He'll be very pleased to have a patient from me and will do as I tell him.   You leave it to me.   I'll send him along on my way back."

\*     \*     \*     \*     \*

Having speeded the parting guest, Jelkes returned to the living-room to find that Mona had disappeared.   She had evidently got no mind for a *tête à tête* with Hugh in his present state.   Jelkes sat down and had a good look at him, and what he saw, he did not like.   He seemed suddenly to have aged in a very curious manner.   When he had first arrived at the shop, immediately after the shock of his wife's death, he had looked a good ten years older than his real age.   That look had passed away as the days went by, and though he had premature lines on his face, probably of many years standing, Hugh, animated, was very boyish.   Now, however, he had a curious look, as if of a man whose work is over and who is waiting for death.   Jelkes had seen it on the faces of men who had been dismissed after a life-time in one job. He did not like it at all.

Neither did he like the way Hugh was sunk in thought, paying no attention to anything.   He spoke to him, just to see if he would respond or not.

" Well, Hugh, what are you going to do ?   Are you going to push on with the furnishing of this place under the circumstances ? "

Hugh roused himself with an effort.

" I am sure I don't know.   Hadn't thought about it," he replied.   " Miss Wilton can get whatever's needful."

Jelkes' quick ear caught the change of name, and queried its significance.

They sat for a while in silence, and then a car was heard once more on the drive.

" That'll be Watney's saw-bones," said Jelkes.   " At least I hope to God it is."

It was.

He proved to be a young fellow, masking nervousness

under over-assurance.

" Mr Watney told you about the case ? " said Jelkes in a low voice as he admitted him.

He nodded.

" Want to see him alone ? "

" Yes, please."

Jelkes grunted, showed him in, and shut the door on him.

The new-comer stood looking at his patient in silence for a moment, and Hugh, sensing the presence of a stranger, suddenly looked up.

" Hullo ?, I beg your pardon," he said. " I didn't know there was anyone there."

" Mr Watney asked me to come and see you. I am Dr Atkins."

" Very good of you, I'm sure," said Hugh, and conversation languished, Dr Atkins trying desperately to remember what had been taught him in his scanty instruction in the care of minds diseased. All he could recall was the law relating to certification. He knew as much about examining a mental case as he did about ballooning.

" Er, can you tell me what day of the week it is ? " he said at length.

" It's been Wednesday all day long, so far as I know," said Hugh, and silence fell again.

Dr Atkins felt himself beginning to perspire. This was his first important case in his first start in practice, and he was hashing it horribly. He felt he knew even less about psychiatry than he did about midwifery, and wished to God he had gone into partnership with an older man, instead of this ambitious start on his own. Private practice, he was discovering, was very different to walking the hospitals. A lot less science and a lot more common sense came into it.

" May I examine you ? " he said at length, hoping to warm up on the accustomed routine.

" Certainly," said Hugh.  " Anything you like."

Dr Atkins got out his stethoscope.

" Would you be good enough to undress ? "

" Undress ? " exclaimed Hugh, suddenly waking up. " Good Lord, man, I'm all right from the neck downwards. This is where my trouble is," and he tapped his head. " You don't want to stethoscope that, do you ? Come and sit down and have a cigarette."

" Thanks," said Dr Atkins, feeling he was showing tact.

" I don't know what we've got in the way of refreshments," said Hugh, " I am afraid there's nothing but bottled beer," and produced some forthwith from the sideboard. Dr Atkins, what with gratitude for the beer and relief at the turn the interview had taken, forgot to be professional and became the decent, inexperienced lad Nature meant him to be, and they settled down on either side of the hearth, he and his patient, with a glass of beer and a cigarette apiece, to the entirely unorthodox method of treating a mental case as if it were human.

It was Hugh who took charge of the interview.

" I suppose Mr Watney told you all there is to tell ? " he said.

" He told me all he knew," said Dr Atkins, grinning. " But I dare say there's plenty more if you care to tell it."

This was not the way cases had been examined at the demonstrations at the asylum, but it was much more comfortable for both parties than the orthodox method —this and the beer.

" I suppose Watney told you they want to certify me ? I daresay they're right, but I don't want to be certified. I'd be glad if you could fix it so that I'm not. I'll do anything you want me to."

Dr Atkins, warmed by the beer, began to feel as if he were under Divine guidance, so successful did he appear to be in the management of mental cases.

"Don't you worry about that," he said. "I'll see you're not certified."

"Have some more beer?" said Hugh.

"Thanks, I will," said Dr Atkins.

Hugh opened another bottle.

"Had a bit of a shock?" said Dr Atkins.

"Yes, the devil of a shock."

"Care to talk about it?"

"Not particularly."

"It'll blow over, given time."

"Hope so. Have some more beer?"

"I don't mind if I do."

Hugh opened another bottle. Dr Atkins contributed a packet of gaspers. They sat in a companionable silence. There are many worse ways than this of doing psychiatry. Hugh had seen some of them, and was duly grateful.

"Know anything about psycho-analysis?" he asked his medical adviser as he filled his glass.

"No, not much."

"Well, I do," said Hugh. "And I'll wring your neck if you try it on me."

"Right-o," said Dr Atkins.

"Have some more beer?"

"No, my Lord, no. I've got to drive home! There's a row of empties on the floor."

And so they parted. Hugh greatly relieved. He liked Dr Atkins personally, and had had his fears laid to rest. Dr Atkins, for his part, drove straight home and looked up the case in his books before he put the car away. He knew he had succeeded, but he did not know how, or why. He had sat like that once with a pal of his after the fellow had had a knock-out blow; but still, that wasn't psychiatry. He made a note of a prescription capable of calming lions and tigers, and hoped for the best. That was all he could do, poor lad. Medical science knows precious little about minds, diseased or healthy, and what it does know it has got hold of by the wrong end.

\*     \*     \*     \*     \*

Jelkes mounted guard over the household all the following day, and the next, but no sign came from the hostile camp. As Mr Watney had surmised, the Power of Attorney stimied them neatly, and they dropped the idea of certification, for the moment, at any rate, and unless Hugh did something really outrageous, he was safe enough.

But even if that sword no longer hung over their heads, there was still a pretty serious problem on their hands, for it could not be denied that there was something very much wrong with Hugh. He had lasped into a peculiar, brooding, spiritless apathy, as if his mind were away in another world and that world not a pleasant one. Jelkes, who had read widely in psychology and had seen a good many cracked-up minds among the Jesuits—a nervous breakdown, politely called surrender to God, being part of their curriculum—didn't like the look of Hugh at all. He had a shrewd suspicion, judging him on type, that he would swing between apathy and excitability. If something got through the skin of his apathy, he would be excitable ; and when his excitement had exhausted him, he would lapse into apathy. After all, the human machine is an internal combustion engine running on spirit. Temperament activated by vitality. Jelkes judged Hugh to be suffering from air-lock, and liable to backfire as the air-lock blew clear. If one were turning the starting-handle when that happened, one could get a broken wrist as easy as kiss hands. Jelkes was deadly uneasy at the idea of leaving Mona alone with Hugh, but for the life of him did not see how he could let his business take care of itself any longer if he expected to have any business left to go back to. What was in

Mona's mind he could not make out. Sometimes he thought she had no appreciation at all of the state of affairs, and sometimes he thought she knew a lot more than she had seen fit to tell him. Mona was blessed with a poker-face.

# CHAPTER XXI

By the end of the week Hugh seemed considerably more normal; the telephone was in, so in case of emergency Mona could get either Mr Watney, the doctor, or the police according to which seemed to be indicated, and was no longer at the mercy of Hugh and his *alter ego*, Ambrosius, who between them might be capable of anything; Jelkes decided to risk it, and leave Monks Farm to its own devices for a few days and see what was happening to his means of livelihood.

"I don't believe in selling one's soul for filthy lucre," he said. "I think the Duke of Wellington had the right idea—put all your letters in a drawer, and they'll answer themselves, given time. But unfortunately you can't do too much of that sort of thing in business—folk don't like it. God knows why."

So Hugh ran him down into the valley in the car, and he caught the evening bus for London.

Having pushed Jelkes into his bus, and his rush-basket after him, Hugh put the big car about and drove up into the hills. He dreaded the first meeting with Mona alone. There was a lot to be thought out. He needed to be clear on his own line of action, and very sure of his ability to carry it out. It was going to take a good deal of self-control, he thought, to go just so far and no further, and not slip into anything that would earn him a snub from Mona, which might cause him, in his strung-up state, to lose his temper and have a row with her that would lead to permanent estrangement. Left to his own devices, Hugh would not have risked it, but he knew that Mona did not intend to leave him to his own devices, and he wondered how much she knew about life, and how much she knew about what she was doing, and whether she would be able to steer round the bends ahead.

The thing he feared was the loss of his own self-control. It was no longer his trouble that he could not grip life, but that he might accidentally strangle it. He knew that the stubbornness of the weak man, the courage of the coward, the binge of the saint are all notorious. He had always known that he had no stomach for a fight, that he was as weak as ditch-water in every relationship of life, and that he sincerely wished to do what was right and was always ready to sacrifice himself for others —and if that isn't the road to sainthood, what is ? But now he found himself getting his head down and going at things like a bull at a gate ; as for righteousness, he knew the thing his whole being ached for—life, more life, fullness of life—the blessing of Pan !

Self-sacrifice ? That was the last thread by which he hung. For Hugh was soft-hearted : keenly alive to the hurt of others. It was very difficult for him to sacrifice anybody, and impossible to sacrifice them to himself. But he knew that the gods are only to be invoked by sacrifice, and that in the case of Pan, self-sacrifice would not serve.

All around him, where he had pulled up his car on the high common, the gorse was in flower, and its sweet almondy odour filled the air. There was a mellowness as of summer in the slow-moving wind of the warm spring dusk. April was ending ; May would soon be here ; and with the last day of April came the Eve of Beltane.

According to tradition, as Hugh had gathered from Jelkes's books, Beltane was the Night of the Witches, and if anything were going to happen, it might be expected to happen then. He wondered what form Pan would take if he appeared ? Would he come crudely, as a materialising stench of goat ? Or would he come

more subtly in the soul ? Hugh inclined to the latter
view. He had always been interested in the uncanny,
and had read all the occult thrillers as they appeared.
He remembered that the great event was invariably one
of two things—a materialisation that does not quite come
off, or a dream from which everybody wakes up in the
last chapter. He suspected that the writers of the thrillers
had diligently taken in each other's washing—in fact
one author went so far as definitely to disclaim all
practical knowledge of the subject on which he wrote
in great detail—and had not exactly gone to Nature. if
such a term could be applied to so unnatural a matter,
for their data.

He, for his part, did not know quite what to expect,
and so could not decide whether he should be disappointed that more that was spectacular had not happened,
or satisfied that so much had already come about.
Looking back over the weeks that had passed since he
had started to break out of the luminous opacity that
was his opal, he could not deny that things had happened
—Ambrosius, for instance—, and Mona had come into
his life, with results that looked as if they were going
to prove harrowing.

Was all this the fruit of his invocation of Pan ? He
began to suspect that it was. For after all, what was an
invocation of Pan, in the first instance, save a resolution
to break out of the opal ? He had given permission to
his own subconscious to come up to the light ; then he
had gone on to invoke the primordial forces of life to
declare themselves ; not only had he let loose the Pan
within, but he had called upon the Great God Pan without. Plenty of people let loose the Pan within—the
most appropriate rite for that was alcoholic—but the
Great God Pan—that was another matter ; he wasn't
often called upon in these materialistic days when folk
had given up believing in spiritual evil even more
thoroughly than they had ceased to believe in spiritual

good. But was the Great God evil? "No!" said Hugh aloud. "He isn't. I repudiate that."

And with that he started the engine, and put the car about once more, and returned to Monks Farm and Mona.

He had a very queer feeling as he turned into the lane, now promoted by the liberal addition of gravel to be a carriage drive. Deep down in him there was a sudden thrill of eagerness, but all on the surface was dead numbness. During the days of brooding, that had passed with Jelkes for apathy, he had made up his mind that to try and make any further advance with Mona Wilton was to lose what he had already got. The side of him that had raised its seven crowned heads out of the kingdoms of unbalanced force, to quote Jelkes's favourite Qabalists, that old serpent Leviathan that is in each one of us, had been thrust back into the place of severest judgments again; what Hugh considered his better self was sitting on the lid, and all was quiet for the moment.

As he came over a rise in the ground that hid the farm from the road and saw the firelight shining out of its uncurtained windows, he felt an exquisite pleasure, and at the same time a tantalised sense of frustration such as a starving man might feel when gazing at a realistic poster advertising plenty. The car slid down the gentle slope by its own weight, and he eased it through the wide doors of the barn without recourse to the engine. The thoroughbred car moved as silently as a ghost, not a spring squeaked, not a window rattled. The newly-rolled gravel hardly crunched, and Hugh returned to his home unobserved.

He cut across the courtyard from the barn, intending to enter by the back door. As he passed the kitchen window he glanced in, and saw there Bill, very much taking his ease by the fire, with Silly Lizzie worshipping him as if he were the Vision Beautiful, which he decidedly was not, in this ungirt mood. Hugh hesitated. To break in on an idyll like that was like smashing a pane of glass. He turned away, re-crossing the courtyard, and entered the chapel.

It was as black as pitch at first, but the lingering after-glow gleamed faintly through the west window, and his eyes gradually became accustomed to the dim light. The great angels in the buttressing bays were hidden in the gloom, but the dark mass of the Tree on the high wall at the eastern end showed up against its lighter background. Hugh stood staring at it, trying to picture it as he knew it to be, with its ten gaudy fruit arranged in their three symmetrical triangles with the odd one at the bottom. He had heard Jelkes discourse of the symbolism of that Tree, representing heaven and earth and the intermediate worlds between, according to the ancient rabbis. He moved slowly up the broad space of the nave, mounted the three shallow steps, and felt under his feet the smooth tessellated pavement of the sanctuary. Around him, though hidden by the darkness, was the rude circle of the Zodiac as designed by the primitive mosaic-workers of Ambrosius' day. His feet were treading the actual flooring that had been trodden by the sandalled feet of the dead monk. He wondered how often Ambrosius had come in thus, alone in the darkness, seeking guidance and strength as the net closed round him, and he thought how narrow his own escape had been from the spiritual equivalent of being walled up alive. He tried to reconstruct in his imagination the cubical altar of the Templars, which, according to their enemies, was the obscene throne of the goat-god, but according to themselves merely symbolised the universe. Of course, if one regarded the universe as the obscene throne of the goat-god, which is what the spiritually-minded seem to do, the Church was amply justified in its attitude towards Ambrosius. If, on the other hand, one regarded the universe as an altar,

Ambrosius was right in his attitude towards the Church.
It all depended on the viewpoint.  If it is true that we
are begotten in sin and brought forth in iniquity, unquestionably the world is a good place to get away from ;
but if, on the other hand, this material universe is the
luminous garment of the Eternal, as the Gnostics
opined, it is a different story.  He remembered a remark
of Jelkes's : " I worship God made manifest in Nature,
and to Hell with the saints ! "

Hugh wished to God he had the pluck to send the
saints to hell and go his own way, as Ambrosius had done.
He wondered what that ruthless rebel would have made
of the present circumstances.  Of one thing he was
certain—he would not have been baulked of Mona
Wilton by any such small circumstance as her disinclination.  He could imagine Ambrosius by sheer will-power
dominating any one who came his way.  And as he
thought, imagining the mind of Ambrosius, it seemed to
him as if something in his own mind opened like a door,
and the two minds coincided, and once again he *was*
Ambrosius.  But this time he knew it.  There was no
closing-down of the one consciousness as the other
opened, they were intercommunicating for a brief
second.

But the door closed again as swiftly as it had opened.
Hugh breathless and sweating, staggered slightly as he
recovered his balance.  But now he understood a good
many things he had not understood before.  Rapidly
his mind pieced together the various scraps of information that had come his way : the crash onto his back in
the upper room at the museum, when he had lost his
balance at the change-over from one mode of consciousness to another—Mrs Macintosh's remark : " Your
face altered completely as you entered the door——."
He wondered whether, had there been a witness to note,
his face would have been observed to change during
these last few minutes, and felt pretty certain that it had.

One thing in particular he had realised however, that he did not ' get ' Ambrosius by concentrating on a mental picture of him, as he had tried to do in the stuffy little parlour at the Green Man, but by meditating on what Ambrosius must have felt or thought or done.

> ' He also looked forth for an hour
> On peopled plains and skies that lower,
> From those few windows in a tower
> That is the head of a man.'

The thing in Hugh that had stirred before under the surface apathy, turned over in its sleep and chuckled. A key had been found, if he had the nerve to use it. Ambrosius could be invoked at will by simply thinking of him in a particular way, which consisted in identifying oneself with him instead of looking at him.

> ' But who shall look from Alfred's hood,
> Or breathe his breath alive ? '

Hugh had a pretty good notion that he was going to look from Ambrosius' hood. Exactly what the consequences would be, he did not know, but suspected that they might be drastic. He might even get himself certified in good earnest if he went on like this. But he did not care. He had an idea that the road to Mona Wilton might lie through Ambrosius' hood, and he didn't care a damn for the consequences. The renegade ecclesiastic had already begun to leave his mark behind him.

Hugh turned and left the chapel and made his way round to the south front of the priory, passing silently over the dew-soaked grass. Glancing in at the window as he passed, he saw Mona sitting over the fire, an unlit lamp beside her, her elbows on her knees and her chin in her hands, staring into the flames, deep in thought.

And anxious thought, too, to judge by the set of her mouth and the lines on her forehead. The door stood open to the mild spring night and he entered unheard. It was not till he spoke to her that she realised his presence, and then she leapt to her feet so startled that she sent her chair over behind her and Hugh was only just in time to catch the lamp, thanking his stars that it was unlit.

" I'm frightfully sorry," he said. " I didn't mean to scare you like that, but what was I to do as you hadn't heard me come ? "

" It's very stupid of me," said Mona. " I don't know why I jumped like that. I can't imagine."

But he knew perfectly well, and so did she. It was the hawk face in the black cowl she dreaded to see.

" This is rather awkward," said Hugh, dropping into his accustomed chair, which engulfed him completely so that he sat on his shoulder-blades. " Sit down, Mona, we've got to face up to this, otherwise we shall never be able to exist together in the same house. You're not scared of me, are you ? No one on God's earth could be scared of me. Is it Ambrosius you're scared of ? "

" Yes—and no," said Mona. " I give reflex jumps at the sight of Ambrosius, but I'm not really scared of him."

" I should have said you were badly scared of him, Mona."

" Yes, perhaps I am ; but all the same, I'm not going to chase Ambrosius off. He has got to come through, you know, Hugh. That is what I have been facing up to while you have been away. He has got to come through."

Hugh was so delighted at her use of his Christian name instead of the formal ' Mr Paston ' which was her usual custom, that he very nearly forgot about Ambrosius forthwith, for it did not matter whether he came or not. It was Mona who recalled him.

" We have got to face up to Ambrosius, Hugh, both
of us."

" Well," said Hugh, " what about him ? "

Mona sat silent for quite a while, staring at the fire,
and Hugh sat watching her.   He could imagine Ambrosius watching like that, from the window in the Abbey
gate-house that overlooked the market-place—watching
the women that were forbidden to him as a Churchman,
himself unobserved.

Mona seemed to have forgotten Hugh's presence, and
he sat watching her in the dying firelight, wondering
whether he dared think of Ambrosius, or whether, if
he did, he would wreck the whole show.   For a moment
it seemed to him that he could almost see with his
physical eyes the arched stone mullions of the gate-house
window through which he looked.

At length she spoke once more.

" Hugh, has it ever occurred to you to wonder exactly
what Ambrosius is ? "

" Well, I took it for granted he was a dead and gone
monk, the poor chap they did to death belowstairs across
the way.   And that I'm more or less mediumistic,
without ever having realised it, and that he'd speak
through me, given half a chance."

" That's one possibility," said Mona.

" Is there any other ?   Beyond my being just plain
loopy ? "

" Yes, there is another.   Ever heard of reincarnation,
Hugh ? "

" Yes, I've heard something.   It means we've lived
before, doesn't it ?   Do you think I knew Ambrosius in
a past life ? "

" Might have," said Mona noncommittally, wondering
how much she dared say without bringing about a general
gaol-delivery of the subconscious contents.   Silence fell
between them again.

Then suddenly Hugh burst out :   " Mona, I wish to

God you'd tell me what you really think. I don't know where I am, and I'll go crazy in good earnest if I don't find out soon."

"All right," said Mona in a low voice, "I'll tell you. Of course I may be wrong, but personally I think you actually are Ambrosius."

"What do you mean? You mean I've just imagined him?"

"No, I mean you've been him. The soul that is now you was once Ambrosius, and before that—some one else again."

"Mona, I don't understand. What do you mean?"

She could tell by his voice that Hugh was very agitated, and hoped to heaven that she had not said too much. But there was no backing out now.

"You've heard Uncle Jelkes talk of reincarnation?" she said quietly, trying to pull him together by her own quietness.

"Yes, I've heard him talk, but I'm not sure I took in very much of it. He's too metaphysical for me. You mean that Ambrosius is part of myself? A kind of split personality?"

"No, not that either. That implies a pathology— something gone wrong. Ambrosius isn't that. At least, he needn't be, if we handle him the right way. He's part of you, Hugh, part of your subconscious that's coming up, not something outside you."

"I wish to God he were, Mona. It seems to me that Ambrosius is everything I ought to be but aren't."

"Yes, he probably is. There's a whole lot of you that has slipped into Ambrosius and got lost. If we get him back, you'll recover it."

"This is the most sensible thing I've heard yet. Every one else stampedes at the mention of Ambrosius. It's only you who've got the pluck to stand up to him. I'm dashed grateful to you, Mona."

She did not answer, but sat staring into the fire, and

he sat watching her, the conviction strengthening all the time that the way to Mona lay through Ambrosius' hood, though how, or why, he could not say.

He broke the silence, which threatened to become permanent, so far away did Mona seem.

" Well now, what about it ? Supposing I was Ambrosius in a past life, what do I do about it in this one ? "

Mona roused herself.

" That was just what I was puzzling over," she said. " So far as I can see, the only thing for you to do is to face up to Ambrosius, and then absorb him. Only I don't quite know how it is to be done."

" I do, though," said Hugh. " I have only got to think of myself as him, and feel him strongly, and I *am* him. I've done it several times for brief moments, and I haven't measured my length, either, on the last two or three occasions."

" If you do that," said Mona, " Ambrosius will absorb you instead of your absorbing him."

" I shouldn't object to that," said Hugh, " he's a dashed sight better specimen than I am. Would you object, Mona, if that happened ? If Ambrosius absorbed me, would it be the end of our friendship ? "

" Goodness only knows," said Mona. " I've no idea. You'll have to chance it."

Hugh sat in silence for a time. At length he spoke :

" I believe you'd like Ambrosius a lot better than you like me, Mona. Oddly enough, you know, it's through you I always get into touch with Ambrosius. He missed a lot in life, and so have I ; and it's when I get comparing what I have missed with what Ambrosius missed that I get in touch with him."

Mona did not offer any comment.

Hugh spoke again :

" If you're game for the experiment, I am. If you and Uncle Jelkes between you will tackle Ambrosius when he comes along, I'll go and fetch him."

" Uncle Jelkes can't do much in this business," said
Mona in a low voice.   " It is I who have got to tackle
Ambrosius, Hugh.   I'm the only person who can do
anything with him."

Hugh looked at her without speaking.

" Yes, you're right," he said at length.   " That is, if
it isn't too much to ask of you."

Silence fell between them again.   After a long pause,
while the fire settled upon its ashes and the room got
dark, Hugh spoke.

" Do you know what I shall do, Mona, if things turn
out all right, and I'm no longer only half there, like I
am now, nor clean bug-house, like Ambrosius ? "

" No ? "

" I shall ask you if you'll marry me.   Now don't you
start getting worried.   There's no need for you to go to
the trouble of refusing me, for I'm not asking you now.
But if things straighten out for me, I shall come and ask
you."

" Rats," said Mona.   " If things straighten out for
you, you won't want to marry me."

" Well, we'll see about that when the time comes.
Anyway, you can count on a square deal, whatever it
may be."

They both did more thinking than sleeping that night.
Mona had said a great deal more than she had meant to,
and was very worried in consequence.   She had merely
been debating possibilities when Hugh had come in,
and taken by surprise and shaken off her poise, had blurted
out what was in her mind.   She could not understand
herself ; at the best of times she was a silent, reserved
person, and on this occasion, when she was decidedly
uneasy and had by no means arrived at any conclusion or
decision, she could not understand why she had committed herself so rashly.   And she had said so much that
it was impossible to back out.   Hugh had been started
off on a line of ideas that would bear fruit in the near

future, if she were not very much mistaken ; any wavering or uncertainty in handling him, and there would be
a crash as surely as if he were a high-powered car driven
at speed.　Only absolute steadiness and an iron nerve
could take Hugh round his corners.

Hugh's suggestion of marriage she did not take
seriously.　She was not in the least attracted by him,
though she liked him and was exceedingly sorry for
him ; but as she had said to Jelkes, a woman of her type
does not make a marriage on such a basis as that.　Mona
had known real, heart-searing passion, and would never
mistake mere emotional twitchings for the great love.

She was old enough, and disillusioned enough, to
consider the possibility of marrying for the sake of a
home, but she felt perfectly certain that Hugh, once
restored to normal, would return to the fleshpots of
Egypt as Jelkes had repeatedly declared.　They came
from such totally different worlds, did she and Hugh,
that he might as well have married a Martian or a Hotten-
tot for all he would have in common with her.　None
of his friends would accept her, and she would loathe his
way of life, to judge, at least, from what she had heard
of it from Mrs Macintosh.　She could not play bridge :
she had not a notion how to give a dinner-party, or even
how to attend one ;　and as for a week-end at a country
house, it would be the death of her.　She could neither
dress nor walk nor talk as did the women of his world,
and her dignity was a thing that Mona valued highly ;
she would not willingly expose herself to the criticisms
of butlers and lady's maids and all the folk who know a
great deal more about the gentry than the gentry know
about themselves.

She had seen enough of the world to know that a man
of Hugh's watery, impressionable, over-sensitive type
will cling to any hand held out to him when in trouble,
but once the trouble is over, will shake that hand very
warmly in thanks and then let go of it.

Mona asked herself how it had come about that she, who considered herself the least impressionable of women, and who from bitter past experience dreaded emotional entanglements as a burnt child dreads fire, should have let herself in for this schemozzle with Hugh? She cast her mind back to the scene as she had sat in the gathering dusk over the fire, and remembered that she had not been thinking of Ambrosius at all at the moment, nor even of Hugh directly, but of the dream of Greece about which Hugh had told her, and of the sun-drenched hill-side above the sea where he had followed a woman clad in a fawn-skin who had had her carriage and walk. Mona, who was well read in modern psychology, knew at once what Hugh's subconscious had up and said in that dream. But she also knew that such a scene as this had been a favourite phantasy of hers all through her childhood and girlhood. As a child she had day-dreamed of racing over sun-warmed rocks beside a boy-comrade, clad in the short Spartan tunic she had seen in her book of Greek legends. As she grew older, the phantasy had grown more romantic, and it was the pursuit of the lover, not the hand in hand running of comrades that she phantasied. Later, when Jelkes introduced her to the knowledge of the ancient Mysteries and what was taught at Eleusis, the phantasy took on yet another content, and she visualised herself as the mænad adoring Dionysos, giver of ecstasy, and following the beautiful god over the mountains in the frenzied running dance. There were times when Mona had taken off her shoes and stockings and danced on the dew-soaked turf. She, who could not dance the modern nigger-inspired ball-room dances, had a rhythmic movement of her own and an inner singing to accompany it, and sometimes, when she was certain of solitude she had given way to it. No one had ever seen her, not even Jelkes, and she would have flown like a mænad at any one who spied upon her. There was another dance she knew, the dance of the priestesses of the sea-goddess whereby the moon is invoked, but she had never dared to try that.

It was odd that Hugh should have had the same phantasy in his dream. And yet not inexplicable. There was no need to look for an esoteric explanation. Hugh had had the usual public school smattering of the classics, and images of ancient Greece and Rome would be lying latent in his mind. No, she must not take the shared phantasy as indicative of twin soulery or any such tosh. That was merely asking for trouble. It was quite a tricky enough business even when handled impersonally, and utterly impossible if she let her feelings in any way become involved.

Remembering Hugh's reactions in his dream, and the face of Ambrosius when he appeared in the upper room of the museum, Mona considered the possibility of some fairly drastic experiences before they had got Hugh safely onto his feet and returned him whence he came. Remembering Freud's dictum that cure proceeds via transference, she faced the possibility of having to become Hugh's mistress for a time, and being a modern maiden, concluded that it wouldn't kill her if she had to. Thanks to the ministrations of Malthus, unpleasant consequences were highly improbable, and Mona cared nothing for conventions and had her own ideas on the subject of morals. She was not a sensual woman, and no passing attraction had any power to stir her senses to flash-point ; she would sooner put her last shilling in the gas and her head in the gas-oven than sell herself for money, however great her need ; but she would give herself for love freely, and under whatever conditions she saw fit ; and oddly enough, she would also give herself out of pity if the need were great enough ; and though she would have agreed, and in fact asserted, that she was unconventional, she would not have admitted that she was immoral. She would have considered that term much more applicable to the woman who claims all the assets of marriage and doesn't give value for money.

Such being Mona's amoral attitude, she contemplated the handling of Hugh in a purely clinical spirit.

Hugh, for his part, stood in front of his low-pitched window with his hands in his pockets staring out into the moonlight hour after hour, totally unconscious of the lapse of time. At first his head was in such a whirl that he could only see pictures and could not think at all. He saw the Greek hill-side and knew that the woman he had been pursuing was beyond all question Mona, and wondered whether in a still earlier incarnation he had enacted just such a scene. He saw Ambrosius walking around the priory as it was a-building, just as he himself had walked around it while it was being restored. He thought of the discovery he had made in the chapel of the trick of looking out of Ambrosius' hood in order to become Ambrosius.

This checked the flight of his imagination and gave him a cold feeling all down his spine. Dared he do that trick? And if it came off, what the devil would happen? He did not care twopence about what happened to himself. The thing that worried him was what he might do to Mona Wilton—scare her into the middle of next week and offend her beyond repair? He had no confidence in Ambrosius' morals. He judged that that repressed celibate would break out pretty badly once he started, and whether he were the result of Greek magic in the past or a marriage gone wrong in the present, the consequences would be the same. Hugh funked the responsibility of evoking Ambrosius.

Finally he went to bed, very bothered and depleted and fed-up, and dreamt unhappy dreams about his mother and the person he now thought of as his first wife.

In the morning Mona met a dispirited Hugh at breakfast, and could have shaken him for the way in which his moods veered with the wind. So far as could be judged from his demeanour, yesterday's conversation might never have taken place. After breakfast he disappeared and she saw him no more.

Her household duties concluded, she took a note-book and measuring-rod and set out to plan the garden she intended to make inside the courtyard of the old farm-house. There should also, she thought, be a wide double herbaceous border leading from the west door out across the pasture to the fir-wood, bordering the faint track that led thither and that was a favourite sunset stroll. There could be no question of stately hollyhocks and regal delphiniums in the shallow, stony soil upon the chalk, but grey, aromatic things such as sea-lavender and old man's beard; goat's rue and thrift; flowering sage, scarlet and blue, and southernwood and rosemary. It was hot in the bright spring sunshine, and Mona wished she had departed from her usual custom and put on a hat.

Fearing a headache if she persevered, she went just inside the door of the chapel to make her notes and calculate her measurements. She was busily engaged in adding and subtracting, and dividing yards into feet, when there stole over her a feeling that she was not alone. She glanced uneasily over her shoulder, cross with herself for being so nervous, and saw Hugh standing bolt upright and motionless in the centre of the crude Zodiac on the tessellated pavement of the sanctuary. She had not noticed him when she came in because her eyes had been too dazzled by the outside glare to see anything in the semi-darkness of the chapel. She wondered how long he had stood like this, and whether he had been there ever since breakfast, for he was so rigid and immobile that it looked as if he would stand for ever.

She half turned on the stone ledge on which she was seated and gave herself over to watching him. That motionless, absorbed figure produced a very queer feeling as one watched it. She wondered whether it were

Ambrosius or Hugh, or a blend of the two, and for some reason she could not define, inclined to the latter idea.

He stood in the centre of the circle of the Zodiac, his feet in a smaller circle which contained the signs of the four elements of earth, air, fire and water. In the compartments formed by the radii of the signs were small holes into which Mona knew the signs representing the seven planets could be fitted according to the manner in which they stood in their heavenly houses as the wheel of the skies revolved. Hugh was standing in the exact centre of the symbolic representation of the universe, and Mona thought that she had never believed it possible that any living being could be so absolutely alone.

All her irritation with Hugh vanished. He was the watery type, under the presidency of the Moon and Aquarius ; it was his nature to be attentive to the wavering images reflected by moonlight on water. She herself was of the earth, being a Virgo, and Virgo, by the way, is not Ever-virgin, but also Many-breasted.

She felt a profound pity for that lonely soul up there in the shadows of the east, unlighted by any window in the sanctuary, for Ambrosius, for some reason best known to himself, had left the eastern end of his church in darkness. She sat waiting, watching, and wondering. It seemed as if Hugh would stand there indefinitely. Finally she could bear the tension no longer, and moving silently on her jute-soled shoes, she passed up the aisle and took her stand behind and a little to one side of him.

After a few moments he, like herself, became aware that he was not alone, looked over his shoulder, and saw her. He looked at her for a moment, and his face took on a very strange expression ; melancholy, fatalistic, and yet with a touch of fire and fanaticism slumbering behind his eyes. She had a queer feeling that more than one pair of eyes were looking out from under Hugh's rather heavy lids.

They looked at each other without speaking. Speech

was impossible. That was a silence that could not be broken. Then Hugh held out his hand and she put hers in it. Her unhesitating response sent a thrill through Hugh, and his face twitched in a manner that Mona knew was a sure indication that he was emotionally moved. Then he turned towards the East again, and drew her to stand beside him within the circle of the Elements, and they stood facing the altar that was not there, and which, if it had been there, would have been the throne of the goat-god, hand in hand, as if being married.

Mona's heart was beating hard in her throat. There was no knowing what was going to happen next. Ambrosius was capable of anything. Then gradually the panic fear passed away and its place was taken by a profound peace. Then the peace gave place to a curious tense thrilling, like a great organ-note sounding in the soul. Then that too gradually died away, and she knew that they were back to normal. Hugh turned and looked at her again, and she felt the tragedy of that man, whether as Hugh or Ambrosius. She stood with her hand in his and looked into his eyes, and he looked back into hers, a thing that, shifty-eyed with shyness, he had never done before, and she felt that the barriers were down between them. Then he dropped her hand and stood helplessly before her, as if all volition had left him.

"Shall we go now?" she said, touching him lightly on the sleeve. He nodded, and fell into step beside her as they went down the aisle together. She felt a hand laid on her shoulder, looked up, and in the light of the doorway saw Hugh looking very lined and grey and worn and much more round-shouldered than usual.

"These things are tearing me to pieces, Mona," he said in a low voice. "God knows what will be the upshot of it."

They sat down on a low bench in the angle of the wall, the heat of the spring sun warming them after the chill of the chapel; Hugh stretched out his long legs and put his hands behind his head and leant back and shut his eyes. Mona gazed at him anxiously. He looked absolutely done.

The obvious, common-sense remedy was for Hugh to refrain from playing about with Ambrosius any more. But Mona had a profound conviction that Hugh had got to work through Ambrosius and come out the other side if things were ever to be right with him, and that if he turned back now it would be to re-enter into the death-in-life that was closing about him when he had first come to the Marylebone bookshop.

At that moment they heard a footstep on the gravel, and Mr Watney appeared. Mona was never so pleased to see anyone in her life.

Hugh pulled himself together and did the polite. Produced cigarettes and went in search of whisky, leaving Mona and the solicitor together.

" Well ? " said Mr Watney as soon as they were alone. " And how is our friend ? "

" I am rather bothered about him," said Mona, " and I don't feel that doctors would be the slightest use. You see, he's had a pretty bad shock, and there is nothing they can give him for that except bromide, is there ? "

" He certainly does not look right, and he has gone downhill since I was here the other evening. Do you know anything of the nature of the shock he has had ? "

" His wife was killed in a motor-smash, and it all came out about how she was carrying on with another man at the time. He had never suspected it and had absolutely believed in her."

" How long ago was this ? "

" It must be getting on for two months now."

" Then I do not think that was the cause of the trouble, for he was not fond of her."

" How do you know ? "

" Because he is obviously very much in love with you."

Mona was too worried to make the indignant repudiation which is the usual reply to such a charge.

" What makes you think that ? " she asked soberly, as if Mr Watney had drawn her attention to an ominous symptom.

He looked at her sharply over his spectacles.

" Hadn't you seen that for yourself ? "

" I had seen it, but I hadn't taken it seriously, knowing his type of man."

" Then you have made a mistake.  He is taking it very seriously."

" How do you know ? "

" I was watching him when you said that there was no marriage in the offing the other afternoon.  It was a knock-out blow for him, or I'm very much mistaken. Whatever other troubles he may have, that is what is causing the flare-up now."

" Oh dear, this is very awkward," said Mona.  " I knew he wanted to flirt with me, but I had no idea it was as serious as all that.  What's to be done about it ?  Do you think I ought to go away ? "

" Don't you care about him ? "

" Not in that way.   It wouldn't work."

" Why not ? "

" We belong to different worlds.  We've got nothing in common.  I'd never settle with him, and he'd never settle with me."

" Well, I suppose you know your own business best, but I'm sorry.  He's a nice fellow, and it would have been the salvation of him."

At that moment Hugh returned with the drinks, shared the whisky with Mr Watney, and gave Mona a cocktail, which she was very glad to have.

They chatted in a desultory manner.  Hugh invited Mr Watney to lunch, which invitation was accepted, and Mona fled to see if there were enough food.  It would never have entered Hugh's head to raise that point before issuing an invitation.

The moment she had turned the corner, Hugh's manner changed.

" I want to make a new will," he said abruptly.

" Do you ? " said the solicitor, wondering what was afoot now. " If you can give me pencil and paper I'll jot down the headings and let you have a draft."

Hugh felt through his pockets, found one of Mr Pinker's marvellous itemised accounts, and handed it to him. Mr Watney turned it over, changed his spectacles, and prepared to take his instructions.

An eighth of Hugh's personal estate was to go to his mother and to each of his three sisters. The remaining half was to be divided equally between Mona and Jelkes. Mona was to have Monks Farm. Mr Watney gasped. The papers had arrived from his predecessors, and he knew the size of that estate.

" That will is certain to be contested," said Hugh. " How can we protect it ? "

" Give Mr Jelkes and Miss Wilton life interests only, with reversion to your sisters' children providing no one gives trouble. The children of anyone giving trouble to lose their share, proceeds to be divided between the children of the legatees who don't give trouble. Then they'll all cut each other's throats. That'll keep 'em quiet. Psychology again."

" That's all right as far as Jelkes goes. He's in the sear and yellow leaf. He's not likely to raise a family. But I should like Miss Wilton to have her share outright in case she ever has any kids."

" Is she likely to marry ? "

" I fancy there's someone in the offing."

" I was chatting to her just now and she implied there wasn't."

" Did she ? " said Hugh, suddenly thoughtful. " Did she ? Oh well, I don't suppose it makes much difference."

He seemed sunk in thought, which to judge from his expression was gloomy.

Then Mona called them to lunch. Everyone did their best, but it was not a cheery meal, and out of the corner of his eye Mr Watney watched Hugh lowering the whisky.

# CHAPTER XXII

AFTER Mr Watney had gone Hugh sat over the fire in the little sitting-room smoking a big cigar that had been given him. As Mona came into the room he heaved it into the fire.

"Can't say I really like cigars," he said. "Got any gaspers, Mona? I've run out."

Mona produced the desired gaspers out of that universal receptacle, the front of her jumper.

Hugh was always running out of gaspers, and out of small change to buy gaspers, and borrowing from Mona. In fact as far as petty cash was concerned, he was in a chronic condition of impecuniosity. He was only a rich man when he had his cheque-book in his hand—and then he invariably paid twice as much for a thing as it was worth because he hated bargaining and money meant nothing to him. This was a thing that riled Mona beyond all bearing, and she had had serious thoughts of marrying him simply to spite the antique furniture trade.

Mona did not take the other big arm-chair on the opposite side of the hearth, as was her usual Darby and Joan custom, but fidgeted about the room. She wanted to talk to Hugh, but found it difficult to make a start. Hugh paid no attention to her. The sun outside was shining gloriously, but he had got all the windows tight shut and was throwing logs on the fire.

"Why don't you come outside?" said Mona. "It's a shame to leave this sunshine running to waste."

"Too much trouble to move," said Hugh, kicking a protruding log impatiently.

Mona, who had scant patience with spoilt children, cleared out and left him, hoping that, what with the large lunch and the many whiskies and the hot room, he would sleep himself sensible by tea-time.

When she returned from her walk as the early spring dusk closed in, Hugh greeted her with the information that there had been a telephone call for her.

" A Mrs Madden," he said. " She said you would know her as Lucy Whitley. She was at school with you. She's in town for a few days and wants you to join her for the week-end. I said you'd go."

" Oh no, I won't," said Mona. " I'm not leaving here at the present moment."

" Why not ? "

" Ambrosius might turn up. I can't leave you to wrestle with that alone."

Hugh did not express either gratitude or deprecation, but sat in silence. The silence lasted so long that when at length he spoke Mona could not think for a moment what he was referring to.

" I can't expect you to dry-nurse me indefinitely," he said.

Common sense bade her return an airy answer, but something that was not sensible welled up from deep in her, and she replied :

" We'll see this through together, Hugh."

Again he made no acknowledgment.

" Tell me, what were you doing in the chapel this morning ? " said Mona.

" Trying to work things out."

" Any luck ? "

" No, not much."

" Did you get Ambrosius ? "

" No, didn't try for him. To tell you the honest truth, Mona, I'm a bit scared of Ambrosius. You see, I feel that when he comes, he'll come with the hell of a rush, and I'm not sure that he's to be trusted. I'm certainly not going to chance his coming through while I'm alone in the house with you. Ambrosius wouldn't take no for an answer, if I know him."

" I've got a notion I could handle Ambrosius," said Mona.

" I've got a notion you couldn't," said Hugh.

" I'll tell you a curious thing, Hugh, do you know that this business goes back long before Ambrosius ? "

" What do you mean ? "

" Do you remember your dream of the Grecian hillside ? Well, that used to be my favourite day-dream when I was a child. Fawn-skin and all."

To her surprise this did not elicit the reaction she had expected ; she looked round at Hugh, and saw that there was a curious tense immobility about him. She waited.

Presently he spoke :

" Do you know what struck me about you when I saw you when I was Ambrosius ? "

" No ? "

" That you were the succuba that had haunted my dreams all my life."

Silence fell between them again as each tried to realise the significance of what the other had said. Mona was well acquainted with what both the old theologians and the modern psychologists have to say about the demons that haunt men's sleep. She knew all about the theory of dream mechanism and wish fulfilment, and all the rest of the psychological bag of tricks. She had also heard Jelkes discourse on time and space as known to the modern philosopher. Whether there was between herself and Hugh a bond of the soul forged in ancient Greece in a bygone life, or whether she was a type that appealed to that particular sex-starved male, depended entirely upon whether one considered time as a mode of consciousness or a matter of clocks.

One thing stood out quite clearly, however, she was the solution of Hugh's problem. If she were unwilling to solve it for him, it would go unsolved. And looking deeply into her own soul she had to face the fact that although Hugh might make no appeal to her as a man, there was a queer kind of fascination about Ambrosius.

She had always had a very strong feeling for the glory that was Greece and was firmly convinced that she had been an initiate of the Mysteries of the Earth Mother. Her childish fantasy of the swift free running in the short slit kirtle that earned the Spartan girls the opprobrious title of Thigh-showers from the rest of Greece, had given place, as she grew older, to a fantasy in which she was a priestess and an initiate, penetrating deep and secret things, and the boy-comrade of the childish day-dream became the priest-initiator of the Mysteries. Not very long before Hugh had appeared on the scene, she had been reading in one of the books borrowed from Jelkes' miscellaneous stock in trade of the interpretation put by modern scholarship upon the scurrilous abuse which the Early Fathers heaped upon the pagan faiths they sought to supplant. She knew that the alleged temple orgies were far from being the *Mi-Carême* they were supposed to be, but were solemn and sacrificial acts into which no human feeling entered.

At the climax of the Mysteries of the Earth Mother all the lights went out, and the high priest and the chief priestess descended in darkness into the crypt and there consummated a union that was a sacrament just as much as eating the Body and drinking the Blood. She knew the curious magical bond that the act of union makes between a man and a woman, whether they love, or whether they hate, or whether they buy and sell in sordid indifference. If such a bond is forged by a simple animal function, what must be the bond that is forged by such a sacramental rite as that of the pastos of Eleusis?

"Do you know what I think, Hugh?" she said, breaking the long silence that had settled upon the darkening room. "I think that there is a path opening before us, if we have the nerve to take it, that will lead us to some very wonderful things. I'll face it if you will,

but remember, once we start on it, there will be no turning back."

"That's what I have begun to suspect," said Hugh.
"I tried to turn back this morning when I got the wind
up over you and Ambrosius, and found it was like
swimming across a river. It's no good thinking you
can't make it after you've got more than half way across.
You've got to make it. The only thing that bothers me
is what Ambrosius will do to you when he comes
through, for I've got absolutely no control over Ambrosius, you know, Mona."

"I'll have to tackle Ambrosius and come to terms
with him," said Mona. "It's the only thing to be done."

"I don't envy you the job," said Hugh, "and I wish
to goodness I knew what you'll have to say to me when
I take over from him again after the interview. Personally, I think Ambrosius is quite capable of strangling
you."

"I'm not worrying about that. It's something else
I'm worrying about."

"What is it, Mona?" Hugh's face had a very queer
look on it as he sat very quiet in his chair watching her.
She had a feeling that Ambrosius was not far off. It was
not easy to begin, however, and she felt her way.

"I am worried about you because I think you're
bothered about something. Can you tell me what it is?"

Hugh shifted uneasily in his chair and looked away.

"Was that why you wouldn't go up to see your pal
over the week-end?"

"Yes."

"You might just as well have gone. I've got to get
used to standing on my own feet."

"No, you haven't. You can't stand on your own feet
without me, Hugh. Not yet, anyway. Don't you know
that?"

"Yes, I know it all right, but I reckoned I'd got to.
I'm not such a fool as not to realise how you feel about

me. You're very kind to me, but if I overstep the limits you've set, you'll drop me like a hot coal. I can have your kindness, and I can have your companionship, as long as I don't transgress ; but if I forget my manners, I'm for it. Well, I accept that, Mona. It's as much as I can hope for, and more than I have any right to expect, and I reckon I can consider myself lucky, and I ought to be damned grateful to have got so much."

He suddenly looked up and faced her.

" It's odd, isn't it, how things recur in one's life ? Those were exactly the terms on which I lived with my wife. I reckon I'm a spiritual diabetic—I can only keep alive provided I'm willing to stick to a starvation diet."

Mona laid her hand on his knee.

" Do you know that there's a bond that binds me to you, just as there's one that binds you to me ? "

" Yes, I know there is. I've watched you straining at it."

" I may have done at first, but I feel differently about it now."

" I suppose you wouldn't care to marry me, Mona ? "

" Not as things are at present. It wouldn't be fair."

" Well, I don't blame you."

" No, I don't mean it like that. I mean I wouldn't care to take advantage of you when you aren't youself. If I didn't really like you, Hugh, I might ; it's naturally a temptation to any one placed as I am, but I'm not going to do it. You're too good a chap to be exploited. If I marry you at all, I'll marry you properly, because I really want to."

Hugh put his hand over hers as it rested on his knee.

" I'd sooner be refused by you for that reason than accepted by anyone else," he said, and they sat silently together hand in hand, looking into the fire.

At length Hugh spoke.

" The only person I've ever known to whom my money made absolutely no difference is old Jelkes."

" It makes no difference whatever to me," said Mona
tartly, trying to withdraw her hand, but Hugh wouldn't
let her.

" Oh yes, it does.  You shy like a frightened horse
whenever you come up against it.  The people I meet
can be divided into two classes, the people who want a
lick at my silver spoon, and hang out their tongues whenever I come near ;  and the people who think I'll think
they want a lick at it, and stick out their tongues whenever I come near.  It may show a healthy spirit in them,
but it's rather trying for me.  There's no possibility of a
natural relationship with anybody when you've got too
much money, and it gets you as suspicious as an electric
hare at a dog-race.  It's a depraved form of royalty, I
suppose.

" The only money I ever made in my life was the tanner
I got selling chuck-outs from old Jelkes' twopenny bin
—and dash it all, if I haven't forgotten to give it to the
old buster and gone and embezzled it !  A sandwich-
board is about my fighting-weight if I were thrown on
my own resources.  I didn't make my money.  I don't
suppose I should have kept it if it hadn't been tied up so
that I couldn't get at it till I married.  I have never done
any good with it, and I've never got any good out of it."

" Don't you ever give anything to charity ? "

" God, yes, I give thousands.  Mother's a whale on
knowing the right things to give to.  The right things
socially, I mean.  She wants me to save up and buy a
peerage.  But I'd sooner give to party funds if I'm going
to do that.  You get better value for your money provided you time it rightly.  No good giving to a party
that's just going into the wilderness for the next five
years."

" Then you've got no political convictions ? "

" Nobody's got any political convictions except
leader-writers, my dear girl, and they change them when
they change their papers.  There are only two parties,

the ins and the outs, and the thing to give to is the just-coming-ins. But you've got to mind you aren't done. You can't sue on a thing like that, you know. The best way is to sign your cheque with the name you mean to take for your title, and then they've got to elevate you to the peerage before they can cash it. No, Mona, charity, as charity, is all my eye. The big charities are just big business in the poverty trade.

"And charity's unsound, anyway. The Warehouse-man's Orphanage comes to me and says : ' Mr Paston, your firm employs over two thousand clerks and ware-housemen, won't you give us something ? ' I give them a cheque for four figures, and everyone says how good I am. But damn it all, if we paid 'em decently, they'd provide for their own widows and orphans. Soothing-syrup for the under-dog, Mona, so's he won't bite the seat out of our pants, that's what charity is. We make the conditions that shove 'em under, and then chuck 'em a life-line lest their corpses get into the water-supply."

"You don't seem to have much faith in human nature."

"I haven't. Not when it's exposed to the tempta-tions it's exposed to when it gets near me. You and Jelkes and Mrs Macintosh are the only people who've ever given me anything like a square deal. And you've none of you got any use for me as a human being. You all think I'm a fool, and I guess you're right."

Mona did not know what to say, for that was exactly what they did think.

"Mona, has it ever struck you that the man isn't breeched who's grateful for kindness from a woman ? "

"But you have just been saying that you were grate-ful ? "

"Oh, damn it all, that's just like biting on a sore tooth. You bite on it because it's sore out of pure cussedness."

Mona rose. The heart to heart talk she had intended

to have with Hugh had not been a success. He had merely been irritable and irritating. If marriage with him were going to be like this, she certainly wasn't having any. Much better to struggle on as she was and keep her freedom.

" I'm afraid I've been a swine, Mona."

" Yes, I'm afraid you have."

" I wish you'd give me a kiss."

· Why in God's name should I give you a kiss after the way you've behaved all afternoon ? "

" If you had Ambrosius to deal with, he wouldn't ask for a kiss, he'd take it. By Jove, why shouldn't I get Ambrosius to kiss you for me ? It would be rather a lark."

" If you do, I'll never forgive you."

Hugh put his back against the door and looked at her fixedly, and as he looked, she watched his face begin to change. But the change had hardly started before it stopped.

" Sorry, that was caddish. Sorry, Mona."

He held the door open for her.

She walked over to it, looked up at him, held out her hand and said :

" Shake ? "

He gripped her hand hard.

" Thanks. That was very sweet of you, Mona."

# CHAPTER XXIII

HUGH was so late getting down next morning that he had to eat his breakfast by himself, which he hated.

He could hear Mona's voice in the back premises talking to Silly Lizzie, who appeared to be in a great state of mind. There were occasional interpolations from Bill Pascoe. There did not seem to be exactly a row going on, but things sounded rather crucial. Gradually it dawned on the listener that the invocation of Pan on which they were engaged had not been without results, and that Mona was engaged in persuading Silly Lizzie that it was her duty to let Bill Pascoe make an honest woman of her, which to his credit he appeared to be quite willing to do. Lizzie appeared to think, however, that as she had fallen into sin it was her bounden duty to stop there, and that nothing could ever be the same again. Hugh was immensely amused at Mona's matter of fact, man-of-the-world attitude in the matter. The reprobate Bill and she were entirely of one mind and seemed to understand each other perfectly and be supporting each other warmly. Lizzie's attitude, on the other hand, was strictly conventional, and she overflowed into a squelching repentance and misery by way of compensating for her previous actions. She was also terrified of Bill's mother.

Hugh was not at all sure that Mona was justified in the line she was taking unless it were absolutely necessary ; Lizzie would be an exceedingly uneugenic wife—but then Bill would be an exceedingly unhygienic husband, so perhaps it was as well that they should pair off and cancel each other out, rather than make better folk miserable. Finally Lizzie's blubbering became less stormy, and Bill's jocular basso more in evidence, and presently Mona left the happy pair to their own devices, and came out to join Hugh where he stood leaning against the door-post, smoking in the sunshine. Together they strolled slowly to the seat in the angle of the wall. Hugh gave Mona a cigarette and lit it for her.

"You have taken on a serious responsibility, Mona. Bill and Lizzie will produce things with tails if family likenesses are anything to go by."

"I think they have got about as good as they could expect, don't you?" said Mona. "It would be awful if either of them married anyone decent."

"Mona, is this the result of the invocation of Pan I did in the chapel yesterday?"

"Yes, I expect so."

"If it affects Silly and Bill like this, what is it going to do to us?"

Mona did not answer.

"I admit we have got better headpieces than they have," Hugh went on, "but it has got to be considered."

Mona scraped the gravel with the toe of her shoe.

"What are you driving at, Hugh?"

"This is what I am driving at, Mona. I think that if Pan comes through in force, he will clear out all the stopped-up inhibitions in me, and I shall be all right after that."

"How do you expect him to come through?"

"As an emotional upheaval. I suppose you don't think you are taking rather a long chance, alone at the farm with me like this, while I am stirring up Pan with a pole?"

"I can take care of myself."

"If I did the right thing by you, I should take you home to your mother; but life is sweet, Mona, and I am afraid I'm not going to."

She did not answer.

Hugh spoke again.

Do you remember Des Esseintes' stunt—in Huysmans' '*A Rebours*', you know? The all-black dinner-party when he wished to feel particularly wicked—or wished his pals to think he was feeling particularly wicked. And the bedroom got up with fawn-coloured watered silk to look like a stone-walled cell with a leaky roof? Well, what about it? Don't you think we ought to be getting on with the job?"

Mona flushed at the sudden recall to the business relationship, which had gone from her mind as completely as if it had never existed.

"Yes, certainly," she said. "What would you like me to start on first?"

"Well, I don't quite know. I'll have to ask your Uncle Jelkes. He's the expert. And I'll have to feel my way a bit. I've a sort of notion things will come clear when we make a move. But there's one thing I wish you would fit me up with, so as I can make a start, and that's a monk's robe like Ambrosius was wearing in the picture in the psalter."

Mona raised startled eyes to his.

"What are you going to do?" she demanded anxiously.

He put his hand over hers.

"Mona, I'm going to bring Ambrosius back in good earnest. You needn't look so scared. It's the safest thing to do; for then we shall know where he is and what he is up to. You fit me up with my monk's robe, and then you clear off up to London and do a bit of shopping, and by the time you get back, I'll have Ambrosius cleared up, or know the reason why. Can you get the gear for a monk's outfit in the town, or must you go up to London for it?"

"I expect we can get it in the town. It's pretty common-place."

"Right-o. If you'll put your bonnet on, I'll run you into the town, and we can get the makings and sling it together temporarily. Then you can clear off and leave me to get on with it."

He drove Mona into the little country town, and waited in the parked car in the market-place and watched her enter a draper's and a saddler's and a shoe-shop. The back view of Mona, as she stalked through the market-day crowds at her unhurried pace, recalled his dream, and something inside him stirred like a quickening child. For a moment he saw Mona's face before him in her green hood—the face of the succuba—and all the crowded market place went strange and unreal and fantastic. It was only the great bell of the Abbey that recalled him to a sense of reality and self-control, and he knew that for a brief moment Ambrosius had come again, and that it was to his eyes that the modern market-place looked strange and fantastic, and it was the familiar sound of the great bell that had recalled him to himself.

The draper, of whom Mona bought half a dozen yards of the coarse black serge affected by country people in mourning, wondered who the poor young lady had lost. The saddler of whom she bought a length of the white cotton rope that is used to halter beasts at shows, wondered what she was exhibiting. The shoe-maker of whom she bought a pair of sandals such as are worn by healthy lifers thought she must have a hefty pair of feet for her size.

Mona spent the afternoon in her bedroom making the coarse black serge into a cowled robe. Where or how Hugh spent it, she did not know, save that he came in to supper looking exhausted.

" I want a fitting," said Mona in her abrupt way as soon as tea was finished.

" Right-o," said Hugh, and followed her upstairs when she went to fetch her handiwork.

He followed her straight into her room, which was not what she had bargained for, coming as she did from a class that do not walk into each other's rooms. However, he seemed to think nothing of it, and it was less trouble to accept the situation at its face value than to give it an importance it did not possess by shooing him out.

He pulled on the voluminous garment over his head like a shirt, tied the white halter-cord round his waist, and Mona knelt down at his feet to adjust the hem. He looked over her head into the mirror on the door of the wardrobe.

It gave him a very odd feeling to see himself in the long black robe with its white girdle and loose cowl around the neck. Raising his hands, he drew the cowl over his head and studied the effect of his own face, dimly seen in its shadow. It seemed extraordinarily natural to wear that kit. He had never felt so at home in anything in his life. He could understand why Jelkes, having once got used to it, always wore a dressing-gown. All his life he had had it rubbed into him, in season and out of season, that he chose his clothes badly, put them on badly, carried himself badly, and generally shuffled through life in a shame-faced fashion. But all that seemed wiped out with the assumption of the monk's robe. The long loose folds gave dignity to his lanky height. His round-shouldered stoop was appropriate in a churchman. The shadow of the cowl gave his hollow-cheeked, sharp-featured face a look of fine-drawn asceticism. He was an utterly different man.

And with the change came a sudden feeling of something dynamic ; of a self-confidence and self-will he had never known before. He looked down at Mona's black head as she knelt at his feet, and prompted by some sudden mischief, he laid his hand on it.

" Pax vobiscum, my daughter," he said.

Mona looked up, startled.

" It's all right, it's all right," he said, patting her on the head, seeing that he had really frightened her. " I'm not Ambrosius. I was only teasing you."

But she continued to crouch at his feet, clutching a fold of his robe.

He bent down and put a hand on her shoulder.

" What's the matter, Mona ? I'm frightfully sorry if I scared you. I was only joking. I'm not Ambrosius, you know, I'm Hugh."

" You're not the Hugh I know," said Mona.

He sat down on the edge of her low divan bed and drew her towards him till she was leaning against his knee. She stared up into his face, fascinated, oblivious of her position.

" What do you mean, Mona ? "

" There was a rush of power through you. I don't know what it means."

The realisation came to Hugh that Mona was completely dominated by him at that moment, and he could do anything he liked with her. The feeling gave him an extraordinary exhilaration and sense of freedom and power. He felt that he must say something, anything, to assert his new dominion and make it lock home.

" This is my bigger self coming through," he said in a low voice.

" I know it is."

" This is the Ambrosius that won't take no for an answer."

" This is the Ambrosius who won't get no for an answer ! " and Mona suddenly smiled at him in a way she had never done before.

Hugh sat motionless, not daring to break the spell ; wondering how long it would last before it faded into the light of common day.

" Do you know what I am going to do as soon as my robe is ready ? " he said at length. " I am going into the chapel, and I'm going to try and reconstruct the whole thing."

" Aren't I coming ? " said Mona.

" No," said Hugh, " you aren't. I'm taking no

chances on Ambrosius. If I were you I'd lock your door."

"But Hugh, you won't solve the problem with Ambrosius. It goes back further than him. It goes back to Greece—on the hill-side. And I want to be there. I'm sure I ought to be there. I'm part of it."

"You're no part of Ambrosius, Mona. You were simply his bad dream."

"That was his trouble, Hugh. That was what was the matter with him. It was because I wasn't there that things went wrong. They'll go wrong again if I'm not there this time."

Hugh laid his hand on the black head that had grown satiny as her health returned and she got decent food.

"We aren't having any human sacrifices in this temple. I'll tackle Ambrosius by myself, and then if anything goes wrong, the results will be minimal."

Mona clutched his wrist and looked up at him with anguished eyes.

"Oh, Hugh, I wish you'd let me come too. I am sure things will go wrong if I don't."

"No, little Mona. I know Ambrosius better than you do, and you just aren't coming."

"Hugh, if I'm not there to act as lightning-conductor, it will be as if you were struck by lightning. I know it will. I felt it on a small scale just now. If I hadn't been touching you when it happened, you'd have gone right off into Ambrosius."

Hugh leant forward and took her by the shoulders. "Mona, that is exactly what I have got to do. I've got to go right off into Ambrosius, and then I've got to bring Ambrosius back into me. But you needn't worry, because the two overlap nowadays, and I shan't get lost in the past, if that is what you are afraid of. Ambrosius and I have been overlapping more and more every time he comes through. A very little more, and we'll coincide, and then the job will be done."

Mona, looking up at his face, hawk-featured in the shadow of the cowl, knew instinctively that his mental attitude was that of a man accustomed to being obeyed, like Ambrosius, who had commanded a monastery as big as a small town, not like Hugh Paston, used to being chivied by his womenfolk.

\*     \*     \*     \*     \*

Mona kept herself busy in the garden during the days that followed. The thing she was doing was a severe strain, and it was telling on her. It was one thing to stand by Hugh with Jelkes beside her ; it was another to go on day after day alone, knowing that he was experimenting all the time, and that Ambrosius was drawing steadily nearer. She was determined not to summon Jelkes because she feared that his little business might tie itself into a knot if he were not there to attend to it, and then he would be without means of livelihood.

She worked steadily at the long border leading out into the field. Dug up by Bill's willing but inexpert efforts, it looked as if it had been shelled by heavy artillery. The grey, aromatic plants were going in one by one, and the sweet sharp scent given off by their foliage as she handled them filled the air as she worked. She concentrated on her planting, knowing that from the contact she was making with the newly-turned earth she was drawing strength and stability. The great Earth-mother, feeling herself tended and served, responded, and virtue flowed from her.

A shadow fell across the moist, sun-warmed soil, and Mona looked up to find Hugh Paston standing over her.

" Where have you put my black dressing-up gown, Mona ? "

" It's hanging over the banisters."

" Thanks."

Mona knew that the thing she greatly feared had now arrived. She watched Hugh walking back towards the house, never turning his head, which was not his usual custom when he was leaving her; unable to concentrate on the gardening any longer, she sat down on a pile of turf and lit a cigarette with fingers that trembled.

She was not troubled about the outcome of the affair for herself; she had little or nothing to lose; it was Hugh she feared for. Would he stand the strain of what they were doing to him, or were they pushing him over the border-line into a breakdown? And were they, after all, upon the right track? The occult philosophy is a very tenuous thing, and there is not much to lay hold of when it comes to putting it into practice. Was it, after all, just intellectual chess, with no relation whatsoever to life, like the speculations of the schoolmen, who debated how many angels could stand on the point of a needle?

So far as she could see, Pan, if stirred up sufficiently, would come into action. Hugh's real nature would break through to the surface, never to be repressed again. But several problems presented themselves. Would the Pan in Hugh be strong enough to break through his inhibitions? And if it did, would Hugh's nature stand the strain, or would it split? And supposing the two sides of Hugh's nature became merged into harmony, and normality were restored, what would the resulting man have to say to her? Would he, being made normal, return whence he came to the life that was habitual to him, as Jelkes had always declared? After all, this life at the farm with her was an absurd one for Hugh, with his position and resources. She was no mate for him if he were normal. It was this realisation that made her reluctant to yield to his advances. Hugh, normal, might, and probably would, be a very different person to the Hugh Paston she had learnt to know and like. Mona feared and distrusted Mayfair, having seen a good deal of its ways and works from the point of view of the under-dog. Old school ties stank to heaven in her nostrils after several unfortunate experiences. Mona's distrust was deep-rooted. From her point of view she could not see what there was to do with Mayfair, except exploit it and avoid its claws.

She sat on in the sun, smoking her cigarette down to the bitter end and burning her lips before she threw it away. She was a courageous creature, and could have steered steadily through the breakers ahead had she had any sort of a chart or compasses. It was the absence of any sea-mark by which she could lay her course that gave her anxiety. She knew the general direction, but she did not know where the water might be expected to shoal and the channel would have to be kept accurately.

But there are many worse sea-marks than a star. She found herself picturing the sea of her metaphor, indigo in the darkness, flecked here and there with foam where it broke on the unseen rocks. Above her head was the night sky and the stars. The sunlight faded out, and Mona was alone with her vision. She could feel the boat of the soul that carried herself and another reaching steadily on its tack; then she put it about, and it paid off on the next long slant of the wind. The night was closing in, the wind freshening, and she thought of the Master Who had walked the waves in the storm. His comforting touch was not for her if she were following after the Wild Goat of the mountains. And then there came to her the vision of Pan with his crook, Pan as the Shepherd; Pan with his pipes—the Nether Apollo— the harmoniser. She saw him, shaggy and wild and kind, leading the creatures of the flock of Ishmael down to the grey and barren shore that lay ahead. And he held out his crook towards her over the dark waters, and she laid the course that would bring her to him where he waited, the creatures of the flock of Ishmael about his feet—creatures for whom there was no place in the world of towns and men. Somehow she knew that steering by that uplifted crook, she would come steadily through the churning white water that marked the unseen rocks.

She held on her course fearlessly, even though she could hear the breakers closing in all round her. Then it seemed to her that the Shepherd of Goats rose up gigantic in the darkness, towering above her small boat, his slanting agate eyes gleaming and kindly. He was the keeper of all wild and hunted souls for which no place could be found in a man-made world, and she and Hugh were running in under the shadow of his crook. They were coming down onto the fundamental realities of life which cannot be shaken, to which all things must come in the end. She began to feel safe and secure. Keeping her eyes fixed on the fundamental reality, let it be what it might, she felt certain that she would steer the right course. This was the real invocation of Pan—the surrender to bed-rock natural fact, the return to Nature, the sinking back into the cosmic life after all the struggle to rise above it into an unnatural humanity. Animal is our beginning, and animal our end, and all our sophistications are carried on the back of the beast and we do ill to forget our humble brother. Uncared-for, collar-galled and filthy, he takes his revenge in the spread of disease. St Francis spoke contemptuously of Brother Ass, but man is a centaur who is related to Pegasus on one side of the family. The wise Cheiron who taught Æsculapius healing was carried swiftly on his four strong hooves. Perhaps there is a lesson in that for us.

Mona awoke from her dream of goats and centaurs and breaking seas to find that the sun had gone in and the wind of spring was cold. All the same, she knew that she had received the Blessing of Pan on her enterprise because she had given her undeviating loyalty to things natural—because she had said : ' What is truth ? ' and set to work to pursue it.

The gong summoned her to lunch, but Hugh did not appear. She sent Silly Lizzie, now radiant—so radiant that Mona could only conclude that she had sinned again

—up to his bedroom to see if he were there, but drew blank. Alarmed, which was hardly reasonable, for to be late for lunch does not necessarily argue tragedy, Mona ran across to the chapel, and drew blank once more. Hurrying back through the cloisters, she noticed that the door into the main building stood ajar with the huge key in the lock. Work on the main building had come to a standstill since Mr Pinker had finished his share of it and departed, and they had not yet begun on the furnishing. Decorating there was none, for all was stone.

The big stove in the cellar had done its work, and the place struck warm as she entered, for stone, once warmed up, holds the heat well. She ran from the one big room to the other, but they were empty ; peered into the cellar, but that was empty too, so far as she could see ; then upstairs, and along the long line of cells—all empty ; up again, to the chapel in the gable—empty also. Mona, now thoroughly scared, for there was a sense of impending evil about the place, ran down the worn twisting steps of the stairs again, and down into the cellar, the only place she had not searched thoroughly. One of the cells, that had probably been used as a coal-bunker by the last tenants, had a door to it, and the door was closed ; Mona pushed it open and looked in.

A single point of dim blue flame flickered in the darkness, giving practically no illumination ; but by the light coming down the stairway behind her she saw that Hugh, clad in his monk's robe, lay on a roughly-made bench, his cowl drawn over his face. The dim blue flame came from his cigarette-lighter, which he had stood burning in a niche high up in the wall. He did not stir at the sound of the opening door.

Anything might have happened in that airless cellar with the closed stove burning anthracite. Mona, terrified, pushed back the cowl from his face, and his eyes opened and looked up at her.

" This was how it should have been," he said, without

moving.

Then Mona knew that he had been deliberately living over again his life and death as Ambrosius in the hope of picking up the lost threads of memory. The atmosphere of doom was all about him, and it was this that she had felt as impending evil and danger. Powerfully and definitely, as only a trained mind could do it, he had created that atmosphere by his picturing, and she, being sensitive, had felt it.

' This was how it should have been,' he had said. This was how the monk Ambrosius, meeting death in his sins, had pictured it. The succuba of his dreams, the woman he had never seen in real life, had come to open the prison doors, and he would be free on the hillside of Greece where the Shepherd of Goats awaited him.

Mona took upon herself the personality of the dream-woman, the succuba, the visitant from the wide free world of the Unseen. She put out her hand and took his, knowing by the heat of his hand in hers how cold hers must feel to him.

" Come," she said, and he rose.

He followed her up the cellar steps, cowl over face, hands in sleeves, but at the top he turned aside from the door.

" I must call them also," he said, and went on up the winding stairs. She followed him, standing with her head just above the topmost step to watch what would happen.

He passed down the long line of the empty cells, some doorless, some with rotting modern doors hanging on broken hinges, for Mr Pinker had been refused permission to work here, and Mona now saw why. Door by door, Hugh paused and called a name. Benedick, Johannes, Gyles—one by one he called the roster of the condemned monks, long since mouldered to dust. Mona wondered what spirits reborn felt a sudden stir of memory within them, a nostalgia for the Unseen.

At the end of the passage Hugh turned, and came back towards her again where she stood on the topmost step of the steep and winding stairs. He walked slowly, as befitted a Churchman, the slow swing of the skirted gown keeping time to his stride; his hands, thrust into the wide sleeves, rested folded on the knot of his girdle; his cowl was pulled forward over his face as monks use when meditating. He came and stood before her, and looking up from below, she saw his face clearly for the first time. In the shadows of the hood it looked dark and saturnine, indefinably different from Hugh Paston, and yet not Ambrosius.

"I am not the same man you have known, Mona, I am something quite different."

"So I see," said Mona in a low voice.

He did not ask her if she minded, as Hugh would have done. He left her to take it or leave it, and in so doing, accomplished his ascendency over her.

"Do you realise what I am?" he said. "I am a Churchman who has mastered the Church. The Church was made for man, not man for the Church, Mona."

She noticed that he did not say: 'Who has renounced the Church,' nor yet: 'Who has been cast out of the Church,' but: 'Who has mastered the Church'.

He came closer to her.

"I shall never wear this gown again," he said. "But there is one thing I mean to do before I put it off."

He took Mona by the shoulders and held her at arm's length, staring down into her face, his own shadowed in the cowl.

He began to speak in a low voice, as if communing with himself, heedless of his listener.

"I have seen you many times, near, very near, but never quite——." He paused. "This is what I have always wanted to do——" and he folded her in his arms. She stood for a while leaning against him, her face buried in the loose harsh folds of the monk's robe, stifled by them, but not caring to move.

" Look up," he said at length, and she raised her head.

The dark hawk's face of Ambrosius, deep in its cowl, hung over hers.

" This is what is forbidden me," he said, " and that is why I am doing it," and he kissed her on the forehead. Then his hands dropped to his sides, and he stood back and looked at her, not as if to see how she had taken it, but as if he had done all he meant to do and had finished. He was perfectly calm, but there was a kind of still intensity about him like the hush before a thunderstorm. Mona felt herself trembling.

They stood face to face, neither moving, and she, looking up at the harsh-featured face in the shadow of the cowl, had a sudden feeling that the fantasy was real, and that they were back in the days of Ambrosius, risking all for love under the shadow of the terrible hand of ecclesiastical power.

The man before her was a prince of the Church, powerful, ambitious ; he was risking everything that made life living—more, he was risking life itself, to talk to her thus, for a few stolen moments.

And she, what was she risking ? In the days of Ambrosius she would have been burnt at the stake ; in the days of the present, she was risking a very nasty, possibly a pretty dangerous, experience, at the hands of an unbalanced man whom she was deliberately inciting. She might even be risking life itself, there in the empty building ; many murders have been done by men in the state Hugh Paston was in. Pan in his most goatlike aspect might appear, and if thwarted, might strangle her.

Mona tried to keep a level head as she gazed back into Hugh's grey-green eyes that regarded her with a fixed, unwavering stare. But under the influence of those fanatical eyes she felt herself unconsciously slipping back into Ambrosius's century, and finding in the renegade monk confronting her a man more magnetic and fascinating than any she had ever known.

With an effort she dragged consciousness back to the present, but the renegade monk came with it, and Mona found herself wanting to rouse the Ambrosius aspect of Hugh and find with him tremendous experiences of the emotions. That aspect of her which she had thought dead began to wake again.

It must have shown in her eyes, for a strange look came into Hugh's for a moment. Then he too dragged himself back to the present. He gave a short laugh, thrust his hands into his wide sleeves after the manner of monks, and stepped back and away from her.

" This, won't do, Mona," he said. " You go on back to the house and wait for me there."

" Aren't you coming ? " she asked, startled, fear rising in her at the thought of what might be afoot in the empty building with Hugh prowling like a ghost.

He shook his head. " No, I am in the full tide of a catharsis, if you know what that is. You've read psycho-analysis, haven't you, Mona ? Well, I am abreacting my complexes. Leave me alone. I'll be all right. Don't worry. There's nothing to worry about."

Mona turned away and he shut the door. She knew she must leave him alone. There was nothing else to be done—but to obey his instruction and not to worry was beyond her power. Neither did she believe that there was nothing to worry about. What Hugh was going through might be truly cathartic—a purge of the soul ; but it put a severe strain on the integrity of the personality and she knew from Jelkes of things that happen in psycho-analyses that never get into the text-books. Personalities sometimes come to pieces at such times, and the results have to be certified.

# CHAPTER XXIV

HUGH climbed up the worn and winding stone stairs till he came to the chapel in the gable. It had been scantily furnished with a Glastonbury chair, a press and a coffer. It was just such an equipment as Ambrosius might have had in his study, save that there was a rush mat to keep the feet from the cold of the stone—a luxury he was unlikely to have enjoyed. Hugh dropped into the Glastonbury chair, resting his elbows in the crutches of its arms, drew his cowl yet closer over his head, and settled down to think.

It had never been his custom to do much thinking, it is a lost art in the modern West, but he had picked up from Jelkes one or two of the tricks of the trade, and as the subject on which he proposed to think was an absorbing one, he had no difficulty in fixing his mind on it, a capacity that in the ordinary way has to be slowly and laboriously acquired.

He wanted to understand; beyond everything else he felt that this was his need. Disjointed scraps of realisation had been coming to him in the weeks that had passed since his wife's death, and he was trying to piece them together. Only so could he reconstruct his house of life upon its faulty foundations. He had learnt from Jelkes the trick of thinking backwards—of tracing a thing to its source, step by step, instead of starting at the imagined cause and trying to see how the effects came about. As he had tracked back through his own life he had been struck again and again by the curious recurrence of the same factors in different forms. His grandfather and Jelkes were of a type; his mother and his wife; his old Scotch nurse and Mrs Macintosh—Mona alone in his experience was unique, he had never met anything like her—and then he remembered his flash of recollection as Ambrosius, who had been haunted by a succuba in her likeness.

He shuddered involuntarily when his thoughts turned to the life of Ambrosius, and his mind shied away like a frightened horse. He had spent two hours in the dark cellar thinking of Ambrosius, thinking of him with an intensity that had reconstructed the whole mediæval scene till he was living in it, and not only experiencing its emotions but feeling its sensations; and now it seemed to him as if Ambrosius' experiences had been his own experiences, many years ago, which though healed, could still pain in the old scar.

He was startled to find how real the thing had become to him. It seemed as if there were not two lives, but two epochs of one life, and that the earlier years of Hugh Paston bore the marks of the experiences that had left Ambrosius shattered. He could imagine that had Ambrosius escaped with his life, a broken man, he would have been in the same nerveless condition that Hugh found himself in. Hugh knew from his reading that there is all the difference in the world between the man whose nerve has been shattered by a devastating experience and the congenital neurotic; that the crisis of the former will pass, but that the latter condition is chronic. Every doctor who had ever seen him had declared Hugh to be neurotic; but if his condition were due to the experiences that had broken him when he was Ambrosius, might not the condition pass as it passes in the normal man who breaks down from overstrain? Once the conditions that produced the breakdown had passed away and the body has rested, the normal man becomes normal again as soon as he can pick up his old interests. In this deeper shattering, that had passed beyond the personality into the immortal soul, might it not be possible that he would once more recover his spiritual strength if he could touch the springs of life that had motived Ambrosius?

He knew what these were. Ambrosius, a misfit in the cloister, pagan at heart for all his priesthood, had seen God made manifest in Nature and rejected the ascetic doctrine which cries 'Unclean, unclean' to natural things. Ambrosius was no malignant devotee of a destructive Satan, after the manner of the old witch-cults; he sought life for deadness and light for the mediæval gloom and narrowness of the cloister. Ambrosius had been broken because he had been born out of due season; he had been blackened and cut off as surely as fruit-blossom flowering too early. But the times had advanced now, and the whole age was reaching out in the same direction as Ambrosius, its way cleared by Freud and the psychologists; supposing he could do as Ambrosius had done, and go back to the prime source of his inspiration, back beyond that disastrous mediæval tragedy, might he not also contact the springs of life and live anew? It was no good stopping at Ambrosius; that would be fatal, he would only reconstruct the tragedy; but to evade and avoid Ambrosius would have been like leaving an unconquered fortress in his rear; this he had known when he had passed that grim hour of hard thinking in the darkness of the cellar, facing all the things he feared.

The essence of Ambrosius' problem had been that, placed as he was, it was exceedingly dangerous for him to break with orthodoxy and claim for his manhood the natural things that were denied to the Churchman. The essence of Hugh Paston's problem had been curiously similar, save that the inhibitions were now in his own soul and not in his circumstances. Hugh was deadly afraid of coming to grips with natural things amid all the artificiality of his life, lest in some unforseen way he let catastrophe loose. In his mind the primitive and the catastrophic were inalienably associated, as they probably had been in the experience of Ambrosius. The burnt soul dreads what seared it, even after reincarnation. Hugh could not grip the things that Ambrosius had burnt his fingers over.

But supposing he could go back beyond that, go back as Ambrosius had tried to do ? That was the game, but how was it to be done ? He thought of his original plan —the evocation of Pan by a combination of the Method of St Ignatius and the very unsainted des Esseintes, Huysmans' decadent hero, and suddenly realised that, all unknown to himself, the thing had come about spontaneously, but had come about backwards. Not only was it possible by a careful ' composition of place ' to evoke the appropriate Presence, but it seemed as if, were one successful in evoking a Presence, that circumstances would produce the appropriate composition of place. This was a startling realisation.

After all, what had his quest of Pan been save a hunger for the primitive and vital amid all the sophistication and devitalisation of his life ? And Pan was leading him back to the primitive along the path of his own evolution. Provided he had the courage to sink down through his own subconsciousness he would pass through the mediæval darkness and tragedy and come out into the radiance that was Greece.

And if Ambrosius were the mediæval reality, what was the Greek reality ? But was Ambrosius reality or was he phantasy ? Hugh had no means of knowing, and was probably the last person to be able to form an unbiassed opinion. But whatever Ambrosius might or might not be, he corresponded to reality as the movements of the hands of a clock correspond to the passage of time. He represented something of vital importance in Hugh's soul.

Hugh was not disposed to worry about the metaphysics of Ambrosius if by means of Ambrosius he could obtain results. Jelkes, arguing about objective and subjective reality, was probably nearer the truth than anybody ; but it was Mona, who took Ambrosius for granted, who alone could handle the situation. Taking the motion of the hands of the clock as time, you would catch your train and get to your destination ; take time as the fourth dimension, and you would land anywhere and nowhere.

Hugh cast his mind back to that night in the cock-eyed old feather-bed in Jelkes' dilapidated establishment when he had invoked Pan and started everything off. Could the operation be repeated at will ? What was the word of power that had brought the god ? What is the word of power that brings any god, save adoration ? It is the heart, not the tongue that invokes. Lift up your heart unto the Lord and never mind about your hands, whether that lord be Adonai or Adonis. When Hugh had asserted to himself the Divine Right of Nature, he had evoked Pan quite effectually. Each time he had renewed the assertion, Pan had answered. Each time he had doubted the natural divinity, the god had withdrawn. When he had kissed Mona because he was man and she was woman, she had yielded as if something deep within her had acknowledged the right ; but when he behaved towards her like a gentleman, she had kept him at arm's length and found nothing in him that attracted her. There is a life behind the personality that uses personalities as masks. There are times when life puts off the mask and deep answers unto deep. Unless there is elemental life behind the personality, the loveliest mask is lifeless. That is why certain marriages go astray, for a man marries a mask or a woman mates with a shadow. Liquor, love and fights are the three great inebriations, and this is a teetotal age in all departments. And at best liquor can only supplement love and fights, but not replace them. The chaste and the mild merely get maudlin in their cups ; the Dionysiac inebriation is not for them.

Hugh had a feeling that in doing what Ambrosius had always wanted to do and never managed—embrace his succuba—the force in himself that he called Ambrosius had found a channel, and the unquiet monk would walk no more. Hugh had done the thing Ambrosius set out to do—or had accomplished the thing for which Ambrosius stood, according to which way one looked at it ; he had picked up the thread of his own past, and the Ambrosius factor was integrated with his personality. Whatever the terminology that might be used, there was a change in him, and he knew it. Names did not matter in face of that.

Ambrosius had started as an idea that had taken hold of his imagination ; then he had passed over into the kind of semi-objective reality of dream ; and on the basis of the dream Hugh had built the entirely subjective structure of the day-dream : and into it all Ambrosius had projected with the peculiar reality of the lunatic's illusion. Where was the line to be drawn between all these things, and what was the influence of the deliberately willed day-dream in the matter ? What was it that made the subjective cross the line and for all practical purposes, objectify ? He did not know, any more than he knew how the pendulum and the escapement correlated with the fourth dimension—and he didn't care, so long as his watch kept time and he caught his train. He knew now, as in his heart he had known all along, whose was the satiny moulded back of the woman who was not his wife, whose appearance in his dream had been the overture to the whole strange affair—the woman who had no use for him in real life but who in the subjective realms had proved responsive. What indeed was the power of the deliberately willed day-dream in this matter ? Could it project itself and be shared by another ? If there was anything in telepathy, it probably could.

Hugh sat up and pushed back his cowl and looked the affair straight in the face. He knew what he wanted, but he did not know whether he was justified in going for it. But after all, can one make custards without breaking eggs ? The great difference between the pagan and the Christian attitudes is that the latter sticks to custard powder.

He groped his way down the worn, winding stairs in the gathering dusk, and made his way through the cloisters to the dwelling-house, forgetting that he still wore the monk's robe. As he crossed the garth a fearful, dreadful yell re-echoed through the twilight, and he saw Bill going for his life down the drive with Lizzie running like a hare behind him. They had seen the famous ghost of Monks Farm ! Hugh with a pang of compunction realised that he had upset all Mona's domestic arrangements. However, the Eleusinian Mysteries do not require an audience. ' Hekas, hekas, este bibeloi ! Be ye far from us, O ye profane——' so perhaps it was just as well.

He could see by Mona's face as he entered the living-room how anxious she had been. She made tea for him, and he drank it with relief, for he remembered a remark of Jelkes to the effect that there is nothing like food to check psychism.

It was pleasant to lie back in the deep chair with his feet on the hearth and a cup of tea beside him and a cigarette between his lips. For the moment, Greece and Ambrosius both seemed a long way off. But the gods are exacting, and he knew that if he strayed from the path at the present moment he might not easily find it again. He must not deviate from the concentration. Now he knew why Jelkes said that occultists trained so carefully in concentration.

" Mona," he said, " did you ever read ' The Corn King and the Spring Queen ' ? "

" Yes."

" What was the meaning of the rite in the ploughing-field, beyond the obvious, that is ? "

" It was supposed to link up with the forces behind the earth and the sun."

" Link up the individuals who took part in it, or the whole tribe ? "

" Link up both, I suppose. The individuals wouldn't be able to link up the tribe unless they first linked up themselves."

" I see."

" It was a sacrament. ' An outward and visible sign of an inward and spiritual grace.' "

" Funny thing," said Hugh, " Christians make a sacrament of taking life, and pagans make a sacrament of giving it."

" They are probably different sides of the same coin, if the truth were known," said Mona.

" The truth never will be known," said Hugh, " because they always fly at each other's throats the minute they catch sight of one another. More's the pity, for we need them both, at least I do. One can't go in for complete unrepression, much as I'd like to. One would only end on the gallows. That's the weak spot in Freudianism."

Mona watching him closely, saw that there was a profound change in him.

" Have you read much psychology, Mona ? "

" Yes, a fair bit. I was very interested in it at one time. Then I got tired of it because it never seemed to get you anywhere."

" I have read a certain amount, and I've seen a good deal of it done. It was all the rage in our set when it first started. So far as I can see, either nothing happens at all, or else you go up with a whizz like a rocket, and come down with a whack like the stick. What's the use of revealing to me that I want to murder my father when he died of natural causes twenty years ago ? Or that I've got a fixation on my mother, when the nearest approach to a mother I've ever known was Allen and Hanbury, and you can't work up much of a crush on them. Or that I'm suffering from repression when—well, we won't go into that. Anyway, I'd no need to be any more repressed than I wished to be. No, Mona, it won't wash. There's more to it than that. I'll make you a present of Freud and never ask for the change. I think that the best thing I can do is to get on with my original idea of an invocation of Pan; if I can get a good rush of life-force through, it will blow all my inhibitions clear."

" Have you ever departed from your original idea ? "

" Well, we haven't been able to do much about it recently, have we ? What with your bronchitis and Mr Pinker and all."

" Hugh, you've never departed from it. As soon as ever you even thought of Pan, you began tracking back into your own subconscious, and then you picked up the trail of Ambrosius."

" I picked up the trail of Ambrosius through coming here, Mona. I can't blame that onto Pan."

" But why did you come here, where Ambrosius was to be picked up ? "

" God knows. Pure chance, I suppose."

" Is there such a thing as pure chance ? Or is it undisclosed causation ? Whatever it was, it was very appropriate."

" It sure was. But I think I've dealt with Ambrosius, you know. I think I've absorbed him. I don't think he'll walk again. You see, I have worked out what he wanted to do, and made up my mind to go and do it, and that settled Ambrosius. He rested quiet in his grave after that. That's the way to lay subconscious ghosts, Mona—fulfil their last wishes."

Mona sat silently staring into the fire, wondering what was going to develop, and whether Hugh had any idea where he was heading. At length she said,

" How do you propose to set about all this ? "

" I don't altogether know. I've got to feel my way. The first thing is to carry out our original plan and equip the place à la Des Esseintes. I haven't felt able to tackle it before ; I don't know why. But I can tackle it now all right, and I'd like to get a move on."

" Do you want me to start collecting Tudor pieces for you ? "

" No, I don't. I'm not after Ambrosius. I'm after the thing that was behind Ambrosius."

" Greek stuff would look ghastly here, Hugh."

" I know it would ; but ultra-modern stuff wouldn't. It would look all right because it is primitive, and this place is primitive. The old craftsmen had to be simple because they were short of tools and materials ; and modern design has gone simple because it was bilious with elaboration. It's on a slimming diet. So extremes meet. You pick up the ultra-modern, stream-lined stuff, and it will go in all right. Ambrosius' fan-arching is stream-lined, if you come to think of it. You mark my words, Mona, Pan is coming into his own again, and the sheer, hard, crude lines of modern design point to it. Pure force with the brake off. It suits Pan fine. Don't you go and dig up any mock-gothic. And look here, Mona, you've got twelve days till Beltane, can you get through with it by then ? "

" What do you want doing ? "

" I want a lot of things doing. Complete reorganisation, in fact. I suggest we turn this end of the building over to Bill and Lizzie. They ought to get married. They can't slosh about as they are indefinitely. The village will come up and tar and feather them. Oh, I forgot to tell you, they've bolted. Caught sight of me in my monk's kit and let out a hoot and fled. But I expect they'll flee back again in due course. They won't get much change out of Mrs Pascoe. We'll let them have these quarters and move in next door. I'll get old Pinker along to knock out all those monks' cells and make two big rooms upstairs same as downstairs. He's itching to do it. Called 'em horse-boxes. It only means a wall and a door across each end, and the job's done. Oh yes, and a few windows. We don't want to be walled up for life. Pinker's got the stone mullions for them sitting in his yard waiting. I think the job will go through all right in time. I'll attend to this end of it if you will go up to London and get busy on the furnishing. I'll have one room, and you have the other, and we'll make the chapel up in the gable into a prophet's chamber for Uncle Jelkes whenever he cares to honour us."

Mona looked at him. Apparently he considered her a permanency at Monks Farm. Neither did he seem to consider the possibility of tarring and feathering for any one except Lizzie and Bill.

A timid knock at the door broke in upon them, and Mona, not wishing Hugh to be seen, for he was still in his monk's robe, muttered ' damn ' and went to answer it. There stood two forlorn figures, who, as Hugh prophesied, had been driven forth ignominiously from The Green Man by its proprietress.

Bill told the sad tale while Silly sniffed. Mrs Pascoe, though she had seen quite fit to saddle Mona with Silly, was horrified at the idea of her as a daughter-in-law, and had cast her to the geese on the common remorselessly, all clad in cap and apron as she was. Bill, who in his dim animal mind now regarded her as his mate, was infuriated by this insult, and had stalked after her, bidding mamma and all his prospects farewell for ever. Rather than put up with such treatment he had returned to Mona, braving the ghost.

Mona, laughing, opened the door and showed them Hugh, the monk's robe hanging loose and ungirt from his shoulders like a dressing-gown, revealing reassuring trousers, and told them that it was Mr Paston who had dressed up for a lark.

Guffaws and general relief was the result. But when asked to swear secrecy, Bill explained that it was too late, as they had already told the tale far and wide. Mrs Pascoe, it was true, had repudiated it as the result of drink, but everyone else had received it open-mouthed. He also informed them that he and Lizzie had been hand in hand to the parson, demanding to put up the banns, and parson had declined, being a friend of Miss Pumfrey's, alleging that Lizzie was under age and must return to her duly appointed guardian forthwith, and had summoned that lady by special messenger. She, being his next door neighbour, had cut off the unhappy couple in the drive and given them a piece of her mind, demanding the instant return of Lizzie and threatening all and sundry with the utmost rigours of the law.

" But I told 'er she was expectin', so she just turned on 'er 'eel and 'opped it," Bill explained lucidly.

Then they returned to the vicarage to have another try for the banns, and parson proving firm, had told him that it didn't matter, as the lady they worked for wasn't really particular. Whereupon the vicar suddenly changed his mind and promised to do the needful.

Bill was immensely proud of his strategy, but Mona was appalled at the wreck of her reputation that now lay all over the village. However she reflected that the persons who were not kept away by the ghost would be maintained at a safe distance by the scandal, so they could be sure of the seclusion that is required for all occult matters.

Hugh unlocked the cellarette and handed Bill two bottles of beer to celebrate with, and the now happy couple retired to their own quarters.

# CHAPTER XXV

Next day Hugh drove Mona up to town and dropped her in Oxford Street, arranging to meet her for tea at Uncle Jelkes'. She disappeared down a side turning into some purlieus known to herself, for Mona never shopped at the obvious, and Hugh, for the first time since the tragedy, went to his club.

It was a club that Trevor Wilmott had chosen for him. In its heyday it had been a notable institution, but it had fallen on hard times since the War, and an effort had been made to introduce some new blood into it. It was even rumoured that something akin to the coupon system had been instituted, and members introducing new blood had their subscriptions reduced on a sliding scale. Perhaps on account of this blood-money not very much discretion had been used in introducing new members, and the club found itself in the same condition as unfortunate invalids in the early days of blood transfusion before donors were tested for ' grouping ', and in consequence dangerous clotting took place in the smoking-room and other vital spots, till in the end there were practically two clubs under one roof, the old originals and the new bloods, and God help anyone who set foot in the wrong department.

Hugh, as usual, belonged nowhere. The new bloods were of the flashy business man type—' something in the City ' trying to graduate into a man about town. The resignation-upon-bankruptcy clause came into action with such distressing frequency that the question was raised as to whether a member's subscription ought not to return to normal when the last of his *protégés* entered Carey Street. The old brigade were of the type of

Frida's father, the fag-end of the old *régime*, hanging on by their eyebrows to privilege and prestige, and keeping up their self-respect by means of mutual admiration. The more difficult they found it to keep up appearances themselves, the more exacting were their standards for other folk. Both parties regarded Hugh as an inoffensive nonentity belonging to the rival camp.

It was the first time he had visited the club since the tragedy, and his appearance created something of a sensation. Frida's father was one of the old brigade, and Trevor had been liaison officer between the two camps and a very leading light in club affairs generally, having, it was rumoured, the run of his teeth in return for his services. The general opinion was that Hugh would resign. All Trevor's friends were there, and all Frida's father's friends were there. No one expected to see him walk into the dining-room and sit down and order lunch, looking particularly sprightly. Like his one-time butler, nobody quite knew the line to take with Hugh. Condolences were obviously out of place, and congratulations not in good taste. Everybody waited to see what other people were going to do, and consequently nobody did anything. Hugh, who felt as if the tragedy belonged to an age more remote than Ambrosius, and had in fact, almost forgotten it, ate his lunch in peace.

He strolled into the smoking-room, reserved for members only, and stood watching the tape machine. It was a huge room with a fire-place at each end. The one at the far end was sacred to the old brigade, the one near the door to the new blood. Hugh, standing with his back to the room watching the tape, was suddenly aware that he, who had always been a most undiscerning person, could clearly distinguish the difference in the spiritual atmosphere at the two ends of the room; he also became aware that he was a focus of attention, and that it was not friendly attention. He wondered why in the world it was not. What had he done ? Hugh, who had always accepted as gospel other people's estimate of his imperfections, experienced the novel sensation of feeling his hackle rise. Why should he be treated like dirt by either old has-beens or young pseudo-bucks? He turned and strolled slowly, hands in trouser-pockets, towards the sacred fire-place at the far end of the room. There, as ill-luck would have it, he came face to face with one of Frida's uncles. The old gentleman stared straight through him with a stony stare. So did all the other old gentlemen, his friends.

This was a surprise for Hugh. He had expected mutual embarrassment, which would be smoothed over by mutual courtesy; he had not expected to be outcasted by these mangy old has-beens who ought to have been apologetic. The devil entered into Hugh, and he deliberately thought of Ambrosius; as he did so, he observed a startled expression come over the faces of the old gentlemen who were supposed not to be looking at him. Hugh stared hard at his uncle-in-law, watching him slowly go from red to magenta. Still no one spoke. They probably could not if they had wanted to by now.

Hugh broke the silence. " You act as if it was I who had seduced your niece," he said, and turned on his heel and walked off.

He went to the cloak-room to have a wash, and was still bending over the basin when he heard a voice behind him speaking his name in icy tones, and turned round to see his brother-in-law, the husband of his youngest sister. This brother-in-law was one of the few things Hugh's family had got out of his marriage; he had married the youngest daughter on the clear understanding that Hugh would do something for them, as Hugh had faithfully done. In return, Robert had added his voice to the general chorus of admonition and disparagement that surrounded Hugh.

" That was a pretty ghastly thing you did just now in the smoking-room, Hugh."

" Was it ? " said Hugh, rinsing his hands under the tap.

" What possessed you to act like that ? "

" The devil, I expect."

" Do you really think you are possessed by the devil ? "

" I shouldn't be surprised.  But even if I am, there is nothing to be made out of certifying me.  There's a power of attorney in existence."

" Do you wish to pick a quarrel with me ? "

" No, not especially.  You can please yourself about that.  I shall be quite content as long as I see the last of you."

" You are insulting ! "

" Well, if you will persist in ladling out unsolicited advice, you must not be surprised if you get sloshed on the nozzle occasionally."

" My *dear* Hugh ! "

" I'm not your dear Hugh.  You hate the sight of me, and you know it."

" Well, if you ask my opinion——"

" I didn't," said Hugh.

" —there is only one thing for you to do, and that is to resign from the club, and then, in your own interests, to go to a nursing-home."

" I'll resign from the club all right, it's no earthly use to me.  And I'll withdraw my guarantee, too."

" What do you mean ? "

" Didn't you know I guaranteed the overdraft at the bank ? "

" No, I didn't."

" I thought you didn't.  I guess I'll withdraw a few other guarantees and subscriptions while I'm at it.  I'm tired of everlastingly paying the piper and never being consulted about the tune."

He straightened his back and flung the damp towel into the bin and looked at Robert.  The same startled look came into Robert's face as had come into the faces of the old gentlemen in the smoking-room. He suddenly lost all his loftiness and looked very much like the towel. Then he turned and walked off. Hugh felt certain he was using all his will-power to walk slowly.

Hugh scribbled his resignation on a half-sheet of paper and tossed it into the secretary's office ; said good-bye to the hall-porter, who also looked startled, got his car, and set out for Marylebone.

In response to the clang of the bell the old bookseller appeared through the ragged curtain just as he done that night so short a while ago that had marked the turn of the lane in Hugh's life.

Hugh walked through into the inner room without waiting to be asked. He was much more at home here than he had ever been in his club.

" Going to give me a cup of tea, T. J. ? " he said, and they indulged in desultory conversation while Jelkes fished a cup out of a pile of dirty crockery and gave it a rinse.

Settled down with the pot on the hob, Hugh got to business.

" Uncle Jelkes," he said, " I'm going to seduce Mona."

" Good God ! " said Jelkes.

" Well, she won't marry me, so there's nothing else for it. Tell me, how had I better set about it ? "

" Are you possessed by the devil, Hugh Paston ? "

" That's the second time I've been asked that today. Would you say I was possessed by the devil, or would you say I was just beginning to be my normal self ? "

Jelkes rubbed his nose thoughtfully.

" Who asked you if you were possessed by the devil ? "

" My brother-in-law."

" Why ? "

" Because I didn't want his advice."

" Is that a sign of diabolical possession ? "

" My family think it is. You see, T. J., I've always taken everybody's advice. A change of disposition is a sign of hydrophobia in dogs."

" What did you quarrel with your brother-in-law about ? "

" He had me on the mat for being rude to my old uncle-in-law."

" And what did you do that for ? "

" Oh God, T. J., if you'd seen the old bird you'd know why ! Only thing to do with him—be rude to him. Look here, Jelkes, I've had a row with every blessed one of my family and resigned from my club. If you'll help me seduce Mona, I swear I'll make an honest woman of her afterwards."

" So this is what comes of invoking Pan, is it ? " said Jelkes quietly.

" Well, what did you expect ? Pan was a whale on nymphs."

Jelkes sighed. He shrewdly suspected that if Mona saw Hugh in his present mood, no assistance would be needed for the seduction. Pan had been evoked most effectually.

" Now look here, T. J., just remember that you are talking to a dashed sight better priest than ever you were. I was running my own monastery before you had cut your pin-feathers, and it took a Pope to scrag me. Yes, I've absorbed Ambrosius, together with all his kick and go. I've only got to look at people and they wilt nowadays."

" Tell me, Hugh, how do you know Ambrosius is you ? "

" That's a facer, Uncle Jelkes," said Hugh, pulled up in mid-career. " How do I know he's me ? Well, I suppose strictly speaking I don't know. I only think he is. But I think it with a kind of inner conviction that I can't describe. If he isn't me, at least he corresponds to something very deep in my subconscious ; and he's worth cultivating whether he's fact or fancy."

Jelkes nodded. " Yes," he said. " We don't know

what these things are, but we know they work. He'll give you self-confidence if he gives you nothing else. Given that, you can get a lot of things out of your sub-conscious that never went into it."

" I don't mind what you call him, T. J. A rose by any name will smell as sweet. He's a dissociated complex, or a past incarnation, or just plain spoof, or anything else you fancy so long as you'll lend me a hand with him, for I know he'll deliver the goods. As you said yourself, time is a mode of consciousness, though what you meant by that, blowed if I know."

" Blowed if I do either," said Jelkes. " We'll take Ambrosius for what he is worth and get on with him. What was your first intimation of him ? "

" My first intimation ? Difficult to say. He didn't seem to have any beginning. He had always been there, only I hadn't realised it. Like when you look up and find someone standing in front of you. Then when I realised what he meant, I gave him his head."

" What do you mean by that ? "

" Well now, there's an awful lot missing from me, isn't there ? And my family chivvy me in consequence till I don't know whether I'm standing on my head or my heels, and then there's still more missing. And I come across Ambrosius, and I take a fancy to him. He seemed to have everything I lack, and I have everything he lacked. That's to say, he'd got guts and no oppor-tunity, and I've got opportunity and no guts. And I say to myself : If Ambrosius had had my opportunities, what couldn't he have made of them ? And if I'd had Am-brosius' guts, what couldn't I have made of them ? Then along comes Mona and says : ' You are Ambrosius. He was you in a past life,' and tells me about reincarnation. And I cotton on to the idea, partly because I like it, and partly because it was Mona who said it. And I say to myself, ' Gosh, if I *am* Ambrosius, I wonder how he'd feel ? ' And I begin to think how Ambrosius would have felt, him being what he was. And then, me being him, or so I think, *I* begin to feel like that. And as soon as I begin to feel like that, other people feel it too, and they begin to treat me as if I were the diabolical prior, and that does me no end of good. It is extraordinary the effect it has on you when people treat you with respect. And the more impressed they are, the more impressive I become. Ambrosius is a dashed effectual method of auto-suggestion, if he's nothing else. But personally I think he is something else. There's a kind of reality about him that I can't describe."

"Very good, then," said Jelkes. "We'll take Ambrosius at his face value, and refrain from looking him in the mouth. If he isn't real now, he very soon will be. Whether he was real or whether he wasn't is a question I don't suppose we shall ever settle ; he stood for something valid in your life, so take him at his face value, same as you would a Bradbury. You don't bite a bank-note to see if it is genuine. It is genuine all right if it will buy goods. I'll do what I can for you, Hugh. The reason I wouldn't help with the job before was because I reckoned you'd just make use of Mona and then go back to your own kind."

"You were wrong, Uncle Jelkes, I'm not that sort."

"What made you suddenly round on all your old associates today, Hugh ? When did you make up your mind you were going bald-headed for this thing ? "

"I've always wanted to go bald-headed for it, but I didn't know which way to go. And you've got such dashed cold feet you wouldn't show me. But yesterday I began to get the hang of the thing and see what could be done with it. Then I knew which way I wanted to go."

"Yes," said Jelkes, "I see now that you have been working with power all along. Anyone who means business always works with power. You got Pan at the first go-off ; whether he is subjective or objective doesn't matter. You mean business, and that is an effectual invocation."

" Can you get any of the gods in that way ? "

" No, you can't, because the rest are highly specialised, and you have got to get each one in his own particular way. But Pan is All. You can get him any old way simply by wanting him. And he can introduce you to Parnassus if he sees fit."

" He introduced me to Ambrosius, which wasn't a bad start."

" He will introduce you to every blessed thing you've got in your subconscious, and to every blessed thing in the racial memory that's behind you, and to the biological memory behind that, to the morphological memory of all your organs, and the physiological memory of all your functions——" Jelkes stopped for breath.

" Odd, isn't it," said Hugh, " that an old billy-goat can teach you all that ? "

" Well, you see," said Jelkes, " the billy-goat stands for unrepression, or at least so I have always understood from those who keep goats."

" Of course the whole thing is simply the opening-up of the subconscious," said Hugh, " only there's a dashed sight more in the subconscious than most people suspect ; or at any rate, than anyone with a reputation to lose is prepared to say on paper."

" Ever read ' The Secret of the Golden Flower ', Hugh ? "

" No."

" It's worth reading. Add Coué and Jung to Iamblichos and St Ignatius, and you will begin to see what has been happening."

" I'll leave the metaphysics to you, Uncle, I want to get on with the composition of place. It is my idea to equip Monks Farm with absolutely modern stuff instead of the mock-gothic, which was my original notion. Mona was disposed to hoot at me at first, but she sees

my point now.   You see, T. J., I think that modern
design embodies the idea of the straight run-through of
force with the brakes off, and what is that but Pan ?  How
do you think Ambrosius will like it ?  Will he turn polter-
geist and start chucking the stuff about ? "

"Well, laddie, he was a modernist in his day.   What
you want to recapture is not Ambrosius' limitations, but
his spirit, just as he was trying to recapture the Greek
spirit."

"Then in that case we might as well go to the fountain-head and see what word the Greeks had for it."

"That is what you will have to do.   But you had to
work through the Ambrosius phase before you could get
there.   Otherwise he and his problems would be like an
unconquered fortress in your rear."

There was a clang of the shop-bell, and Jelkes dived
through the curtain to deal with the customer, but
returned instead with Mona.   He watched the pair of
them closely as they greeted each other.   It seemed to
him that there was a humorous twinkle in Hugh's eye,
as if he had got something up his sleeve for Mona, but
she herself was carefully noncommittal.

"Well, what luck have you had ? " said Hugh.

Mona did not reply, but began to unpack a small
brown paper parcel she was carrying, and there appeared
a little terra cotta figure of the dancing Pan, skipping
along with his pipes and glancing over his shoulder with
a very come-hither look in his eye indeed.

"Huh," said Jelkes.   "Very suitable. But I should
keep him done up in brown paper for the present, if I
were you."

# CHAPTER XXVI

THE days that followed were fascinating ones for Hugh and Mona. She took him among the craft-workers, disdaining shop-fronts and show-cases, and he realised the peculiar life conveyed to an article by the hand of a creative worker who is putting himself into it. But she was not of those who believe in the sanctity of handwork, however crude. There is no particular point in doing by hand what can be done as well and better by machine. The industrial designer also puts life into a thing provided he is doing creative and not hack-work. Then the man masters the machine instead of the machine dictating to the man.

Always, everywhere, through all the studios and workshops, Mona went looking for the creative spirit. Hugh was amazed to see how much of it was abroad.

" This is period furniture," said Mona, looking at a number of newly-turned chair-legs lying among the shavings. " And if you choose it carefully it will become antique in time. After all, the only reason why antiques were so highly prized was because Victorian design was so vile. And I'll tell you what made it so vile, if you like, Hugh, it was the repressions of the Victorian Age. All force was twisted out of shape, or cut off from its roots and left hanging limply. There was no elemental drive behind anything. The only thing that really flourished in the Victorian Age was the music-hall, where they became unrepressed for a bit. Say what you like, Hugh, it was the only art-form that really developed."

The cold grey stone of the old buildings made a wonderful background for the modern colours—which are the colours of the semi-precious stones—the green of the turquoise, the yellow of amber, the red of the garnet, the blue of the aquamarine.  The stark line of modern design was at home with the simplicity of the ancient builders, though their simplicity was of necessity dictated by primitive tools and materials.  The simplicity of limitation had been fed full by expansion and invention, and now, from a surfeit of richness, it was going onto an eliminatory diet for the good of its health.  Civilisation had lost touch with its foundations, and, sick in heart and head in consequence, was groping desperately for fundamentals.  Everything was ripe for the return of Pan, as Pan had probably known when he answered the cry of his invoker.

The nuptials of Bill and Lizzie were due for celebration in the near future—(officially, that is.  Unofficially, of course, they had been in full blast for some time), and the problem of housing had to be considered.  Bill and Lizzie, in their dunder-headed, shuffle-footed, faithful, easy-going fashion, suited the Monks Farm *ménage* uncommonly well—suited it in a way that Miss Pumfrey's parlour-maid or Mrs Macintosh would never have done. The obvious thing was for the newly-married couple to move into the farm-house end of Monks Farm, and for Mona and Hugh to move out into the main building and settle down as they meant to go on.

Jelkes had given Mona a straight talking-to, but as he expected, she had declined to be sensible.

" I won't be a party to any hanky-panky, Mona.  Do you mean to marry Hugh or not ? "

" Not at the moment, Uncle."

" Why not ? "

" Difficult to say.  I like Hugh very much.  There is something awfully nice about him ; in fact, I might say I am very fond of him ; but I wouldn't worry if I never saw him again.  It doesn't do to marry a man on those terms, does it ?  Not fair to the man, don't you think ? Especially a very rich man like Hugh and a church mouse like me."

" Lots of women have made happy marriages on much
less raw material."

" Maybe, but not folk like me, who's been a cat on the
tiles.   You see, Uncle, if Hugh didn't give me all I
needed in marriage, I'd find it very difficult to stick to
him.   I've not got the makings of a Penelope in me.   It
is no good promising what I can't perform.   Another
dud marriage would be a poisonous thing for poor old
Hugh.   He would never hold up his head again."

" You could make him a good wife if you made up
your mind to it."

" Oh no, I couldn't.   I am not the stuff of which good
wives are made.   I'd be a top-hole mistress to the right
kind of man, but I'd be a domestic fiend to the wrong
one."

" Mona, my dear, how can you say such things ! "

" What a pity it is, Uncle," said Mona, looking at him
meditatively, " that you suffer so much from repression
and all your occult knowledge is wasted."

" After all, Mona, the whole of our social life is built
on repressions ; if you pull out the underpinning, down
comes the whole structure."

Mona shrugged her shoulders.   " It is one thing to
build on repressions, but it is quite another to build on
dissociations.   Modern social life is a slum property, if
you ask me ; all divided up into maisonnettes, with bad
tenants in the basement.   A celestial sanitary inspector
ought to come along and condemn it."

" You are a very immoral young woman, as I've told
you before," Jelkes said.

" On the contrary," said Mona.   " I am exceedingly
moral.   If I were what you say I am, I'd marry Hugh,
and do him down, and clear out on the alimony."

The Eve of Beltane drew near ; the moon was waxing
towards the full, and everyone knew, though no one
said a word, that a crisis of some sort was approaching.

Finally Jelkes heaved a sigh that came from the depths of his heart, for he liked a quiet life and preferred theory to practice in occultism, packed his rush basket, locked up the shop, and took a Green Line bus.

Getting off where the lane met the by-pass, he trudged the three long uphill miles to Monks Farm, his rush basket under his arm, and arrived rather weary, for the day was close and he was not as young as he had been. However, the warmth of his welcome offset the heat of the day.

" How's the furnishing going ? " asked the old man, as they sat on the bench in the angle of the wall, listening to distant church bells and bees.

" First-rate," said Hugh. " You wouldn't believe how well modern stream-lined stuff fits in with Ambrosius' notion of what was appropriate in a monastic establishment. The only things that look out of place are the beds. But I'm not going to sleep on a plank bed in order to imagine I'm Ambrosius. I'm going to sleep on a decent mattress, and Ambrosius can imagine he's me."

" I shouldn't make the drains too realistic, either, if I were you," said Jelkes.

The sun sank red behind the fir-trees ; the bees packed up and went home, and the church bells stopped ringing. Mona went in to prod the loving couple in the kitchen into activity, tactfully treading heavily as she approached the back premises.

Jelkes turned to Hugh. " Laddie, we're tackling the job this evening."

" What's the plan of campaign, T. J. ? "

" Go into the chapel, open up our subconsciouses, and see what comes."

" Right you are. I'll go and put things into some sort of shape in the chapel."

They parted, Hugh to the chapel, and Jelkes returning to the farm-house. There Mona joined him.

" Where's Hugh ? " she demanded possessively.

Jelkes cocked his eyebrow at her. There was a strong atmosphere of domesticity in the living-room of the smaller building, not yet handed over to Bill and Silly, pending their wedding, which was fast becoming a work of supererogation.

" Hugh's gone to get the chapel ready."

" Is tonight the night ? "

" Yes."

" What do you propose to do ? "

" Take Hugh into the chapel, build up the Ambrosius phantasy, and then psycho-analyse it."

" And me ? Do I come on in this act ? "

" Yes, you come on all right. You will sit opposite Hugh and pick up the transference as it comes across. What you do with it after you've got it is your look-out. I'm tired of your haverings, and so's Hugh."

' Was ever woman in this manner wooed ? ' It was an odd mixture of ' Richard III ' and ' The Courtship of Miles Standish ', and Jelkes hoped it would prove efficacious.

Mona answered not a word, but turned on her heel and went upstairs.

Arrived in her own room, she lit every candle she possessed, dragged a battered cabin-trunk into the middle of the floor, and took out a brown paper parcel, tore it open, and held up a green crêpe dress and inspected it. It was badly creased, having lain a considerable time on the shelves of the uncle who was not Jelkes, and not having been unpacked since it was redeemed, but it would have to do. She stripped off her dingy brown jumper and skirt and slipped the clinging, flowing green over her head. It fell in long straight folds, held in place by a loose girdle with a barbaric jewelled clasp, a cheap enough thing, but effective, as so many cheap things are nowadays.

She dived into her trunk again, and fetched out a pair of tarnished gold cocktail sandals, a tip from a client that had riled Mona unspeakably at the time, but which she had not dared to fling back at the donor for fear of giving offence and losing future jobs. They would come in handy now, however. Mona pulled off her stockings and inspected her toes. They would pass muster, thanks to her taste for brogues.

She strapped the cocktail sandals round her bare ankles. Smoothed her thick, page-cropped hair with her brush, and bound round her sleek black head a broad swathe of the green crêpe of the dress. Then once again she dived into the ancient trunk, and brought forth a hand-bag, once handsome, also a tip from a client, fished about in the vanity-case it contained and produced a compactum of powder and a lip-stick. Now the bag had been an unappreciated gift to the donor, who was a blonde, and consequently the make-up kit it contained was designed for a blonde, and by the time Mona had applied the powder and lip-stick to herself with a generous hand, the result was startling. But Mona didn't care. Something in her, that Jelkes had always known was there, had taken the bit between its teeth and was running blind.

She went downstairs to give instructions concerning supper, and was greeted with round-eyed amazement, for whatever was in Silly Lizzie had to come out.

" Oh, my, Miss, ain't you lovely ! " gasped poor Silly Lizzie, quite overcome, and slowly pouring a stream of boiling water from the kettle perilously near her own toes. Mona rescued the kettle, gave her instructions, and retreated, lest the distraction of her presence should do more harm than good.

She opened the door of the sitting-room and walked in defiantly. Jelkes looked at her amazed and raised his eyebrows. Hugh had his back to her, but at the sight of Jelkes' scandalised expression he turned round, as was only natural, to see the cause of the scandal. Mona heard him gasp and saw him stiffen, and in another moment

Ambrosius was in the midst of them.

The change-over was so quick that there was no moment of dazed uncertainty; so quick, in fact, that the two personalities coincided and Hugh himself was conscious of the change. Then suddenly, in the hall, clanged the gong for supper.

For a moment the hawk-eyes in Hugh's head wavered, then they steadied and regained their calm. He stood looking down at Mona with a fixed regard. Then he turned to Jelkes.

" Now I understand something I never understood before," he said. They both gasped, for this was Hugh, whereas they had thought it was Ambrosius.

" I understand why I went in for dangerous sports. It was because as soon as ever the fun began, Ambrosius took charge. Everyone always wondered how a mut like me managed it. But it wasn't me, it was me plus Ambrosius."

" Then who is it now, Hugh ? " said Jelkes, watching him closely.

" God knows. I suppose it's the same thing. I'm feeling just like I used to on the track. Never mind supper, I'll put on my Ambrosius kit and we'll go to the chapel and tackle the job before the effect wears off."

They made their way round the west front to the chapel, the brilliant moonlight making electric torches needless. Hugh leading the way, robed and cowled and sandalled ; Jelkes following, looking like a great moulting bird in his Inverness cape ; and Mona with a dark velvety rug from the car thrown cloak-wise over her thin dress.

When they reached the chapel they saw how Hugh had spent his time. Upon the altar of the double cube that represents the universe—'as above, so below'— stood the figure of the Piping Pan. The Glastonbury chairs formed a triangle in the sanctuary, one facing the east, and the other two facing each other. High triple candlesticks stood on either side of the altar, and in a small niche in the wall beside it was a large brass censer and the necessary equipment for getting it going.

Hugh lit up the candles and switched off his electric torch, leaving their soft radiance to penetrate the gloom into the wavering shadows beyond.

" Do you understand this ? " he said to Jelkes, and Mona sat watching them, two weird figures in the uncertain light, as they wrestled with the reluctant charcoal in the censer. Then Jelkes rose upright and whirled the thing on its yard-long clashing chains round and round his head, clouds of smoke and showers of sparks flying in every direction ; his enormous shadow stretched far across the vaulting of the roof, grotesque and demoniac, the cloak of his ulster flapping like the wings of a bat. Hugh, his face invisible in the shadow of his cowl, stood silently watching him. Mona clutched the arms of her chair, her heart beating in her throat and nearly suffocating her. Jelkes and Hugh, tall men in any case, looked enormous in the uncertain light. Hugh was in very deed the renegade monk returned from the tomb ; Jelkes a being of another order of creation altogether.

Hugh put out his hand, and Jelkes handed the censer to him. Now a censer is a thing in which the inexperienced can get very badly tangled, but Mona, who had expected to see red-hot charcoal all over the sanctuary, observed that Hugh handled it with the silence of an expert ; there was no clashing of metal as it swung to the steady jerk of the wrist ; no looping or twisting of the perverse tangle of the chains. Standing in front of the cubical altar, he censed it in due form, catching the fuming censer with a musical clash on its own chains at each return. Five swings to the left, and five to the right, instead of the orthodox three that affirms the Trinity : for five is the number of man, and ten is the number of Earth, according to the Qabalists. Ten musical clangs rang out in the shadowy darkness, regular as the chiming of a clock.

This task finished, he looked round helplessly at Jelkes, as if not knowing what to do next. All his experience lay in his hands. Little or nothing came through to the surface of the brain.

"Go and sit down over there, Hugh," said the old bookseller. Hugh did as he was bid, taking the chair facing Mona, and setting the smoking censer carefully down on the stone floor beside him. Jelkes watched the hands that remembered arrange the trailing chains in such a manner that it could be picked up again without capsizing, and wondered what would be coming to the surface as the barriers went down.

"Now," said Jelkes. "Make a mental picture of Ambrosius, and look at it, and tell me what comes into your head."

Hugh dutifully did as he was bid. They sat for a few minutes in silence. Mona could not take her eyes off the black cowled figure, sitting with bowed head intent, across on the opposite side of the sanctuary. Hugh's bare foot in its thonged sandal showed under the hem of his robe in just the same way that Ambrosius' foot had shown in the minute vignette in the psalter. Hugh she could like and pity, but Ambrosius—Ambrosius was an altogether different story.

At length Hugh raised his head and spoke.

"I keep on sliding off onto myself when I try to think of Ambrosius," he said.

"Never mind," said Jelkes. "Let's have whatever comes. We'll get through the surface layers presently."

"I think of Ambrosius going round this place keeping an eye on things while it was building, and then I think of myself doing the same thing. I think of him planning the chapel for his stunts, and I think of the kind of stunts that I'd like to have here. I think of him barging into all sorts of restrictions because he was a Churchman, and I think of myself up against things because—well, because of the way I was placed."

" I shouldn't have thought you would have bumped into many restrictions with your resources," said Jelkes.

" Well then, because of the way I was built," said Hugh sulkily, and silence fell again. It is not easy to do psycho-analysis in front of a third person, especially if that person is one for whose opinion you care very deeply.

" Go on, Hugh," said Jelkes. " It's like a tooth-pulling, but go through with it."

" I was just thinking," said Hugh, " what Ambrosius would have done if he'd been me. That's to say, if I'd had Ambrosius' temperament, or he'd had my oppor-tunities. I think he'd have gone through my restrictions like a clown through a paper hoop."

" What would he have done ? "

" Well, to start with, he'd have made short work of my family."

" You seem to have made pretty short work of them yourself recently."

" That's Mona's doing. They tried to come between her and me——." Hugh pulled up abruptly, furious at his unguarded utterance.

" What else would Ambrosius have done, as well as turf your family ? " said Jelkes tactfully, easing him off the sore point before the resistances could rise and jam it.

" Well," Hugh hesitated, " I expect he'd have got onto my wife's game early in the proceedings, and turfed her too."

" Do you think he'd ever have married her at all ? "

" Difficult to say. I was only a youngster, and by Jove, she knew how to get her fingers on your nerves. I doubt if any man that ever wore trousers would have seen through her right away. Women would, I dare say, but men wouldn't. It's awfully easy to throw dust in a man's eyes, so far as I can see. But I don't suppose you realise that, T. J., being three parts of a priest yourself."

" No, that was never one of my problems.  Plain as a pikestaff and poor as Job.  How long do you suppose Ambrosius would have stood your wife ? "

" Not long, I reckon, if she played him up the way she played me.  But then she mightn't have played Ambrosius up."

Mona gasped.  That was so exactly her sentiment.

" How do you reckon he'd have disposed of her ? " said Jelkes.

" Same way I did—killed her."

" Good God, Hugh, what do you mean ? "

" Hadn't you realised I'd killed my wife ? "

" But you didn't.  You're imagining things.  She died in a motor-smash when you were miles away."

" I bought a car for Trevor that I knew he couldn't handle.  It was a kind of practical joke ; and a sixty horse-power practical joke is—well—not funny."

" Did you realise what you were doing ? "

" There's a little imp inside me, T. J., that does things occasionally while I look the other way.  And there's another thing you'd better know, if I had a row with someone I—really cared about, I could imagine myself turning pretty nasty."

" I couldn't imagine you doing that, Hugh."

" You ask Mona, she knows me better than you do ; she's got no delusions about me, if you have.  I could imagine myself getting my hands onto someone's throat and—and not taking no for an answer.  That is, if I were in my Ambrosius personality."

" What is the relationship between you and Ambrosius, Hugh ? "

" Dunno, T. J.  He bloweth where he listeth.  I've got to the point where I can invoke him, but I can't control him, and therefore I'm afraid to invoke because of the consequences to—to other people."

" Don't you worry about that, laddie, you fetch Ambrosius along and I'll undertake to control him."

" T. J., I'm thirty-four and you're rising seventy.
Besides, you aren't here all the time."

There was an awkward silence.   Then Mona's voice
came to them out of the shadows.

" I can manage Ambrosius."

Hugh gave a short laugh that had no mirth in it.

" Yes, I bet you can—by letting him have his own
way."

Mona's voice came again.

" What would Ambrosius do if you gave him his head,
Hugh ? "

" It is no good thinking about that, Mona, because it
isn't a practical proposition."

" Then what would you do if Ambrosius backed you
up ? "

Hugh thought for a moment.

" I'd go for the invocation of Pan that was my original
idea.   Only that isn't a practical proposition either, for if
I go for the invocation of Pan, Ambrosius would get the
bit between his teeth."

" Then Pan and Ambrosius are really the same
person ? "

" No, I don't think so.   Pan is a god, isn't he ? "

" Have you ever heard of the idea of the Christ
Within ? "

" Yes."

" Well, there is a Pan Within as well, you know."

" I see, and my Pan Within is Ambrosius ?   Then
Ambrosius never had any real existence ?   Oh, but he
must have had.   He's historical, and they painted him."

" What is time, Hugh ? "

" God knows.   I don't.   What's time, Uncle Jelkes ? "

" A mode of consciousness, laddie."

" I suppose that explains it, though I'm not sure that
I'm any the wiser.   I suppose we've caught time bending,
same as Einstein caught light.   Well I don't pretend to
understand either time or space apart from clocks and

tape-measures. It's all so much talk to me, but I'll take your word for it, T. J. I suppose for all practical purposes Ambrosius is the foundation on which I am built. He's my subconscious, or part of it, anyway, and when anything happens to bring my subconscious to the surface, Ambrosius comes up with it and takes charge."

" That's about it, laddie."

" Well, what's to do about it ? I don't know that I'm any better off now that I've been labelled. That is the grouse I've always had against psycho-analysis. But I'll tell you one thing, T. J., it's my solemn conviction that Ambrosius is normal, and it is Hugh Paston who is the pathology."

" Hugh, you've spoken the sober truth, and if psycho-analysts went to work on that assumption, they'd get some cures, which is more than they do now. Ambrosius is the real you, and he was made what he is by experiences in a past life."

" But hang it all, T. J., we can't let Ambrosius loose on polite society. I know Ambrosius if you don't."

" Aye, that's the difficulty."

" I can cope with Ambrosius," came Mona's voice from the shadows.

" No, you can't," said both men, hastily and simultaneously.

" Yes, I can," said Mona. " I'm not afraid of Pan if you are."

" I'd never dream of letting you try to cope with Ambrosius, Mona," said Hugh. " He's not a man, he's a fiend."

" ' Starving men are dangerous men '," said Mona.

" And liable to turn cannibal," added Jelkes. " Tell me, Hugh," he continued hastily, hoping to change the subject, " what are the things that bring Ambrosius up with you ? "

" Danger, anger, and Mona," said Hugh curtly.

Before poor Jelkes could make another cast, Mona

spoke again.

"It is my turn to be psycho-analysed now," she said. "And I'm going to psycho-analyse my day-dreams. They are just as useful as night-dreams if you know how to take them. When I was little I used to imagine myself racing over hills with a boy who was my brother. As we lived in the very centre of an industrial town in the Black Country and I was an only child, it isn't difficult to trace the root of that dream. When I got older and went to school I was tremendously fascinated by the Greek myths and legends. Fairy tales did not amuse me in the least; neither did stories from English history; but the Greek myths fascinated me, and I fitted my day-dream into them. Instead of running over the hills hand in hand with a brother, I was a Bacchante going out to look for Dionysos and the boy playmate was a Greek athlete who followed me because he admired me. I wore nothing but the fawn-skin because I loved to feel the sun and air."

"What do you trace that to?" said Jelkes.

"Mother making me wear wool next the skin," said Mona tartly.

"That day-dream lasted a long time," she went on. "I put myself to sleep with it every night for years. Then, when I learnt of the Mysteries from you, I became a priestess, a pythoness, and the Greek athlete became the high priest who used me as a pythoness. That is all I remember. I have got no mediæval memories, but Hugh has. Now Hugh, you take up the tale. What were your day-dreams?"

"Good Lord, I never had any. I haven't got an imagination like yours."

"Treat Ambrosius as a day-dream, and tell us about him."

"Yes, I might do that. That's a bright idea. When I think of Ambrosius as real, he scares me; and when I think of him as imagination, I feel foolish, but I can treat him as a day-dream all right. Well, I think Ambrosius was a solitary, supercilious sort of blighter when he was a lad. Kept himself to himself and felt superior, in spite of being looked down upon locally because he was a flight of fancy. I think that wherever he was, he felt he didn't belong. Then they wanted to shove him in the Church, and that suited him well enough because he had got nothing to hold him outside it. Then, I think, as he got older he got it in the neck over women. Not because the old Abbot didn't ride him on a loose rein, but because he couldn't find a woman to suit him. He used to have a nightmare of a particular type of woman, and he couldn't find her in the flesh, and no one else was any use to him. It's a funny thing, but if you don't get just the right type of woman, rows of others are no use to you. I know, because I've tried. I'm not such a fool as to believe in one life one love sort of thing, but there's one type—or at any rate there's one particular factor you look for without quite knowing what it is. You *don't* know what you *do* want, but you *do* know what you *don't* want. Sorry, Mona, to be spilling my innermost Gubbins in front of you like this, but if Uncle J. *will* stir up my subconscious with a pole, what do you expect ? ''

" Have you got anything about Greece ? " said Mona abruptly.

" Well now, I'll tell you, but you're getting onto ticklish ground again. What with a few ideas I'd picked up from you and Uncle Jelkes, and the remains of what was called by courtesy my education, I had as a matter of fact been constructing a Greek fantasy. I was thinking how awfully interesting it would be to try you out as a pythoness, or priestess, or whatever it is. I could see you walking in a procession, looking as if you came off a Greek vase, and carrying whatever it was that the priestesses carried in the processions. And I could see you and me up at an altar, doing a ceremony together and bringing Pan through into manifestation. Getting a descent of power, don't you know, like the tongues of flame at Pentecost."

Jelkes thanked his stars that even in the classics a public school education has its limits. He hastily cast about in his mind for some siding into which he could shunt Hugh out of harm's way, but before he found it Mona spoke again.

" So your day-dreams and mine have met, Hugh ? "

" Yes," came in a low voice from under the cowl.

" Then let's go through with it. If you will come outside, I will dance the Moon-dance for you on the grass in the moonlight."

" I'd sooner not, if you don't mind," said Hugh in a low voice.

" Come," said Mona, and dropping her heavy dark wrap, she went walking down the aisle, her thin soft draperies fluttering and her golden sandals gleaming under the hem. Hugh came.

Jelkes hastily extinguished the candles lest there should be a fire, and hurried after them.

# CHAPTER XXVII

MONA stood erect in the moonlight on the short grass of the barren pasture ; the pallid light taking all colour from grass and gown and face so that she looked like a wraith. Hugh, tall and gaunt in his black cowled robe, stood a dozen yards away from her on the edge of the shadow thrown by the chapel, and even in the darkness the knuckles showed white on his clenched hands.

Then Mona began her dance. It was not so much a dance as a series of mime-gestures, for she never moved more than a few steps forward or back. A low, rhythmical humming that hardly seemed to come from human lips at all was her accompaniment, and to its rise and fall she swayed and gestured. Jelkes, knowing the symbol-language of the ancient faiths, was able to read her meaning, and with his heart sinking within him, wondered how much of it Hugh was picking up subconsciously. The shades of the seminary had not altogether lifted from Jelkes' soul, and to him there was something rather startling in seeing the man in the garb of the Church watching the oldest dance in the world being danced for him. He had wanted Mona to come to an understanding with Hugh, but he had not bargained for anything quite so primitive.

He knew perfectly well that Hugh was not a priest ; had taken no vows ; that the black cowled gown was only a symbolic representation of his inhibitions ; he knew that Mona's dance was perfectly decorous and unexceptionable ; and yet he knew that she was deliberately drawing magnetism out of the man with her weaving hands. It was all make-believe, he told himself over and over again. Mona and Hugh were simply play-acting, and knew it. There was no more in it than if they had taken part in amateur theatricals together. It was perfectly decorous, and he was there to play propriety—and yet there was a vivid kind of reality about it. He could tell by Hugh's clenched, white-knuckled hands that it was real to him. Mona was playing with fire, and it was a diabolical thing to do, especially with a man in Hugh's unbalanced state. Mona was a syren, drawing his very soul out of him. Hugh would never look at any other woman after this. What was Mona playing at? She had frankly declared she wanted none of Hugh, but she would never rid herself of him now without smashing the fellow.

But gradually, as the dance went on, the sense of reality grew upon Jelkes. The dance was mime and make-believe, yes, admitted. But it corresponded to certain other kinds of realities as the movements of the hands of a clock correspond to the passage of time. And Jelkes began to recognise that reality and admit its validity. The wild upheave in him died down. He was too old for this game. Emotions were short-lived at his time of life. His head cleared, and he stood watching the other two—the green, swaying, moving creature of life and dream, and the gaunt, black-cowled, solitary figure, set apart in the shadow of the chapel. There was always about Hugh Paston a peculiar solitariness. As he had said of Ambrosius, he never seemed to belong anywhere, but always to be an alien and an exile. And now, standing in the shadows in his cowled black robe, that lonely apartness was intensified to the *nth* degree.

Was it in Hugh's power to come out of the shadow of the chapel into the moonlight? Jelkes felt that Mona was trying to lure him. Why did he not respond if she wanted him to? It was only make-believe. It wouldn't hurt anybody. But Jelkes knew in his heart, and felt that Hugh knew also, that what was going on was very far from make-believe. Jelkes was not psychic; he had never seen anything in his life; but he could picture Mona's etheric hands going out and touching Hugh and drawing him to her, for he knew that that was what she was doing in her imagination.

He pictured to himself the weaving hands drawing lines of light upon the air, and then reaching right out, like tenuous silvery tentacles, and stroking Hugh. He could see Mona's hands on Hugh's shoulders, although she was a dozen yards away. And then he saw what he had never expected to see—he saw a grey, shadowy replica of Hugh standing a yard or so in front of himself, so that there were two Hughs, one black and one silvery grey. Jelkes gasped, feeling as if the universe were turning round on him. He had only been picturing in his imagination what he knew Mona was picturing, being familiar with the technique of that operation; he had never visualised Hugh moving out of his physical body—then why had he seen it? True, he had only seen it in his mind's eye, but nevertheless, he *had* seen it, and he certainly had not formulated it. The picture had risen spontaneously without any volition on his part, and it set Jelkes thinking.

The momentary distraction had caused him to lose sight of the two he was watching, and when he looked at them again he found that Mona had ceased her dance and was walking towards them with her normal step, no longer the curious processional pacing with which she had passed down the length of the chapel.

Jelkes knew at once that Mona had done as much as she meant to do for the moment, and was now pulling Hugh back to normal. But Hugh did not respond. He stood silently, looking down from his ungainly height upon Mona's face, upturned in the moonlight, his own completely hidden in the shadow of his cowl. Jelkes held his breath, wondering what was going to happen next; knowing that Mona had unleashed the wind and must now be prepared to ride the whirlwind.

Suddenly Hugh seized her by the shoulders, left bare by the loose drapery of her sleeves. Then rigid once more, he stared down at her, the expression of his own face invisible inside the cowl. Jelkes was thankful that Mona was spared the sight of that face ; he thought it would be a thing to haunt one's dreams. Mona stood quite still, looking back at Hugh, her features clear in the bright moonlight shining over his shoulder. Her eyes were calm and steadfast, but her mouth was twitching slightly. It is a terrible thing deliberately to raise such a conflagration in a man when no answering spark responds in oneself.

Hugh was speaking rapidly in a low vice. " Why are you doing this, Mona ? What are you driving at with me ? You know you don't want me. I had been hoping against hope, but I'm not such a fool that I can't see when I'm not really wanted. You are going to have trouble on your hands if you go on like this. It is a bit too much of a good thing."

Hugh's grip was tightening painfully on her arms. She had a feeling that if she did not speak, did not command the situation, those hands would shift to her throat.

" If I knew what I was driving at," she said in a level voice, " I would tell you, but I am feeling my way, and you must be content to feel your way with me. But I do not think I am taking you up a blind alley, Hugh."

" Where are you taking me ? "

" Back to the beginning of things, I think. Back to elemental nature."

" And when we get there, Mona ? "

" That I don't know ; but Nature is natural, we ¹ ₁ve got to trust her. I think we will distentangle all ₁ight when we get down to bed-rock. We have got to take a chance on it anyway."

" I'll take a chance on it all right. As many as you like. But what about you ? I suppose you are doing this with your eyes open ? "

" Yes, I know what I am about."

" Well, I hope you do. There is going to be the hell of a crash if you don't."

As he spoke, Mona felt the curious cold thrill of fear in the solar plexus that heralds the coming of the god. She caught hold of Hugh's wrists as he held her, and they stood waiting and listening. The wind was rising and rustling the thicket of overgrown laurels that flanked the chapel, and the moon, sinking to her setting, was just tipping the high gable. The weather-worn remains of the cross that had lost its arms cut the bright disk and threw its pagan shadow across them. They waited ; the wind freshened ; the moon slowly passed behind the gable and sank from sight.

Jelkes heard Hugh say in a low voice, " Where is all this going to end, Mona ? "

And Mona answered, " I don't know. We have just got to trust and follow on."

" All right. Lead on. I'll follow. I'll follow you anywhere, Mona, you know that. All I hope is that at the end it won't be absolutely good-bye."

Jelkes could see they had forgotten they had an audience. He wished he could see Hugh's face, but it was deep in his cowl and the light was behind him.

It grew darker as the moon sank behind the trees and the shadows deepened.

Jelkes could hardly see the two in the shadows now. Mona's drapery, grey and wraith-like, shone faintly in the dim, diffused light of the setting moon. Hugh in his black gown was invisible save for the pale blur of his face in the folds of the cowl. His two hands on Mona's shoulders alone showed up white and distinct. Jelkes expected every second to see the tense immobility of the two shadowy figures change into a desperate struggle as the forces evoked from the depths of the man's nature broke loose and took charge, and doubted whether his own strength would be sufficient to protect Mona. Had he not better interfere before the storm broke ? He opened his lips, but no words came. He tried to take a step forward, but found himself unable to move. The whole scene had changed into nightmare. Mona and Hugh were real enough ; but that which lay around them was not real ; another dimension had opened.

It seemed to Jelkes as if the shadows all around him were alive with forms that Hugh and Mona between them, playing with strange forces, had called to life. It was like a cinema without a screen, with all the films moving in and out of each other. Was it possible that they had re-awakened the magic done by Ambrosius ? Up here, at the chapel, he must have performed his rites, and things that are made with ritual live on in the memory of Nature.

This was the old magic all right, thought Jelkes, fascinated and horrified ; this was what Ambrosius had been up to ! That was not Hugh at all, that was Ambrosius, and he had got his hands on Mona. But what was Mona ? Jelkes did not know, for that was not Mona either. It was something that was not human, something disembodied that Ambrosius had created with his magic.

All around them, and passing overhead, was the concourse of the elemental forces ; powers of the air and spirits of elemental fire ; souls of the waters, guardians of the treasures hidden in the veins of the earth, and all the strange familiars that served the mediæval magicians. In the middle of it all stood Ambrosius with the thing he had created in his hands—the woman-form built up by his own desires ; and around him were the forms of his familiars, keeping the circle secure from intrusion.

Jelkes felt the hair on his neck rising like a dog's. He strove desperately to make the Sign of the Cross and banish it all, but he was bound in the circle of that sorcery and could move neither hand nor foot, but only watch with horrified eyes what was going on before him—a renegade monk caressing the woman-form he had made by forbidden arts.

Then slowly the sight faded ; the buildings and the starlight re-appeared. Hugh stepped back from Mona. No one spoke. Hugh looked half-stunned. Mona seemed paralysed. Jelkes felt as if he were coming round from an anæsthetic. He had a suspicion that Mona had actually been in Hugh's arms.

Hugh raised his hands uncertainly and pushed back his cowl ; Mona drew a deep gasping breath and the rigidity of her attitude relaxed. Jelkes called up all his will-power and broke through the spell. He walked up to them, put a hand on the shoulder of each and turned them about.

"Come along," he said. "We're going in. We've had enough of this."

They walked beside him without word spoken ; his hands on their shoulders guiding them as if they were sleep-walkers.

Back in the stuffy warmth of the living-room, Jelkes turned up the lamp as high as it would go and threw an armful of kindling on the fire. Hugh stared dazedly at the flame of the lamp and rubbed his eyes ; then he dived in among the folds of his draperies and got a handkerchief out of his trouser pocket and wiped his face, which was dripping with sweat as if he had dipped it in a basin of water. He looked round at Mona, who looked back at him with non-committal eyes. She had better control of herself than either of the two men, and was like the core of calm at the heart of a cyclone.

Slowly Hugh ungirt his robe, rolled it into a bundle, and threw it into a corner of the sofa. Then he mopped his neck.

"Gosh !" he said. "Is there anything in the cupboard ?" and moved uncertainly towards the sideboard.

"No, there isn't anything in the cupboard," said Jelkes firmly ; "and if there was, I wouldn't let you have it.  Mona will make us some tea."

Mona, only too thankful to make her escape, disappeared in the direction of the kitchen.  Jelkes turned to Hugh.

" Well, what happened ? " he demanded.

" God only knows, T. J.  I don't.  It was like a dream. I hope to goodness I haven't upset Mona."

" She asked for it.  She's got to put up with it."

" She sure did, T. J.  I never meant to let things go as far as this.  This is what I have been scared of all along.  This mustn't happen again, Jelkes, it isn't fair to anybody."

Mona entered with a tray of crockery.  She did not look at them, and they did not look at her.

" What are we going to do about it ? " asked Hugh as she went out again.

" I'll speak to her," said Jelkes.

" I wish you would," said Hugh.  " Somebody certainly ought to.  I don't think she knows what she's about."

Mona came in again, a big brown earthenware bowl between her two hands.  She paused in the doorway and stood looking at them.  Still in her green dress and with the fillet about her hair, she looked, as Hugh had said, like something off a Greek vase.  Jelkes looked at Hugh. He was staring at her fascinated, oblivious of all else. He looked at Mona.  She stood looking down at Hugh as he half sat, half crouched in the deep chair.  Her face was calm.  Her eyes were steady, but the usual close-held line of her mouth was relaxed, and her lips were full and very scarlet and in the hollow of her neck a pulse was beating visibly.  Jelkes came to the conclusion that Mona knew exactly what she was doing, and that it was not the slightest use to speak to her.

The meal was eaten in silence, save for the necessities of the table.  Jelkes and Mona drank the everlasting tea, and Hugh, though he forewent spirits out of deference to

Jelkes, felt he owed himself something, and opened a bottle of beer. After all, the hop is the northern analogue of the vine, and Pan was due for a libation. Jelkes, observing his companions out of the corner of his eye, saw Mona look up, and finding Hugh Paston's eyes on her, look down again hastily, to look up no more for the rest of the meal.

The party broke up and went to their rooms as soon as the meal was over. Jelkes wondered whether it was his duty to patrol the passages, but concluded that it was better to leave things to nature and pulled the bed-clothes over his head with a profound sigh. What would be, would be, *Dei et Diaboli volunti*.

# CHAPTER XXVIII

MONA sat up in bed, her arms tight folded round her knees to prevent them from shaking, and asked herself what in the world had possessed her to act as she had. The reaction had set in and was proportionate to the previous exaltation. Not having the kind of conscience that prevaricates with herself, Mona did not deny that Ambrosius, the renegade monk, had a diabolical fascination for her; but to stir up the Ambrosius aspect of Hugh was to play with fire. In her reaction she swung over to the psychological explanation of the whole thing. Ambrosius was Hugh's repressed subconscious, built up into a secondary personality. He ought to go and be psycho-analysed and get it cleared up. If she played the fool with him any more, he might have a nasty breakdown, and even come within genuine reach of certification. She blamed herself bitterly. She had believed herself to be single-hearted in her desire to help Jelkes with his *protégé*, and then had fallen so low as to start messing about with him. Mona, whose standard of morality, though peculiar, was definite, was exceedingly angry with herself. Why had she let herself get carried away like this? She had thought she had learnt her lesson once and for all. She knew, too, that Jelkes was angry with her, and that vexed her still more, for she had a very great respect for him, and valued his good opinion highly. In the mood she was now in, she was disposed to be exceedingly angry with the unfortunate Hugh, and to find him not merely unattractive, but positively repulsive. Then, realising that tomorrow had got to be faced, and that it was steadily drawing nearer while she cogitated, she took two aspirins and set to work to try to go to sleep, but, as might have been expected, without much success. Finally she arrived at the state when all her life passed in review before her and she wept hopelessly into her pillow.

After that she thought she felt calmer, though exhausted, and another mood set in. After all Hugh was a dear, and life was very hard ; she would certainly miss him if she broke with him, probably more than she realised. Why shouldn't she marry him ? It would make him happy, and lift her from her the intolerable strain of the struggle for a livelihood.

Then back once more her mood reacted. After all, the post-War depression could not last for ever, and once she could earn a decent living again, there was nothing she would love better than her cat-on-the-tiles existence ; nothing she would hate more than trying to be a good wife to Hugh. More tears began to flow, but tears of rage this time. Mona was furious with herself, with Hugh, but above all, with Jelkes, whom she recognised as acting as a kind of conscience to the pair of them. She felt certain that Jelkes hated Pan, if the truth were known, and was perpetually making the Sign of the Cross inside himself, thus preventing Pan from manifesting and so throwing everything into confusion, just as Mrs Macintosh's promise to pray for her had done. Mona flung angrily away from all restraints, and yet her self-respect prevented her from yielding to Pan in his satyric aspect. The tears of rage gave place to tears of self-pity, and then, beaten down to her foundations, to forlorn tears of humility before life and its problems. The world was too much for her, and she longed for the vales of Arcady.

Hugh, on his side, had not got any aspirins, and stood with his hands in his dressing-gown pockets staring out of the window at the starlight. He had had a pretty thorough shake-up, and sleep was far from him. He might be a fool in dealing with people because too easily swayed and influenced, but he was by no means a fool in summing them up, his plastic nature rendering him intuitive to a high degree. He knew with a sense of delighted triumph that Mona had let herself go far more than she had ever meant to ; but he had also sensed the reaction that had been coming on steadily all through supper. He was quite alive to the fact that it was Mona's fixed intention not to involve herself with him, firstly, because she did not like him well enough, and secondly, because her pride stood like a lion in the way. He, for his part, felt that everything life held for him was bound up with Mona. His negative, hypersensitive nature clung to Mona's dynamism as the one thing that would enable it to go on living in a world that had been all darkness and coldness, but that under her touch became golden. He had come to the point when he was beginning to feel pretty desperate ; if Mona wouldn't have him, he didn't know what he was going to do.

It did not seem to Hugh to be a subject which one could very well lay before a Heaven where there is neither marrying nor giving in marriage ; there was more to be hoped of the infinite richness and everlasting fecundity of the earth. Surely out of all her richness and abundance the Great Mother of us all could meet his need ? Why do we forget the Mother in the worship of the Father ? What particular virtue is there in virgin begetting ? Are the descending Paraclete and the up-rising Pan two opposing forces locked in an everlasting struggle, or are they an alternating current playing between the two poles of spirit and matter ?

Hugh did not know. Metaphysics had never been his strong point. He knew what his need was, and he considered it to be a legitimate need, and he did not see why he should be expected to deny it fulfilment as a matter of principle. He was going to fulfil it if he could, and that was that !

He began to consider how it could be fulfilled. What

was the real thing in Mona's heart ? Why had she never
mated during her thirty-odd years ? What was she
asking of men that they did not give her ? Wherein did
the reality fail to match the ideal ? Were there no priest-
initiates now to work with her the rites of Eleusis ?
Perhaps that was the trouble. And he debated whether
it was feasible for him, Hugh Paston, to assume the part
of the priest of the Mysteries as Iamblichos said the priests
assumed the part of the god ? Could he, by imagining
himself to be the Greek priest-initiate, identify himself
with Pan ? It was a bold concept, but after all, it was a
traditional one, and no novelty.

But if he did this, what would be the repercussion ?
He and Mona were not boy and girl on the hills in the
sun, but mature man and woman, who asked more of
mating than would have satisfied the Greek athlete and
his lass. They were priest and priestess. In Mona's
phantasy the priest had been the initiator who had
admitted her to the Mysteries. What was to be done
about it ? How was he to fill the bill ? He could not
very well enquire of the celibate monk in the bookshop ;
to ask Mona what secrets he ought to reveal to her was
a contradiction in terms. Then came to him the remem-
brance of Ignatius' dictum—' Put yourself in the posture
of prayer and you will soon feel prayerful '. If he played
the part of the high-priest he would soon feel sacerdotal :
especially if he could inveigle Mona into playing the part
of the pythoness. It was the Froebel method, the action-
song—' This is the way we mow the wheat '—education
by doing. That, according to Jelkes, was the way the
ancients initiated.

Lost in his day-dream, Hugh stood on, oblivious of
the passage of time. The bare grey stone of the English
building gave place to the white marble of a Greek
temple ; the pale starlight of an English night to flicker-
ing Greek torches. He was the high-priest in the sanctuary awaiting the coming of the priestess. Beyond the

curtains, Tyrian-dyed, he could hear the murmur of the crowded, excited temple. The curtains parted, and Mona stood before him in her robe as priestess of Ceres, the curtains falling again immediately behind her. The crowded temple hushed and held its breath. This was the sacrament, the bringing through of power. This was the sacerdotal office. Behind him was the All-Father, the First-Begotten Love, behind her was the Earth-Mother. As in the phantasy, he had become the priest, now the priest became the god—spontaneously, without any volition on his part. He felt power come upon him, he felt himself part of a larger whole, made one with the earth as she swung through the circling heavens. And then he checked and stayed. He could go no further. He lacked his priestess. The power that had sought expression through him could find no passage, for the circuit did not lead to earth but remained insulated in empty space. The reaction hit him hard. He knew that he had been within an ace of the thing he sought, and the missing of it gave him a sense of irritated frustration that promised badly for his nerves next day.

He tried to get hold of himself. After all, it was only phantasy he had been indulging in ; there was no need to be so upheaved over a day-dream that had missed fire. He tried to concentrate his mind on the problem of his relationship with Mona. He suspected that the happenings of the last few hours had given him a distinct advantage, if he only knew how to use it. But he was so hopelessly inept with women, he was always either missing his chance or over-reaching himself. Hugh found himself slipping into his old condition of miserable self-hating. Desperately he struggled out of it. That way lay paralysis—he must not yield to it. He thought of Ambrosius. A little smile twiched the corner of his mouth. He suspected that Mona liked Ambrosius. Supposing he were deliberately to slip into his Ambrosius personality, as he could pretty nearly do at will now, would he be able to dominate Mona? It was a tempting proposition, but all the same, he had his doubts of it. Any relationship between Mona and Ambrosius implied frustration. The diabolical prior drew his dynamism from the very fact of his frustration.

Then there came to him an inexplicable but very definite feeling that he would never again turn into Ambrosius, for the good and excellent reason that Ambrosius had turned into him! As he had said to Mona, he was engaged in carrying out the last wishes of the renegade prior, and his unquiet ghost had no longer anything to walk for. Or in other words, he was engaged in fulfilling the thing for which Ambrosius stood in his soul. It is a curious fact that the inner self is satisfied if we ' show willing ', and it is not necessary actually to carry out its urges. It is the attitude that counts in the subjective kingdom, as the ancients knew when they made use of ritual.

The formidable prior could help him no longer. He had to stand on his own feet. It was no use dramatising a frustration.

There came to his mind the memory of that strange scene in the chapel when, goaded to despair by his sisters' innuendoes, he had phantasied the death of Ambrosius, and with it had come the strange certainty of a promise. What was it that had been promised to Ambrosius? What was it that he had sought? Was he, Hugh, entitled to claim the fulfilment of that promise?

His mind turned back to Arcady. There, and there alone, lay the fulfilment of both promise and dream. The Arcadian Pan with his shepherd's pipe was no diabolical deity, like the sinister Goat of Mendes of the inflamed mediæval imagination. It was the thing behind Ambrosius he must go after—the Greek inspiration that had awakened Ambrosius to his manhood. It is a curious fact that when men began to re-assemble the fragments

of Greek culture—the peerless statues of the gods and
the ageless wisdom of the sages—a Renaissance came to
the civilisation that had sat in intellectual darkness since
the days when the gods had withdrawn before the assaults
of the Galileans. What is going to happen in our own
day, now that Freud has come along crying: " Great
Pan is risen ! "—? Hugh wondered whether his own
problems were not part of a universal problem, and his
own awakening part of a much wider awakening? He
wondered how far the realisation of an idea by one man,
even if he spoke no word, might not inject that idea into
the group-mind of the race and set it working like a
ferment ?

Supposing, thought Hugh, absorbed and completely
oblivious of his surroundings—supposing he were to
phantasy the part of the Greek high-priest of Mona's
day-dream until it became alive in him even as Ambrosius had done, might not Mona answer to it ? A
famous film-star, who is also a great artist, has said that
something enters into him and takes possession of him
when he plays a part, and he changes, and the character
he represents becomes alive in him. Hugh remembered
Mona's words in the chapel concerning the Greek athlete
of her phantasy who had followed her because he admired
her. That, of course, was his own dream precisely. He
remembered the tense look on Mona's face when he had
casually told that dream as they were looking at the
dusty old books in the museum. She had recognised it
all right, and for some reason best known to herself had
made open confession when they were psycho-analysing
themselves in the chapel. Now why had she done that ?
Was there something in Mona that was saying, ' Yes, I
will worship Pan with you provided you are of the true
faith ' ?

It seemed to him that if he could pull this thing off
with Mona—this curious experience of time as a mode
of consciousness, and this even more curious experiment

in the power of the day-dream—something would be brought through into the group-mind of the race and added to the racial heritage. He had no need to appeal to his fellow-men or seek their suffrage and support; he had only got to *be* something—*do* something, and the thing would start in the group-soul of the race and they would feel it subconsciously—that, at any rate, was the way Jelkes said the adepts worked.

There came to him, as he stared at the marvel of the night-sky, a realisation that he was part of a larger whole and that a vast life found expression through him, and that in his fulfilment it would find a measure of its fulfilment, and in his frustration it was frustrated. It was not a question of Hugh Paston being in love with a woman who did not respond to him, it was a question of unbalanced force in the universe, and he knew that the whole universe was striving to adjust that unbalance, and that if he would but lean back and let himself be borne by the cosmic tides, they would bring him to the place where he would be. But to achieve that, he must lean back, and let go, and allow the cosmic forces to adjust themselves in their own way. Not otherwise could he take advantage of them.

He felt that he had stumbled on a very important key when he had realised that the way of approach to the dynamic reality lay by the path of phantasy, the most dynamic of all auto-suggestions. The orthodox psychologists had never spotted that. It might be pure imagination, but nevertheless it was the way to set the invisible causes in motion, provided it lay along the line of their course.

This was indeed a discovery worth making, thought Hugh, forgetting his frustration as he saw the way opening up in front of him once more. He had only to become the priest and he could command his priestess.

It was not a case of dominating Mona; it was a case of himself becoming the thing that would answer to the need in her.   She knew too much to be contented with a commonplace mating ; what she wanted was the priest-initiator.   If he could make himself this, she would marry him all right, no need to worry about that.   It was not Mona that was his problem, but he that was Mona's problem.   But how was he to do this thing ?   How was he to ordain himself to the priesthood of a forgotten rite ?   How save by letting the power of which it was the expression rise up with its own peculiar magnetism, so that deep called unto deep ?   Mona had played a rite on him for reasons best known to herself and Jelkes ; he would play a rite on Mona !

He thought he could see his way through, and determined that in the morning he would get on with it.

# CHAPTER XXIX

THE sun rose next day through the morning mists with a promise of heat, one of those brief miniature heat-waves that sometimes come in the days between spring and summer, and Hugh, feeling the breathing warmth coming in at his open window as he dressed, felt a strong disinclination for heavy stuffs and stiff collars, and clad himself in an old pair of khaki shorts left over from his African expedition, a short-sleeved khaki mesh shirt minus most of its buttons, and Ambrosius' sandals. In this disreputable kit he descended to breakfast.

He moved silently in the heelless sandals, and came into the living-room without Mona being aware of his presence. As upon the day of their first morning meal at the farm, the door leading out to the garden was wide open to admit the morning sun and the table stood before it, a small oak gate-legged table covered with a gaily-coloured, coarse-textured, hand-woven cloth on which stood the hand-thrown earthenware breakfast set, all yellow and orange on the greyish-buff ground of the natural clay. As before, the brown velvety faces of polyanthuses rose from their little honey-pot, but whereas on that day they had been the first bold venturers from under a sunny wall, these were the last lingering laggards from a shady corner. Mona, singing softly to herself, was re-arranging the haphazard efforts of Silly Lizzie in the way of table decoration, and the song she sang was a curious one.

> " Bowl of oak and earthen jar,
> Honey of the honey-bee ;
> Milk of kine and Grecian wine,

Golden corn from neighbouring lea—
These our offerings, Pan, to thee,
Goat-foot god of Arcady.

" Horned head and cloven hoof—
Fawns who seek and nymphs that flee—
Piping clear that draweth near
Through the vales of Arcady—
These the gifts we have of thee,
God of joyous ecstasy.

" Come, great Pan, and bless us all :
Bless the corn and honey-bee.
Bless the kine and bless the vine,
Bless the vales of Arcady.
Bless the nymphs that laugh and flee,
God of all fertility."

It was oddly appropriate to the simple breakfast-table set there in the sun, from which only the Grecian wine was lacking, and Mona, who, like Hugh, had felt the early heat and put on her thin green frock, was the appropriate priestess. She had her old brown sandals on her stockingless feet, and there was no fillet on her hair, but save for that, she was exactly as she had been the previous evening when she had danced the moon-dance for the drawing-out of Hugh's soul.

She looked up and saw him there and stood clutching the little bowl of flowers in her hands helplessly. Sleep and the sunshine had enabled her to put her problems behind her for the moment and escape into the vales of Arcady. She had not expected Hugh to be down just yet, and, taken by surprise, could find no word to say save : " Hello, Hugh ? "

" Hello, Mona ? " he replied.

She tried desperately to discern from his bearing what his interpretation might be of the previous evening's happenings. They meant much or little according to how one looked at them.  But there were times when Hugh was as impassive as an effigy on a tomb, and the present was one of them.  Mona thought that her best course was to make light of the previous evening's doings and trust to his following her lead.

" Isn't it a lovely morning ? " she said nervously.

" Very lovely, very lovely indeed, Mona.  I think "— a smile appeared at the corner of his mouth—" that Pan must be pleased with us."

Then, to Mona's intense relief, Jelkes joined them, clad in the everlasting Inverness, despite the warmth, and they sat down to the milk and the honey and the porridge and the new-laid eggs and whole-meal bread in the sunshine—a truly Arcadian meal.

Mona departed to the back premises to start Silly Lizzie off with a push ; Jelkes sat himself down in the sun with a sensational Sunday paper and proceeded to soak his soul in scandal, and Hugh wandered off across the pasture smoking his after-breakfast cigarette.

He had an instinctive feeling that the chapel was not a suitable place for the invocation of Pan—he doubted if any roofed place ever could be.  The great archangels in the buttress bays were the austere regents of the elemental forces and the mystical Tree in the east had meanings to meditate upon for a lifetime, but Pan was another matter.  It was in Hugh's mind that a coffer, up-ended, would serve as a cubical altar, and it was in his mind to shift it out into the pine-wood if he could find a place unobserved from both the house and the road.

He strolled slowly down the broad grassy way between Mona's newly-planted herb-beds, plucking here and there grey aromatic leaves, crushing them in his hands, and inhaling their clean, sharp odour from between his cupped palms.  At the end of the walk, where the desert met the sown and there was no more any sustenance even for the grey herbs in the shallow black stony soil above the chalk, two round grey-green bushes stood sentinel. Hugh plucked a delicate maidenhair sprig from one of them, crushed it between his palms, and immediately the rank stench of the billy-goat assailed his nostrils. Hastily he rubbed his hands on the seat of his shorts, but this failed to improve matters, merely distributing the odour fore and aft. Frida had always insisted on his changing his shoes after he had visited the stables, and he wondered whether Mona would require him to get back into tweeds on this scorching day over which the heat-haze already hung luminous. He could apply Vim to his hands, but would it be a success applied to the seat of his pants ? He doubted it, sat down for a few minutes in a patch of damp grass, and thought he would suggest having lunch out of doors.

Assured by the chill to his spine that the dew had done all that was to be expected of it, he rose from his uncomfortable seat, only to find, however, that the damp had made matters considerably worse. He gave it up as a bad job, muttered ' damn,' lit a cigarette, and strolled on down the path, a crying temptation to all the nanny-goats in the neighbourhood.

The little wood was of Scotch firs ; but as these go bare about the legs as they get on in years, and at this point the road, though at a little distance, ran along rising ground, whatever was done in the wood was clearly visible from the road, and the prospect of finding a secluded site for the altar of Pan was not very good. The bare ground out of sight of the road was overlooked by a scattered hamlet on the opposite side of the valley, so it must be here or nowhere. They had never explored the wood very thoroughly because it was beset with brambles, but Hugh, taking giant's strides, lifted his long bare legs over these and reached its shade, hoping to find some sort of cover among the undergrowth.

He pushed on, finding it easier going now that the shade made all growth scanty, and saw ahead of him a dense mass of dark foliage among red-brown trunks.

This looked hopeful, and he headed towards it, to find a close-set belt of yews blocking his path. The yew is a long-lived, slow-growing tree, and from the girth of these he judged they must be pretty ancient, and with a sudden quickening of heart-beat, wondered whether they dated from Ambrosius' day, and if so, why they had been planted?

He ducked under the low-hanging outer branches, and with some difficulty forced his way through, to come out into a little open glade entirely surrounded by yews. Here was the very privacy he desired ! He took stock of his surroundings while he picked the yew-needles out of his hair and shirt-collar.

All round him the green-black branches of the yews swept the very ground in a long narrow oval. The glade was the exact shape of the space made by two intersecting circles, and had evidently been laid out with mathematical precision. In the exact centre of the rabbit-nibbled turf an oblong boulder reclined upon its side. Hugh examined it. It was difficult to tell, so weather-worn it was, whether it was a natural outcrop or a tooled stone brought thither by the hand of man. The chalk, however, does not produce such stones as this, and Hugh, looking at the long narrow rock at his feet, guessed that it was one of those standing-stones of which Mona had spoken—a sighting-stone along a line of power. The little stream in the valley was dammed, and on the dam grew ancient oaks. There was no point in such a dam. It watered no flocks. It turned no mill. But if a straight line were drawn between the dam in the valley and the old abbey, it would pass immediately over this stone. Scotch firs were new-comers in this part of the country. Before their day the barren hilltop stood bare, and a man standing beside the dam in one valley bottom could sight over here to the dam in the next valley, and so on to where the green roads of England converged on Avebury : Ambrosius had chosen his site well. Around the ancient standing-stone he had planted his grove of yew, thus ensuring it being right in the track of one of the lines of force of the ancient worship.

Hugh considered the great stone as it lay humbled in the dust. It would not take a great deal of work to set it up again. He thought he could do it single-handed, with luck. Pushing his way through the yews, he set off at a dog-trot for the house, skirted round to the potting-shed unobserved, and returned with pick and spade. The loose sandy soil worked easily, but up-ending the great stone was another matter, and sorely against his will, Hugh had to go and fetch Bill.

Amiable as the bob-tailed sheep-dog he so closely resembled in everything save intelligence, Bill shoved through the bushes in his Sunday best in the wake of his employer. When he saw the stone, however, he pushed his peaked cap onto the back of his head and scratched it.

" Oy," he said. " That's one of the Devil's skittles. 'Adn't we better leave it alone, Mister ? "

" Do you believe in the Devil ? " said Hugh.

" Well, I dunno. 'E's never done me no 'arm, and 'e's bin arst to often enough. I've got nuthin' to complain of."

" All right then. Up-end his stone and put it tidy for him, since he's always treated you decently."

" Aye, aye, sir," said Bill, gave the stone a mighty heave, and set it upright in the hole that Hugh had dug under its base. Together they filled in the loose earth and trod it firm. Then they straightened their backs and surveyed their handiwork, each wondering in his different way how the Devil would take it. Something attracted Bill's attention and he sniffed suspiciously.

" Gawd," he said. " Someone's got a bleedin' billy-goat ! "

" Have they really ? " said Hugh, edging to leeward.

Bill shouldered the pick and spade and ambled off, leaving Hugh to consider the next move. Having a standing-stone in the centre of the glade, he needed no other altar. He examined it closely, and decided that it was certainly a worked stone—a short, blunt pillar with a rounded top, it was too symmetrical to be anything else.

Well, he had got his temple, and now what about the rite ? Was it done at high noon, or full moon, or the dark of the moon ? He did not know. He would wait till the spirit moved him, and then bring Mona here— and Pan could speak for himself.

But supposing after all that Pan were the Devil, as Bill had opined ? The Devil, taken so seriously by all good Christians, was certainly a very goat-like individual if the illustrations in the Sunday-school books were to be believed. And yet there was a geniality and kindliness about the celestial billy-goat that did not seem consonant with utter badness.

And after all, if God objected to the Devil, why did He tolerate him ? And if God tolerated him, did He not connive thereby at his devilishness and share the responsibility therefor ? It was beyond Hugh. His philosophy split on a rock that has sunk many stout theological ships. After all, why should Nature be at perpetual war with its Creator ? It wasn't reasonable, unless, of course, the act of creation had been badly botched. Was it not more reasonable, as well as more reverent, to presume that God had made Nature as He meant it to be, and the saints, trying to improve upon God's handiwork, had made a mess of it ? A distant gong called to lunch, and with a friendly nod to the standing-stone, Hugh pushed his way through the circling yews and departed.

In response to his message sent by Bill, lunch was in the open, but even so, Mona circled round Hugh, sniffing.

" Hugh," she said, " have you been playing with my rues ? "

Hugh, trying to look innocent, demanded what rues

might be.

" The two grey bushes at the end of the herb-walk—
the goat-herbs."

Hugh sheepishly explained his misadventure. The
Vim had been efficacious enough applied to his hands,
but neither dew nor Vim had had any effect on the seat
of his pants.

Jelkes roared. " Well, I knew girls bathed their faces
in dew for the sake of their complexions——" he said.

Mona cast a scathing glance at him.

" Better sit down, Hugh," she said, " and then it won't
be so noticeable."

Mona served them—it was no use getting Silly Lizzie
to wait at table if you did not like your food down your
neck—and they settled down to their meal.  Suddenly
old Jelkes looked up, and breaking his usual rule of
silence while feeding said :

" I reckon you are right to go through with this thing,
Hugh, and I'll do anything I can to help you, even if I do
get knotted up in my own complexes sometimes.  It's
that monk's cowl that does for me.  Dash it all, I was
very nearly one myself ! "

" Hugh said a true thing once," said Mona.  " Or
maybe it wasn't Hugh but Ambrosius.  I can't tell them
apart these days.  He said that the Church was made for
man, not man for the Church."

" I reckon that's about it," said Jelkes.  " After all
religion is simply our speculation about what lies below
the horizon of life.  We don't know.  In the very nature
of things, we can't know.  The only way you can judge
a theology, so far as I can see, is by its effect on character.
You have no means of knowing how God views it save
by what its opponents say He says about it ; but you
can see its effect on human life, and that is what I sum
religions up by.  I look at their adherents—the general
run of them—not the saints—not the black sheep, but
the bulk.  Christianity produces too many fiends and

tolerates too many fools. Now why does it do that, I ask myself? It's the worst persecutor of the whole bunch. Islam goes in for jehads and massacres, but there's no petty spite about it. I reckon that group-souls get neuroses, same as individuals, and that Christianity is suffering from old-maid's insanity from too much repression; that's what makes it so damned unchristian."

" You are blaspheming abominably, Uncle," said Mona. " If I said the half of this, you'd screw my neck."

" It isn't as bad as it sounds, my dear," said Jelkes. " It is the Church I'm slanging, not the Christ."

" When you have had a hearty sickener of the whole business it is very difficult to separate the Church from the Christ," said Hugh. " For all practical purposes the Church exercises proprietary rights."

" I don't admit those rights," said Jelkes. " In the opinion of all impartial scholars, those deeds are forged. It is function, not charter, that confers rights in religion. I defer to the man with genuine spiritual power, and I don't care a hoot in hell whether he has been ordained or not."

Sitting on the low, broad bench, with the man and the girl on either side of him, Jelkes stared out towards the sun that hung golden over the pine-wood.

" What is going to be the next move in the game ? " he said at length.

" The next move," said Hugh, " is to return to our original plan, and invoke Pan by a blend of Ignatius and Huysmans."

" Have you ever departed from it ? " said Jelkes.

" Well, we haven't been able to give it much attention while Mona had a cold on the chest, and I was getting the farm tidy, and Ambrosius was cutting his capers."

" You have never departed from it, Hugh. The old

buildings evoked Ambrosius and Ambrosius invoked Pan absolutely according to plan."

" Good Lord ! " said Hugh, and fell silent.

" Will living here make Hugh permanently Ambrosius ? " asked Mona, a note of anxiety in her voice.

" It would if he had equipped the place on mediæval lines. Put any mediæval stuff you have got into the chapel. You can't live with it, any more than you could live with Ambrosius' drains or menus."

" Then—ought Hugh to live here at all ? But he's so awfully fond of the place. And it's such a fascinating place," said Mona with a sigh, thinking of the happy beginnings of a garden in the cloister garth.

" A house is what you make it," said Jelkes. " My predecessor ran the business as a cover for receiving stolen goods, but it doesn't follow that I have to receive stolen goods. One or two of his customers turned up at first, but when I said : ' Nothing doing,' they soon got out of the way of calling. After all, the person in possession has the last word on the subject of atmospheres unless he lets the place dominate his imagination. You get busy and dominate it ; don't let it dominate you."

" It is in my mind," said Hugh, " that we've travelled a good long way already ; perhaps further than any of us realise."

Jelkes cocked an eyebrow at him. " What makes you think that ? " he said.

Hugh pushed back his seat and rested his sinewy elbows on his great gaunt knees—he looked much bigger and more formidable thus sketchily clad than in his ordinary clothes.

" Difficult to say," he said at length. " Very difficult to say. One expects psychic phenomena to be reasonably tangible and to have something of the miraculous about them. We've had nothing of that. Not even up to the standard of an ordinary home circle with someone playing hymns on a harmonium. We've had nothing that you can't father onto the subconscious if you have a mind to. Nothing you could call evidential if you'd got any notion of the nature of evidence. But all the same we've had—or at any rate, I've had, some pretty drastic experiences. I couldn't prove them to anybody else, and I'm not such a fool as to try to ; but I'm quite satisfied about them in my own mind. Anyway, whatever they are, subconscious, super-conscious, hallucinations, telepathy, suggestion, auto-suggestion, cosmic experiences, bunk, spoof or hokum, I feel as if I had been born again. Not saved. Or ever likely to be. Or ever likely to want to be. But born into a wider life and a bigger personality. That's good enough for me, T. J., and I'll make anybody who wants it a present of the rest."

"How do you know it isn't all your imagination, Hugh ? " asked Jelkes, watching him.

"I don't know, T. J., and don't care. It probably is, for I've used my imagination diligently enough over the job. But *via* the imagination I've got extended consciousness, which I probably should never have been able to make a start on if I'd stuck to hard facts all along and rejected everything I couldn't prove at the first go-off. It's no use doing that. You've got to take the Unseen as a working hypothesis, and then things you can't prove at the first go-off prove themselves later.

"It isn't real as tables and chairs are real : that's to say, I wouldn't bark my shins if I fell over it in the dark ; but no one but the very naive holds by that kind of reality nowadays. By going ahead 'as if', I've got in touch with another kind of reality to the popular one— and in that kind of reality I can pull the strings that make things happen—and damn it all, Jelkes, I'm going to ! "

"How are you proposing to set about it, Hugh ? " Jelkes had in the back of his mind certain words about a seduction, and it seemed to him he might be wise to rush out and lay in a stock of wedding-rings.

" You've got to handle it along its own lines, T. J. That's the mistake people make—expecting miracles. Thinking if they say the word of power things will happen. But they won't unless you've worked up the power of the word first of all. Old Ignatius was right, if it was him who said it—Live the life and you'll develop the faith. I want to invoke Pan, so I've got to live Panishly—hence these gooseberry shanks that I saw you gazing at so reproachfully from the depths of your Inverness."

" If you call at Billings Street in a dappled fawn-skin, you'll draw a crowd, and probably catch a cold into the bargain ! "

" You choose to misunderstand me, T. J., I'm not going in for any play-acting. You won't catch me prancing down Piccadilly with a something or a lily. It's the spirit of the thing, not its outward trappings, that counts. My shirt and shorts are the modern equivalent of an ancient Greek athlete cleared for action. All the modern stream-lined furniture is sophisticated primitive. When they wanted a really antiquated throne for Eochaid in the 'Immortal Hour', they gave him a modern arm-chair without the cushions. It makes me feel unrepressed just to look at our cretonnes. Whereas if I look at Mrs Macintosh's rosebuds in the new part of the house, first I feel as pure as anything, and then presently I feel perfectly hateful. Oh yes, Mona's done her job all right. There are times when the devil enters into that girl—if he isn't there permanently." He rubbed his chin thoughtfully. " That's what I like about her," he added.

" It appears to me," said Jelkes, " that if Mona is to remain here alone with you, she would be well advised to lock her door."

" That's what I told her," said Hugh. " But she doesn't do it."

"How do you know I don't?" cried Mona indignantly.

"Because I took the key away some time ago, and you've never missed it."

Mona sprang to her feet with the heavy earthenware pitcher in her hand.

"If you throw that water over me, you'll get what's coming to you," said Hugh, grinning delightedly.

Jelkes got onto his feet and pounded the table like a chairman at a disorderly meeting.

"I will not put up with such behaviour, Hugh Paston! This sort of thing may go on in the kind of houses you're accustomed to, but we're not going to have it here."

"Well, I've offered to make an honest woman of her, but she doesn't take it on. I can't do more than that, can I? The offer still stands open. It's for Mona to say what she'd like. I'll dispense with the ceremony if she'd prefer it!"

They felt there was a snag in the logic somewhere, but they couldn't put their fingers on it on the spur of the moment, and could only stand and glare at Hugh. Jelkes got his wits in hand first. There was no question as to what ought to be done, no matter by what route they arrived there.

"You'd better marry him, Mona, and be done with it. It will save us all a lot of trouble."

Mona, speechless with rage, poised the heavy pitcher in her hand as if about to heave it at them both simultaneously.

"It doesn't matter to me," said Hugh airily. "I'm not Silly Lizzie. The ceremony is not of overwhelming importance in the circles in which I move."

"Nor in the circles in which I move," said Mona. "But I'm damned if I'm going to be bounced in this manner."

"Well, will you marry me or not? That's civil

enough, isn't it ? "

" No, blast you, I won't ! "

" All right, then, don't."

" Oh, my Gawd ! " said Jelkes, dropping down on the
bench and resting his head on his hands.

Hugh patted him on the back. " Cheer up, Uncle ;
we're enjoying it, even if you aren't. This is love as she
is spoke among the moderns. Look at Mona, she's
thriving on it—Hi, you little devil ! " He fielded the
pitcher neatly, but the water went all over Jelkes, who
rose and shook himself like a wet cat, looking most
indignant.

" If this is love among the moderns, give me hate,"
he said. " I don't know how you tell 'em apart," and
stalked off into the house, slamming the door behind
him.

Hugh set down the pitcher out of Mona's reach.

" Well, what about it ? Will you marry me, old
thing ? "

" *NO ! ! ! !* "

" Splendid, I'll see about the licence."

" It will be wasted."

" Doesn't matter if it is. It's only seven-and-six. If
you throw that dinner-plate, I'll spank you with it."

Mona sank down on the bench as Jelkes had done, and
clutched her head.

" Oh, my God ! I wouldn't have believed it of you,
Hugh. I suppose I may as well. I'll get no peace till
I do. But it was taking that key away that annoyed
me."

" No, it wasn't. It was not having locked your door
after you'd had fair warning."

" Well, it was a rotten thing to do, anyway, to take
my key."

" But I didn't do it. I only said I'd done it."

" Then you're a damned liar ! Whatever possessed you
to say that ? "

" I wanted to see if you really had locked your door after I warned you.   I betted you hadn't."

" What point was there in finding out that ? "

" Because, dear heart, if you hadn't, it was safe to bully you into a wedding, for your subcon had up and spoke," and he bent down and kissed her.

# CHAPTER XXX

PENDING the three intervening weeks, while the vicar would be sulkily announcing the banns of employers and employees, Hugh bid Mona collect a suitable trousseau in which, he said, green should predominate as she was being dedicated to Pan.

Mona agreed, while doing hasty mental arithmetic, too proud to ask for a halfpenny. But when the post came in, she waved before him a printed form in speechless indignation : five hundred pounds had been placed to her credit at her bank.

" What's the meaning of this ? " she demanded, as if direly insulted.

" Well, dear heart, I didn't want you to take my instructions too literally and turn out in a fig-leaf, not in this uncertain weather, anyway. I want you to do the thing properly, *à la Huysmans*. Now come along, put your heart into it."

" Indeed ? " said Mona, " and what would you consider to be garments appropriate to Pan ? "

" Well, strictly speaking, none at all, but as it's an English spring——."

" I wish Uncle were here to tell you what he thought of you."

" I wish he were, too. He's well worth listening to when he's roused. But with regard to your outfit, Mona——"

" Well ? "

" Can't you design something for yourself, same as you did for the house ? You've made a champion job of the house. I feel unrepressed whenever I go into it."

" And you want to feel unrepressed whenever you look

371

at me ? "

" Oh no, you can take that for granted. I do that in any case. What I want is for you to feel unrepressed."

" I *am* unrepressed ! " snarled Mona, furious at this aspersion on her modernity.

" No, you aren't, darling, or you wouldn't snarl. Unrepressed people have sweet tempers, for they are absolutely spontaneous and free from conflict."

" If I were absolutely spontaneous and free from conflict, you'd be lying dead at the moment."

" Oh no, I shouldn't. For the moment you slogged me, I'd slog you, and then we'd both feel lovely."

" I don't know that I should be feeling lovely," said Mona, " if you gave me one on the jaw and put your weight behind it. It's not possible to have more than one unrepressed person in a family, so far as I can see. Everyone else has to spend their time cleaning up after him if the place is to be habitable. All the unrepressed people I've ever known had to live in unfurnished bed-sitting-rooms without attendance, and move every quarter-day."

" It is a curious thing," said Hugh, " that in the days when I was a decent citizen, you posed as a cat on the tiles, and now that I've taken you at your word and joined you on the tiles, you bolt for the hearth-rug."

" All right. Anything for a quiet life. I'll do what you want, but I hate you giving me money."

" I shall be responsible for your debts and torts in eighteen days' time. Surely we can anticipate the cere-mony, to this extent, anyway. You've got a frightfully middle class mind, Mona."

" All right. I'll do what you want, but I'll do it in my own way."

What she proposed to do he neither knew nor enquired ; but he returned one afternoon from a session with Mr Whatney to find the farm-house standing empty, and felt a sudden chill feeling of hurt, for it was the first time he had ever returned to the farm and Mona had not been there to welcome him. He could not conceive of the farm without her—in fact, he could not conceive of life without her. Then a sound in the old part of the building caught his ear, and he went quickly towards it. At the foot of the beautiful spiral stair stood a woman of the Renaissance.

He halted, completely taken aback. He adored Mona, but it had never occurred to him before to consider her beautiful. She was dressed in a full-skirted, tight-bodiced robe of heavy brocade—not the discreet brocade of the dress-materials, but the heavy, handsome, gorgeous stuff of the soft furnishings. The ground colour was fawn, faintly dusted with gold by an occasional gold thread in the warp, and peacocks and passion flowers interlaced all over it in a dazzle of green and blue. The neck of the tight-fitting bodice was cut square and low, and behind Mona's smooth dark head rose a high collar of gold—white linen, bought ready-made at the village shop and gilded, if Hugh had known. She was astonishingly like Beatrice d'Este, but all her splendour had cost under thirty shillings. Mona was proud. She wanted to please Hugh, but she wouldn't surrender her independence. His five hundred would not be touched till after the wedding. What she did, she would do with her own resources, and when those came to an end, she would stop.

Hugh came towards her. " What are you doing in here ? " he demanded, to cover his emotion, for the sight of her in her *cinquecento* robes affected him beyond all reason. She was a woman of Ambrosius' age !

" I am trying on my frocks against their proper background," said Mona with dignity, but as red as a pæony. " I had not expected you back so soon."

" So you've chosen the Renaissance for your period ? " said Hugh slowly. " Now why that, and not Greek draperies ? "

" Because I *am* Renaissance," snapped Mona, tossing her head.

He looked at her without speaking. " Yes," he said at length, " I think you are. I know a picture of some-one very like you." He wondered how the story would have ended if a certain Italian princess had visited Eng-land, or a certain English prelate had made the pilgrimage to Rome, as he certainly would have done if his enemies had not prevailed against him. Supposing Ambrosius had got his abbacy, made his pilgrimage to Rome, and met there his princess, rich with the influence of a power-ful house, might not the history of European thought have been different ? For the Renaissance was two-sided—whereas life is a trinity, like the God who made it.

Might it be that he and Mona were making an experi-ment that would bear not only fruit but seed ? He knew from the talk in the old book-shop how little is needed to infect the group-mind with a new idea. The thing they were doing was not desperately daring,—widowers have remarried before now ; but although they were complying with convention, they were rendering no lip-service to it. If this were a remedy for sin, it was a homœopathic remedy. The Greeks quite simply, and perfectly politely, carried a phallus on a pole in the wedding processions—and after all, why not ? thought Hugh ; for if not, why marry ? And if you marry at all, why not do it properly ? Why waste seven-and-six? A line from Arnold Bennett's poem came to his mind— ' Knowing naught of the trade of a wife——.' The Anglo-Saxons are a curious people, and God made them a lot madder than the Kelts, despite Chesterton's state-ment to the contrary.

Thrown in a heap on a broad divan were a pile of gar-ments ; there was a rust-red robe with a bold gold pattern of dragons upon it ; there was a deep, intense blue, patterned in silver like a moonlight night ; these

were heavy and stiff brocades, full-skirted, tight-bodiced.
But there were also diaphanous stuffs that flowed like
water, cloud-blue, dusk-grey and leaf-green. The whole
pile was shimmering and opalescent, for the diaphanous
stuffs seemed to have under-dresses of silver and gold
tissues.

Hugh looked at them. His masculine eye was not to
know the few scanty shillings that had provided the whole
pile, for the hand and eye of an artist had been at work,
and they glowed like the gardens of Paradise.

" You shall have jewels to go with these, Mona," he
said abruptly. His mind had seized upon a new idea that
had suddenly sprung up in it. The Renaissance princess
should have a Renaissance palace somewhere in London
where Bohemia gathers. He would house her as Ambrosius, if he had got his cardinal's hat, would have
housed his mistress. He had not heard Mona's revealing
remark that she would be an unsatisfactory wife but a
top-hole mistress, but he was shrewd enough, and had
seen enough of the world, even if only as a spectator, to
guess this for himself. To introduce Mona to his social
circle would be disastrous to both Mona and the social
circle. Mona would always be a cat upon the tiles for
whom a window must be left open. They would picnic
with Bill and Silly at the farm ; they would live as artists
live in London ; they would, in fact, live for themselves,
and not for their neighbours, their set, their relations, or
posterity. Why, in fact, should we do anything for
posterity ? What has posterity ever done for us ?

Mona disappeared behind the stairs, to return in a
moment clad in her usual garments with her glory over
her arm, gathered up the heap of opalescence, and stalked
off in her usual sturdy manner across the cloister garth to
the farm-house, Hugh behind her. The glory was
departed ; Mona was back to her normal, matter of fact
self again ; but Hugh had had a glimpse of that other
self in her, the Renaissance self, that lay there under all,

waiting to be called into life, and he was not likely to forget.

*    *    *    *    *

There came a day when they all packed into the Rolls-Royce and turned up at the village church to supervise the making one of Bill and Silly. Mr and Mrs Huggins were there; they delighted in doing anything that could possibly annoy Miss Pumfrey, who continued ineradicably haughty, however much she owed them; moreover, they considered Hugh their private property. Mr Pinker was not there, though he turned up at the wedding break-fast and did his share and something over, explaining apologetically that he could not afford to quarrel with Miss Pumfrey and the vicar. Even Mrs Pascoe was there, to Silly Lizzie's horror, who was certain she had come to forbid the banns, and was with difficulty prevented from turning back and bolting forthwith. But Mrs Pascoe had proved a ready convert when told that Miss Pumfrey was infuriated at the idea of any orphan of hers getting married, and had threatened to invoke the power of the law to prevent such an indecency. Once converted, she showed all a convert's zeal—for the time being, at any rate. The vicar eyed them with a sour eye and broke the speed record for the diocese. Thereafter there was a noble binge at the Green Man, and Mr Huggins had to be driven home round the common in Mr Pinker's gig because he was incapable of walking across it; such a thing had never occurred before within living memory, and probably was directly due to the Dionysiac influence introduced by the Monks Farm contingent. Bill and Silly then went off for a week at Southend at Hugh's expense, and stopped on for another week at the rate-payers' expense for having been drunk and disorderly.

Thereafter Hugh and Mona were free to attend to their own affairs. They drove up to town, collected Jelkes from among his books, and as Mona's flat was just over the Marylebone boundary, set off for the registry office so symbolically situated half-way between the Lock Hospital and the police station, with the workhouse immediately behind and a pawn-shop directly opposite, and which, as you ascend the handsome staircase of the building that houses it, offers you the choice of the registrar and the relieving officer. Having paid this tribute to the gods of England, they both kissed the blushing Jelkes and returned to Monks Farm and the gods of Greece.

# CHAPTER XXXI

THE full moon rode high and cloudless over Monks
Farm as Hugh and his bride stacked the dirty crockery
of their wedding supper into the sink to await the morning's wash-up *à la* Jelkes. As far as their outward
demeanour was concerned, this evening in no way
differed from any other evening at Monks Farm, save that
Lizzie was not there to do her little jobs with such pains-
taking care and incompetency, she and Bill being at the
moment spending pennies on the Southend pier trying to
see What the Butler Saw, and what it was the Curate Did
In Paris. These penny bioscopes, however, proved to
be quite inoffensive except for their titles, and Bill put
another penny in, and then another, in case the first one
had given out before they had finished, like the gas.

Monks Farm was quiet with a quietness that seemed
almost uncanny to the ears that had rung with the noise
of London all day. A dog barked on a far-off farm ; a
misguided rooster crowed ; and between each sound
there were long spaces of warm scented stillness as a
faint breeze stirred soundlessly in a line of ancient
thorns, laden with blossom. The afterglow faded from
the west, and a bright low star came out over the pines.
Then from the furthest thorn came : " Gluck, gluck,
gluck ! " and a long liquid bubble.

" Our wedding-march," said Hugh, squeezing Mona's
arm where his hand lay. "Come along, I've got something to show you. But first we must assume our
wedding-garments or we'll get chucked out, same as the
fellow in Scripture."

When Mona rejoined him she wore floating green, but
the moonlight took all colour from it and she looked like

a grey wraith. Hugh himself wore the traditional fawn-skin.

They went down between the herb borders, hoary silver in the dusk, crossed the bare pasture, and entered the pine-wood, now cleared of brambles. In the dense belt of yews an arch had been cut and an oak door fitted, an iron-studded door, reminiscent of Ambrosius. They came out into the little, lozenge-shaped glade bathed in moonlight, and away scurried dozens of rabbits, all except one baby thing that lost its head and took refuge in the shadow of the pillar and stayed there throughout the proceedings, as if representing its Master, the Lord of the Wild.

Hugh offered no explanation, and Mona offered no comment. Neither were needed. He placed her at one end of the enclosure, and took up his own position at the other, the new-risen moon behind them. Then he waited for inspiration, for he had no idea what a rite of Pan might be.

Silently they waited, and time went by, but it did not seem to drag. Both were thinking of the ancient rites of Eleusis, and wondering in what form the power of the god would come upon them. Once only Hugh stirred, to raise his arms in invocation. Mona never moved. The turf beneath their feet retained the heat of the day, though the air was slowly chilling with the evening damp.

Hugh's thoughts went back to his dream of the hills of Greece : perhaps there he would pick up the trail. He followed in his mind the path of the dream, up the steep hill-side, through the sparse wood, and then, almost involuntarily, he entered the deeper wood and felt the cold pang of fear that lurked there waiting for him. He felt it in the solar plexus, like a hand gripping, and a shudder went all over him. He saw the hanging points of Mona's drapery flicker, and knew that she had shuddered too. Then he saw that between them was a path of pale gold light, and it was not moonlight.

A breath of wind began to stir in the narrow space between the encircling yews, a little cold breath of air that moved softly over them, as if feeling them, paused, and moved again and was gone. Then the temperature began to rise. It rose steadily, rapidly, till Hugh wondered when it was going to stop, and whether they had indeed landed themselves in the Hell the parsons prophesied; he felt the sweat break out on his chest, left bare by the fawn-skin; he found it hard to breathe, and his breath came short and quick. The band of light across the turf rose hip-high. It bound him to Mona as the current binds a man to the live rail. It was far stronger than he expected, and again came the pang of fear.

Then the place began to fill with light, overpowering the oppressive heat so that they thought only of the light and forgot the heat. It was a curious light, neither of the sun, nor of the moon, nor of the stars; more silvery than the golden band that still shone amid it; less silvery than the pale moon-glow and the stars. And in this light all things were reflected. The earth spread away into space in a great curve, with their grove upon it. It swung through the heavens in a yet greater curve, the planets circling around it, and it was ringed like Saturn with luminous bands. This was the earth-aura, and within it was lived their life. Their psychic selves breathed in those bands of light as their physical selves breathed in the atmosphere. And within the earth was the earth-soul, all alive and sentient, and from it they drew their vitality.

Mona knew that these things were there all the time, though in their normal state they were unaware of them; but Hugh thought that they had come at his invocation, and felt that the whole swinging sphere circled about him, and for a brief moment knew godhead.

Then the light returned to focus on the glade, leaving behind, like a receding tide, the memory of the environ-

ing infinity, never to be effaced. For ever after Hugh
would live his life against that background and measure
all things by it.

The glade was softly luminous, very hot, and a band
of glowing gold, like illuminated smoke, stretched from
Hugh to Mona, flowing around the pillar, whose conical
top rose just above it. Behind Hugh was the newly-risen
moon and his face was in darkness, but Mona's showed
clear in the moonlight. He could see her eyes, but she
could not see his, and her look had a blankness in consequence, as if she were looking beyond him at something
that stood behind. Perhaps she was : for at that moment
a gradually dawning awareness made itself felt, and Hugh
knew that something was behind him, vast and over-
shadowing, and that from it emanated the band of light
that passed through him and fell upon Mona. He felt
himself getting vaster and vaster, and about to burst with
the force that was upon him. He was towering up, his
head among the stars ; below him, Mona and the earth
lay in darkness. But over the earth-bend the advancing
line of dawn was creeping up. Dimly he wondered if
they had been in the grove all night, unconscious of the
passage of time ; then he realised that this was no earthly
dawn, but the coming of the sun-god.

Yes, it was not the goat-god, crude and earthy. It
was the sun ! But not the sun of the sophisticated Apollo,
but an older, earlier, primordial sun, the sun of Helios
the Titan. Hugh had not known what Freudian deeps
they would work through in the name of the goat-god,
and was prepared for anything ; but this golden exaltation of high space took him completely by surprise. Then
he remembered the favourite phrase of old Jelkes : ' All
the gods are one god, and all the goddesses are one god-
dess, and there is one initiator.' The All-Father was
celestial Zeus—and woodland Pan—and Helios the Life-
giver. He was all these things, and having known Pan,
a man might pass on to the heavenly gate where Helios

waits beside the Dawn.

Hugh felt his feet winged with fire, and knew that he was coming as the Angel of the Annunciation came to the Virgin : he was coming as the messenger of the Life-giver. Far below him Mona waited in the earth-shadow, and it seemed to him that she was in some way lying back upon the earth and sunk in it, like a swimmer floating in water.

And he knew that he was coming swiftly on the wings of the dawn, coming up with the dawn-wind as it circled the earth. He could see the line of golden light advance, and knew that his return to the grove would coincide with its coming.

Then he found himself standing in the grove, in his own body, clad in the fawn-skin, and the line of light was just beyond his feet. For the first time since the vision began he moved, taking a step forward. The line of light advanced with him. He took another step forward ; it advanced again. Mona also had taken two paces forward. He moved again, and the light and the woman moved also.

Now they were standing face to face upon either side of the pillar. Hugh raised his sinewy bare arms and stretched them over Mona's head, and the light that had enveloped him spread over her also. Then, raising his right hand in the Salute of the Sun as the Roman legions raised it, he lowered the left, tingling and burning with a strange heat, and laid the flat palm between Mona's breasts and cried the ancient cry—" Hekas, Hekas, este bibeloi ! Be ye far from us, O ye profane."

# A MAGICAL INVOCATION OF PAN

I AM She who ere the earth was formed
  Rose from the sea.
O First-begotten Love, come unto me,
And let the worlds be formed of me and thee.

Giver of vine and wine and ecstasy,
God of the garden, shepherd of the lea—
Bringer of fear, who maketh men to flee,
 I am thy priestess, answer unto me !

Lo, I receive the gifts thou bringest me—
Life, and more life, in fullest ecstasy.
I am the moon, the moon that draweth thee.
I am the waiting earth that needeth thee.
 Come unto me, Great Pan, come unto me !

     (from " The Rite of Pan.")

Dion Fortune (1891–1946), founder of The Society of Inner Light, is recognized as one of the most luminous and significant figures of 20th-century esoteric thought. A prolific writer, pioneer psychologist, and powerful psychic, she dedicated her life to the revival of the Mystery Tradition of the West. She left behind a solidly established system of teaching and a school of initiation based on her knowledge of many systems, ancient and modern. Her books were published before World War II, and have been continuously in demand since that time.

The Society of the Inner Light, founded by the late Dion Fortune, has courses for those who wish seriously to pursue the study of the Western Esoteric Tradition. Information about the society may be obtained by writing to the address below. Please enclose British stamps or international postal coupons in your letter if you wish a response.

The Secretary
The Society of the Inner Light
38 Steele's Road
London NW3 4RG, England

CPSIA information can be obtained at www.ICGtesting.com
Printed in the USA
LVOW07s1404030915

452704LV00001B/28/P

9 780877 285007